A LONG JOURNEY HOME - SHANNON

A Long Journey Home - Shannon

Melody Lavrakas

To persistent and dedicated women through the ages.

Contents

PART ONE – A College Woman

1

Life at Berkeley

Shannon Baker stood on the steps of South Hall at the University of California in Berkeley, patiently waiting for Matthew Taylor, her best friend. It was January 1915, the first day of classes after the winter break, and the cold crisp air chilled her hands. Matthew promised to meet her for lunch, but as usual, he was late. Shannon had made an important decision over the break and wanted to discuss it with Matthew, and she wanted a promise from him.

Shannon and Matthew had known each other ever since they were infants. Lalani, Shannon's mother and Katherine, Matthew's mother, were best friends and had traveled the world together, long before either was married. Katherine and Lalani had settled in the town of Oak Ridge, California in 1890 to be close to Katherine's family and ended up marrying local ranchers. Both Shannon and Matthew were born in Oak Ridge only a year apart. When Matthew, at one year's old, first saw Shannon, Shay Shay came out of his mouth, and it instantly stuck as her nickname. A year later Shannon would give him the nickname Matty.

When Shannon was almost three, the Bakers moved to a small cattle ranch on Oahu, Lalani's native home. Matthew 's family stayed on their large cattle ranch in Oak Ridge. Their mothers stayed in constant contact, writing each other weekly about their life and children. In addition to writing, the families visited every couple of years, making the long voyage from the mainland to the island. From their mothers, Shannon and Matthew grew up hearing all about each other and what they were doing. When they visited over the years, it was as if they had never been apart. They knew everything about each other, and they shared secrets that even their families didn't know about.

Now twenty years later, Shannon had a charming quiet beauty of her own with dark wavy hair and tan complexion embracing a rather pretty torso. One could easily see she inherited her mother's Hawaiian features, all but her nose, which was longer, more English, like her father's. While Matthew, at a tall six-foot one, with brown hair, and light tan skin, from his mother's half American Indian heritage, was slender yet muscular, a dashing young man.

As Shannon stood looking for Matty, her thoughts turned back to her earliest memory of him, seeing Matty's eyes crying out as the ship taking her to Oahu departed. His four-year-old face shouting "Shay Shay," as his father held him in his arms, and the ship's whistle blew for the final time. Shannon would never forget that parting, the feeling she was losing part of herself, the only other little person she knew at the time.

Shannon still remembered that awful feeling of being parted from him, and now dreaded to think she would go through that unbearable emotion again. Matthew was a senior at Cal and would graduate come June. Shannon was only a junior, but they had been together for the past two and half years, sharing all their accomplishments and failures. Come June, Matthew would be off into the big world and Shannon would be without him again.

They had both started college a year later than most, as Matthew was now twenty-two and Shannon twenty-one. Shannon had travelled around the world with her parents after graduating from high school, crossing the United States, to Europe, through the Suez Canal to Australia, then to the Marquesas Islands on the way back to Hawaii in 1911. Matthew also postponed college, helping his father run the family ranch, until he realized that his younger brother Andrew was much more suited to take over than he was. Matthew's interests lay in creating and building things. Ever since he was a small boy, he loved watching a barn or house being built. Now with the modern age of automobiles and more people traveling, he could see the need for roads, bridges, hotels and so much more. He wanted to be an architect.

Shannon, on the other hand, grew up on the east side of Oahu, riding horses and exploring the hills and beaches of Kahalu'u Valley. Shannon grew up among the ancient Hawaiian ruins in the valley and by the Kahalu'u lagoon. She was fascinated by the native stories about how the native people came to Hawaii. Upon coming to the university, she wanted to continue her quest to know how ancient cultures could be valued in the modern world.

Now in 1915, as she started the new semester, Shannon had made the decision of what her major would be.

"You're late!" Shannon teased as Matty rushed up. "Where are you taking me for lunch?"

"Hello, to you too. I'm sorry I'm late. I had to get supplies for my senior project. Hopefully this will make up for it," he said holding up a picnic basket. "Since you have such an important decision to tell me, I thought your thinking spot out past California Hall, away from noise and people would suit you," he said as he extended his arm to escort her.

"Matty, that's a wonderful idea."

"Well, did you make a decision?"

"Oh, no. You made me wait, now it's your turn. I'll tell you when we get there," she teased.

They walked out to a small wood cabin at the edge of the eucalyptus grove. The campus groundskeeper had given Shannon the key to the original homestead, a one room cabin, and she would steal away there to think and read when she wanted to be alone. The cabin wasn't big, but she had cleaned it up and the groundskeeper kept the stove working and the wood bin filled. There was a large multi-paned window to let in light and a small table and chair. Once inside,

Matthew started a fire in the potbelly stove and spread a blanket on the floor in front. Shannon sat down, opening the basket and found Matthew had thought of everything: ham sandwiches, a container of hot chocolate, apples and cookies, plates, cups and even napkins. She set things out, then took a sandwich with one hand while warming the other by the stove. Matthew just sat watching and smiling. Shannon's dark wavy hair glistened in the soft light shining through the window. Her light tan face glowed with excitement, yet her dark almond shaped eyes had a hint of uncertainty.

"Well, what have you decided?" he asked

"Historical archaeology! It's the logical course, since I'm interested in old ruins from the 6th century forward, and who and how they were built. I'm just not sure what era I will concentrate on, medieval or modern," she announced smugly.

"Is that practical for a woman?" Matthew said, knowing this field of work would require roughing it and traveling to out of the way places.

"What do you mean 'practical'? You know I'm just as capable as a man when it comes to finding things, if not better. And I love to travel. I can hike, climb, and dig post holes just as well as a man. Matter of fact a woman's touch is better when it comes to carefully digging things out of the ground."

She always could read my mind. "True, but how many women are actually in the field with men digging things up. Most men don't see woman as rugged, and I know for a fact you're not accustomed to roughing it. Never once did you sleep on the ground when we camped out," he said, challenging her.

"Why should I, when I didn't have to? I can wear pants just as well as a man. I'm not my mother," she said, just loud enough to be proud of the fact but soft enough so that it didn't sound like she didn't respect her mother, for indeed she admired her a great deal.

"That's for sure, I don't think I have ever seen her in pants, even when riding a horse. Mom says it's one of her quirks. But we digress, so it's historical archaeology. Fine. Lots of woman work in museums and a few on archaeological sites."

Shannon stopped and took another bite of the ham sandwich and thought. "Yes. Ever since we stopped at the island Ua Pou in the Marquesas Islands, on our way back to Hawaii, I've thought about the similarities in the ruins there and the Hawaiian culture. I was taught the Hawaiian people are descendants of the Polynesians explorers, and for the first time I saw it. It was exciting to see," she said with enthusiasm.

"Okay, I'm sure any museum will want you. People can bring you ancient artifacts or shards from various digs to compare. It's better than if you were a paleontologist studying bones and evolution. Safer too. Evolution is still controversial with most churches. Plus, when you get married your husband won't want you galivanting all over with strange men," he added smiling.

The word marriage riled Shannon. "Married? This is the twentieth century; women aren't looking to get married at eighteen any more. We're looking for new possibilities and the right to a life other than mothering. Besides, I can take care of myself, if father and mother would just stop worrying about me. I had hoped to get my own place with Maureen this year, but father is insisting I stay at Aunt Joanna and Uncle Richard's again. Now look at what you did, you have distracted me. I'm excited about my choice, and Professor Kroeber, my adviser and anthropology instructor, is now teaching archaeology."

Matty just laughed. "You do want to get married someday, don't you? And it doesn't take much to sidetrack you, Shay Shay."

"That's not true. I have aways been interested in my Hawaiian ancestry. I like exploring the old ruins at home. Archaeology isn't a distraction. It's an integral part of finding and comparing ancient cultures. Marriage would be a distraction."

"Okay, you're right. You have a one-track mind when it comes to ancient ruins. But didn't you want to ask me something else?" he said, not wanting to debate any longer.

Shannon looked out the window for a moment, trying to collect her thoughts and how to approach the subject of what was happening in the world. There was a war raging in Europe. Germany had invaded Belgium and France. Russia was involved in helping Serbia fight the Austro-Hungarians, and England had gone to help France, because of the alliance they had made. Some American men were joining the British to fight the war. Shannon didn't like the thought of Matthew as a soldier in a war.

"Matty, you will be graduating come June. What are your plans?" Before Matthew could answer, she blurted out, "Please, promise me you won't volunteer and go fight with the British or French!" Her voice was pained with anguish.

"Shay Shay! I have no plans to join the army. What gave you that idea?" Matthew said putting his arm around her.

"Well, your mother has family and good friends in Britain and France. And you're always reading the newspaper about the war," she said quietly.

"Oh, I see. Yes, Thomas, Jessie and Charles are in a difficult situation, being so close to the war. But they are not near the fighting. That's partly why I read the paper to make sure they're not in harm's way. Mother is quite concerned about Charles since he is French and his estate is near Paris. We've offered to have him come here several times since the war broke out. But he won't leave. As for me going to fight, it's not our country's war. President Wilson has not joined the Allied Powers. Only if he does and I'm required to go, only then will I join the army. So, stop worrying," he said with a reassuring look.

"Good! I hope he never signs an agreement to help. I'm just used to you being around all the time. Just the fact that you're graduating and leaving has got me missing you already. You know I always hated saying good bye when we were kids."

"Well, I haven't left yet, and I'm only going to Sacramento, where I think I might have a job lined up with Lionaski Architectural Firm, a very new firm. I didn't want to say anything until I was sure, knowing how you hate it when we part," Matthew said, trying to comfort her.

Just then there was a knock on the door. It was Maureen Campbell, Shannon's roommate. Maureen was an art major, studying the classic masters of art, while trying to create her own oil landscapes. She had a bubbly outgoing bohemian personality, while Shannon was more reserved, introverted at times. Maureen had an overwhelmingly adventurous side to her. She was rather short, with soft reddish hair and a quite fair complexion. Shannon in contrast was five foot eight inches. Together the girls were a carefree courageous force, with a side of common sense thrown in.

"There you are!" Maureen said as she came through the cabin door. "Time to go!" she announced as she reached for Shannon's hand to help her to her feet. "By the way, Matt, Lars is looking for you to help set up the firewood for tonight's bonfire."

"Okay! That's my cue to leave you two until tonight. Shay Shay, I promise," and with that Matt jumped up, kissed Shannon on the head, and was off.

"What about the picnic basket?" she called after him.

"I'll get it from you tonight when I pick you up at 6:00 o'clock!" he yelled back.

"Promise? What promise?" Maureen asked.

"Oh, nothing I'll tell you later," Shannon said as she packed up the basket and blanket and headed back to the Malcomb's place where they were rooming.

~~

Joanna and Richard Malcomb were good friends with Matt's mother, Katherine. Joanna had been Katherine's roommate at boarding school, and Shannon's mother Lalani knew Joanna at that time as well. Shannon had grown up calling them Aunt Joanna and Uncle Richard. Richard and Joanna had lived in San Francisco until 1906, when the great earthquake destroyed most of the city, including the hospital where Richard practiced. Their home was also badly damaged beyond repair, so like many people, they left the city and moved across the bay to Berkeley. They purchased a large five-bedroom, craftsman style house on Chestnut and Rose, about a mile from the university. Their daughters were now grown and married, and the Malcombs were happy to have Shannon and Maureen in the house. Richard tried keeping an eye on the girls, but they weren't little girls anymore and had the right to come and go as they desired, at least within reason, according to the girl's parents.

The bonfire rally that evening was in celebration of Cal's basketball team joining the Pacific Conference, the season's opening game being against Nebraska. The girls dressed in warm sweaters and long skirts, and they gathered their scarves and mittens, along with their coats, as the weather was a brisk forty-eight degrees. They met Matt and Lars in the parlor just after six o'clock. "I don't see what the big fuss is over watching men chase after a bouncing ball," Maureen squealed as Lars hurried her out to the car.

Lars grabbed the door and helped Maureen into the back while Shannon sat up front. Milton Larson was Matt's roommate. They met their first day at Berkeley and quickly became best friends. As early as four years old, Lars disliked his first name Milton, and proudly announced he wanted to go by his last name, which was quickly shortened to Lars, with his approval. Lars was from a wealthy family in San Diego, who ran an accounting firm that handled the accounts for various shipping and merchant companies. Lars was tall and lanky, while Matt was as tall and muscular. Lars had a big grin that reeked of playful antics, that could be seen in his hazel brown eyes.

Matt and Lars shared a small apartment only a few blocks from the university, and Matt had a car, a 1914 Packard roadster his parents had given him. Everyone in Berkeley knew the Taylor gang: Matthew, Shannon, Maureen and Lars. When Shannon decided to attend Cal Berkeley, Matthew was delighted, knowing she would add fun and adventure to his and Lars' boyish pranks. It was Maureen and Lars that teamed up to create the most mischief, but they didn't seem to want to be more than good friends. Shannon added the common sense to this little band, while Matt had the calm reserve to keep things from getting too far out of hand. Many an afternoon, the four of them could be seen driving off in Matt's roadster heading for some rally or to a sporting event, depending on who won the coin toss or protested the loudest. Tonight, the boys had won the coin toss and they were headed for the bonfire to mark the start of basketball season for the Pacific Coast Conference.

By the time they arrived at the beach, the fire was in full blaze. Matt didn't remember building the stack quite so high earlier that day. Someone apparently had added several short logs to the top. They now burned like the top of a torch. Classmates were cheering and sitting on blankets on the sand around the fire, watching an effigy of the opposing team's mascot go up in flames. The four of them quickly joined a few other couples standing there, trying to stay warm.

"Why do they always burn a paper effigy of the mascot? Why don't we just go steal the mascot like other schools?" Maureen asked.

"We used to steal the mascots, but the rivalry got out of hand with putting them in trees and on top of buildings, and stuffing cannons with cement. Our mascot, Oski, is difficult to steal. One guy even got clawed! Stealing a live bear is a lot more difficult than stealing a live Irish terrier from Notre Dame or Biff the wolverine from Michigan," Matt explained.

"And what is that supposed to be?" Maureen asked, pointing to the green effigy.

"That's Corncob Man, he's a husker from Nebraska. Basically, he's half a corn cob with corn silk for hair, wearing green overalls. A Nebraska farmer," Lars laughed.

"If I was from Nebraska, I'd be burning it too. That's a terrible mascot," Shannon added.

Matt spread a blanket next to a few others and Shannon joined him on the ground. Maureen stood behind them not wanting to get too close to the fire, and Lars behind her, attempting to put his arms around her. The fire had been burning for some time and the top logs now teetered, ready to slide down the stack.

"Oski Wow Wow, Oski Wow Wow, Oski Wow Wow!" the crowd began to yell.

A group of basketball players arrived with ears of corn and shouted, "Roast the Huskers!" The team captain threw a large ear of corn onto the top of the stack, hitting one of the teetering logs. "Basket!" he yelled as it struck the top log. Sparks went flying into the night air as the log shifted, knocking a second log loose. He threw a second large ear, hitting the top logs again. They teetered for a moment, then crashed down the stack, causing the third log to come with them. Gasps and aahhs went up from the onlookers as sparks flew. The logs went end over end down the burning stack and bounced into the crowd. The girls began to scream as a log came crashing between their blankets. Lars instantly reacted pulling Maureen back out of the way of a second log coming towards them. Matt rolled over the top of Shannon to protect her as the log slammed into the sand just in front of them.

The third log hit one of the rocks surrounding the fire and bounced towards two freshmen girls. Colleen Atkins screamed as the log landed next to her with a blast of red sparks. She got up to escape the burning log, but her skirt was full of hot embers. A boy pulled Colleen back to the ground and was stomping on her dress, trying to get the embers to go out.

Matt rushed to help, grabbing a shovel standing upright in the sand, and moved toward Colleen. He dug the shovel into the sand and flung a heavy load at Colleen's skirt. She sputtered as the sand hit her face as well as the dress. A second shovel of sand smothered the final embers. Her friend managed to scamper out of the way unharmed, and was being held by the player who had tossed the ear, now with a horrified look on his face. The first log was still burning on the blanket where it landed, and Matt swung around with another shovel of sand and dumped it onto the log and the burning blanket. With a few more shovels of sand the dislodged burning wood was snuffed out, yet still very hot. Shannon and several other girls went to Colleen to check on her.

"Are you hurt? Did your legs get burned?" Shannon asked.

Colleen now sat upright, sand covering her clothes and her hair. "I don't think so, just scared out of my wits."

Matt came and helped her up, feeling embarrassed he had flung sand in her face. Shannon checked to make sure her dress was cold and her petticoat as well. Her friend rejoined them, assuring them she was fine, and that the embers had not landed on her.

Two of the basketball players managed to get the extinguished logs back inside the fire ring and collected the remaining ears of corn to prevent other logs from being dislodged. Another player came and asked if he could take Colleen and her friend home, apologizing profusely for what had happened. Colleen looked at Matt, hoping he would take her home. "Colleen, Carl is a good guy, you'll be fine with him. I need to stay and make sure the fire is put out," Matt said. Carl took her arm and helped her and her friend to his car.

"Well, that was exciting," Maureen said, now joining Matt and Shannon.

"Only you would think it exciting," Matt sneered.

After all the commotion, the other students began to depart. Only a few remained. Matt decided it was best to put the remaining fire out. He, Lars, and a few others began to shovel sand onto the fire. Once the flames were knocked down, they took the remaining logs and pulled them apart. Lars had gone to the water with two buckets and was now pouring the water onto the smoldering logs. It took them another half hour to make sure the fire was out and safe to leave it.

Matt asked Shannon if she was ready to go home, but Maureen insisted on going to the café for sodas. "Matt, it's too early to go home," Lars joined in protesting.

At the Coffee Club they found other students gathered around talking about what happened. After a drink with the girls, Matt and

Lars gravitated to the group of senior classmates, while Shannon and Maureen joined several other junior girls. By ten o'clock, Maureen was finally ready to go home. Lars was quite happy after four beers and grabbed Maureen around the waist, "Are you my girl?"

"Don't be silly. Shannon and I are no one's girls," she declared. "But I can be your date anytime. Just not now, it's time to go home." Taking his arm from around her waist, she led him out to the car and they tumbled into the back seat. Matt was more composed, helping Shannon into the front. By the time they reached the Malcomb's, Lars had fallen asleep on Maureen's lap. She lifted his head and wiggled out, letting it thump to the seat in hopes to get a disgruntled response to laugh at. But all she got was a short sleepy groan.

"Good luck in Professor Kroeber's class tomorrow," Matt said as he watched them head for the door. Once they were inside, he motioned to Lars it was safe to come up front.

Lars grinned as he took the front, "I couldn't give her the satisfaction of getting the last word and laugh."

Matt just shook his head and drove the few blocks back to their place.

Matt lay in bed thinking about Maureen's remark about them not wanting to be any one's girls and laughed, *she indeed is controlling her courtships. She has Lars right where she wants him and he doesn't seem to mind. They're like two young horses, chasing each other around the pasture, nuzzling up to each other, then charging off again, but when the time comes, I wonder if she will give in to him. Once we're not on campus I bet Maureen will sow her oats with some other stud.*

And then there's Shannon. When she arrived on campus, I was compelled to show her the ropes and protect her from the seedier side of college jocks. But I found myself thoroughly enjoying taking her to the dances and escorting her to her rallies. She was a fresh change from the other girls I'd dated. I don't know if it's because I can be myself around her and don't have to pretend to please her. Or if it's because she's unpretentious, not expecting any-

thing, willing to take what I offer and not expecting more, that makes her desirable. Let alone how pretty she is.

It's easy to be with her, to tell her anything that's bothering me. Well, just about everything, except that I might be in love with her. I wish I had the courage to really kiss her, just one long embracing kiss, to see how it feels. Then I'd truly know.

She's not ready for that! And I'm not ready to find out and have my love rejected. Best to continue to be best friends. I will have a lifetime full of future opportunities with Shay Shay. You don't want to go messing things up now. What would the families say if I do something she doesn't want? I can just hear mother, 'Matthew Taylor, how could you? Shay Shay's your best friend, not your lover.' Little brother Andrew on the other hand would be quite sympathetic, he's had a crush on her since he was ten. He would have kissed her by now, if he thought she would have let him.

Oh, Matt! just let it go for now, it's only the first week of the semester. Holding her close will have to do and what does any of us know about true love?

Matt turned over to sleep. His mind flashing to the log coming towards them. *I'm glad she didn't get hurt. Nor anyone else for that matter. Stop! Get some sleep, in the morning Lars's hangover will be enough to deal with and getting him to class.*

~~

The next morning, Lars was rather grumpy and difficult to get moving to class. Shannon on the other hand was up early and headed for the college pool for a morning swim before the freshmen boys arrived to ogle the women swimmers. Shannon had swum in the lagoon of Kaneohe Bay all her life and was an excellent swimmer and diver. Sporting her tight-fitting swim suit with knee length trousers she would arrive about 6:10 a.m. and swim laps for about forty minutes at the Olympic woman's pool on the south end of campus, and then return home to shower and dress for her classes. By 7:30, Maureen would be up and ready for class, and the girls would catch the bus to campus.

This morning was no different, except as she was about to climb out, the coach from the women's swim team extended a hand and helped her out. "Good morning, Miss Baker, still doing your morning swim I see. We sure could use a strong swimmer like you. What do you say?" Coach Paulsen smiled.

"Good morning. The water's a lot cooler than Hawaii, but still not so bad that I can't get a few laps in. Isn't Hazel Langenburg still swimming for you?"

"Yes, but Hazel's a long-distance swimmer. I need a good strong sprinter, and I think you could be just that."

"Sprinter? I don't think I have the arm reach to cut the distance quickly. I'll pass, but thanks for asking." Shannon wrapped the towel around her and headed to Richard's car she had borrowed.

"Do think about it!" Coach called back.

Shannon caught Aunt Joanna and Maureen sitting in the kitchen, drinking their morning coffee upon her return. "Coach asked me to be on the swim team again." Maureen pooh-poohed the idea. "I'll never see you, and what about weekend outings? You'd be at meets every weekend. Swimming should be for fun not competition. You're not competitive!"

"I'm competitive! I hate to be outsmarted," Shannon rebutted.

"Only with Matty, and it's more you want the last word," Maureen pointed out.

"Well, maybe you're right, but I do like a good debate," Shannon conceded.

2

The Final Everything

The first week went quickly. Shannon met with Professor Kroeber about what era of archaeology to pursue, settling on modern archaeology, since medieval concentrates on Europe. The era of modern archaeology would give her the freedom and technology to explore more of the Pacific Island sites she was interested in.

The first Friday night dance arrived. The girls bought new dresses over the winter break for the dances and couldn't wait to show them off. Lars and Matthew arrived at seven o'clock to escort them, looking as handsome as ever. Shannon was wearing a silky, rather straight, cap sleeve blue dress, which showed her pretty curves, and Matthew's eyes lit up when she walked into the room. Lars let out a whistle.

"Milton Larson, what about me?" Maureen huffed as she came in behind Shannon wearing a scoop neck green chiffon bodice with a skirt about two inches shorter than customary.

Lars swaggered up to her and took a look at her pretty little ankles and small waist, "A sight to behold, me goddess." He bowed and kissed her hand, causing her to giggle.

As they arrived at the dance, Matthew snatched up Shannon's dance card and wrote his name on the first and last lines, knowing all her dances would be taken, especially in that dress. There was a small orchestra playing, and the large reception room in South Hall was decorated with blue and gold balloons and streamers. Matthew immediately took Shannon in his arms and began to dance slowly, holding

17

her as close to him as he dared. "You look smashing tonight. I think I'll keep you all to myself and make the other guys jealous."

"You wouldn't dare. If you do, they will think I'm your gal, as they did last year. No one will ever ask me out, and then what will I do next year when you're gone? I happen to like Freddie Wrightman in my archaeology logistics class, and I'm hoping he will be here tonight."

Matt's heart sank a little upon hearing her words, "Would it be so bad to be my girl?" he whispered.

Shannon stared at him with a surprised questioning look. "Matty, don't be a tease."

"I'm not teasing, I'm protecting you from all the wolves out there. Just for the rest of the year. Once I'm gone and you're older, I'm sure there will be plenty of men knocking on your door."

"Now, you are teasing. I'm perfectly capable of weeding out the wolves and holding them at bay. I had plenty of them at the swim club in Oahu circling when I was a senior in high school."

"Ok, forget I said it! Let's just enjoy the dancing," he said as he spun her around and picked up the pace. Before Shannon could comment the dance ended and Byron Forsythe was asking to sign her dance card. Matthew knew he had lost the pursuit of making her his gal and quickly retreated before he said something more that he shouldn't. *Matthew, it's best to be satisfied with always having the first and last dance with her. I really should give Sylvia a second chance, I liked her the best of all the girls I've escorted.* Matthew looked around the room for Sylvia as Shannon sent Byron for punch while she caught up with Maureen and Allison talking. The young men, from bold freshmen to seniors, lined up to sign Shannon's dance card, including Freddie. Byron returned and he proved to be an excellent foxtrot partner.

After an hour of dancing and various partners from great to mediocre, Shannon was glad the orchestra took a small break and she could take time with the girls to gossip about their partners and who was dreamy and who to avoid.

Freddie approached Shannon as the band started back up. "I believe my name is next on your card, is it not?" he said, offering his hand.

"Why, yes, it is!" she smiled. Shannon had been looking forward to this dance. *I hope he's as good a dancer as he looks. I would really like to get to know him better.*

Freddie was a good dancer and together they made perfect two step partners. So much that she hoped Maxwell next on her list would have forgotten and she could continue with Freddie. But no luck. Maxwell swept in with both left feet and was eager to try his luck at a waltz.

Maxwell was six foot two and his stride was far too wide for Shannon's straight cut dress. At one point she wasn't quick enough and he landed squarely on her foot. "Auw!" She could feel the slit to her skirt give and become an inch higher as she tried to widen her stride. After the second near mishap, she suggested they get a drink. "Maxwell, my friend I think it's best you stay with a two-step or one-step or else find a very tall partner that can match your stride."

"Stride? It's my turn to match your stride," Lars said from behind them. Shannon was most grateful for the rescue and that it was Lars with whom she could easily dance.

"Thanks for rescuing me. My feet need a break from the toe crushers." He smiled and spun her around as they two-stepped their way around the floor.

Shannon had spotted Matty dancing with several pretty girls as she danced with more young men. They gave each other a friendly smile. On one occasion a "when is this dance going to end" glance came from Matty. He had picked a pretty girl, but she was a talker with a shrill giggle. In reality at the end of the dance, both Shannon and Matty were glad to be back with each other for the final dance. They didn't have to make small talk and they could hold each other comfortably without worrying about being too close. Shannon leaned in, putting her cheek against his chin. *Matt, this is your chance. Just turn your head down and kiss her. Her lips are right there.* Matt pulled his head back and down about to kiss her, when 'BANG.' Startled they turned their heads in the direction of the noise. There, stood Maureen and Lars, about to pop another balloon. BANG.

Matt gave Lars a look that could kill, then spun Shannon around and finished their dance.

After the dance, Lars and Maureen hooked up with another couple to go dancing in town. Shannon declined, and Matthew offered to take her for a sweet at the coffee club, wanting to spend more time together. At the club the conversation wasn't exactly what he was hoping for. Shannon ran through her dance partner's pros and cons. Maxwell was as awkward as he appeared, and Mitchell was decent until he had too much to drink. Freddie was all she hoped for as a dancer, but not much at conversation. Shannon quizzed Matty about the girls he danced with and who the redhead was that he danced with twice, wondering if she was an old flame. *They seemed pretty friendly. I could tell she had a crush on him. Still, he didn't seem too interested in her. I wonder why he hasn't got a girl?*

"Matty, who was the redhead you danced with? Seems you enjoyed her company."

Matt was lost in thought about Freddie, "Who?"

"The redhead you danced with twice," Shannon repeated.

"Oh, Margo. She's a friend, we went out several times when we were sophomores. But we're just friends now. Nice girl, but has big dreams of being a newspaper reporter. Far too ambitious for me. Pretty though, and a good dancer. Why? Are you jealous?"

"Me? Jealous? Of course not. Just curious why you don't have a steady girl."

"You're my steady girl, didn't you know that?" he said with a wink. *It would be nice if she took me seriously on this, but she won't. She'll just laugh.*

"That's silly, Matty. I've known you too long to be your girl. And no, I won't say sister either," she laughed, as she stood taking her coat.

Childhood sweethearts maybe? "It's getting late, and if we want to get to the stable early to ride and then watch the race horses practice, we'd best go." Matt just smiled with a sigh.

At times when growing up, Shannon and Matty were so close, strangers would have thought they were brother and sister. But neither of them felt that way. Instead, they were very special friends. Matt had two siblings, Andrew two years younger, and Abigail four years younger. Shannon had one brother, Evan, some twenty years older than her.

When Shannon's parents moved to the ranch on Oahu, Evan, their twenty-three-year-old ranch hand, came with them and lived in the main house as a family member. Jim and Lalani Baker eventually adopted Evan when he was twenty-five and he officially became Shannon's older brother. When the Bakers and Taylor families were together, it was Shay Shay and Matty that were always off somewhere together, exploring and sharing secrets. She never shared secrets with Evan. He was more of a second father figure than brother. Perhaps that's why she never thought of Matthew as a brother, being so close in age and sharing secrets. But this time, Matty would keep his thoughts about her to himself, only giving her his usual peck on the cheek and "Goodnight," when leaving her at her door.

~~

The next morning Shannon was up early, dressed in trousers, a plaid shirt, and cowboy boots. A cowboy hat, leather gloves, scarf, and a change of clothes sat on the hall table waiting. At about 6:30 a.m. Shannon heard the sound of Matt's roadster pull up. She snatched up the thermos of hot coffee and grabbed the things on the hall table and was out the door before Matt was halfway up the walkway. It was still dark out and the air was chilly. "Good morning, Matty. Maureen got in this morning about three so I didn't want the bell to wake anyone. I've got hot coffee if you need it."

Matty gave Shannon a quick kiss to the cheek and took the thermos. "No, thanks. Had two cups, already. I put the top up on the roadster since the wind will be quite chilly." He tucked the thermos in the back seat on the floor along with Shay Shay's hat. It took them about an hour and a half to get to the riding stables. Matthew's mother bred horses and knew the owner of Pleasanton Stable, Roger Mackenzie. Pleasanton Stables was a training track for race horses, and Roger was happy to have Matt come ride some of the extra workout horses. This morning he would be riding a gelding name Ben and Shannon a mare named Mable. These horses were calm strong horses that would run with the thoroughbreds.

At the stables, Sam reminded them not to try and race the horses, as they still needed them to work with the race horses that afternoon. Sam was glad to hear Shannon had grown up on a cattle ranch on Oahu, and had her own horse, Ginger. She stroked Mable's white blaze and spoke softly as the two of them got to know each other. Matt had ridden Ben before and checked his cinch. Holding his breath while it was being buckled was a trick of Ben's. Once buckled, he let out the air so it wasn't so tight. It was a common trick of riding horses and one Matt had learned the hard way when he was ten. The saddle slid around, and he fell to the ground as he raced his brother Andrew, breaking his arm. Ben snorted as Matt elbowed him in the girth and tightened the cinch another notch. After checking the horse's hooves for any stones, Matt gave Shannon a two-handed foot lift up, as Mable was rather tall. They headed down the trail to the open park area along Alameda Creek, then picked up the pace. Shannon sprinted ahead at a gallop for a short distance stopping by a large tree while Matt caught up.

"We can't do that too much, otherwise Sam will get after me."

"I know, I just couldn't resist. It's been two weeks since I let it all out."

"Tell you what. We can do mother and father's game of matching paces. You ride a little faster, not a lot, until I've matched the pace. Then we switch, changing the pace and waiting for the horses to come together. Slow or fast, we have to match. Just nothing faster than an easy cantor, else the horses will get too sweaty and Sam won't be happy," Matt said as he adjusted his hat tighter to his head.

"Alright, you're on. I'll start. Bet you can't get ahead of me. I'm quick to notice a change," Shannon replied.

Shannon started off at a trot and Matt quickly matched it. Then he squeezed Ben with his thigh, signally to pick up the pace. Shannon quickly caught up. Finally, Shannon kicked Mable into a cantor and took the lead. Matt quickly caught up, bringing Ben into a gallop for a short moment. "Hey, that's not fair, you galloped. I win," Shannon protested. "I was slowing down so you could catch up, a cantor would have gotten you here." They were now along a narrow sandy edge of the creek as they stood.

They dismounted and let the horses drink from the creek and nibble on grass. Matt came up behind Shannon, looking out across the water to a grove of cottonwood trees turning yellow.

"Not the same as your island, is it?" he said softly.

"No, not exactly!" she sighed.

"Do you miss home?" Matty asked.

"Parts of it. I miss swims with mom and evening rides with dad. Mom used to go with him but since Genevieve died, she doesn't ride much anymore."

"She always did prefer a horse and carriage. Bet she's not too fond of cars either," Matt laughed.

"Not so much, but she will let dad take the car when they go into Honolulu. How about you? You've been away from the ranch for four years now. Do you plan to go back to Oak Ridge when you graduate?"

"Heavens, no. Oak Ridge has grown, but it's still a small town. Dad wants me to talk to the Cattlemen's Association in Sacramento once I'm there."

"Really! Why?"

"Something to do with lobbying for better prices and shipping fees. The meat packing houses have too much say in the price the cattlemen get and what kind of beef the public gets. One group shouldn't control the meat source for the whole country. Cattlemen, stockyards, meat packers, and butchers should all work together with equal say on setting prices and processing."

"You would do that for your dad and give up your dream of building things? The market on the mainland is very different than that on Oahu. At home my dad has more trouble keeping up with the demand, and the ranches can pretty much set their own prices. But what about building bridges and buildings?"

"Lobbying may be something I do on the side if Father insists. If I get a job with the Lionaski firm, of course, that will come first. But if we can't get some control over the cattle pricing, a lot of ranchers will be forced to stop ranching. I just hope I can manage both. Once a compromise is accomplished, I can go back to architecture full time," Matt said with a half-smile. "Enough about cattle and jobs, are you going to miss me when I'm gone?" Matt asked teasingly. *I hope she does.*

"Miss you? I think about it now and then. I always miss you at first when we go back to Oahu, and if you're in Sacramento, that's not that far. You can drive up on weekends. On the other hand, maybe I can finally meet some other men. Alice says I need to find a husband. Of course, that's the last thing I'm looking for at the moment. Father says I should enjoy school and find something I'm passionate about. Something other than getting the right to vote for women in Hawaii, that is."

"You are passionate about that alright. But at least you go about it in a civilized manner. It is odd that your dad can vote, and your mom, who is the native Hawaiian, cannot." Matt shook his head. *Great, I shouldn't have said that, I've given her an opening for an oration on women's rights.*

"Exactly! If the US wanted Hawaii so badly, then they should at least give the native people the right to vote like other US citizens," Shannon bristled back.

"Okay, I agree, let's not turn this lovely spot into a pulpit for woman's rights. Let's enjoy the warm day while we can. It's rare in winter to have such a nice day as this. Soon enough we will be knee deep in term papers so this may be our last chance to ride." Matt put his arms around Shannon holding her in front of him. "You know I'm always here for you, right?"

"Yes, I know. Still, I have to admit I will miss you once you graduate, just as I always do when you leave."

Matt gave her a squeeze. *I should kiss her now, right here while we're alone.* He started to turn her around, but chickened out and only kissed her on her forehead.

"What was that for?"

"Just because I felt like it. Come on, it's time we head back."

They gathered the horses up from the stream where they had wandered, then mounted and began a slow easy ride back to the stable. The cottonwood trees were thick here, and they created a brilliant yellowish-brown canopy as they rode beneath them. As they came to a meadow, Shannon returned to the game of matching paces with a cantor then back to a trot, finally, arriving back at the stable with a slow easy walk. They didn't have to stable and brush down the horses. Stable boys were waiting to do it.

Shannon took a moment and washed up in the washroom, changing into the skirt she had brought. They decided not to stay and watch the race horses work out. Shannon was now hungry, having missed breakfast, and Matt had promised to take her to lunch on their way back to campus. At lunch they discussed plans for Matt's graduation, knowing it would be a big deal for the Taylor family. Shannon wished her folks could be there, but the trips from Oahu still took a week's sailing and there would be too much to do at Mau Loa with spring round up. Matt's question about missing him came floating across her mind as she sipped her tea. *It will be different this time when Matty leaves. I've gotten used to him being close all this time. I will miss him. I won't tell him that, I don't want to inflate his ego. At least not at this moment.*

Matthew looked at Shannon in deep thought, "Penny for your thoughts."

"Oh, no, they're far too precious to sell," she said teasingly. "Nothing really. Just about not going home this summer. Father thinks I should stay here, since so many ships have been torpedoed by the Germans. I keep writing that the war is in the Atlantic and not the Pacific. That shipping between the islands and here is safe."

"I think you're right, but I'm sure your dad just wants to make sure you're safe. I know the Malcombs will be happy to have you over the summer or you could come stay in Oak Ridge. Mother would be happy to have you."

"I could spend the summer with you and the family. That way we can spend a little more time together before you go out on you own. It might be the last time we really spend time with each other. You may find a girl and get engaged or move to Washington D.C. to lobby Congress or who knows where to build a bridge or opera house."

"So, you will miss me?" Matt smiled.

"Only if you don't write," she chuckled.

It was getting late and they both had classwork waiting, so they skipped dessert and headed out. It had been a crazy first week and now it was time to settle into a routine of classwork. Matt had a final architecture project to propose to his professor and Shannon had a full load with both geology and archaeology classes along with ancient art history and upper division math.

The first part of the spring semester went by quickly. Shannon found she enjoyed her geology classes and archaeology field studies class, especially the digging part. But she loved the research part of archaeology, looking for clues to connect various geological events and cultures together. She was now quite familiar with several libraries in town and in San Francisco. She also understood the importance of her ancient civilizations course and was glad she had done well and kept the book. The History of Art class was also becoming valuable to her understanding pottery and how important shards were to archaeology. She was very interested to get a hold of Captain Cook's journals of his second voyage, which included stops in Tahiti, the Society Islands and the South Marquesas Islands. She hoped to use them to support her senior project on Hawaiian ruins in her final year. She needed to write to London to obtain them, hopefully with Annie Alexander's help. Annie was a paleontology and geology graduate which had a lot of influence, had funded several expeditions and liked to help undergraduate students with their research.

While Shannon spent her time at the libraries, Maureen spent a great deal of time painting at a little studio that a fellow artist had rented. So much that her grades in her other academic classes had dropped, and the school was recommending she consider leaving and just take up freelance painting. Her grades on her finals would determine her future at Cal.

Both Matt and Lars were busy with senior projects. Matt had decided to enter the school's competition for a new classroom building to be added to the university. The school was growing and they were planning several new buildings. The school governing board agreed to allow graduating architecture students to submit their designs for consideration.

As spring rolled around, Maureen became more interested in attending plays and movies before leaving for home. Shannon kept trying to get her to be more serious about her classes, but Maureen had lost interest and felt she had learned all she needed to know. Her natural ability in painting would allow her to do what she wanted, and going to the movies twice a week became more important. Of course, she wanted Shannon to go with her. There was a new cinema in town and Charlie Chaplain films were her favorite. At first Shannon and Lars traded off going with her, but as the semester work got busier, Lars had to decline and Shannon wanted to spend more time with the suffragist group on campus.

Shannon had actively participated in the suffragist movement, advocating for the ratification of the new nineteen amendment at home in Hawaii. The campus chapter was more about writing letters and strategy than the suffragettes marching and violence. California had passed the amendment in 1911, but Hawaii was still holding out, therefore Shannon could not vote but Maureen could. Shannon liked the method the local suffragists had taken to get the passage of the amendment in California. They had looked at how it could help the towns, rather than force them into it, often meeting with various groups to quietly and professionally discuss the pros and cons of the amendment. Shannon was a good writer and with the help of others, drafted many persuasive letters to Hawaiian officials and business-men, hoping this method would work in Hawaii as it did in Califor-nia. Her biggest problem was that she was not in Hawaii and therefore it was difficult to know what kind of impact her letters had.

As the last few weeks of the semester approached, Shannon saw little of anyone. Maureen had made up her mind to leave Cal and spent most of her time out painting or at the movies. Lars was fed up with her and stopped coming around. Matthew had sequestered himself in the dining room of his apartment, building a model of the classroom building for Cal and finalizing the blueprints. He had one more week before it all had to be turned in. It was beginning to dawn on Shannon that Matty would be gone soon. He was pretty certain he would get the position with the architectural firm in Sacramento and would be starting in July. Therefore, if she did go to the Taylor ranch for summer, she still wouldn't see much of him.

On a warm May evening she walked over to Matt's with dinner and they took it outside on the lawn to eat, the house being rather a mess at this point.

"Your building looks amazing. Will you have everything finished for your presentation next week?" Shannon asked as she handed Matt a piece of fried chicken.

"I better have it finished. My whole grade and future depends on it. Lionaski has made a job offer on the basis I retain top standing in my class. I know I haven't been much fun lately. It's just that I need to get this right and done on time." Matt said, running his free hand through his hair.

"I understand. I have been busy doing a lot of research myself. Not that my future depends on it right now, but I'm fascinated with the way I can examine a piece of pottery and determine what it was made of, which then leads me to where it was made. I'm also beginning to recognize certain commonalities between certain cultures. I'm especially excited now that Annie has arranged to get transcripts of Cook's journal about the Marquesas and Society Islands. They wouldn't do the entire journal; it was too extensive. But what they are sending will be significant to my senior project for next year."

"That's great! You should enjoy what you're studying, then you know you've picked the right field," Matt said, as he watched the sparkle in her eyes.

"Matt, I don't think I am going to go to Oak Ridge this summer. Professor Kroeber is taking a group of students to Mesa Verde Indian ruins in Colorado to help with the restoration and to study some of the artifacts they are digging up. He says it will give us good experience.

"Others are going up to the Presidio to check out where they're building the World's Fair site, looking for things left after the great earthquake. Many people camped out and left lots of things behind. The families were from all sorts of cultures and by looking at the artifacts, they should be able to determine what cultures they came from. It's not as exciting as Mesa Verde, but not everyone can go on that trip," Shannon explained.

Matt was surprised and a little disappointed by this announcement. *But what about spending time together? I'd hoped to have a couple of weeks together at the ranch before I left for Sacramento.* "Really! I thought you wanted to go to the ranch?"

"I did. But you're going to be there only for a few weeks and then what will I do? It's a great opportunity to be part of the Mesa Verde work or the Presidio. But I do feel bad about asking the Malcombs if I can stay. I had hoped to find a place Maureen and I could share. But she will be going back to Julian and I can't afford a place on my own."

"Why move from the Malcombs? They love having you there."

"They do, but their daughter and grandkids have been visiting more often, and they need the rooms. Plus, trying to study with screaming two-year-olds around is just not helpful. I'm going be twenty-three this year, and I think it's time I get my own place. Your place will be coming available, I wish I could move in there. With everyone leaving, -- you, Lars and Maureen, -- and without a house-mate, I can't afford it. I thought I might ask Alice if she would be interested."

"You could move in with me here for the few weeks I'm here and then find a new housemate," Matthew said with a wink.

"Matthew Taylor, that would be scandalous! I'd couldn't do that even if I wanted to, which I don't. You're far too messy. When was the last time you cleaned?" she said, giving him a swat.

"We've been a little busy lately. You know it's not usually that messy," he said in defense.

"You're right, I'm sorry. I would love to have your place when you move out, it's so close to campus I could walk and not need to take the bus."

"Well, I can see if the landlord has anyone else lined up to move in after us. If he doesn't, I'll have him hold it for you. I'm sure Alice or even Grace would be agreeable to sharing the place. I'm just hoping you will come down to the ranch for the few weeks I'm there. I have missed you this past month and will miss you terribly once we're miles apart. When will the Mesa Verde trip begin?" he added as his voice tapered off.

"I'm not sure when the Mesa Verde trip will leave, probably early June, I may not even be invited to go. I'll think about coming to the ranch."

"You will be invited to Mesa Verde, I'm sure. But you could come to the ranch for a few weeks before you leave," Matt reassured her.

"Maybe I can come for a week. And I'll ask Alice about rooming. Let me know if your place will be available." She leaned over and gave him a kiss to the cheek.

Matthew smiled and wanted to pull her into his arms and give her a firm kiss to the lips but refrained himself, once again. This was not the time. *If she comes to the ranch that will be the time. Then or never.*

Shannon was glad when senior finals week arrived. Matthew had been a frantic mess for days trying to finish his designs, model, and term papers. She was afraid at one point he might collapse from exhaustion. Lars was no help as he had procrastinated with two of his term papers and was burning the midnight oil as well. Lars preferred the campus library to the house because Matthew had taken over every room but his. Shannon continued to come with supper and began to wash up the piles of dishes stacked around so when Matt's parents arrived at least the place wouldn't smell like the pig's trough it had become with leftover food bowls and dirty shirts.

Matthew painstakingly managed to get his classroom model to South Hall's auditorium where competition models were being presented. Lars was there to help carry the four foot by five foot board, holding the model while Shannon carried all the support documents and papers for the presentation. There were six applicants for the building project, and each had an assigned time to present. Matthew was to begin precisely at 11:00 with thirty minutes prior for set up. There were six members to the selection panel, two architects, two professors, the college chancellor and the city of Berkeley's city planner. Lars wanted to stay and watch the presentation but had a final to attend. "You'll do great, it's a masterpiece," he said as he patted Matt on the shoulder before leaving.

Shannon helped Matt check that his presentation papers were in order, straightened his tie and smoothed a lock of hair down that was sticking up. Then just before 11:00 o'clock as he stood waiting for the panel to come in, Shannon turned to him and taking his face in her two hands said, "Matthew, it's a beautiful and practical design and you can be very proud of it. Your professor said so. Remember that. And if nothing else I love you." Then she gave him a smile and kissed him on the cheek "for good luck" and went and took a seat in the second row of the auditorium.

Matthew was still reeling from her words "I love you," when the six members came in and took their seats. The college chancellor cleared his throat, "You may begin, Mr. Taylor." This snapped Matthew back to reality, and for the next hour he presented his blueprints explained his modern ideas and architectural design to harmonize with South Hall. He had created a building with a similar Napoleon style and with the same mansard roof to blend with South Hall. At the entrance, there were tall square pillars for the gabled pediment having a façade in red brick with striking cast iron arched windows. He answered most questions with confidence. Only once did an "Um" come hesitatingly out, then silence. Fortunately, he recovered and pulled out a sketch that covered exactly their question about using gas in the labs and ventilation. At the end of his hour, the six men were gathered around his model and commenting on this and that with what Shannon could observe were approving nods and looks.

"Thank you, Mr. Taylor, for a job well done. Once we have reviewed the remaining proposal, we will announce our decision. "

Two students came in after the panel left and carefully moved Matt's model to a side wall where another model stood. Matt hadn't noticed it when he came in, and now he took a good look. It was impressive, a different architectural design than South Hall, but impressive with its colonial round columns flanking the entrance.

Shannon came down from her seat. "Yours is much better than that one. You did a remarkable, … no, amazing job. They were impressed, I could tell by the looks on their faces. You've got this. So, stop worrying. It's done. Now take me to lunch," she said, grabbing his arm.

Matt was quiet at lunch and Shannon did most of the talking. She knew for a fact that his mother and Joanna had been in contact and were planning a big graduation celebration after the ceremony. His family would be arriving in Berkeley the day before graduation. But Matt didn't hear much of what Shannon was saying. His mind was still on the competition and who the other presenters might be. He knew the other senior architecture student who was competing and didn't think he had the creative style needed. "Matt, your mother is going to march around in cowboy boots and riding pants at the ceremony," Shannon said trying to get his attention.

"What about my mother?" he said as he realized he was being rude. "I'm sorry, my mind is still on the competition and who the other presenters might be."

"I understand, but there's nothing you can do at this point. Best to be positive and you can be very proud of your design. Do you have any idea who you're up against?"

"I know Conrad Abrams is the other senior, and I'm sure Lionaski will bid for it, as well as John Howard who built South Hall. I don't think I'm good enough to compete with Howard or Polk," he said, holding his hands to his face and then pulling them back through his hair. In reality he was exhausted, the last week of all work and little sleep was beginning to catch up with him.

"Of course, you are! Maybe you don't have the experience, but you are just as knowledgeable and creative as they are. You wait and see. When will they make the announcement?" Shannon said with a reassuring smile.

"There's a dinner tonight at the school of architecture. Sometime then."

"Tonight! You are going, right? And you didn't invite me?" Shannon shook her head in surprise.

Matthew immediately knew he had made a mistake by not telling her. "I... I wasn't sure I wanted anyone there, especially if I came in last."

"Matthew don't be silly. You're just tired. You are not going to come in last. Now we need to get you home so you can sleep for a few hours and then wash and dress. I'll pick you up tonight, say seven o'clock." She took a final sip of her tea as Matt finished the last bit of brisket. Shannon took the keys to the roadster, "I'll drive. You're too tired. I'll bring it back when I pick you up."

Matt started to protest, but Shannon was right. He was exhausted emotionally and physically. "Make it 6:30. I think dinner is seated at seven."

Shannon showed up right on time, dressed in a smartly tailored blue dress she thought fitting for the event. Matthew had managed to shave and dress in his blue suit. Upon seeing Shannon, his mood picked up, "You look beautiful tonight. I'm glad you're coming." He reached out his hand for the keys to the roadster and Shannon dropped them in with a nod. They arrived at South Hall about 6:45, which was already crowded with college dignitaries. As Matt suspected, John Howard was there as well as Mr. Lionaski and Henry Polk. The head of the school of architecture, William Wurster, was there with his wife, who stood talking with the chancellor's wife.

"Matthew, glad to see you made it," said Mr. Lionaski. "I like what you did. I think you're going to be a good asset to the firm. You've got to get some experience, but I think we can make sure that happens."

"Thank you, Mr. Lionaski, this must mean I'm hired?" Matthew gave a small smile while inside he was letting out a sigh of relief to know he had done well enough to get the job.

"Uh, hum." Shannon tugged at his arm.

"My apologies, Mr. Lionaski I'd like to introduce my good friend, Miss Baker. She's an archaeology student here at Berkeley," Matthew said as he turned to her.

"Delighted to make your acquaintance, Miss Baker," Mr. Lionaski said politely.

"I'm delighted to see you realize what great potential Matthew has as an architect. I told him he was brilliant."

"I wouldn't go as far as brilliant, but we do see the great potential," Mr. Lionaski replied.

Just then the dinner gong sounded and everyone made their way to the tables. Matthew and Conrad were seated at the same table, along with Mr. Thompkins, the city planner and his wife, and William and Catherine Wurster. Dinner was served, and Shannon managed to keep up with the architectural discussion much better than Conrad's date. Mr. Thompkins and Professor Wurster commended both Matthew and Conrad for their excellent work. Shannon was trying to determine who had done better by the comments they made. But it was hard to tell, until she saw Catherine Wurster smile as she talked about Matt's design and didn't do the same when taking about Conrad's. Now she was certain Matthew had won. Finally, after dessert was served, Chancellor Henry Durant got up to announce the architect for the new classroom building. He began his comments by thanking Mr. Thompkins and Professors Wurster and Etcheverry for their participation. Finally, he reviewed the candidate's work. Starting with Conrad for his gallant effort, then Mr. Julian Morgan and Mr. Polk for their excellent presentations, but said the projects were over the budget approved. Finally, Mr. Lionaski for his practical and efficient design, but said the board preferred to work with a local firm. Shannon reached under the table and took Matthew's hand, His and Mr. Howard's were the final two.

After what seemed to be an infinitely long moment, Chancellor Durant asked Matthew to stand, and pointed out that his design was exceptional with forward thinking ideas and a complementary but unique design that would harmonize with the current buildings. "Matthew, it was a job well done, and this young man deserves a round of applause for his work." Matthew nodded his head in acknowledgement and forced a tight lipped smile as he felt his insides crumble with disappointment. *It makes sense Howard would win.* After a brief moment, he sat down and looked at Mr. Howard and nodded. Mr. Durant then announced, "The panel has decided to go with John Howard's design which continues the style and feel Cal expresses now and in the future. Congratulations, John, we look forward to construction beginning in the fall."

Shannon could feel the disappointment in Matthew as she reached for his arm. "Matt, you came in ahead of two well known professional firms. That's quite an accomplishment."

"She's right, son," Mr. Thompkins added. "We had a long debate over yours and Mr. Howard's design. You should know the first vote was a tie, but the Chancellor convinced us that time was of the essence and Howard's firm would be ready to start by fall. But Matt, it is an exceptional design. You can be proud of it."

"To the best architect at the table," Conrad said, raising his glass, but forgetting the Wursters were present. They graciously raised their glasses with the others.

After a short time, John Howard came over to Matthew and congratulated him for being a very strong competitor. and he would be happy to have him come work for him anytime. Hearing this from such a well known architect helped lifted Matthew's spirits as he graciously declined the offer, having already accepted Mr. Lionaski's position.

3

Going Separate Ways

The final week was done and Matthew's family had arrived. The Taylors didn't stay with Joanna and Richard, instead taking a room at the Claremont Hotel in town. Shannon had been busy finishing finals and arranging to go to Colorado, since she had been selected. She hadn't seen much of Matthew or his parents. Matthew's mother, Katherine, and Abby, his little sister, had come to see Joanna early on the morning of graduation and finally caught up with Shannon. Joanna served coffee and biscuits as they all sat in the parlor discussing the graduation activities. Matthew's graduation class had over a thousand students, but only twenty from the school of architecture. The commencement ceremony would be at ten o'clock and a small private school of architecture ceremony at one o'clock.

"Shay Shay, you have to come to the ranch this summer. Your folks don't want you taking a ship home. Mother says it would be too dangerous because of the war in Europe," Abby insisted.

"It's only dangerous for ships in the Atlantic. Ships going between here and Hawaii are just fine. Life is changing, Abby. I have a career to work towards and the Mesa Verde dig will do just that.

"I did promised Matt that I would come with him the first two weeks, so I'll travel down with him this weekend, but I will join the archaeological internship group and my professor on site in Colorado come the first week of June," Shannon explained.

"I got a letter from your mother yesterday, and she's relieved to hear you plan to stay on the mainland, but she hopes you're not working too hard," Katherine added.

"It won't be that much work. It's rather exciting to be doing my first actual dig. The internship is only for six weeks and then I'll have a month before classes start again."

"Where will you be staying?" asked Abby.

"Grace, an anthropology student, and I will be sharing a tent at the site. The archaeology department has a base camp for students, which includes tents with sleeping cots and they provide meals as well. The outdoor latrines and showers will be the worst part. But I'm sure I can manage for six weeks," Shannon said with confidence.

"Does that mean you will come back to the ranch afterwards? Even if Matthew isn't there?" Abby asked.

"Well, no. Grace and I have arranged to take Matt and Lars's apartment once they move out. The landlord wants to paint and do some repairs so it wasn't going to be ready to rent again until August, which is perfect for Grace and me." Seeing Abby's disappointed face, "but I could come down for a few days so you and I can go riding. Looks like you will have to be my riding partner after Matt leaves for Sacramento."

"Perfect!" Abby gleamed, "I think it's wonderful you are going to have your own place. Maybe I can stay with you and Grace and do some fun grown up things with you when I come up to visit Uncle Eric and Nancy."

"I think Shannon and Grace's activities are a little too grown up for you at the moment. You need to finish high school first before joining their activities," Katherine announced to Abby's dismay and Shannon's glance of thank you.

Shannon, Abby, and Katherine met the Taylor men at the hotel and together went to the ceremony. It was crowded and warm sitting with all the families on the main lawn in front of South Hall. The graduation class of 1915 was 1014 students. *He would be a T. It's going to take forever to announce Matthew Taylor.* Abby fidgeted in her chair and even Andrew began making comments about how long it was taking. Shannon cheered, "Go Lars!" as Milton Larson was announced and looked around to see if she could spot his family, but they must have been behind her. Finally, after over an hour of announcing names, Matthew Taylor was called. He was tall and dashing in the long black robe with yellow trim navy sash. Katherine and Clay were proud as they announced *Magna Cum Laude* for the School of Architecture. The whole family cheered and Matt waved his diploma.

The small ceremony at the School of Architecture was much more informal under a large tent. Special awards were handed out, as well as specific certificates for the degree for Architecture. Abby was delighted there was punch and cake to celebrate, and Lars and his family came to congratulate Matt. At one point, Lars took Matt aside, "Matty, old man, this European war is getting out of hand and if we're not careful President Wilson will have us joining the war. So, keep that promise to Shay Shay and don't go joining up and if you do, you better make it the Army Corps of Engineers. My grandfather was army, so I'll have no choice but to go army. And if we have to serve, it would be best to be in the same service where we can watch out for each other. You also need to let Shay Shay know you're in love with her before then, too.

"I'm going to miss your squirming around her. I'm also going to miss the roadster. Oh, yeah, you too. Promise you will keep in touch and you'll tell her. You know where to find me at my family accounting firm in San Diego."

Matt gave Lars a long embrace and upon departing, a hearty handshake. "I promise and I will be in touch."

"What promise?" Shannon asked.

"Oh, just that we would keep in touch, that's all. Are you ready to head to the ranch?"

"Almost. Joanna's daughter and children are coming for the summer, so I need to clear my room completely. I have a few more books to pack up and then store the things I won't need in the basement out of the way. When I get back from the dig, I can take them to the apartment."

Joanna insisted on hosting a celebratory dinner at home. Eric and Nancy, Clay's brother and niece, joined the party. Joanna had outdone herself with liver *paté* and duck *á l'orange*, wild rice, and spring asparagus. Champagne poured freely for everyone but Abby.

After supper, while gathered in the parlor, Clay and Katherine presented Matt with a gold pocket watch. It was etched with a sun shining just behind a bridge spanning two mountains. On the back they had inscribed his name. The clock face was simple with roman numerals and a fleur-de-lis in the center. Shannon had known about the gift, something Katherine gave to all her special men, and asked if she could provide the chain for the watch.

Matt held the watch admiring it as Shannon presented her gift, "You might need this to go with it."

Matt opened the small box and inside was a solid gold watch chain made of tiny interlocking boxes. At the end was a small oblong shaped locket. Matt took it out and rubbed the chain through his fingers stopping at the locket. The locket was simple with only the tiniest of sapphire in the center. Matt opened it and smiled as he saw Shannon's picture inside. *This I will treasure forever and keep close to my heart.*

"So, you won't forget me as you venture out to make your mark on the world."

Matt took the chain and clipped it to the watch, "Forget you? Never!" he said as he leaned over and gave her a kiss on the cheek.

After Matt thanked his parents and showed the others the watch, stories of Matt and Shannon's wilder moments at school began to come out. First Shannon, about Matty and Lars staging all of the administrative officer's chairs on the roof of South Hall, leaving clues like a treasure hunt as how to retrieve them. Matt came back with Shannon's midnight swims in the men's pool, and things escalated from there until both were laughing about the time they lost at tug of war and fell into the mud pit, only to be tossed into the lake to get washed off. It was Matty's retelling of their changing out of wet clothes in the bushes that raised Joanna and Katherine's brows slightly.

As the evening wound down, Joanna encouraged Katherine and Matt to the piano for a duet. Katherine was happy to do so, as she thought it might be a long time before they played together again. Shannon loved to hear them play piano together.

Finally, Matt and Andrew went up to Shannon's room to help move boxes to the basement. As they took a large trunk down, Andrew commented, "And who is going to get this out of the basement and to the apartment for you?"

"Oh, Grace and I will find some strapping freshmen, I'm sure, willing to help two helpless women," Shannon teased.

Matt gave her a look and shook his head, "Helpless? Since when?" *Regrettably, I'm sure she will. I fear there will be no lack of young men lined up to assist her, to take what has always been my job and pleasure. I'll just have to make her understand how I feel about us before she leaves the ranch.*

~~

The next morning, the Taylor family boarded the train for Oak Ridge, while Shannon and Matthew drove in the roadster to the ranch. Matt and Shannon arrived at the ranch just past two o'clock, about an hour after the family arrived. Shannon took the guest bedroom next to Abby's room as usual. It had only been since Christmas since she had been there. Matt's room was at the end of hall. He waited for Shannon to emerge from her room, where she had gone to freshen up before dinner.

Suddenly, they heard a commotion downstairs. Uncle Morgan, Clay's half-brother, and Aunt Amanda, Morgan's wife, and their sons, arrived for dinner and to continue the congratulations. Morgan Taylor and family lived at Kalau'ana Ranch, a short distance from the main Taylor ranch house. The Bakers had lived at Kalau'ana, and Shannon always loved visiting the house where her parents had met and she was born. Morgan and Amanda now lived in it and had added an east wing of bedrooms for the boys. Morgan wasn't as loud as Clay, but his boys made up for his reserve. "Matt, where are you?" yelled Patrick, the older son. Patrick was six years younger than Matt but they were close. Shannon came from her room just as Matt started down the stairs, but then he stopped to escort her down.

"Shay Shay, you're here too!" Patrick smiled.

"Yes, Patrick. We're all here, so no need to shout," Katherine scolded.

Patrick and Thomas greeted Matt with a slap on the shoulder, and handshake. "Good to see you, too!" Matt said.

Just then Benson, the butler, announced dinner was served. There were lots of questions about Matt's plans and his new job during dinner.

"For now, I'll be staying at a boarding house, until I can find something permanent."

"Shannon should go with you and help pick out a house," Abby piped up with a giggle.

"I don't think so, Abby. Shay Shay has her own travels; she will be in Colorado," Katherine said in an attempt to rescue Shannon and Matt from Abby's teasing.

Matt continued, "Mr. Lionaski hinted about a new justice building in Sacramento, or possibly a new bridge further south near Santa Barbara."

"It sounds quite exciting," Amanda remarked.

It had been a long day, after a long week and Shannon retired early. The following morning, Matt saddled horses for Shannon and him so they could ride out to the tree with her parent's name carved in it. The tree marked the edge of the ranch that was once theirs, but now marked the entrance to the reservoir and land that served as winter overflow. Upon reaching the tree, Shannon found the carving her father had etched, "Here lies the Baker Ranch – J&L", J & L for Jim and

Lalani, her parents. They walked the horses down to the edge of the water and stood looking.

"Do you want to swim out to the Olsen house rooftop?" Shannon asked. The Olsen ranch had been bought up, like her parents' ranch, to accommodate the reservoir waters the dam would create. In the process, the Olsen's houses and barn, being close to the dam, were soon underwater. Shannon and Matt, in their teens would often swim out and find the old house roof, which during drier years sat just below the water line and they could stand on it.

"No, not today. I have something important to tell you, to ask you, Shay Shay," Matt said turning and looking at her. He took the horses' reins and tied them off to a shrub and then took her hand and walked to a clearing. *This must be serious, Matty's never been this quiet out here at the lake,* Shannon thought. Almost hesitant to ask and waiting for Matt to say something, she took his other hand and faced him, looking up into his green eyes.

Matt smiled, *there's no going back now, she's expecting something important,* then he took a deep breath, "Shannon, I've known you all my life. Even though we were apart for two years at a time, I have always felt close to you. At first as best friends and now since we've been together these past two years, I have wanted more." Matt looked down at the ground for a moment, *If I tell her I'm in love with her, am I going to ruin everything? will I lose her completely?* He took her chin and looked into her eyes, and couldn't help himself as he quickly and tenderly kissed her on the lips. *This will change everything.* But as he was still mulling his words over in his mind, he heard himself say "Shay Shay, I'm in love with you and have been for years, even before college," and he kissed her again, completely, as a man kisses a woman.

Shannon felt a tingle go through her body, her eyes wide with surprise, but she didn't pull away as he still held her hands and had pulled her close to him. Years earlier she had wondered what it would be like to kiss Matthew, but like him didn't want to ruin a friendship and make things awkward, thus putting it out of her mind. Now here she was tingling from his touch, her heart racing, thoroughly caught up in this second kiss. Matt slowly pulled away, watching Shannon's face. Was it just surprise, hopefully delight? But also confusion he saw.

Shannon turned and looked at the water, her whole body tingled, and her heart felt as if it was going to burst from her chest. *Is it because I'm so surprised or is it because of something hidden between us. I've always sensed he had deeper feelings towards me than just childhood friendship. And Shannon Baker, what about your true feelings toward him? I have always loved him, but is it truly in this way? Do you allow yourself to be swept up in passion. Is there more to it than passion, is there love as man and woman? How do I know, is it only because he's leaving?*

As she thought about this last thought, Matt turned her back towards him. "Say something." *Please don't say I've ruined things.* She put her hand to the side of his face. She saw such tenderness, then she reached up and kissed his lips, as tenderly as he had first kissed her. Matthew put his arms around her and kissed her long and passionately. Shannon could feel the warmth of his body against hers, the desire of his lips on hers, and her breath leave her body as she suddenly experienced something she had never felt before. She had been kissed before and deeply, but nothing that touched her soul the way this kiss did. After a moment she pulled back putting her hands on his chest, "Oh, Matty, … What are we doing?"

Matthew took a step back, now afraid of what he had done, that he had ruined everything, that she didn't want him. "I'm sorry, Shay Shay. I shouldn't have done that."

Shannon was still stunned by the emotions and warmth surging through her, her face flushed, unable to say anything. Only managing to put a finger to his lips so he wouldn't say anything more. Matt was now more confused. *She's mad and doesn't want an apology, but she kissed me back and she didn't pull away. Have I embarrassed her and she doesn't know what to say or how to get out this?*

As her senses came back to her and her heart stopped pounding, "Matty, no, there is nothing to apologize for. I...I have felt you have loved me for a long time, but I was afraid to let it be more. If I'm honest now, I'm still afraid. I'm not sure really how I feel for you. I've hidden the thought of loving you for so long. I had to put it out of my mind." Seeing the disappointment come into Matt's eyes and posture, she quickly added, "But your kiss and embrace just now, sparked something I have never felt. Something well, I'm going to keep to myself, but I will tell you, a love, I have never felt from any other man I have kissed deeply." *Shannon, stop talking, you're making matters worse.*

"What do you mean other men, kissing you deeply. How many other men?" Matt asked suddenly, confused as to whether she did nor didn't love him.

"Matty, don't go there, we both have been kissed and kissed others affectionately, more than a friendly kiss. What we need to talk about, and I need to think about is what we're going to do about these feelings between us … this confession we just made to each other."

Now that her head had cleared following the kiss, Shannon began to think more rationally. "Matty, I know I love you. I got jealous every time I saw you with another girl, and I couldn't wait for the last dance to be back in your arms. I just didn't want to admit it, and ruin things between us. And now you tell me the same and stir up that hidden feeling. But you're going off to a career and I'm going back to school. How can I let that kind of love take over? I can't figure this out in a week or two. Love just doesn't happen. It can't be forced, but it can grow. But how can it, if we're apart?"

Matthew had been standing close, just letting her get it all out. His disappointment had been given hope when she said 'I know I love you'. That was a good start. "Shay Shay, I know I have sprung this on you from out of the blue. I told you now, so we could have the next few weeks together, to show you how much I love you, in hope that you would love me as much. I had to take the chance now.

Oh Matty! I don't know. Well, do you or don't you Shannon Baker? I want to, but can I? He being in Sacramento and me at Berkeley. Shannon looked at Matt for a long moment, and he didn't say anything at first.

"Shay Shay, I should have told you two years ago, thus giving us time to fall in love together. I'm sorry we only have two weeks now before we part. I would love to have you come with me." He put up his finger before she objected. "I know you need to finish school. I just hope you won't run off to some foreign country to dig up old ruins and fall in love with a paleontologist, and leave me behind."

Shannon smiled at him sweetly, "I would never do that! You would just come with us."

"Shannon, I'm serious. And I hate to bring it up, but there is the war in Europe, one of these days if things don't end, America will be drawn into it just as England was on Belgium's behalf. The French came to our aid and they are expecting us to do the same for them. In a year from now, I could be fighting in France."

"Don't say that, you promised you would stay out of the war. I can't even think about that. You just being in Sacramento has made me sad and missing you already."

"And I will keep my promise, unless Wilson requires me to go."

"How can we make this work? You have terrible timing, Matthew Taylor. You tell me you love me and then have to leave me, for a year, maybe more. I don't know if I should go ahead and love you now and spend the next few years pining or keep it hidden until I can be sure you're mine."

"Just hearing you would be pining for me, makes me happy."

"Matty, now I'm serious."

Matthew reached down and took her hand, "Walk with me."

Shannon reached over and put her other hand on his arm and smiled, trying to reestablish a normalcy between them, but deep down she felt a new warmth and concern. Something she had been afraid to feel, and something she had not let herself feel before. They walked along the shoreline for a few minutes in silence. *This is all so… so confusing. I hate the idea of him going to war. The idea of losing him. I can't lose him… I must love him if the thought of losing him terrifies me so much. I wish I knew what true romantic love was; is this it?*

Shannon stopped and looked out across the water to some ducks, and Matt came up behind her and gently put his arms around her. "Are you alright? Have I ruined things?" he whispered.

"No, I mean yes, we're good, you haven't ruined things. You've just brought to the surface what has been hiding between us this past year. I'm just not sure how to react. I can't just flip a switch and be head over heels in love. Plus, what will your parents say?" Shannon was grasping at straws, still reeling over everything said and felt.

"I'm sure my parents will be fine with it. Andrew will say, 'it's about time'," he said, smiling.

Shannon didn't pull away from Matt's embrace but for the first time took a moment to enjoy it in a new way. *I'm not sure I'm ready to have the family's attention on all this. If I ask to keep this between us, will he be okay with that?* Matt knew she was running through things in her mind. He wanted her to share them with him so they could work things out together. "Shannon, you can tell me what your concerns are. I know you have them."

She turned around and smiled, "It's unfair that you know me so well. I... I just think I need a little time to sort out my feelings before everyone else does it for me. Would you be alright keeping this just between the two us for now?"

"I understand that, just between us for now. But I'm sure mother will notice something has changed. So, for how long? I kind of want everyone to know. To be honest I'd shout it from the rooftop if you would let me."

"You wouldn't!" She put her hand to his cheek, "Just give me a few days. Our time is so short, I promise I'll figure it all out soon. I do love you, and not just as a friend."

Matt leaned down and kissed her lovingly one more time before taking her hand again and returning to the horses.

As they reached the ranch house Matthew could sense an uneasiness come over Shannon. "Hey, don't worry, just be and do what you want for us. I'm not going to push things. The family doesn't need to know how we feel. As far as they're concerned, we're still good child-hood friends." *How does he know that is exactly what I needed to hear?*

She dismounted and they led the horses to the barn and unsaddled them. As they cleared the stall, Shannon reached out to Matthew and reached up, quickly kissing him on the lips, "Just checking. Yep, there's definitely something there. But let's keep it between us for now," she smiled. Matt grinned with delight and winked, "Just between us! Mother would be shocked at your forwardness."

~~

For the next week Shannon and Matthew carried on doing the usual things they did when together. At the barn dance perhaps, he held her a little closer than usual and took her hand when walking in the meadow or along the stream. Shannon had never let herself fall in love with Matthew as a teenager, and now she found it easy to allow this to happen. He was handsome, with striking masculine features, and strong hands. His green eyes said he loved her. She loved his long slender fingers as they glided across the piano keys as he played for her. Matthew was an excellent pianist, having been taught by his mother, a retired concert pianist. He was charming and gallant when he wanted to be, but a fun and delightful tease when she was in the mood to be silly.

As Katherine and Clay watched the two of them over the week, they could see their son had fallen in love and that both were quite well suited for each other. Both had grown up on cattle ranches, but neither had a hankering to stay on their family's ranches. Their prospective interests were the opposite of each other and yet similar: Matt building new things while Shannon dug up the old and forgot-ten. Yet they fit, both putting things together, figuring out puzzles, how to make the new work and how the old did work.

There was no doubt in Katherine's mind that Shannon would re-turn to school and finish her degree while Matthew went to Sacra-mento to start his career. Katherine wrote to Lalani about what was transpiring between the two of them and wanted her advice as to how to help Shannon, once Matt left for Sacramento and she found herself alone. Lalani wrote that Shannon preferred to be left alone with her troubles rather than fussed over, that she would find a special place and brood or cry, and when she was ready, she would come to her.

As the time for Matthew's departure drew near, they spent more time out riding and sitting at their favorite spot along the river. Matt had not taken Shannon there when he told her he loved her, not wanting to ruin this place for them, if she rebuffed him. But now they found themselves there every day, talking about what they wanted for each other, what they expected of each other when apart, how they would write and Matthew would come visit when he could.

The one thing Matthew knew, Shannon was not ready to discuss marriage and so he carefully avoided the subject, for which she was grateful.

By the time Matthew was due to leave, everyone at the ranch knew he was in love and she seemingly loved him, though nothing had been said and only a friendly peck to the cheek or a hand being held was seen. But Shannon had let herself indulge in the idea of being in love and expressed many of the signs to Matthew without actually realizing it. Yet she had another full year of school and then wanted to work for a year or two on a dig before settling in one place, always assuming that place would be home in Hawaii.

The morning before Matt was due to leave, Shannon insisted they take a ride, not to their favorite spot but to the reservoir. She tried to be chipper, but Matt could tell something heavy weighed on her mind.

They dismounted and Shannon walked to the water's edge. "Shay Shay, what is it? I know I'm leaving tomorrow, but we talked about how we will stay in touch," Matt said.

"Matt, that's just it. We will be apart for a full year. I've let myself fall in love you, but what I feel, is it truly love or just hopeful wishing? My heart says love, but my mind says it's not practical to be tying myself down at this point."

"What are you saying? You have just been pretending these past weeks? But you have let me hold you close and kiss you. We talked about you working at the museum in Sacramento after you graduate. Was all that a game to you?"

Shannon didn't like the tone Matt's voice had taken on. She knew he was hurt and now confused. *He's confused...I'm so confused too. I wish I had not lay awake last night thinking about being at school without him. How all the boys will want to take me out and dance. And the thing is I'm sure I will want to go with them. And yet every time I get his letter or see him, I know I will get butterflies, but after so long apart, will they just flitter away? I just don't know and it seems so unfair to Matt to give him false hope. Is that what I have been doing? .... fooling myself and him?*

"Shannon, say something! Tell me that's not true." Matt said as he lifted her chin to look at him with a gentle concern.

"No, of course not, by no means was it a game to me. I wanted to let myself fall in love with you, I wanted to make plans for a life together eventually. The timing is just terrible. You're leaving and I'll be back at school where I'll be asked out and to dance with various men." She paused and looked down, but before he said anything, she took a deep breath and continued. "Matt, I know I am going to want to accept some of the invitations. If I promised to be your girl, I'll feel guilty accepting their invitations, guilty for wanting to go with them."

Matt took her in his arms, "I never want you to feel guilty because of me. You're right, for one thing I can't expect you to sit and stay at home while Grace and Alice are out dancing. You should accept their invitations. I just hope you discover how much more in love with me you are than persuaded by their good looks and charm."

I'm glad to see he understands the situation. But what about him. "Matt, what about you? If I accept invitations, then so should you." *Now that I've said that, I hate the idea.* "I appreciate the offer, but it doesn't quite work that way. Ladies don't go asking men out, at least decent women," Matt said with a chuckle.

"Matt, I'm serious. You can't wait for me to show up, you should ask others out. Life will become very lonely if you don't, and you might resent me for not coming with you now," Shannon said, again turning to face him.

"Lonely, yes, but resent the fact that you want to finish your degree? I could never be resentful. I'm proud of you for staying with it. I always knew there would be a period of time we would be apart, that's why I had to make my feelings clear now. So, you wouldn't go off and fall in love with someone else."

"So, what are we to do?" Shannon asked, looking for an answer from Matthew to make her heart and mind peaceful.

Matthew looked out across the water and with a deep sigh, "I guess we just hope we are in love enough with each other to not find anyone else more infatuating. We know each other better than anyone else and have always been the best of friends. Let's hold on to that and let it work to our advantage. I know I would rather be with you than any other girl. You have more intelligence, enthusiasm and caring qualities than anyone else I've met. That's what made me fall in love with you. You're not bad to look at either and can ride a horse better than any other girl I've met."

"Thank you for the lovely compliments. I too feel the same way. But I have to admit you didn't give me much chance to date other men, since I've been at Cal. And most of those I've danced with or talked to in class can't compare to you. Maybe that's why it was so easy to let myself fall in love you now."

"So, you admit you love me, as your lover," Matt said, with a glee in his voice.

"Lover sounds so risqué, as if we'd been to bed together." *Oh no, now I've put me foot in it. Before he even gets the idea, I'd better change the subject, but to what?* "Forget I even said that, but you know what I mean. And that won't be happening. You just have to wait for a wedding night." *Am I getting myself in deeper? Just stop talking.*

"Okay, let's back up a step before lover came up," Matt said. "Just know that I love you and take the next year to make sure you love me. Perhaps being away from each other and seeing a few other people will prove they can't compare to us, that we are meant for each other." Matt put his arms back around her to reassure himself, feeling the tension in her body begin to melt again.

"Oh, Matty, why are you so understanding? You're too loving. No wonder I love you more and more." She turned to him and put her arms around his neck and waited. Matt didn't disappoint her, but kissed her long and passionately.

With a much clearer understanding, they mounted their horses and took a long ride together through the ranch, knowing this wouldn't happen again for some time.

~~

The final evening at the ranch was busy with packing things up for Matthew as well as for Shannon, who would be leaving for the dig in Colorado in another three days.

It was ten o'clock in the morning, the sun was streaming down on the powerful black train engine, snorting its steam as it waited for its passengers to board. As Shannon stood on the train station platform with Katherine, Clay and Abby, she found herself uncertain as to where she wanted to be. She so desperately wanted to go with Matthew, to continue to let herself fall in love with him. *I can't believe he is really leaving, and I won't see him every day. Our lives have been such a coming and going from each other, and here we are again saying good bye. I hate good byes!*

Matthew finished saying good bye to his folks and little sister, then took Shannon's hand and walked to the end of the platform. "I know we agreed you should go ahead and attend the dances and have the proper escorts to events, but I want you to have this to remind you, you're my girl," and he handed her a small box. Seeing the fear in her eyes, he quickly said, "Don't worry, it's not a ring. It's not time for that."

She opened the box and found a lovely heart shaped locket engraved with flowers and inside was a picture of Matthew, his warm smile and assuring eyes looking back at her. "It's beautiful, and I'm so glad to have this picture that I can keep with me." The train whistle blew, causing Shannon to jump. Matthew quickly put the necklace around her neck, then grabbed her in his arms and kissed her deeply and she returned the embrace. As the conductor called the final 'All Aboard', Matthew let go and stepped onto the train as it slowly began to pull away.

"You're my girl, right?!" he said over the noise of the engine.

"Yes, I'm your girl," Shannon called back as she could feel the tears welling up inside her and with her last breath called out, "I love you, Matthew Taylor. Don't forget me."

Over the rumble of the train, she could hear Matt's faint reply, "I love you always."

Shannon turned back once the train was out of sight and found Clay and Katherine waiting at the car. Clay put his arm around her and held her in a fatherly fashion and whispered, "It will be alright, you two always find your way back to each other." Shannon didn't say anything but hugged him back and then smiled.

Back at the ranch, the house seemed quiet and empty even though Abby and Andrew were still there. Shannon proved to be a poor cribbage player for Abby that evening, her thoughts still on Matthew's leaving and the ache she felt. Finally, she forced herself to concentrate on what she was going to do next and she turned her thoughts to getting herself to Mesa Verde and the dig site.

4

Becoming an Archaeologist

Shannon arrived at Mesa Verde on the third of June. It was a long three-day trip from Oak Ridge, first by train to Los Angeles, transferring to the Santa Fe Railway which took her to Gallup, New Mexico, then a long, bumpy dusty car ride north to the Mesa Verde site. Peter Gonzalez was sent to Gallup to pick up supplies and to meet her at the train. Pete was a friendly man in his thirties. He had been working as a supply clerk for the dig for the past five years. Shannon had all kinds of questions for him, but he didn't have much to say. "Miss, I'm not one of the scientists. I do know they keep finding pieces of pottery and charcoal remains, but I can't tell you much more, other that they think it will be years before they completely discover everything. Dr. Fewkes' main goal is to restore what sites have been found. Dr. Fewkes is in charge of the dig, hired by the Smithsonian, friendly enough, but Mr. Wetherill, who found the dwellings, feels he's not going about it in the right way."

This last statement made Shannon curious. Was he carelessly digging things up with shovels or was he not looking for more sites? She had heard there were many sites yet unknown as the ancient civilization seem to stretch throughout the area. The robbing and reckless destruction of a dig site caused the archaeologists the greatest grief.

And if restoring a site, would there be enough original materials there to reconstruct a site correctly?

Grace had arrived a few days earlier and met her as the car arrived in camp. "You made it! You are going to be amazed at what's going on here. Professor Kroeber is immersed in all the artifacts that were found. I just started photographing and cataloging some of them today. But first you need to learn the ropes and rules of camp. Come on let's get you settled." Grace took Shannon's arm and led her off to their tent.

Grace explained the first rule is to always check your boots for scorpions, and before getting into bed, your blankets for rattlesnakes. "Poor Murry was surprised last week with a rattler under his pillow."

Shannon's eyes widened and shook her head. "Got it! What else?"

Grace explained water was to be used sparingly. Showers everyday were frowned upon but not forbidden, sponge baths were encouraged. The best time to shower was late afternoon, when the water would be warmed by the sun. Early morning it could be pretty cold.

Grace then continued, "Only authorized people are allowed in the artifact storage tent. Dr. Fewkes, if possible, is better to avoid. Winn or Professor Kroeber will be giving most of the day's assignments. Most of all, never offer an opinion to either Fewkes or Kroeber unless asked. At the dig sites, never open anything without checking for scorpions or baby rattlers first. If you are bit, don't run. Yell for help, and Winn will come as fast as possible with a snakebite kit. Well, that's it for now. There's more but you'll figure them out as you go. Breakfast is served at seven a.m. and lunch and supper are set up from noon to eight o'clock. You grab those meals when you're done for the day, or pull yourself away from what you're doing. Hot coffee is always available, tea is something they don't even consider, and the water is usually warm to tepid. The food's not too bad, but the cook is Mexican and so is most of the food. You best change out of that skirt and pack it away until you leave. We live in trousers here. Then we can go get you something to eat. "

Shannon quickly changed into trousers and a plaid shirt, checked her boots for critters, and grabbed her cowboy hat. The sun still had several hours of light, so the mess tent was sparsely occupied. Grace introduced her to Carlos the cook, and upon Grace's recommendation, she took a tamale and what looked like chopped tomatoes and onions. *I had best work hard, seeing all the beans and rice. I could be ten pounds heavier by the time I leave. Matt might not recognize me.* Shannon felt a little guilty for not thinking about Matt all day, but she was so wrapped up in arriving, her mind didn't miss him.

They found a long table and sat down. After just a few minutes Winn Wetherill came in, and seeing Grace with a new face, came to say hello. "You must be Shannon Baker, Professor Kroeber's archaeology student. Welcome to Mesa Verde. We have lots for you to do."

"Thank you. I'm excited to be here."

Grace explained that it was Winn and his brothers that discovered the cliff dwelling. "I was much younger then, and we didn't know what we had found or what we should do. After a few mistakes, we had the sites made into a national park and got the protection and help we needed. I hope you know what you're getting into. It's hot and dirty at the sites. You sure you don't want to work with Grace in the cataloging tent?"

"I assure you I'm tougher than I look, I grew up on a cattle ranch in Hawaii. The weather may be extremely different, but my quest to see how ancient civilizations built things and used them will keep me on task."

"Good, that fits well with the massive restoration going on. We're attempting to reconstruct the main building on three of the main ridges. You will get a hands-on look at how they were made. You can start at the Pithouse dig. Meet me here at seven a.m. and I'll show you to the site. Just make sure you take water. You do have a canteen?" he said with a warning. He then left Shannon and Grace to catch up and get settled.

Clay had given Shannon two things before leaving, a canteen and a small handgun. He didn't like the idea of her being unchaperoned at a dig site, and knew from cattle drives that men could get out of hand. Shannon said she would be fine. She was not the only woman, but took the gun in case she needed to shoot snakes or coyotes that got too close.

That evening as Shannon undressed for the night, Grace spotted the locket hanging around her neck. "Something new. Can I guess? ... it's from Matthew," Grace said gleefully.

"Yes, a parting gift." *I have his locket and he has mine. Should I tell her we have fallen in love?*

"Just a parting? With that far away look, you're thinking of Matthew. Don't tell me you finally let him kiss you? Have you finally admitted you're in love with him?"

Shannon blushed, "Well, I think so, we spent the last two weeks together and he told me he loved me and I finally let myself love him back."

"You let him kiss you, and more?" Grace said cocking her head with wide eyes.

"Yes, No! Grace, Matthew is too much of a gentleman and his mother would have killed us both. There was definitely no 'more.' But... he did kiss me, not just a peck but a real kiss, and it was heavenly." Again, Shannon blushed as she began to giggle.

The girls slipped into their beds and talked a while longer. Shannon asked Grace about being interested in any of the men at the camp, but she yawned a "course not" and then turned over to sleep. Shannon lay awake thinking of Matthew, wishing he was there to share all that she was going to be doing. She quickly rose and wrote a quick note to him, feeling guilty again for not writing sooner. *I assume they have mail service here.*

The next morning Winn met Shannon at breakfast. She was standing by the coffee in her cowboy hat and gloves hanging from her back pocket. "Good morning, Miss Baker. You say you grew up on a cattle ranch. Does that mean you can ride a horse comfortably on a narrow trail?"

"Well, yes, I can ride. As long as the horse has some common sense, I manage quite well!" she replied.

"Good! Originally, I thought I would have you join the men at Long House, but since you can ride, we will go out to Kodak House. It's a little out of the way and the only way to get there is by foot or horseback."

"Oh, I thought most of the restoration work was at Step House and Spruce Tree House," she said, forgetting not to challenge those in charge.

"True, but Dr. Fewkes has been concentrating on those sites for years and they're almost complete. My brothers and I would like to see Kodak House restored. It's located on Wetherill Mesa," he said with a grin.

"I see. What does Kodak mean in the Pueblo language?" she asked.

"Nothing! We gave it that name because Baron Nordenskiold, our first archaeologist, kept leaving his camera at the site. It was to photograph things. He left it at the site and never came back for it. On the cover it says Kodak. My brothers and I just got used to calling it the Kodak House. It's not a very big site, in pretty bad shape from Nordenskiold digging. But I'd like to see it restored, so if you don't mind working with Murry Danvers, I'll take the two of you out there and you can assess the damages."

Once Shannon had finished her breakfast, she met Winn and Murry at the corral. Winn had a pretty little chestnut bay, named Molly, for her to ride. "She's sure footed and takes command easily. You should have no problem with her," Winn said.

Murry held the reins to a paint gelding named Chief. "Welcome, I hear we're going to be working together." Murry was from Leadville, Colorado and had been working at Mesa Verde for the past two years. He had worked in the mines, and knew rock: what it was made of, how made, rock hardness and uses. But he didn't like being underground all day. There at Verde, he could still work with rock but above ground. He had large rugged hands and light brown hair that hung in his brown eyes. They mounted up, and it took about an hour to get to the site, which was comprised of two levels of sandstone cliffs. The few buildings still standing were also made of sandstone clay bricks and Murry was encouraged to see so many still lying about that could be used to rebuild.

Since they had come in on the top of the mesa, and the sites lay below them on the alcove ledges, the only way down was by a rope ladder. They tied off the horses near a small grove of cedar trees that they could have shade by. "Murry, you go first, then I'll help Miss Baker down; that way if she starts to fall you can catch her," Winn said, more serious than not. It was only about thirty feet to the floor of the top ledge. A ladder was secured at the top by two large heavy metal poles. It was also secured at the bottom to the floor.

Murry went first, while Winn made sure Shannon had a good hold on the poles and her feet stood firmly on the first rung. Shannon had flipped her cowboy hat to her back and made sure her little pick ax was tightly attached to her belt. She didn't look down but slowly reached with her foot for the next rung. As she worked her way down, the ladder swayed slightly and she tightened her grip. *I'm glad I have good leather gloves and my boots have just enough heel to prevent my foot from sliding through the rungs.* When she was about five feet off the floor, she felt a pair of hands grab her around the waist.

"You can let go now, I've got you," Murry said as he lifted her down to the ground. He could see the surprise in Shannon's face, "Sorry miss, I should have warned you. I didn't mean to be disrespectful. "

Before Shannon could reply that it was fine, Winn arrived jumping the last five feet and landing just behind them. "Good, you managed that ladder just fine. But make sure Murry is first going down and you go first coming up, Miss Baker."

"Fine, but please call me Shannon, I think as I work, my hair will be rather disheveled, and I'll be quite dirty, so calling me miss will somehow be unbefitting my appearance."

"Alright, Shannon," Winn smiled. *Oh, I like his smile.*

Winn and Murry showed her the upper level sites: what they believed to be the remains of a house, a long meeting hall similar to Long House, and a pit house. They made their way via a rather slippery path with the help of a rope that led down to the lower cliff. It was here the Kodak House remains stood. These remains were in better shape and had several partial walls still standing. At the far end of this cliff was a pit house and small kiva.

"So now you have the general layout of the Pueblo community that lived here. But the building we want you and Murry to restore is the actual Kodak House. It looks like it had a small kiva within it and several small chambers. We're not sure what they were used for. You can excavate those and bring me whatever artifacts you might find. Kodak House, being so remote, wasn't ransacked the way Spruce and Longhouse were."

"Sounds good to me. Can I ask, did Nordenskiold take pictures of the house and do you have copies we can study? Pictures taken ten years ago will be helpful, since I'm sure weather has eroded the site since then," Shannon inquired.

"Of course, we have a large library of photos taken of all the sites. I'll pull the ones for these cliffs and you can study them back at camp. Look, it's getting late, and it takes almost an hour to get back to camp. With sunset at seven thirty, you will have to get out here early in order to get any real work done. I want you both leaving no later than five o'clock each afternoon. I don't want to have to come looking for you in the dark, not out this far," Winn warned.

Murry picked up a small broken brick and stuck it in his pack and then helped Shannon back up the slippery path to the upper cliff. The group made it back to camp just before lunch. Winn went off to gather photos for the project, while Murry and Shannon went to the mess tent for lunch and planned how they would approach the project. Just as they were finishing their meal, Winn arrived with a stack of photos of Kodak House. They quickly took over the table, laying out the photos and discussing where to start the reconstruction.

That evening Shannon could hardly sleep as the photos and ideas ran through her mind. For the next several days Murry and Shannon made sketches and checked notes on artifacts found and the photos taken at Kodak House. Murry had Joseph, the camp geologist, meet with them to discuss the geological aspect of the cliff. The cliff was mostly sandstone. The bricks from the site were heavy with an iron oxide type clay sandstone, and the clay mortar was mixed with a fine silt rather than a coarser sand.

On the third day, Murry and Shannon returned to the site and began meticulously to clear bricks that had fallen from a wall, placing them into wood boxes marked with numbers corresponding with numbered sticks indicating where the bricks had been taken from at the site. These then could be used later to rebuild the wall from where they came. Murry and Shannon found they worked easily with each other, and Shannon was pleased Murry didn't coddle her or think her incompetent to the work needing to be done.

After a month at Mesa Verde, Shannon began to form a routine: rise early, go to the site by eight a.m. with Murry, clear and organize the site materials for four hours until the sun was overhead. Then take a break to eat their sack lunch and check that the horses had water, then return to finish working until five o'clock.

Shannon returned to camp dirty, and with aching knees and back from stooping and lifting bricks, rock and sand. The only thing that helped relieve her aches were letters from Matt. On the evenings she received his letters, she lay in bed realizing how much she missed him and sharing her days with him. Matt was now busy helping design the new Justice Building for Sacramento and exploring the social life in the capital. Shannon just hoped it wasn't too social and not too many pretty women were vying for his attention. Of course, she had written about working with Murry, saying he was ten years older than she, and she was such a mess each night that the other men wouldn't even want to look at her.

One afternoon, as they worked on the back room on the south side of the Kodak House, she was clearing a large pile of bricks when she began to realize it was hiding a small archway to a space in the cliff. Shannon and Murry spent the next day clearing this area, that turned out to be a long narrow passage way to nowhere, with only a small pile of bricks at the far end. The corridor appeared to be carved out of the sandstone cliff and they wondered what it was used for. A storage area for food or for bricks, possibly, because of the pile still there. The next day, Murry led the way through the corridor, as they planned to box up the bricks. It was cool in the passage compared to the hot July sun. Murry held the lantern up high as they made their way down the fifteen foot passage. He suddenly heard that distinct rattling noise. Swinging the lantern towards the noise, he spotted a large rattlesnake coiled high on the bricks with its eyes large and staring right at him. Murry froze and held the lantern out away from his body, hoping that if the snake struck, it would go for the light. Shannon wasn't far behind him and hearing the noise realized what it was. She stepped slowly back and then hurried back to her pack and retrieved the small revolver Clay had given her. She rushed halfway back down the corridor and then slowed, seeing Murry still standing and the snake still coiled. She took a few more steps closer and pressed her body against the wall until she could clear Murry and have an unobstructed view of the snake.

"Don't move," she said. "I've got..."

Suddenly the snake's head shifted her direction, and she knew it had caught her scent. Its head reared back and Shannon and Murry knew it was going to strike. Bang! Bang! echoed loudly in the space. The gun in Shannon hand went off, causing Murry to jump backward, dropping the lantern. There was a thud. "Murry, Murry, are you alright?" Shannon shouted, unable to see him or the snake clearly.

Once the ringing of the gun shots died away everything was silent with only a soft low light along the floor. Shannon scrambled to Murry now lying on the floor holding his head. "Oh, my God, did the second bullet hit you?"

Murry rolled toward her. "No, I just hit my head hard on the floor. The shot scared the living daylights out of me, and I jumped back, stumbling over something and fell hitting my head on the floor. I'll be fine, I'm glad I can't say the same for the rattler, from the looks of it, you completely killed the life out of him. Where did you get the gun?"

Shannon was relieved to see she had hit her mark and not Murry and explained it was a gift from her uncle. "He intended for it to fight off men, but I took it to kill vermin like that," as she pointed to the dead snake.

Shannon said they should call it a day, worried that Murry might be hurt more than he was letting on. As she handed the lantern to Murry, she saw she was covered with dirt. Rubbing the grit from her hair with her fingers, she realized it wasn't sandstone dust from the cliff but it was clay, clay silt mortar. *Why would there be clay mortar on the ceiling? The ceiling is the cliff's' natural sandstone, isn't it?* As she took a few steps back towards the end of the corridor, where the dead snake now lay, she could hear and feel the crunching of earth beneath her feet. As Shannon turned to leave, tiny specks of light caught her eye. At first, she thought it was coming from the lantern light bouncing off the walls.

"Murry, wait! Do you see those specks of light?" pointing to a spot on the floor. "Can you bring the lantern closer?" He set it on the ground and they could see it wasn't the sand dirt floor that most of the corridor had, but there were small chunks of reddish clay scattered around. Shannon looked up at the ceiling some ten feet above and could just make out a tiny beam of light coming in. Murry took the lantern and held it closer to the ceiling, and it revealed a partial clay brick ceiling. He took the lantern and surveyed the surrounding walls, coming across what appeared to be notches in the wall.

"Shannon, look, these notches line up and are evenly spaced. I think they're steps to go from this level to the upper cliff. For some reason they closed up the passage."

"You think so? What's above this?"

"I don't think anything. I think the ruins of the long common area is nearby, but we can check on our way out. Which if you don't mind, I think I would like to go ahead and leave now. I have a splitting headache, from the bang ringing in my ears and my head hitting the ground."

"Of course, we need to get you back to camp and have Doc look at you."

They made their way to the upper level and stopped just long enough to pace off the distance they estimated where the corridor ended. There was a small pile of rubble from the walls of a small room. Shannon wanted to clear the rubble, but then remembered Murry's headache. "Best to wait until tomorrow. I wouldn't want either of us falling through the weakened ceiling or floor from this viewpoint."

They made their way back to camp and reported to Winn what had happened and what they had found.

Winn sent Murry to the anthropology tent to see Dr. Schneider, the camp physician as well, to make sure there wasn't a concussion.

First, they agreed to meet up in the morning and Winn would come with them and bring the Kodak camera to take pictures of their find. The word of their discovery spread quickly through camp. A passageway between one level to the next had never been found at any of the other mesas. Even Dr. Fewkes was eager to see the photos and see the space once it was open and clear.

Shannon went and took a shower for once and tried to wash the clay silt from her hair and the dirt from her face. Once dry, she pulled back her wet hair and put on her semi clean flower blouse for dinner in an effort to look a little more presentable for the evening. Grace was all excited to hear about what they had found. After supper, Shannon checked on Murry to make sure he was okay, since he had not come to the tent to eat. Doc had given him a couple of aspirins, saying he would be fine by morning. He said, "His head aches much less and he just wants to get a good night's sleep." It had been an exciting day in more ways than one.

Shannon and Grace hunkered down in their tent and wrote letters. Grace wrote to her grandfather, Frank Monroe grandson of President Monroe, with whom she was very close, but seldom saw as he lived in New York and she in California. Before her father moved the family to the west, she spent a great deal of time with her grandfather listening to stories about his grandfather and how he fought in the Revolutionary War and what he did as President of the United States.

Shannon wrote to her folks leaving out the part about the rattlesnake and the scorpion she found in her boot the week before, but she did write about how exciting it was to find something no one else had discovered. She also wrote to Matthew, sharing all her joys and some of the hardships, how her hands and fingernails may never be beautiful again, there being so much red clay on and under them. She also shared how wonderful it was to take a long warm shower after several days of being hot and dusty. *I probably shouldn't tell him about how good the shower felt, it will just cause him to imagine something he shouldn't.* She didn't include Winn's offer to stay until winter and keep working on the site. *Both mother, father and Matthew would not approve of me staying and not completing my degree. It probably is not the best plan either. As exciting as it has been learning about the Pueblo culture and dwellings, I still have a deep desire to explore my native Hawaiian ruins. And Hawaii doesn't have rattlesnakes.*

Shannon now realized she only had three more weeks at Mesa Verde before she was due back in Oak Ridge before returning to Berkeley. She lay awake thinking about what had yet to be done at Kodak House, uncovering and documenting the new passageway, at least beginning to start the reconstruction of the west wall, and they still wanted to explore the canyon below for displaced bricks that would have tumbled from the ruins. There was so much to do and no time to do it.

Winn, Murry and Shannon took the next week and carefully exposed the opening that was only big enough for one person to climb through. They carefully removed the clay bricks from the upper level, taking photos and measurements of the upper ruins to determine what type of building the opening came into. It appeared to have a fairly small foundation layout. Winn figured it must have been a tower of some sort. It appeared that the west wall had fallen as a single chunk covering the small opening, thus from below it looked like it had deliberately been made into a brick ceiling.

Winn was excited. It was a big discovery, and nothing like it had been found before. The other cliff foundations had all proved to be too thick. Shannon thought it might have started out be to a pit house. As they dug down, they broke through the shelf, seeing that it provided a perfectly safe means for going from one level to the other.

Shannon decided to extend her stay at Mesa Verde for an extra week, but that was the best she could do. She had promised to stop back at the Taylor's ranch, and Matthew was planning to come for the weekend. After that she had to get to Berkeley to set up the apartment and be ready for classes to start. Grace, as much as she liked working with the artifacts, found the tent hot and stifling and would leave as planned at the end of July. She also found some of the laymen annoying, pinching her as she went by at dinner. Only once did Big Kelly try it on Shannon and was met with her elbow to his stomach in return. The passes and remarks quickly stopped. Most of the men were older than she and Grace, and didn't bother socializing with them. Lou was the one other woman at camp and helped keep the boys in line around them. Shannon by no means was drawn to any of the men, though she was fond of Murry and admired Winn.

Shannon's final two weeks were spent beginning to reconstruct the west wall of Kodak House. She didn't realize it was going to be such a messy job. They had cleaned and organized the bricks to be used, but now they had to make the clay mortar to hold them in place. Murry hauled in water in large canvas bags and had collected silt and clay from nearby hills, then they began testing the mix for the right consistency to hold the brick. Murry had experience creating the mortar mix, having worked on Long House. He made the mortar and then handed Shannon the bucket. She would place the sticky thick mortar in place, and then Murry would hand her the right brick to fit. Shannon's heavy work gloves proved to be too awkward and the mortar clung easily to them. She borrowed a pair of Grace's artifact handling gloves which were made of a silky cotton and much thinner. The clay stained the white cotton instantly and stuck just as much, but were less bulky than the leather gloves. These gloves allowed her to work faster in spreading the mortar and then, with a trowel, tap bricks into place, repeating this process as Murry handed the right pieces to recreate the wall.

By the end of the first day, they had a good rhythm going. *I didn't realize I would become a mason, but I guess I can add that to my resume.* Shannon had spent most of the day on her knees, and her trousers were caked with clay. By the time they returned to camp, the clay had dried and she could take a rug beater to her trousers and flake the dry clay coating off. Winn, seeing how grungy she was, said she could go and shower every evening until she was due to leave. As she stood in the warm water with the red clay stream flowing off her legs and hands, she was most grateful to Winn.

At the end of July, Professor Kroeber, Grace and his other students all headed back to Berkeley. It seemed the anthropologists didn't get as much out of the experience as Shannon did and were ready to head back to Berkeley's clean, cooler anthropology department artifacts. Shannon wanted to stay the extra week, since she and Murry were close to joining the twenty-foot-long west wall with the front south wall. They had raised the west wall two feet and now the west end of the front was just one layer higher.

On Monday of her last week, Murry and Shannon mounted up but didn't head out for the top of the ridge. Instead, they made their way to the canyon bottom below the cliffs. Although they had found numerous bricks from the ruined walls, there still were a great many missing. Kodak being a small site compared to the others, no one had explored the canyon below for pieces of wall that might have fallen. Slowly they made their way through the thick brush until they were below Kodak House and dismounted.

They listened carefully for any sound of a rattlesnake hiding under a bush out of the morning sun. *Please no snakes today, we don't have time for them.* Shannon stood looking at the slope of the canyon and noticed a small fan shaped area between two shallow ravines near the bottom of the canyon. She made her way toward it and scrambled up through the brush, stopping suddenly to watch a scorpion scurry under a rock. *Mental note, don't pick up the reddish rock the size of a grapefruit.* She then continued until she reached what she thought was the fan shape. It was covered with dry grass, sandstone gravel, and dirt.

She stood observing the site for several minutes, then began to see a pattern, clumps of grass clustering around very small mounds that had the appearance of rock. Could they be fallen bricks rather than rocks? She pulled her small pick from her back pocket, selecting a well-established tuft of grass, and dug it out. It didn't take much of a tug to dislodge the grass, roots and all. The layer of dirt below didn't reveal anything other than more pebbles and dirt. Shannon took the pick and began to dig at the spot, uncovering darker rich silt, then hit something hard. Now on her knees, she cleared the three inches of dirt with her hand until it revealed a brownish round shape. *It looks like river rock, as I would expect to find.* She was about to abandon the spot and try another when she noticed a faint black line across the tannish brown surface. *Maybe it's not a rock. That looks like something stained onto it.* She then carefully cleared more of the dirt from the object, and as she did, a definite faint black line appeared.

"There you are. You find something?" Murry asked. He had lost her in the tall brush for a moment until coming upon her.

"I think so. What do you think?" she said standing and moving aside.

Murry stooped and cleared more dirt, "Oh, definitely, it looks like part of a pot, a nice piece of shard. This is going to lead to this whole area being excavated, you just watch and see."

Murry stood back, "It's your find. Go ahead and finish digging it out." Shannon continued to dig out around the shard until it lay completely exposed. "We need to photograph this and mark the spot," she said. Murry went and retrieved the Kodak camera and one of the burlap bags they had planned to gather bricks in. Once the photo was taken and the place properly marked, Shannon very slowly and carefully lifted the shard from its resting place and set it onto the burlap.

"How does it feel to find your first piece of ancient history?" Murry smiled.

As she held it, observing her find, "It's unbelievable, exciting. If my research is right, this would be at least over a century old or perhaps even five hundred years old." The shard was only about eight inches wide and four inches high with a single black painted line across the bottom third. *Well, I hoped we'd find brick artifacts, I never dreamed of finding a pottery shard.* Shannon carefully wrapped the piece in the burlap and set it aside, now wanting to pull other tufts of grass to see what was hiding beneath.

Now they knew they were in the right spot, and the soil layer wasn't too thick. The annual rains probably prevented the buildup of soil and the artifacts from being buried deeper. They spent another twenty minutes pulling up clumps of grass and poking into the soil, when finally, Murry found the first brick remnant. It was about fifteen feet further down from the shard location. As they pulled out their shovels and carefully cleared the area, they hit several more pieces of brick, some still in good usable shape. Shannon marked and took pictures of the clearing and then packed bricks into the bags. She stood back and looked up to the dwelling trying to determine which house the brick might have come from. Kodak House was twenty feet to the west, at the end of the ledge. *These bricks must be from Kodak, or maybe the small tower above it. The slope of the canyon probably carried them further east as they tumbled down. And the shard? It seems to be more directly below Kodak. Could it be part of a dumping area where the inhabitants tossed garbage and waste, broken items. Now I wish I had more time to stay and work. This is a whole other project in itself.*

They worked for another hour, and then the heat became unbearable at 102 degrees. "It's time to call it a day. It's August and the heat will get to you faster than you realize," Murry said. "Anyway Dr. Fewkes will want to see your find and get the photos developed. Just be sure not to say where you found them. Everyone at camp will be over here claiming their part in the find. Best to keep it for yourself and let it be part of your resume. Fewkes I'm sure will take the credit, but will be happy to have you stay or come back to work the area."

They loaded up the bricks, and Shannon mounted Molly, then Murry carefully handed her the wrapped shard. They traversed the canyon up to the top of the mesa to deposit the bricks they had found, then made their way back to camp. Shannon went directly to her tent and put the shard in her trunk until she could find Fewkes. Since Grace had already gone, no one else would be in the tent. She quickly washed up and met Murry at the mess tent. They'd hoped to find Fewkes or Winn there. Cook said the Doctor, as he called Dr. Fewkes, had come and gone, but Mr. Winn should be around soon for lunch. They grabbed a few enchiladas and a Coke and sat to wait. It was easier to wait in the shade of the tent than to be running around the camp and to the other sites in the sun. It was only twenty minutes when Winn came in, dripping wet with perspiration. The tent was very quiet and once he had grabbed a Coke and a plate of food, Winn came over to Shannon, noticing her wave to come join them.

"Hot day out there. It's only going to get worse now that August is here. Glad to see you two had the common sense to come back early," Winn said.

Shannon wasn't sure how to tell Winn what they had found and only replied, "That it is. But considering the day we had, I'm almost wish I were able to stay longer."

"Oh?" Winn said raising his eyebrow and looking at Murry for more elucidation.

Murry looked at Shannon, "It's your find, you tell the man and your theory."

Now Winn knew they had found something of importance and, realizing where they were, said "Maybe we should go to my tent to discuss this."

They left the mess tent and Shannon then said her tent would be the best place, considering. Once they arrived, she pulled out the burlap from her trunk and laid it on her bed and unwrapped it.

Winn's eyes lit up. "Where?" was all he said, and he took and examined it.

Shannon then explained where they had found it and her theory about it being a dump site; that the bricks were further east and they hadn't taken more time to dig up where they had found this piece.

"Well, looks like you have something worth looking into alright. From the looks of this, it could be from the early dwellers at Kodak House. Let's take it to the artifact tent and compare it to other Kodak artifact shards. The artifact tent was manned by Felix Schneider, the main anthropologist for the project. He took one look at the find and confirmed it was early Pueblo pottery. He pulled a piece from the archive box marked Kodak and sure enough they looked quite similar, the clay composition and the stain being of the same intensity and texture.

The final week at Mesa Verde for Shannon was a whirlwind. Her find was the buzz of the camp and Dr. Fewkes had his own people out surveying the area, and a few more shards and even animal bones had been found, further supporting Shannon's theory of a dump site. Shannon was officially credited with finding the new site and Winn made sure the shard was filed with her name as founder, the camp now referring to it as the Baker shard. While Fewkes and his men worked on the shard site, Shannon and Murry took another day locating brick ruins and hauling them up to the mesa. Shannon was proud of the work they had done on Kodak House and wanted to finish the west wall and its connection to the front wall. It would take one more full day of mixing mortar and getting dirty to complete the wall to the point she was satisfied she had left her mark.

On her last night there, the only other woman in camp, Lou, short for Louise, an archaeologist that had been there for three years, took Shannon aside and told her, "It's an exciting life when you can get to work on a dig like this, but for women it doesn't happen very often. It took me ten years of trying to prove my worth before Dr. Fewkes agreed to let me dig. Not because I didn't have the knowledge or skill. He needed to wait until I grew old enough, that I wouldn't be bothered by the men. You and Grace were quite the talk the first week, until Kroeber and Fewkes put the wrath of God into them. Take a good look at me, I'm only thirty, but the heat and working with the earth has turned the soft skin I once had dry and wrinkled. I don't get the looks I used to and I've learned to be tough and how to shove off the unwanted men. Winn paired you with Murry because he's one of the gentlemen in the group, so don't be fooled. You could be a good archaeologist, but think twice about the life. It's lonely for a woman, dirty as you have found, and always in the middle of nowhere with heat in a desert or rain in a jungle. Now I've said my peace, and it's up to you as to what you want in life."

Shannon smiled. *I wondered why the ogling the first week we were here ended so abruptly.* "Thanks for the warning, Lou. I know you mean well, but I've come this far. I have to see where it will take me. I hope to work on ruins on my native Hawaiian island of Oahu. First, I've got to get the degree if anyone is going to take me seriously."

Lou laughed, "When has a man ever taken a woman seriously, especially if she's wearing a skirt. I haven't worn a dress in years and changed my name to Lou, just to begin to be taken seriously."

The next morning Shannon, now clean, as much as one could be in camp, wore the skirt and blouse she had when she first arrived. She picked up her journal from the bunkbed and a small bag, and took one last look to ingrain the meager beginnings of being an archaeologist into her mind. *The cot wasn't that bad and so many nights lying on it planning the next day activities. Even the scorpions became tolerable, not the snakes though. I wonder, if that footlocker that held my first find, will hold someone else's first find? If only that wash basin with its warm water could have had cold fresh water this past month. Oh, well, farewell tent, perhaps I'll be back.* Shannon turned and headed past the mess tent. Cook waved a farewell and Winn, quite a few yards away, shouted, "Good luck, Miss Baker, thanks for the good work." She then met Murry at the truck. Winn said he would take her to the train. It would give them a last chance to discuss what should be done next at Kodak House. Now that they had begun the work, Winn wanted to see it completed. Murry took her trunk and placed it in the back of truck, going around and opened her door.

Shannon grinned; *he is a true gentleman.*

"What's that grin for?" he asked as he started the engine.

"Oh nothing, just something Lou said."

The ride to town was still bumpy and dusty. They talked about Kodak House and what order was best for it to be completed. Murry said it would still be a couple of years, if he was to be the only one working, and that Shannon should come back as soon as she could to help finish it. As they pulled into Gallup, the big black Santa Fe train stood waiting.

Murry took her trunk and gave it to the conductor to load into her compartment, while Shannon purchased her ticket to Los Angeles, California where she would change trains to head north to Oak Ridge. It was just after eleven o'clock in the morning and Shannon quickly took a moment to send a telegram to Aunt Katherine that she was at the train and should be in Oak Ridge late the next evening.

Murry waited on the platform, and just before she was to board, took an envelope from his shirt. "This is for you, not that you won't forget your first dig, or me," he said rather shyly.

Shannon opened the envelope and took out two pictures, one of the pieces of shard she had found, labeled with her name on it, and the second a picture of the two of them at Kodak House, taken the day Dr. Fewkes came with the camera. "Oh, Murry, how did you manage to get these? I will cherish them for sure, especially the one of us. How did you ever get Fewkes to take it?"

"It pays to be on his good side, and Winn wanted you to have the other," he smiled. Just then the whistle blew and the 'All Aboard' was called out. Shannon gave Murry a big hug. " You have my address in Berkeley. I expect you to write and tell me how the work is going. I'll write back," and with that she gave him a quick kiss to the cheek and stepped up onto the train. Murry blushed but smiled big, nodding his head. Shannon stood waving as the train pulled out, then made her way to her compartment where the conductor had placed her trunk. She sat holding the photos, *I will never forget this summer or Murry.*

The train roared into Los Angeles Union Station about eight o'clock the next morning. She stepped from the train onto the platform and surprisingly heard a shout, "Shay Shay, over here." She spun around to see Matthew heading towards her. She stood shaking her head, eyes smiling wide with delight and a big grin on her lips. He swept her up and kissed her squarely on the lips, swinging her around as he did. The other disembarking passengers stopped and watched, some with delight, but an older woman walked past muttering, "Shame on you both, such public display is not right."

Shannon chuckled as it dawned on her what the woman had said. *If she thought this was shameful, what would she think of my digging in the dirt, disheveled appearance, and alone with a man for the past two months.*

5

Finishing

Shannon was delighted by Matthew's surprise to meet her in Los Angeles and travel back to Oak Ridge together. All the warm feelings she had for him came flooding back as he held her in their first embrace. Now on the train to Oak Ridge, she sat close and held his hand as she chattered away with all the stories and excitement she had experienced while at Mesa Verde. Matthew sat just listening, loving the smiles on her face and enthusiasm in her voice. He was glad to hear that same enthusiasm as she told him what a wonderful surprise it was to have him there. Even though they had written to each other over the past two months, there was still lots to share. Finally, Shannon realized she had been dominating the conversation and apologized, feeling guilty that she hadn't asked Matt about his new job, the project he was working on or if he had finally found a place of his own. Teasingly Matt said, "Oh, you do care about what I have been doing."

"Don't be mean and ruin a perfect reunion," she scolded back.

Matt then proceeded to tell her about the Hall of Justice he and others were designing, where they hoped to build it, starting in November. Shannon turned all her attention to listening and asking questions about his work. She could see he was as excited about this project, as she had been about hers. She was slightly envious that he would see his to completion and she would not.

After several hours of talking, Matt was hungry and they made their way to the dining car. Over a meal of veal scaloppini and fresh vegetables, Matthew asked about her plans at Berkeley and for the apartment. While she was with Dr. Kroeber at Mesa Verde, they discussed the final classes she would need to complete and her senior project. She had most of her classwork done, except for advanced research. This class she would tie to her senior project on Hawaiian ruins. Matt raised an eyebrow. *Is she thinking of going back to Hawaii for her final semester?* Seeing concern come across his face, "No, I'm not going back to Hawaii for the year. There are classes for one thing, and there is a lot of research to obtain at Berkeley and several sources back east, such as Harvard's Polynesian collection and the Metropolitan Museum in New York." Seeing this still did not appease his concerns, she added, "I can call the museums and ask questions via telephone and perhaps even have them loan me photographs. I will be at Berkeley most of the time." Now this caused Matthew to relax somewhat, but she could sense he still had something on his mind.

Matthew then changed the subject, indicating he needed a woman's thought on something. He suggested they return to their compartment and escorted her back. Once again sitting next to her, he took her hand, "I've found a house in Sacramento overlooking the river that I'm thinking about buying. But I wanted you to see it first. I need a place I can entertain clients and have room for you, when you come to visit." Quickly realizing how that came out, he added, "with Grace or Abby, of course." Shannon's eyes widened; *doesn't he realize that's still inappropriate, two women in a single man's house, what would the neighbors think?* Matthew knew he still had said the wrong thing but wanted to get past it. "The train will be stopping in Sacramento for an hour before going on to Oak Ridge, and I made arrangements for us to see the house during the layover."

"Two women in your house, now that would be scandalous! What would your neighbors think?" she said teasing, but with an undertone of seriousness. *Just because I was in a field camp with a bunch of men, didn't mean I was sharing the same tent with them. Has he lost his mind? This better not be his way of proposing marriage. Something I'm definitely not ready to consider let alone talk about.*

Matt hearing her tone knew instantly he was still in trouble. He was so used to her just being in the same house with him when she visited the ranch, in his mind he knew he couldn't just have a woman stay, but a friend chaperoned by another woman. Now that he had said it out loud, *Matthew what were you thinking? Shay Shay and I are not children any more, she's a woman. Of course, she can't stay. But you really want her to see the house and approve of it, for someday it might be hers as my wife. Matthew there you go again, getting ahead of yourself. You know better than to even bring up the subject of marriage. That would really be putting your foot in your mouth. Shay Shay is definitely not ready for that. You heard how excited she was about her work; she has to finish school first.*

As he reprimanded himself in his head, Shannon sat quietly giving him time to come up with the right words and apologize for his brazen remark.

After a moment and wiping the side of his face with his free hand, "Will you come see the house? I really want your approval. I think you will like it."

Shannon smiled, "Yes, I'll come. Tell me about it."

Matthew then relieved, told her about the pale green two story craftsman style house. There was a large parlor at the front of the house. Adjoining the parlor was a large dining room with built in glass front China cupboard. A large kitchen and a small servant's room was at the back of the house. Upstairs there was a small study with bookshelves and a fireplace. There was a large master bedroom, three smaller rooms and a large bath. It sounded like more house than Matthew would need, but she knew in the back of his mind he had selected a place big enough for the family he would want.

They talked a little longer about the architectural changes he wanted to make, but that he would need help with decorating, that he hoped she would help since she already knew his taste and didn't want a stranger picking out things. "You just want free help, that's all. Let me see the place first, and then I'll let you know if I have time," she laughed back.

It was another three hours to Sacramento and Shannon wanted to write a letter to her folks, so she could post it from Sacramento. Matt pulled up a small table from below the window for her to write on, lifted her small case down for her to retrieve paper and then took out a book he had been reading on the way down, stretching out on the seat opposite her.

After an hour Shannon looked up and saw Matt sound asleep. She folded the table back down and sat watching him sleep. A young man dressed in a soldier's uniform walked by the glass door and smiled, reminding her that there was a war going on. She had been so far removed from civilization; she hadn't heard much news about the war in France. Shannon looked back at Matt. *This war has been going on for over a year now. So many British and French boys and men have been killed. I was heartbroken when mother wrote and said Thomas Ballard's son had been killed, within months of his enlistment, he was only twenty. It just seems the trench warfare is not getting anyone anywhere other than dead. Why was that young man fighting in a war that didn't involve him? He must have family in France or England. That was why my friend from school, Marie's brother went and fought. Everyone thinks the Americans can beat the Kaiser, will Wilson give in and finally send troops?* Focusing back on Matty, *he promised he wouldn't volunteer. No, he wouldn't. He wants to buy a house and is thinking about a family, a man thinking about volunteering wouldn't want to be buying a house.* Shannon didn't like thinking about war and turned to the window and looked out at the passing landscape, and willed her mind back to the house Matt wanted and what she might do to it.

Shannon's thoughts were interrupted by Matthew's stirring. Rather than spend more time talking about houses and work, she asked if he'd play a game of cribbage. It was about four o'clock when the train pulled into Sacramento. Shannon quickly posted her letter before they grabbed a cab to go see the house.

It was a charming house and reminded Shannon of the house her mother grew up in in Honolulu. With enthusiasm, Matt explained its qualities and the changes he would make. They finished the tour standing back in the parlor looking out the large window toward the park across the way. "Do you like it?"

"Yes, it's a good house and this view is wonderful." Just then a clock on the mantle chimed three quarters past four and they knew it was time to get back to the train. Boarding just as the last call was made, they went directly to the dining car for supper and they spent the rest of the trip talking about the house. They returned to their compartment just as the train pulled into Oak Ridge. As Shannon turned to leave the train, she stopped and whispered to Matty, "Don't take this the wrong way, but make sure you buy the house for what you want and not me," and she stepped onto the platform before he could say anything.

It was still light at half past seven, and Uncle Morgan and Matt's brother Andrew stood on the platform waiting. *What does she mean by that? She doesn't want to settle down with me, no, no... she's just not ready for marriage yet. You know that.* His thoughts were scattered, by the sound of Andrew's voice and his waves.

"Uncle Morgan, I thought for sure mother would be here to greet us," Matt said, giving him a handshake.

"She's home cooking a late supper and your favorite dessert."

Matt grinned and looked at Shannon, *Oh, shoot, we're not hungry. I forgot mother wrote she would have supper for us.*

"You need to come home more often, brother. We don't get chocolate cake unless you're here," Andrew said, slapping Matt on the shoulder. "Shay Shay, you're looking as beautiful as ever. Doesn't look like the hot desert did any harm."

"Not much, but I sure could use a hot bubble bath with some silky coconut oil."

Matt sat with Shannon in the back seat of Morgan's new car, trying not to think about Shannon's comment about the house. They headed for the Taylor ranch once the luggage was secure on the back. Warm welcomes were waiting from Clay, Katherine, Aunt Amanda, and Abby upon arrival. Katherine scolded Matt for eating on the train. Shannon and Matt sat and nibbled at the food, and did most of the talking during dinner while the others ate. Afterward, Morgan and Amanda headed back to their house, while the others settled in the parlor for cake, with brandy for the men and sherry for the ladies. Abby was now nineteen and entitled to join them with sherry. It was late by the time everyone headed for bed. Matt took Shannon's hand and they climbed the stairs together. At her door he leaned forward and kissed her on the lips, "I'm glad you're back. I'll have the horses ready by seven," then opened her door and let her enter alone. They would ride in the morning and then join the family for breakfast.

Matt only had two days before he was needed back in Sacramento, therefore he and Shannon spent most of their time together. He sat and played piano for her, as he was the better player of the two. Matt had a piano lesson every day for twelve years of his life from the time he was four years old. Shannon was basically self-taught and didn't start playing until she was nine, when Katherine had a piano sent to Oahu. Shannon only had lessons during the time she and Aunt Katherine were together, once every two years for a month or two.

It was a typical hot August in Oak Ridge and the reservoir was a busy place for picnics and swimming.

Shannon had hoped to swim out to the Olsen rooftop and sit in the cool water away from the smaller children playing on the shore. She and Matt went down late the second afternoon and swam out to the roof, but before they knew it Andrew and Abby had joined them, along with two other boys around the age of fourteen. Not before long a game of who could stay on the roof was in full swing, Shannon and Abby being the losers against the boys.

Matt and Shannon swam back to shore to escape the ruckus. "Do you ever wonder what our friendship would have been if my parents had never moved from here, if the dam was built at its originally proposed site?" Shannon asked.

"I'm sure it would have been different. You would have been friends with the Olsen girls, and some of the other girls I went to school with. I would like to think we would have been good friends, riding horses and swimming together. But it would have been different. I'm almost glad you didn't live next door, that we had an ocean between us to keep our friendship something special. But let me make it very clear I'd rather not have an ocean between us now, eighty miles is far enough."

Matt took Shannon to dinner in town the night he had to leave, so they could be alone. Shannon looked lovely in a blue chiffon summer dress, with Matt's locket around her neck. They didn't talk about serious things, no career talk or campaigning for woman or cattlemen's rights. Just little things and when they would see each other next. Matt would come to Berkeley when he could. After supper they strolled down toward the new gazebo that was erected in the town park. Finally, Matt pulled his pocket watch and realized it was time for him to catch his train. In the shadow of a large tree next to the station, Matt took Shannon in his arms and kissed her long and longingly.

The train whistle blew and they reluctantly pulled apart. She smiled and took his hand and led him to the platform. As he stepped onto the train, he whispered, "I love and will marry you someday."

Shannon stepped back, smiled and whispered, "Someday."

~~

Shannon stayed at the Taylor ranch for another week, riding with Abby as she had promised, and visiting Kalau'ana with Morgan and Amanda. Andrew escorted her to the end-of-summer barn dance, before he and his father became immersed in fall round up. Matt went ahead and purchased the house. Shannon was openly delighted for him, and secretly she truly thought it was lovely and could imagine herself there with him.

By late August, Shannon was back at Berkeley with Grace, settling into their new apartment. Getting her things from Aunt Joanna's was not difficult. Several young men, friends, were happy to assist her and Grace with trunks, a small sofa and dining table and anything else in exchange for a dance at the opening gala. As she sized up the young men, appreciative of their help and attention, none of them were equal to Matthew, except perhaps Freddie Wrightman, whom she had always admired.

Freddie was tall and slender, with sandy blond hair that framed his handsome face. He was from a good family in San Francisco and had a decent wit about him, when he finally had something to say. Still his aspirations were different than hers. Freddie, a fellow archaeology student and senior, had his sights set on the emerging Egyptian dig sites and planned to go to Cairo after graduation. But in the meantime, Shannon found Freddie the perfect escort to the dances and social activities.

While Shannon liked Freddie a lot, he still came in second to Matthew. There was no tingle or palpitating heartbeat when Freddie took her hand or danced close to her. Shannon wrote to Matty twice a week, sometimes teasing about a boy that wanted her attention, but quickly adding Matt was still her main love.

Shannon resumed her commitment to the suffrage movement on campus, recruiting new freshmen to join them and explaining that violence and force were not this chapter's means of operation, even though a good march and rally often got loud. Shannon was still disappointed the 19th amendment introduced to Congress over thirty-five years earlier still had not be ratified by all the states, including Hawaii, New York, Pennsylvania and Massachusetts. When the chancellors from Harvard, Columbia, or University Pennsylvania came to Cal, the top leaders of their suffrage chapter would request a meeting to discuss what they were doing to move the ratification forward in their state. Most of the men were agreeable to meet and were sympathetic to the cause. They were appreciative of the manner in which the chapter rationally presented the issues and argued logical and concise points, but warned that the leading men in their state would never see a woman as equal, and it would be a while before they would even see them at best capable. They did admit the woman attending their schools were like them, bright and intelligent.

Shannon was glad to have Grace as her new roommate. Each viewed a nonviolent passage of a women's rights amendments the best way, even if it took longer. Maureen, as she slid into her more bohemian life style, had joined the more radical suffragette's group in San Francisco and was held overnight in jail for disorderly conduct. Grace and Shannon were committed to the cause, but now as seniors found the demands of graduation taking priority.

Grace was deep into reconstructing a Greek vase that had been given to the university, and Shannon was busy gathering information on Polynesian architecture.

Shannon found her advanced research class an invaluable source of information for how to locate and request transcripts and photos of journals, rather than having to go to the sites. When she was a sophomore, she had requested Cook's journal on his second voyage, by using the name of her professor, but the archivist replied she was unable to fulfill her request.

~~

Years previously on Oahu, when Shannon was allowed to ride the ranch on her own, at the age of ten she had come across a thicket of philodendron and koa trees when she was stalking a small mongoose. The animal scurried into a moss and vine covered mound beneath a thicket of philodendrons. Shannon cleared a few large philodendra leaves and some of the vines hoping to catch the mongoose, and was surprised to find a partial structure, a small stone square about five feet by five feet. Three of the walls were only partially standing, part of the back wall stood four feet tall. Several small mounds covered in moss lay on the ground inside and around the structure. The mongoose had long gone but the shape and hidden location of her find had Shannon intrigued. As she pulled some of the thick moss from the structure, she found hard compacted pumice rock. The mounds were piles of fallen rocks.

This became Shannon's secret spot. The only other person who knew about it was Matty and he had been sworn to secrecy, not even her parents or brother Evan knew about this spot. Shannon spent that year creating a small passageway through the thicket and then clearing the pumice stone off of the vines and moss. She discovered the stones were about eight inches long, nine inches wide and eight inches high. They were all exact in measurement and were stacked to create a small structure about three or four feet tall.

As a child, she imagined it to be the remains of a child's playhouse and brought cups and a teapot so she could play afternoon tea there. Other times she thought it a snare where hunters would come to catch wild pigs. As she learned about Hawaiian history at the Royal school, she thought it was most likely a lookout for invading ships from Maui or the island of Hawaii. To finds its origin and purpose would be her senior project.

Dr. Kroeber did not have any expertise in Polynesian culture, but a find like hers would be a good project to research. He pointed her to the Harvard Library, and Oxford University in England which held Cook's journals from his Hawaii expedition. She explained how she had tried to get the journal in her sophomore year.

"Try again, just use the skills and techniques you've learned. Miss Cartwell will be more helpful to a graduating senior with her own research, than an inquisitive sophomore."

Shannon got busy writing institutions for any information they may have on structures such as hers and on occasion make a phone call. She corresponded with Miss Cartwell, at the Oxford archives, for several months and then finally paid for a very expensive twenty-minute phone call to her, to have her read several pages from his journal that described a similar structure off the shore of Ua Pou island, part of the Marquesas Islands. Shannon took copious notes as the librarian read the journal, finally asking if she knew of any other reports or documents on that site. Regrettably she did not, but she invited Shannon to come and look through the Polynesian archives and the artifacts they did have. Shannon thanked her but said with the war on it wasn't likely she would be coming to England any time soon.

~~

Shannon spent Thanksgiving at the Taylor ranch with Matt and family. Both Abby and Shannon had ideas about how Matt should decorate his house. But Matt wanted to make some architectural changes before he did any painting. He wanted to add a breakfast nook off the kitchen that overlooked the river and led to a patio. He and Shannon poured over catalogs and selected a sofa, chairs and dining set for the main room. Matt had already purchased a bed and bureau. Thanksgiving Day was the usual feast, and the long weekend went far too fast for everyone.

Matt was disheartened to hear Shannon had made plans to go home for winter break. She needed to get home and take pictures and obtain more accurate measurements of their secret spot now that she was doing research on it. She tried persuading him to go with her, but he would need at least three weeks off of work if he went. It was two weeks of sailing just to get there and back and if she was going to be working on the ruin's site most of the time, he would only be in the way. Matthew declined, as he also was needed at work, since the Justice Building was now under construction. He promised to come up to Berkeley the weekend before her ship sailed.

Shannon was frantically rushing around finishing her reports and preparing for finals the second week of December. Matt was due in on Friday night to take her to the Christmas Gala. That Friday morning, she took her last final examination and sat in the little log cabin in the eucalyptus grove, putting the finishing touches on her report for her Advanced Ancient Archaeology class. By two o'clock she walked over to South Hall and handed it to Professor Kroeber. Sitting on his desk was a Kodak 3A folding camera and film that he had promised she could use to photograph her site. He handed her the camera and reminded her if the site was of historical value, she should make sure to register it with the National Registry of Historical Places. She confirmed it was on her list to do and thanked him for the use of the camera. It was a brisk walk back to the apartment. Grace was there with hot tea and biscuits waiting.

"All done?" Grace asked as Shannon came through the door. "Come sit and warm up, before you start rushing to do whatever's next."

Shannon hung up her coat and hat, sat on the sofa and poured a cup of hot tea. "What's next? I'm supposed to be dressed and delightful for Matty, that's what next. But at the moment all I want to do is curl up and sleep. I still have to pack the research documents I'm going to need while I'm home, let alone pack clothes," Shannon said with a sigh.

"Well, enjoy your tea first, then go get a hot bath and relax. We can help each other dress and do our hair, and if we're lucky, Matt won't show up too early," Grace said with a wink.

Shannon laid out a beautiful dark forest green brocade gown and finished it off with Matty's locket and small pearl earrings. Grace wore a sapphire satin dress and a lace collar necklace. As Shannon put the last pin in place for Grace, they both heard the old familiar sound of Matt's roadster.

"The roadster! Isn't it a little cold for the roadster? What was he thinking?" Grace scowled.

Matt was early as Shannon suspected he would be. He was staying at his Uncle Eric's house in town only five minutes away. Matt took one look at Shannon and fell in love with her all over again. He had always thought she was a pretty girl who had grown into a pretty woman, but seeing her now, she wasn't just pretty. She was beautiful, her soft tan coloring glowing against the deep green and her eyes deep pools of dark chocolate. He swept her up in his arms and gave her a kiss.

"Matthew Taylor, you're going to muss her hair and dress if you keep on like that. Put her down and behave," Grace demanded.

Matt put her down, looked and winked at Grace, "I see you're still playing big sister, but you do look lovely tonight. Who's the lucky fellow?"

"If you must know, Freddie!" she said gleefully.

He looked at Shannon, "Freddie?"

"Yes, since he couldn't escort me because you were here, he asked Grace. Now you be nice to Freddie. He has been the perfect gentleman and knows I'm still your girl."

Matt grinned and shook his head, but there was mischief in his eyes. Just then there was a knock at the door. "Ah, it's for you, Miss Grace," Matt turned and opened the door.

Freddie was surprised to see Matt, but Matt was cordial and shook his hand, "Grace is all yours tonight, Freddie. Shannon and I are off, see you at the dance," and he picked up her cloak and held it out for her.

He had been practical to a point and had the top up on the roadster with the window shields buttoned down tightly. While Shannon adjusted her hair upon arriving, Matt picked up a dance card and filled out the first and the last four dances with his name. Upon seeing the card Shannon smiled, "Matt, that only leaves me three open dances."

"What three?" He took the card and filled in his name on the third dance. "I think two dances with Freddie will be enough to thank him for escorting you so far this year." Shannon shook her head and smiled; *I really don't want to dance with anyone other than Matty tonight. It's been far too long since we danced.*

Monday morning rolled around and Shannon was tossing gowns and undergarments into her suitcase, having neglected to do so all weekend.

Once again, Shannon and Matt found themselves at the dock in San Francisco saying good bye. She could see the displeasure in his eyes that they would not be together for Christmas or the New Year celebration.

"I wish you could be coming with me. Life with jobs and responsibilities is so much more complicated. But I miss home, my folks. I haven't been home in two years. Evan's boys will be all grown up and Lizzie a young lady ready for her first dance. I'm sure mother has lots of special plans. I'm just hoping Kiki will be free to visit." Matt put his finger to her lips, "I know, you have to go. No need to justify going. Just hurry back." The whistle blew and Shannon reached up and pulled Matt to her and kissed him long and hard. The whistle blew again and she pulled away and ran for the boarding ramp. Once again, they stood, forcing smiles and waving to each other, as the ship pulled away from the dock. *I hope he understands and that he hates saying good bye as much as I do.*

~~

Shannon's parents and big brother Evan stood on the Honolulu pier as her ship's anchor lines were secured. Within minutes she was embraced by her mother's warm arms and smiling eyes, wet with joy at seeing her daughter. Her father gave her a kiss, "Welcome home, so glad you made it safely."

Shannon smiled, "Of course, I made it. It's not like we haven't done that crossing a million times." Turning to her brother, delighted to see him, "Evan, how sweet of you to be here too. Are you keeping things up for me at Mau Loa?" She laughed, knowing it was he that kept everything running at the ranch. In Hawaii, homes were given names. Lalani had named the ranch Mau Loa, meaning forever. Their forever place.

He reached down and swept her up in a hug, "Of course, baby sister; I'm really only here to carry the luggage," he whispered. Now Evan was tall and gangly in stature, with a quiet and reserved manner like their father Jim.

"Now that's the smart-alecky brother I love. Where are the kids?"

"Home! They wanted to come but I was afraid there wouldn't be room in the car with all your luggage."

"I only have one trunk, we could have at least squeezed Lizzy in. She can't have grown that much since I've been away."

Three years after they moved to Hawaii, Evan had married an English girl, Sarah, raised on the island. They built a house near the main house of Mau Loa. Evan's oldest son Jeremy was born when Shannon was nine, Henry two years later and Lizzy three years after that. Lizzy was eight when Shannon last saw her.

"I warn you. Lizzy is all into Christmas decoration. She's been making red anthurium garlands that are everywhere."

It was a warm welcome home. Shannon was happy to be in her childhood room again. It had been eight years since she had truly lived at home. When she was fifteen, she boarded at the Royal School in Honolulu until she was eighteen and graduated, then she spent almost a year traveling the world with her parents. Upon returning, it was only a few months before she was off to Berkeley and that was over three years ago now.

The house had the cool spicy smells she loved. Lizzy had indeed decorated: the stair railing, the fireplace mantels, and doorways with lei leaves and red anthuriums. In the front window stood a pine, just waiting to be decorated. It was only a few days before Christmas and there would be several parties to visit with friends.

Shannon had one special friend growing up in Ahuimanu, the small town on the east coast of Oahu. Kiki Akamu, a Hawaiian native, lived on a farm just down from Mau Loa. They had gone to elementary school in Kailua and spent most days playing, swimming, or exploring. Kiki didn't have a horse like Shannon so they spent most of their time at the beach or each other's *hule* or house.

Kiki had dark curly hair and dark eyes, standing only five foot two inches, comparatively smaller to Shannon's five foot eight inches. She had a quiet mischievousness about her and a way of finding a funny story in whatever situation arose or object she found. As much as Shannon enjoyed Maureen's zeal for fun, Kiki's was more earnest and simpler.

Kiki could take an urchin and create a story about how it journeyed to Maui by asking a whale if it could hitch a ride, that it was on a search to find true love, and that all the urchins in its pool just weren't adventurous enough. By the end of her story, her listeners would be laughing so hard, it would bring tears to their eyes. Shannon had missed this.

Kiki did not go to college, but married a local farmer and lived in Kailua nearby. Shannon was anxious to be with Kiki and find out about married life and to tell her about falling in love with Matty. Kiki of course knew Matty. They had often been together when he was on Oahu.

At four o'clock, Shannon finally had a free moment, and called Kiki to arrange a visit. By 1915, most of the residences on Oahu had telephones. Kiki picked up on the first ring. "Well, it's about time! I've been waiting all day, *Ho okipa I ka* home. Welcome home." They didn't talk long, both had meals to help prepare, but arranged to meet at Lupilo pub for coffee in the morning. Shannon then went off to help her mother prepare dinner. She found her humming a Hawaiian tune and picked up an apron to help. *Boy I miss her humming and the smell of her baking. She must have Hawaiian sweet rolls baking.*

That evening was just family. Evan and Sarah and children came. The boys wanted to know what the wild west of Colorado was like. "Hot and dry, kind of like the east side of the Big Island," Shannon explained. Everyone was excited about her work, but the boys mostly about her shooting the rattlesnake. It had been a long day, and after decorating the pine tree with everyone, Shannon retired early. The next day was Christmas Eve, when the family celebrated with friends.

Shannon met Kiki in the morning, and they took up as if they hadn't been apart. Kiki was enjoying married life and working with Pauli on their farm. Shannon told her about being in love with Matty, that he wanted more. "I'm just not ready for marriage, no matter how good you say it is. I have a secret I need to tell you."

Shannon then proceeded to tell Kiki about the ancient ruins she had found, and how she and Matt would play up there when kids, but now she wanted to uncover it and place it on the National Registry of Historical Sites.

"All this time, it was there and you never told me, you never took me there, why?" Kiki asked with a hurt tone to her voice.

"Oh, Kiki, … you didn't have a horse and it's too far to walk. I'm not sure why. I shared it with Matty, because I knew he wouldn't tell anyone, being on the mainland. I confess I was a little concerned if you knew. You would tell your father and he would tell one of the island elders and they would want the ruins for the people. It was my treasure and my secret spot. I didn't want them to take it."

Kiki could understand that reasoning as a child, but now it should be revealed and the Oahu cultural commission should be apprised. Shannon said she would be contacting them once it was excavated, and she was sure of the origins. It was on Mau Loa land, but it was part of native culture.

Kiki then turned the conversation to what was going on between Shannon and Matt. Shannon confessed concealing her feelings ever since they had been together at college. "Kiki, what was it like for you when you fell in love with Pauli? Sometimes I can't stand being away from Matt, my whole being wants to be with him. Then when I'm away from him at a ruin, I don't even think about him. I just don't know if I'm truly in love with him or just missing our old comfortable friendship."

Kiki laughed, "Oh, you're in love with Matty, I'm sure of that! The last time he was here, you couldn't keep your eyes off him. You two fit together as easily as Pauli and I do. Some people are just meant to be together. I didn't think of Pauli all the time when we first got engaged. But when he was with me, my heart quickened and I was the happiest."

Shannon blushed, "Ever since Matty kissed me, I feel the same. Wishing he would do it again. Sometimes when we're alone and he puts his arms around me, my heart feels like it will burst from within me. When I realize I haven't thought about him during the day, I feel ashamed and miss him. So, you felt this way when you and Pauli were courting, and now that you have been married for a year?"

"Oh, it's different, yet the same. Lying in bed, we're comfortable together, until he touches me romantically, then I tingle and my heart bounds. But as we go about our day, we don't think about each other when were busy. It's only when we have a moment and wonder what the other may be doing. Of course, working the farm together, we can go find each other. Shay Shay, it's natural not to think of people when you're consumed doing other things."

"I hope so. Thanks, you're a good friend. In one way I wished we had stayed friends until after I graduated and had some time to pursue my career and then he confessed his love. Now I'm torn as to where and what I should be doing. Matty's in Sacramento and I'm at Berkeley or will be working who knows where."

"Matty's a patient man, like your father. If I had a career, I would have made Pauli wait a year or two before I said yes. No, I would have said yes, but requested a long engagement."

It was midmorning when they finished catching up. They would see each other later that evening at the Christmas Eve party her parents were hosting. Shannon returned home and found her mother in the kitchen, preparing food. Shannon felt better after talking with Kiki. For some reason it was easier to talk to Kiki than her mother regarding Matty. Shannon grabbed an apron and helped to make macadamia nut cookies and iced ginger Christmas cookies. As she rolled out the dough, she confessed that her relationship with Matty had progressed into something more than just friendship. Lalani just smiled and listened as Shannon expounded on her feelings and concerns. She didn't let on that Katherine had written to warn her about the blossoming love. That afternoon at tea, Shannon told her father.

He shared how Lalani didn't want to rush into marriage either and how patient but persistent he had been. Jim shook his head, "Daughter like mother."

The evening festivities were joyous and everyone was happy to see Shannon. She wore the same green brocade dress that she had worn with Matthew. Christmas in Hawaii was very different than on the mainland. The weather was warm with sunshine and the red hibiscus were in bloom. The evening air was comfortable, and the outdoor lanai was lit by soft lantern lights and tiki torches. The long tables were decorated with green and red floral garlands. The neighboring ranchers and farms brought food and musical instruments to play. Lalani and Moria, a close neighbor, performed traditional Hawaiian dances as Sam and Keanu, Moria's husband and son, played ukulele and Hawaiian drum. Lizzie and two other girls showed off the hula they had learned. A fiddle joined in and everyone began to dance, the two step, a waltz. Keanu, Pauli, and Evan took turns dancing with Shannon, bringing a joy to her. *It's been a lovely evening with good friends, but I so wish Matty were here.*

The families with younger children departed first, wanting to get them to bed, "before Santa came." Evan and Sarah wanted to helped clear the dishes, but Lalani insisted they take the boys and a sleepy Lizzy home. Kiki and Pauli stayed until most of the mess was in order and the torches in the yard were extinguished. Once everyone was gone, Jim and Lalani said goodnight to Shannon, then Jim took Lalani's hand and went upstairs. Shannon smiled as she watched her parents climb the stairs. *They had been good friends first, and now look at them, in love and oh, so happy after all these years. That could be Matty and me someday, or at least I hope so.*

Christmas morning was always quiet with just the three of them and a few presents. Christmas Eve was the big festivity for the season. Shannon was up first preparing the coffee and warming cinnamon rolls, made the day before. Shannon sat looking out the window sipping on coffee; *it's so nice to be home for Christmas. It would be perfect if*

Matty was here. I bet Abby is dragging him out of bed soon, eager to get to the presents. The Taylor Christmas morning is so different from ours, lots of family, packages and noise. What will Matty and my Christmas be like I wonder. Or will we even have "our Christmas"? Or just family Christmases?

I have so much I want to do before marrying. Will Matty wait or can I do it and be married?

"*Mele Kalikimaka!* my darling girl," Jim said as he entered the parlor.

"Merry Christmas to you too, papa." They sat talking about the ranch and her plans to uncover the ancient ruins. It turned out he knew they were there for many years. He had followed her when she was ten and found her there. Since she didn't mention it, well, every child needs a secret hideaway. Lalani joined them and talked about the party and friends, reminisced about last Christmas, and finally they opened presents. A telegram arrived from Matt in the afternoon, wishing Shannon a Merry Christmas.

Evan, Sarah and the children joined them that evening for a more traditional English supper of goose and mashed potatoes.

With the holiday activities finished, Shannon was anxious to get to the ruins and start clearing the vegetation. She only had six days before her ship sailed back to San Francisco and there was so much to do. It had been two years since anyone had been there, and the vegetation had covered things again. Shannon hoped to get the vines cleared so she could photograph the ancient structure. She knew there wouldn't be time to get the photographs developed there in Hawaii. The local photographer was extremely busy developing the Christmas family portraits and would have no time for her film. It would have to wait until she got back to school. She wanted to recruit her cousin Jeremy and Kiki's brothers, Koa and Toni, to help clear the plants and vines. She would just have to supervise them, since fourteen and fifteen year old boys would take a bulldozer approach rather than the fastidious hair styling approach that would be needed.

Shannon set out early with her father and Evan, hauling an axe and shears to start the clearing. The horses were sure footed as they climbed the last steep five hundred feet. Shannon pulled the Kodak 3A out and took a photograph of the jumble before clearing began. Work went quickly the first two days, as the large overgrowth was cleared, then on the third day, vines clinging to the stones were slowly pulled away, making sure not to dislodge loose stones. The five by five foot structure now lay covered only with a mat of moss having only traces of the black pumice stone showing. There were piles of moss-covered rocks from the fallen walls, stacked on the outside of the structure. Shannon and Matt had cleared them from inside so they could play. Now she wished they had left them where they had fallen. Eventually she would use them to rebuild the two shorter side walls. Shannon figured pumice stone was used since it was readily available and lightweight, making hauling to the top of the hill easy. Again, Shannon took a photograph before she showed Jeremy and Toni how to carefully clear the moss from the stones. It wasn't a quick process as the moss roots had grown into the pores of the pumice, and the sharp pumice easily chewed up one's hands and gloves. She worked on the entrance wall that had a narrow two-foot gap for entering, what she now called the lookout blind. It wasn't tall enough to call a tower, standing only four feet tall. Shannon took more photographs, measurements, and sample rocks to take back to Berkeley. Her mother warned not to take the rock from the island, "It's bad luck! But perhaps the gods won't be too angry with only a small piece taken, as long as you return it when you're done."

There didn't seem to be any artifacts in the area, but she had no time to excavate below the structure for hidden shards or weapons. The evening before Shannon was to leave, they had removed most of the moss, and cleared enough of the vegetation on the ocean side to confirm that this was most likely a watch post for invading ships from the other islands, a common occurrence before King Kamehameha arrived.

Shannon celebrated the New Year 1916 with family and friends at Mau Loa. To her surprise, just before midnight, her father handed her another telegram.

"Happy New Year my darling! I'm counting the days until you return," it read. Matt had sent it earlier with instructions to give it to Shannon just before midnight.

Shannon's heart bounded as she read. Once again, she hadn't missed him during the week of working on the ruins, but suddenly tears welled up at the thought of being with him again. "*Hau oli Makahiki Hou*, Happy New Year," she whispered. *I hope you hear this in your heart. I will be with you in six short days.*

On the voyage back to the mainland, much of the discussion at dinner amongst the passengers was about the war in Europe. It had been raging for over two years now, and too many had been killed. The men felt it was time to change tactics from trench warfare to attack forces. It wasn't just bullets killing the men but the influenza running rampant in the trenches and towns. The men finally realized this was not a proper topic in the presence of ladies and quickly reassured them their voyage was safe, saying no U-boats had been seen in the Pacific, before changing the topic.

On a misty afternoon, Matty waved from the dock, holding flowers for Shannon as the boat came into port. Forty minutes later he was kissing Shay Shay and holding her close. Shannon blushed as onlookers passed by them. "Flowers in the middle of winter, how lovely. The carnations are beautiful."

Matthew didn't want to go directly to Shannon's apartment, knowing Grace was there, but instead they went to Delmonico's for lunch in San Francisco. This time, Shannon didn't chatter on about her work at the ruins, like she had upon returning from Mesa Verde. Instead, she asked about Matt's work and Christmas activities. After lunch, they drove out to the Presidio where the remains of the World's Fair stood. It was empty, and a few people wandered through the empty buildings. He held her hand as they walked, and they didn't say much. Both just enjoying being together again. The air now was crisp with an afternoon breeze beginning to blow. Shannon hadn't yet adjusted to the cooler weather of the city. Matt could feel her shiver and put his arm around her and suggested they head back to the car. "Grace will be wondering where we are," Matt said. The day went far too fast for both of them as he said goodnight to her on the apartment porch. Matt would stay at his uncle's overnight and planned to meet Shannon for breakfast at the Coffee Café. Before they knew it, they were at the train station once again, saying good bye.

"We have to stop saying good bye. Once you graduate, I hope you can move to Sacramento and continue your research from there." Matt meant the first part but was only hoping for the second part when it came out of his mouth. *Did I just say that out loud? I hope she takes it in a good way, that I don't want to prevent her from a career, just that I miss her when we are apart.*

Shannon started to react in a huff to his comment, then stopped. *He did say continue your research and after graduation. Not to stop working toward a career and come do what he wants me to do. I'm sure he feels the same and just misses me when we're apart. I haven't truly thought much about where I will end up after graduation. I guess it will depend on how much I can accomplish this final semester on my ruins project. Stop mulling over things and give him a response, he's waiting.* Shannon smiled, "I miss you too, when we're apart."

Oh, thank God, she understands and didn't take it the wrong way. "Let me know how the project goes, and I'll let you know how my projects at the house are going." That old familiar train whistle blew and they knew it was time. Matt took her face in his hands and kissed gently but for a lingering moment, and she longingly kissed him back. Then separating, he smiled, "I'll call you later in the week." Stepping onto the train, he added," I love you always."

Shannon pursed her lips and smiled, feeling sad at his leaving and finally replied, "I love you now and always too."

6

Research and Mysteries

The first thing Shannon did on Monday morning was drop off the film of the ruins to be developed, then she went to see Professor Kroeber. The Professor was excited to hear about her find and they sat down and outlined what she wanted to prove about it for her senior project. Like all mysteries, there were the six basic questions to answer. What was it; she was pretty sure it was some sort of lookout but she would need to prove it by finding a similar structure. Why it was built; again, she had a good idea that it was to warn the natives of invaders. Where it was; of course, this was already answered. When it was made; this might be difficult to determine, as well as how old. How it was made; this would be one of the easier things to determine, by looking at the striation on the rock, which would indicate what was used to cut the stone. Who made them? This was to her the most important, as she wanted to connect the structure to the Marquesas Island culture. Shannon had a lot of work to do in the next five months.

There was going to be a lot of corresponding with institutes that had Polynesian collections. Yet, she already had a start with the information she obtained from Oxford regarding the Cook expedition. Now she needed to get to the lab and see if there were any radioactive elements in the rock to determine its age. Unfortunately, pumice was not known to contain such elements, and Shannon had neglected to secure any nearby igneous rock that would have it. She would have to rely on historical records on when the volcano last erupted.

Shannon and Grace set up a research library in the apartment's dining area. They brought in book shelves, a large corkboard and a map of the Pacific Ocean. Grace claimed one corner for her own research on the Greek vase she was reconstructing. When the photographs were printed, Shannon pinned them to the cork for study. She first had written to Harvard for information and photos. It was a slow process that took weeks to get answers, and she was running out of time. California just didn't have the institutions with the needed information that the east coast had. She contemplated going to Boston, New York and Washington D.C. herself in order to see their collections and compare their findings to hers.

By spring break, Shannon realized she was not going to get all her answers in time for presenting her project. But she had developed good and concise hypotheses regarding the six W's. Professor Kroeber reminded her that research such as hers, had often taken a lifetime to prove. What he was really looking for in her presentation was her logic, methodology, and potential conclusions. The actual proving would take years, and he hoped she would stick to it and prove it, noting many women abandoned their work for marriage and family.

On the first day of spring, Shannon sat in the little cabin behind South Hall, contemplating Professor Kroeber's comments about abandoning the project after graduating. *Lou at Mesa Verde warned me it took years and sacrifice to be taken seriously as an archaeologist. I can't abandon my ruins. Lou said archaeology would take me all over the world. I didn't realize it was more for information gathering than for actually finding ruins. What will Matty think if I run off in search of answers? He's been so understanding and has come up here every month to see me. I'm sure he will ask me to marry once I graduate. He's expecting me to work at some museum in Sacramento. Would he really ask me to abandon my search to connect my lookout ruins to the cultures in the Marquesas Islands? Oh, I wish I knew what to do. Maybe I limit my quest to just establishing the blind to a specific era of Oahu history. Could just finding out who built it and why be enough? Hawaiian folklore already ties our culture to French Polynesian Island cultures. Do I really need to prove this ruin is part of a specific island culture?*

Shannon had been sitting arguing with herself for some time when she realized it was getting dark out. She would settle for who and why within Oahu for now. Upon arriving back at the apartment, she found Grace all in a tizzy and a large box standing in the middle of the sitting area.

"Grace, what's the matter?" she asked as she tried to maneuver around the large table size crate.

"It's not his!" Grace said, as tears ran down her face.

"What's not his, and who is his?" Shannon asked, as she took Grace into her arms and sat her down on the sofa.

"It's not my grandfather's desk. I was promised his desk. It was his grandfather's, from Highland."

Shannon began to piece things together. Grace's grandfather had passed away just after the new year. And the desk was his grandfather's, President James Monroe, a small writing desk. Highland was President Monroe's small farm in Virginia. Shannon looked inside the crate at the small table desk.

"Are you sure this isn't his desk? When was the last time you saw it?"

Grace gave her a bewildered look, "Of course, it's not his. I used to pretend to write letters to his grandfather on the desk. His has a ledge where you can put pens and an inkwell. It has an inlaid leather top that lifts so you can store stationery. In addition, it has two small side by side drawers. One of the drawers is shorter than the other, because there is a secret compartment. Grandfather said he put something special in the secret compartment for me. He and I were the only family members that knew about the compartment. As you can see this is not a writing desk, but simply a writing table. How could this have happened?" Grace began to cry again.

"Now, now. It's only a mix-up, a rather big mix-up, but I'm sure your grandmother was overwhelmed from her loss and just had the wrong item sent."

"That's just it, Shannon, when I saw it was the wrong desk, I called my great aunt. Grandfather lived with his sister since Grandmother died. She said she had his writing desk crated and sent. She's as upset as I am. Somewhere in shipping someone has switched the crates."

"Well, something this big doesn't just go missing, it has simply been delivered to the wrong person. You got their crate and they got yours. If we contact the shipping company, I'm sure they will be able to get things corrected."

"I hope you're right, but I'm sure my great aunt will not be able to deal with trying to find it. Shannon, you're good at finding things. Will you please help me trace the desk to where it went?" Grace pleaded and took Shannon's hand.

"Of course, I will, but it's getting late and there's nothing we can do tonight."

Shannon and Grace managed to move the crate to the side wall out of the way and then went to the kitchen to find something for dinner.

~~

The next morning Shannon found the shipping receipt, to learn what company had made the delivery. *I sure hope that the Monroe desk is here in Berkeley and not halfway across the country. I have too much of my own research to do and can't be spending too much time hunting down a desk. Still Grace is such a good friend.*

Shannon studied the label on the box. The label was addressed to Grace Monroe at 15 Chestnut Ave, Berkeley, California from Mrs. Emma Kelly at 221 Fifty-first Street New York City, New York. This was not good news. *If the label is correct then whoever closed up the crate put the wrong label on it. Could there have been two crates of similar size being shipped to two different locations?*

"Grace, did your aunt indicate she had another crate sent to someone else?" Shannon asked as Grace came into the room with a cup of coffee.

"No, she was so upset to hear the desk wasn't here, she just said they made a mistake on the label and didn't know what to do."

"We will need to call her and ask if she had several things shipped and to whom," Shannon said, hoping it would be that simple. *Something tells me it's not going to be simple.*

Grace had a class to attend, but would contact Aunt Emma, after lunch. Meanwhile Shannon was pouring over notes from her call to Oxford in hope of connecting a structure on Cook's stop at the Marquesas Islands of Ua Pou with her structure. Cook's journal described lookout structures attached to the side of the majestic outcroppings on Ua Pou. There were no drawings of them and he described them as being made of a limestone material rather than black volcanic stones. *They sound like my ruin, only bigger and higher in the mountains. I need to compare the elevation of Ua Pou to my site on Oahu.*

Shannon then opened the letter from Harvard's anthropology department. She had written them regarding their Polynesian collection and requested information on anything that might be related to what she had found. In this letter, Dr. Dixon also described a rock stack house structure found on Ua Pou, in the Marquesas Islands. On Cook's second voyage, he found ancient *Kehu vaka* or rock houses made of small stones skillfully stacked, the stone being mostly igneous and pumice volcanic rock. The letter went on to say they had samples and photographs of the stones and artifacts in their collection. This was the best lead she had come across so far. She was also waiting to hear from the New York Metropolitan Museum.

Later that afternoon, Grace contacted her Aunt Emma. Grace had learned that calling the east coast wasn't easy. It required many telephone operators to link up various switchboards and then hope the connections would be clear enough to hear and not be dropped by an impatient operator. She managed to get through to her great aunt and found out that she indeed had sent two large items: the desk and a small Louis XVI chair to the Richmond, Virginia Museum. Grace was convinced this was where her desk was and a simple trade would be possible. Shannon was not so sure it was that simple.

"Grace, if it was a crate mix up, then we would be looking at a Louis XVI chair and not a Chippendale table desk," Shannon pointed out.

"True! Are you saying that someone deliberately stole the desk?" Grace said, now very concerned.

Not wanting to worry Grace more, "Well, maybe, but the museum may have gotten both crates and put yours out for shipping with others, and they just picked up the wrong crate." *Though I doubt this. Two mix-ups on one crate, most unlikely.* "We need to contact the museum and hear what they did receive from your aunt." Shannon with her research was familiar on how best to ask questions from various museum curators and told Grace she would call. With the time difference, the museum would be closed, and they would have to wait until morning.

Grace set off to the Berkeley Library to locate a directory with telephone numbers. After an hour she was able to obtain the Richmond Historical Society telephone number and the name of William Glover Standard, the librarian. As soon as Shannon returned from classes, Grace was eager to place the call. It took almost thirty minutes for the call to go through, but now at half past one o'clock Shannon had Mr. Standard on the line. She explained the situation and asked about receiving the chair.

"Yes, we received the chair, but I assure you that is all. We are trying to establish an exhibit on President Monroe, he being a Virginian. But it is comprised mostly of letters. We would love to have the desk," Mr. Standard replied with an air of seriousness to his voice.

"Pardon for confirming, but you're sure your people didn't receive the second crate and just sent it on," Shannon asked as timidly and politely as she could.

"Yes, I'm sure. Brian who receives our donations would have told me if there was a second crate. He would want to know what to do with it and ask. Since he did not, I'm can assure you again we did not receive a second crate from Mrs. Emma Kelly."

Realizing there wasn't much hope, Shannon thanked Mr. Standard for his time.

"Now what do we do?" Grace asked, disappointed.

"I'm not sure, we're back at square one. Mr. Standard said he did not receive the crate, that his man Brian received the crates. This makes me wonder did your aunt actually see the two crates packed or did she leave it to a servant? I think you need to talk to her again."

Graced sighed, "It's so hard to be calling the east coast from here. I'm sure she left it to her servant; they would have been too big for her to pack and then get to the train for shipping."

"I'm sure you're right, but did she check the shipping labels on the crates before they left the house? The servant could have mismarked the station destination. Richmond is RVM and here is BKY. Could they have put something else like, BBY for Boston's Back Bay." *But that doesn't explain the crate with this desk. I'm at a loss and I don't have the time for all this. I'm presenting my project in two weeks.*

"I'll keep trying. I'll call your aunt tomorrow and ask to talk to her servant."

Shannon did follow up the next day and as she suspected Aunt Emma had not inspected the labels, but was quite confident in her man Tyron. Upon speaking with him, Shannon knew the labels were correct. But she had learned one interesting tidbit. Tyron said there was a man that came to the house asking about items from the Monroe estate that he would be interested in buying for his collection of Presidential memorabilia. He added that the man was quite taken by the desk and very disappointed when Mrs. Kelly declined his generous offer. Shannon had inquired about the man's name, but Tyron didn't know, saying he would ask the butler who received him and send a telegram with the name.

Shannon tried working on her final paper for her senior project, but little nagging questions about the desk kept intruding. *Is it possible this man stole the desk? That he somehow got his hands on the original crate and substituted it with the one Grace received? But how and when? Who actually took the crates to the station for shipping?*

Getting nowhere with her writing, Shannon made her way to the train station to ask questions. First, she sent a telegram to Tyron asking if he took the crate to the station himself. Then she asked the stationmaster about how crates were sent to their destinations. The stationmaster said they open the crate to verify the goods, then add the shipping paperwork inside before nailing the crate closed. Then a large address label is adhered to the crate. Shannon had pulled their label from the crate to show him, in case he could spot an alteration of some kind.

Instantly he remarked, "Miss, this is not one of our labels. We use heavy duty glue. You would not have been able to peel it off in one piece like this. Plus, they spelled out Berkeley. We use a code in large print that's easy to spot. The BKY is missing." He said as he pointed to a crate in the corner. Sure enough, you could see BKY clearly from across the room.

Shannon thanked him and was about to leave when the telegraph line began to tap. Shannon stopped, hoping it might be for her. She wasn't disappointed. It was her response from Tyron. He had not taken the crates, rather a hauling firm had been hired – O'Rourke and Son. Tyron had included the telephone number as well. This is becoming an expensive investigation with all these calls to the east coast. Shannon turned and took a slip of paper for a new telegram. It took her several tries before she felt the wording was brief, yet asking the right questions of O'Rourke and Son. She then paid the twenty cents and had it sent.

Shannon returned home and told Grace about the telegrams, and that she was once again waiting for a response. Grace felt guilty taking so much of Shannon's time, especially since Matthew was coming up for the weekend.

They heard back from O'Rourke saying they only picked up one crate, marked for Richmond, that it had been sitting on the back walkway. Now Shannon was certain there was no mistake in labeling, but the desk had been deliberately taken and by whom. *I just wish I had more information on the gentleman that wanted the desk so badly.*

Matthew arrived on Friday to take Shannon to the senior gala, the last dance of the year. He again stayed with his Uncle Eric and borrowed his car. Upon arriving, he presented Shannon with a wrist nosegay of small pink and purple orchids which harmonized with her lavender silk organdy gown. Shannon was delighted to be with Matty again. She was looking forward to an evening of romance. *He looks so handsome in his tuxedo! His green eyes danced with delight and mischief. I haven't realized how much until now I want to be in his arms and dance with him, kiss him....*

Matt had arranged a quiet dinner at one of Berkeley's finer restaurants. At first, they sat and talked about what each was doing, his building was almost finished, and she, of the missing desk. As the main course was served and Shannon looked around at the beautiful setting, the soft lights of the chandelier, the white tablecloths and sparkling champagne glasses, she suddenly didn't want to talk about jobs and the desk.

"I've missed you, Matty. Once I graduate, can we go to the ranch and spend some time together? Just riding to our favorite spot and listening to you play piano, just simple things."

He reached across and took her hand, "That would be perfect. But it might have to wait a week, your family will all be here for graduation and there will be so much to do as to where you are going to settle. Please tell me you have considered the job at the museum in Sacramento."

Shannon was quiet, *Oh, I wish I had, but it's been so chaotic.* "I'm sorry Matty, I haven't had time, I will inquire, I promise." *Please let it go at that. I'm not sure where I need to be after graduating. I'm pretty sure I will want to go home and finalize the ruins project and have it registered as a national site. That is going to take time. And then there's finding Grace's desk, I'm beginning to think I might need to go east to accomplish that. Yet I so want to be with Matty. Maybe I set the other aside for the moment and take a job in Sacramento.*

Shannon was lost in thought and didn't hear Matty's reply. Matty repeated his toast to them together in Sacramento, bringing Shannon to the surface again. She quickly picked up her glass and added "to us together," before taking a sip.

They arrived at the dance and everyone was happy to see Matthew. He filled Shannon's dance card as usual, leaving only two dances open, one for Freddie, and one for the young freshman that had been helping with all the manly chores at the house. Grace and Alice swept Shannon up at one point and asked if Matty was going to ask the question. Shannon shushed them with a 'don't be ridiculous, he knows I'm not ready.'

He held her tight as they glided across the dance floor. She laid her head on his shoulder on the last dance, feeling comforted, yet roused by the warmth of his body against hers and the desire to be fully kissed by him. Grace and Freddie, along with Alice and her date William, invited them go on to a club for more dancing and drinking, but Matty took one look at Shannon and seeing in her eyes that she also wanted to be alone, declined. Now knowing Grace would not be home for some time, they went back to Shannon's.

Matty poured a brandy, then a sherry for her and came and sat on the sofa. They sipped their drinks for a moment in silence and then Matty took the glasses and set them down. He pulled her to him and gently stroked her cheek, her smile showing the yearning she had. He kissed her and then again and again, as she let herself be enveloped in each touch and kiss. He picked her up and carried her to her room. Setting her down by the bed, he looked at her, "Just lie with me, I promise not to compromise your virginity, but I so want..." Shannon put her finger to his lips, "I trust you," she whispered and turned so he could undo her dress. It slid to the floor and she stood in her undergarment. She turned back around and unbuttoned his jacket and shirt and he let them fall. He swept her up and laid her gently on the bed. He came and lay next to her, gently taking her hand and laying it on his bare chest, letting her lead the way as to how they would proceed. They spent time gently exploring the curves of each other's body and then exploding into a passion of kisses and heavy petting. Finally, Matty pulled away and excused himself to the bathroom. Shannon lay on the bed, cherishing the intimacy. *Oh, Shannon, you shouldn't have, but how wonderful it all is. The warmth of his body and feel... he does love me so very much.*

Matthew returned and cleared his throat as he stood in the doorway, Shannon now looked up and saw he had his shirt back on and his coat in his hand. She smiled, "Time to go..." She rose and retrieved a dressing gown from her chair, slipping it on and then walked with him to the parlor.

They both knew Grace would be home soon. He pulled a curl back behind her ear and caressed her face with his hand, then gently kissed her and softly asked, "No regret?"

She looked into his eye, "No regrets, thank you for being such a gentleman."

Matty laughed softly, "If I were a true gentleman, I would have never gone that far. But fortunately for us, we're both part heathen."

Shannon knew he was referring to her native and his Indian heritages and smiled. Her eyes narrowed with a loving stare as she watched him walk down the path to the car. Closing the door, she turned and hugged herself, tingling in the warmth of his love. They would see each other for lunch before he had to return to Sacramento. He would stay longer, but Shannon still had a lot of work to do before graduating in three weeks. Grace returned home shortly after Matty departed to find Shannon sitting on the sofa, twiddling with the locket Matt had given her. Shannon had brushed her hair and pulled it neatly back as she usually did before bed.

Grace was suspicious about what went on, but didn't ask. "Well, after a romantic night like this, you sure you don't want to get married this June?"

Shannon smiled and tossed a pillow at her.

~~

The following weeks, Shannon concentrated on her senior project and graduating, as did Grace. Grace was sure they knew where the desk had gone and once school was over, she would go back east and track the man down that had taken it. At least that was what she was hoping, and that Shannon would go with her.

Shannon had been in contact with Harvard several times in regards to comparing artifacts relating to her ruins on Oahu and those they had from the Marquesas Islands. They had been gracious enough to send photographs of various objects and ruins on Ua Pou. She had Evan go up to the ruins on the ranch and take more pictures and do some digging around the inside for any artifacts. Nothing was found inside the ruins, but he did find a carved wooden stick, under one of the mounds of rocks outside, and sent it along with the photos, to her at Berkeley. Shannon was pretty sure it was a warrior's club of some sort. With only a few days left before her dissertation to her professors, Dr. Kroeber and Dr. Gifford, she frantically finished her presentation of methodology, logic and hypothesis on the ruins in Oahu being linked to those in Ua Pou and the migration of the Marquesas natives to Oahu. Grace helped her set up her display of photos and small model at South Hall, then sat quietly with Shannon and waited for the professors.

Shannon recalled Matthew's senior presentation and how nervous he was at the time. *Matthew had such a more impressive presentation and purpose to his project. Somehow mine seems so insignificant. What is my contribution to society? Is it important? I guess it depends on how you ask. It's important to me, and it seemed to be very important to the governor of Oahu when I told him about it. It's important to the people it involves, to their heritage, to who they are.*

Shannon sat gathering her thoughts on what she had spent four years studying and to her native ruin, as the professors came in and took their seats. Shannon had made a simple model of the ruins on Oahu that she had covered for presenting later in her talk. First, she would start with what she had just thought of, that archaeology is important to the people whose lives it touches. She then proceeded to defend her logic and hypotheses using photos and the model she had constructed to bring her points into focus. It took just over an hour and the professors seemed pleased but challenged her with one final question.

"Miss Baker, your presentation and hypotheses are very probable. Will you pursue your quest to prove them and establish the ruins on Oahu as a national site for the Hawaiian people?"

Shannon was taken back by the question. *Was I serious about proving the connection I had hypothesized or would I finish the archaeological dig?* Gathering her thoughts and trying to figure out the real question behind this question, she hesitated for another moment. Professor Kroeber was about to ask again when Shannon began to answer. "If you're asking, will I return to Oahu and finish the excavation of the site, I most definitely will. Whether I can go to Ua Pou and see for myself if their ruins and mine are connected. I'm not sure."

Just then a voice from the back of the room was heard. "If money is the problem, I will be happy to fund the expedition," Annie Alexander said.

Shannon spun around and smiled at her old mentor from her sophomore year. Annie was an experienced graduate archaeologist from Berkeley and a very wealthy woman. Upon hearing Ann, Professor Kroeber remarked, "Well then, I guess you will be. This has been a worthwhile report and we look forward to reading about your final outcome in the *American Journal of Archaeology.*"

Shannon thanked the professors and gathered up her things. Annie invited both Grace and Shannon to join her for lunch where they could discuss the future.

They spent a pleasant several hours listening to Annie tell about her archaeological digs around the world and her plans for a new library at Berkeley. Shannon confirmed she would finish the site on Oahu first and wait for the war in Europe to end before venturing to Ua Pou or any foreign site for now. Annie reiterated she would help fund the expedition when the time arose. Annie paid the check, then hurried off to an appointment, again congratulating Shannon on a job well done. Grace sat watching Shannon, knowing the conflict raging in her mind. "Well, are you going to go to Oahu right away or are you going to Sacramento?"

Shannon looked at her with eyes glazed with uncertainty. Her heart was aching with the pain of being torn between love and self-accomplishment.

"I so want to go and do the work to finish the Oahu site, but I promised Matty I would look into the museum job. I do love him so very much. I really don't want to be an ocean apart from him, yet if I take the job, will I be so unhappy? I will resent him and never want to marry him. Grace, a week ago if he had asked me to marry him, I would have said yes, but now with what Annie has offered and Professor Kroeber's expectations, what do I want to do? ... Will he wait?"

"Of course, he will wait! Come on, let's go home and clean up the mess. I need to prepare for my presentation tomorrow. It won't be as difficult as yours. My restoration piece is complete, and if I do say so myself, it looks magnificent."

Shannon went with Grace the next morning to her presentation and listened as she explained the research and techniques she used to restore the Greek urn. She had done an incredible job matching dyes and smoothing the pieces together without sacrificing the integrity of the piece. Professor Kroeber and Annie Alexander were both pleased and would feature it in the next addition of the Berkeley Anthropology Journal.

Now the work was done, and it was time to celebrate. Parents would be arriving in the next day or two. Grace's parents were coming from Pasadena and Shannon's would arrive on Thursday in San Francisco. Matty and Aunt Katherine, Uncle Clay and Abby would arrive on Friday. Shannon was almost embarrassed by all the people coming to see her graduate. To her surprise, Evan, Sarah, the boys and Lizzy had come along with her parents. Her father beamed with pride. Shannon would be the first with a college education in the family. He knew her generation would be doing great things and she would be part of it. Joanna and Richard held a pre-graduation celebration on Friday night once everyone arrived. Matty of course couldn't keep his eyes off Shannon, he was so proud of her, and now she was free to be with him.

Graduation on Saturday was a typical warm sunny morning. The stage was set with flowers and the Berkeley Blue and Gold banners. Shannon's family and friends took up two rows of chairs close behind where the graduates sat. There were just over a thousand graduates for 1916. Shannon looked regal in her cap and gown. She didn't sport the blue and gold braids for *magna cum laude* that Matty had worn, but her parents were just as proud. Shannon was disappointed she and Grace couldn't sit next to each other, but Baker and Monroe had about two hundred names between them. Shannon was seated between Tom Bacon, a mathematics major and Colleen Bemis, an Education major. Fortunately for Matty, Baker was at the beginning of the alphabet and he didn't have long to wait to cheer for her. When Shannon walked up to accept her diploma, a large round of applause broke out with Jeremy and Henry shrieking out loud with shrill whistles. As the dean handed her her certificate, he winked, "Glad to hear you're loved, congratulations!" Shannon blushed and as she stepped past, held up her diploma and shouted, "For women everywhere!" For which an even louder applause burst out. From the corner of the crowd, she caught Mabel Craft, one of the leaders of the California Suffragists smiling and nodding her head.

Shannon and Grace had arranged to keep the apartment for two weeks after graduation as Shannon was uncertain where she would be going. Grace had also insisted that Shannon keep her informed of where she would be, and any marriage proposal. Grace was returning to Pasadena. Grace's family was staying in Berkeley for the weekend, but everyone in Shannon's group would catch the four o'clock train to Oak Ridge and make their way to the Taylor Ranch. Evan and his family would stay with Uncle Morgan and Aunt Amanda, while Lalani, Jim, Shannon and Matthew would stay at the main house.

Once all the family was gone, Shannon would return to Berkeley and pack things to send home or to Sacramento. Grace and Shannon caught up briefly after the ceremony to congratulate each other and to confirm they would call each other the following week. Grace still wanted her help in locating the desk.

For now, the Baker and Taylor clans were headed for the train station and the Taylor's private railroad car, where everyone could relax and be comfortable, as champagne poured freely during the two hour ride to Oak Ridge, where Morgan and Andrew would be waiting with cars. Jim and Lalani would spend the month with the Taylors, while Evan and family would go on to see Yellowstone National Park before returning to Oahu. Matthew again only had a few days off, before he was needed back at work. He and Shannon made the most of their time together, taking morning rides and swimming at the reservoir with many others. After dinner the men adjourned to the study and often discussed the war in Europe that seemed to be going badly and how France and Britain were applying more pressure for America to come help. Eric and Nancy had also come down, and Eric indicated that the war was now hampering the trade between Europe, India and China. It was harder to get certain goods, and American tobacco and cotton goods were no longer being shipped to Europe, which was impacting prices and the industry. President Wilson would need to do something soon.

Jim wasn't concerned that Evan would have to go fight, as he was too old and his boys too young. The same was for true for Morgan, as his boys were in their late teens, but they all worried for Matthew and Andrew who would be drafted if America got into the war. Clay was also concerned about a shortage of men to work the ranch. He was too old to do most of the hard work and relied on Andrew and the younger ranch hands. They tried not to talk about it in front of the women, but the women, alone in the sitting room, couldn't help worrying about losing the boys to war. As much as Amanda, Katherine and Lalani wanted to talk about marriage for Shannon and Abby, who would be turning nineteen, they avoided that topic, knowing Shannon's concerns, not wanting to marry yet. They talked about gowns and how it was no longer possible to get the French designs and Chinese silks because of the war.

Matt extended his stay until Monday afternoon, wanting the morning to talk seriously and alone with Shannon. It was a cooler morning as they rode out. Shannon had spent the night fretting over what to do. She finally decided to give Sacramento a chance, but first go east to help Grace locate the desk.

She was sure Matty would be happy with that decision, but she still wondered if she would. *I'm sure I can still work on the Oahu project from Sacramento and when I'm on the east coast I can visit Harvard and get the information I need, first hand. I'm sure Matty won't mind, or at least I hope so.*

They stopped and tied up the horses as they sat at their spot looking out over the valley. Matt took her hand, "Shannon, please come to Sacramento with me. I can find you a place of your own, not too far from me. Leon Lionaski says he know the curator of the museum and assures me you can get a job there." Pausing for a moment, Shannon still didn't say anything as she mulled over her decision one more time in her mind. "Shay Shay, you know I love you and want to marry you, but I don't feel it's the right time for us to marry yet. You want to do your research and I have a war hanging over my head. I'm convinced that the US will enter the war before this time next year and I will be drafted. I don't want to make promises I can't keep."

Shannon looked at him surprised and alarmed at the thought of him going to war. "Matty, you promised! I also promised I would contact the museum and look into a job. We have never gone back on any promise we have made to each other. I made up my mind last night I will come to Sacramento, after I help Grace locate her desk."

"Shay Shay, I promised I wouldn't enlist, but if I'm drafted, I will have to go. And I don't want you to take the job in Sacramento because you promised me. You have to do it of your own free will."

"Of course. It is my own decision. I want to be with you, Matty. I have hated being apart from you this past year. I still want my freedom to do as I desire, but I desire to be near you, to see you and share everything with you."

"You're wonderful! You just made me a very happy man. We can take the train to Sacramento and find you a place, and you can apply for the job," he said smiling and giving her a lingering kiss.

Shannon didn't kiss firmly back, however, and Matt knew there was a but coming. "BUT! You have to help Grace first, is that it?"

Shannon pursed her lips and smiled with her eyes. Only Matty could know me so well and not be mad. "Yes, I will try to make the search as quickly as we can, I promise to be back within a month."

"A month!"

"Ok, let's say three weeks, it will take us ten days just to get to the east coast and back, then a week there to find it and go to Harvard for what I need. After that I'll collect my things from Berkeley and be in Sacramento. You can find a place for me in the meantime. I trust your taste, just not too big and something I can afford."

Matty still didn't like the terms but he knew this was the best he was going to get. *At least she's coming and we will be together again. I guess I can find her a place, she'd never agree to living with me.* Matty took her in his arms and held her tight just taking in the smell of her hair and the feel of her body. Shannon did the same.

"Are you sure? Oahu isn't calling you home?" Matt hesitantly whispered.

Shannon laid her head against his chest, "Yes, I'm sure. For now, Oahu is sleeping."

The horses stirred and they realized it was time they headed back.

Upon arriving in the parlor, both mothers were waiting. "Well, what's the verdict?" her mother asked.

Shannon grinned, "I'm taking a few weeks to go back east to help Grace locate her desk and to do some final research at Harvard. When I return, I'll apply for the job in Sacramento. In the meantime, Matty will either build me a house or find me one," she said teasingly.

She could see delight in Katherine's grin but a slight disappointment in her mother's. She went to her and reassured her mother she would be back at Mau Loa before long, maybe for Christmas. Clay and Shannon took Matt to the train station at four o'clock and once again they said their good byes.

"You will keep in touch and let me know where you are. I'll worry every minute you're away. When you get back, I'll meet you, and we can go to Berkeley together and pack up things."

"That sounds perfect." Shannon said giving him a final kiss as he was about to step onto the train.

Matty looked at Shannon, "I love you and…" he was about to say marry me, but stopped himself and added, "And I'll see you in three weeks tops."

Clay just shook his head and grinned. *Timing, having to wait is the hardest thing but the right thing to do!*

PART TWO –
Establishing a Career

7

The Hunt!

Shannon stood watching the train grow smaller and smaller in the distance, the longing to be on that train welling up inside her. Clay suggested she inquire into the next train east and corresponding connections to New York. She also sent a telegram to Grace, now in Pasadena, saying she was ready to go to New York to search for the desk and wanted to leave as soon as possible.

Within two days, Grace had joined Shannon in Oak Ridge. Evan and his family had gone on to Wyoming. Jim and Lalani had decided to stay until Shannon returned from the east, but by mid-July they would need to be back at Mau Loa to prepare for fall round up. Lalani wasn't keen on the girls travelling alone, but Jim could see his daughter had become a strong independent woman, and had a good sense of things. Clay confirmed she still had the hand pistol he had given her for Mesa Verde, and she knew how to handle it if necessary.

Both Katherine and Lalani knew the route the girls would be taking and warned them not to get off the train in Elko, Nevada and be leery of strange men. Grace had sent a telegram to her great aunt about when they would arrive and stay with her. Tyron, Aunt Emma's groom, would be at the station to meet them. Emma was old fashioned and preferred a horse-drawn carriage to the new modern automobile. Shannon had made the journey once before when she was seventeen. Grace was seven the last she visited her grandfather at his home in New York. As he grew older and less able to get around, he moved into his sister's home.

After five days Grace and Shannon arrived at Aunt Emma's. It was a large two-story brick colonial style house near the south end of Central Park.

Her aunt was pleased to see Grace, but confessed she had a busy social schedule and wouldn't have much time for the girls.

"I apologize for imposing, Aunt. I wish I didn't feel so attached to the desk, but I just have to find it. I can still hear Grandfather's voice telling me stories about your grandfather writing important letters on the desk."

"I'm glad you have fond memories with him. Grandfather was not at Highland when we knew him. After his presidency he moved to Oak Hills in Virginia. I too can remember him writing letters at the desk there. Regretfully, I'm not sure it's possible to find the desk now, but if you want to try, by all means. Tyron is free to help as much as possible, as long as he doesn't neglect his responsibilities here. I will need him and the carriage part of each day."

The girls had lovely rooms on the second floor, each with its own fireplace, but the weather was far too warm for them to be needed. Once they were settled, Grace and Shannon joined Aunt Emma for a light supper in the dining room. The girls told her about college and their adventure at Mesa Verde. Aunt Emma had no idea why they studied anthropology or archaeology and how they could possibly use the information they had learned. But she admitted it was a new century and things were changing, "A little too much and too fast for my taste," she added.

After supper, Shannon wanted to talk to Tyron about shipping the desk and found him in the kitchen, helping the cook, Mrs. Piedmont, with drying the dishes. Shannon took a seat at the table and waited. Tyron joined her after a moment, and he told her everything he could remember about packing the two crates, and writing out the bills of lading for the railroad. He wasn't home when they picked up the crates, but had them set on the back path so the hauling company could easily retrieve them without bothering Mrs. Piedmont. She told them she heard the truck pull up, but didn't look out as she had a cake in the oven that needed to be taken out. Shannon planned to visit O'Rourke's in the morning to confirm the pickup. She then asked Tyron about the man who came looking for President Monroe's memorabilia.

"I don't know much, as I didn't see him. The madam spoke with him and was rather miffed after he left. Said he was far too pushy and insistent, that he tried to bribe her with an inordinate amount of money for the desk. But the madam had promised Master William she would send the desk to you. And she doesn't go back on a promise."

Edmond, the butler, had come in for an evening cup of tea and sat listening. "I remember that chap. Rather self-important he was."

"Do you remember his name, where he came from?" Shannon asked rather excitedly.

"I don't remember his last name, but his first name was funny sounding. He didn't leave a card either. What was it? Um.... started with a G. Gerald, no Germaine, ... no it was Gran something. Grandale, I think, I'd never heard of such a name. All I can remember about his last name is that it was short, foreign."

"That certainly helps. Do you remember what he looked like, where he was from?" Shannon asked.

"He was rather a short stout man, with thinning light brown hair. He was well dressed, carried a walking stick with an ivory knob handle. He wasn't from New York, sounded more like he was from Boston, kept dropping his r's. I heard him say he was staying at the Ames Hotel near the 'pahk'."

Shannon thanked the staff for their help and said she would follow up in the morning.

After breakfast, Shannon and Grace headed out to O'Rourke and Son. Aunt Emma didn't need the carriage that morning and offered it to the girls, as long as they were back in time for afternoon tea at Mrs. Gardner's.

Mr. O'Rourke greeted Shannon and Grace cordially, and upon hearing what happened expressed concern, but was convinced nothing on their part was done wrong. He called in his worker Gus to verify the pickup. Gus remembered knocking on the door but no one answered, so he went around back to the servant's entrance and found the two crates sitting on the walkway, and that everything seemed in order. "It was my last pickup and I took them directly to the train station and set them on the loading dock. I rang the bell as usual and the stationmaster came and checked the crates. Said fine, Mrs. Kelly had made the payment and all the necessary arrangements, and I left." Mr. O'Rourke thanked him and told him he could go back to work.

Shannon now was puzzled. *If the crates were picked up and delivered, when and where was the one crate switched?*

"One last question. Do you verify what is in the crate when you pick it up?"

"Do you mean do we open them? No, there's no need. The stationmaster does that, as part of the arrangements. The stationmaster opens the crate and adds a bill of lading for the receiver, then nails it back up and places the corresponding delivery label onto the crate."

Shannon thanked Mr. O'Rourke for his time and for the service, reassuring him they had done exactly as asked.

Shannon now wanted to go to the station and talk to the stationmaster. As she and Grace were leaving, she spotted Gus standing by some crates waiting to be loaded. *Is it possible there was another wagon there watching for the crate?* Shannon went over to Gus, "Gus, one more question. Was there another wagon at the dock dropping off a crate when you were?"

Gus thought for a moment, "Aye, miss, he seemed to be watching intently at what me and the stationmaster was saying. But he only had one crate to deliver, that I could see." Shannon thanked him again and they went on their way.

It was only a few minutes to the train station, the cargo loading dock was south of the central passenger station. Grace pulled the carriage to a side area and waited for the stationmaster to finish with a wagon unloading. The dock was littered with broken crates and ropes. There were several dock workers milling about, large rather intimidating poorly dressed men. Therefore, Shannon felt it best to stay in the carriage until they could pull up next to the loading dock.

Once the wagon pulled away, Shannon and Grace pulled up close and climbed the stairs to the platform. The stationmaster was himself a rather large burley man, but his hair was now gray and his face lined with years of hard work. As Shannon and Grace approached, wolf whistles and shouts came from several of the workers. Grace grabbed Shannon's arm and began to quicken her pace, but Shannon held her stride and straightened her back, trying not to be frightened by the men's attention. The stationmaster, busy with inspecting the crate, upon hearing the whistles looked up, and was startled to see two neatly dressed ladies standing there. He gave the men a sharp glare and jerk of his head, indicating they should get back to work. "I'm sorry miss, miss, but the passenger station is another block up, this is the cargo loading dock."

Shannon smiled, "Yes, I know, I think you are the one we are looking for, the stationmaster?"

He nodded, "And how can I possibly help you?"

Grace explained the mix up in crates and showed him the bill of lading that had come with the table desk. "Is this your writing? Do you recall seeing the desk?"

He took the sheet and looked for a moment, pinching his chin in thought. "This is my handwriting alright. But I see so many crates a day, it's hard to remember something from weeks ago."

Grace gave him a forlorn look, "Please try, a small desk."

He looked at the lading bill again, reviewing the names and addresses. When he saw the name Monroe in the receiving line, a memory flicker through his mind. "Monroe, that looks familiar...yes, I remember thinking is this desk possibly going to William Monroe's daughter. I recognized the sending address as being where President Monroe's grandson lived. I read about his passing in the paper."

"So, you do recall seeing a desk in the crate?" Shannon asked.

"Oh, yes, miss. A nice small writing desk."

"Was it a writing desk with pen and inkwell or just a small table-type writing desk?" Shannon asked.

He looked at the shipping slip. It just listed a small desk, no description. Then rubbing his chin again, "Well, I'm pretty sure it was just a small mahogany table. The paperwork said desk so I assumed it meant table type desk, and I was looking at the right item. There was a chair too, and I thought it odd that Mrs. Kelly was splitting up the set."

Shannon was reluctant to ask, not wanting to offend or feel like she was accusing the man, but she proceeded. "Once you inspected and closed the crates, what did you do? Do they stay on the dock until loading on the train or do they get moved to a holding area?"

"Oh, things are definitely moved to a holding area. Nothing is left on the dock for long, too many wagons coming and going." Again, he became contemplative for a moment. "You know I was pulled away from the dock, that day, just after the crates arrived. It wasn't for long mind you. But there was a gentleman inside, insisting I take care of a package he wanted to send and that I do it personally. He was making a raucous of a fuss about it. I left the crates for about ten, no longer than fifteen minutes, while I dealt with him. But as soon as I was done, I returned to the dock. Another wagon was there waiting to make a delivery. He had already off loaded his crate. "

"Do you recall what was in his crate and where it was going?" Grace eagerly questioned.

"No, I don't remember that one, the name was unfamiliar. I hadn't done the paperwork for it. When I finished, I had one of the workers retrieve a dolly and place the first crate in the area for the west coast train, the other for the southbound, and the new one to the northbound train. And no, I don't remember specifically where they were going."

Shannon now had an idea of what happened and thanked the stationmaster for his time. Grace still had one final question to asked, "What did the man casing the scene look like?" she said quickly.

"He was rather short. I remember it was odd he was wearing a cape on such a warm day. He wore a hat too, so I only saw a wisp of hair that looked to be a shade of brown." Grace thanked him and then followed Shannon back to the carriage. It was getting late and they needed to get the carriage back for Mrs. Kelly's afternoon tea. Shannon explained to Grace what she thought had occurred.

"This Mr. Grandale must have paid someone to switch crates. He created a scene to get the stationmaster distracted away from the dock. I bet the driver waiting was the one who switched the crate labels when he left the crate we got and changed the label on your aunt's crate to go to him. "

"So now we have to find this Mr. Grandale, but how?" Grace said, rather bewildered.

"I'm not sure, but we have a few clues. We need to stop at the Ames Hotel on our way back."

The desk clerk at the Ames was a stately formal gentleman. When Grace asked about a guest Grandale, he politely told her there was no one by that name, first or last registered. Grace put on her most demure look and described Grandale in hopes the clerk would share more." That's a very vague description and could be several of our guests." Once again Grace, with a longing desperate look, asked if he would share the name of the possible men. This time the clerk straightened to his five-foot eight height and with an authoritative voice informed her, "I'm sorry miss, but our clientele's information is private. I regret once again I cannot help you. Unless you have a name or a room number, I cannot put you in contact with anyone."

Shannon could tell by his manner they would not get anywhere with him. She thanked him for his time and tugged at Grace's sleeve to leave. The doorman opened the door for them as they left. Their carriage stood waiting, and Grace reached for the reins, when she stopped and jumped down, and hurried back to the doorman. Giving the young man a smile, "Sir, do you have a short stout man with thin brown hair staying here by the name of Grandale." He was taken by surprise at first, "Well, miss, that could be any of two or three men, here, but none with that name. Sorry miss, I think two of them checked out this morning. The other's last name is Smithfield, but he has gray hair." Grace curtsied and thanked him for his time and returned to Shannon waiting in the carriage.

Grace pulled up to Aunt Emma's. Edmond had been watching for them and was out the front door before they had descended the carriage. "Just in time, another ten minutes and Mrs. Kelly would be late to her tea." Grace and Shannon went inside to the parlor and asked Edmond if the cook could fix them some sandwiches since they had missed lunch.

Shannon was convinced this Grandale had the desk and, since he had checked out of the hotel, was no longer in New York. Their next move was to head to Boston. That their Mr. Grandale most likely was from there, since he had a Boston accent and the third crate was sent north. Grace thought it was a slim lead, but she had nothing to add. Edmond arrived with a tray of sandwiches and tea which he poured and then left the room. Grace snatched up a sandwich as her stomach growled, while Shannon explained she had planned to go to Boston anyway to see the Harvard Polynesian collection. Shannon also picked up a sandwich as they made plans to leave the next day.

Later that evening at supper with Aunt Emma, Grace expounded on what they had learned and their plan to go to Boston. Aunt Emma gave them the name of Mr. Stark, a good friend of her husband that lived there. She would send a telegram asking him to assist if he could. After supper, Shannon retired to her room to write Matty a letter, explaining they had arrived safe and were making progress, but going to

Boston. That they would be staying at the Eliot Hotel in the back bay area of the city. Finally adding 'I miss you and love you.'

The train from New York arrived in Boston just after five in the evening. Shannon had the porter hail them a cab. This time it was a motor car, and the driver seemed to know his way and not take them out of their way. They arrived at the hotel just in time for the last seating for supper.

Grace and Shannon confirmed the plans they had made on the train ride, as they enjoyed fresh crab cakes with a tangy aioli sauce. Grace would visit Mr. Stark, since he was well connected to Boston's Brahman elite. Her thought being Mr. Grandale, who appeared to be wealthy, would also be part of that group. While Grace visited Mr. Stark, Shannon would go to Harvard and meet with Professor Dixon about the Polynesian collection. Shannon warned Grace not to go after Grandale, if she happens to find out who he was and where he lived. *I truly doubt she will, but luck might be on our side.* She warned her he wouldn't want to give up the desk and she didn't have much proof it was hers.

~~

Shannon arrived at the Peabody Museum on Harvard's massive campus just before her ten o'clock appointment with Dr. Dixon. Unfortunately, the doors were still locked. As she waited, she found it a little hard to breathe. The anxiety of finally seeing concrete proof of her ruins directly tied to those in Ua Pou was growing with every beat of her heart. She held her photos in a small satchel along with the wooden artifacts Evan had sent, staring out across the campus looking for someone to come.

Suddenly, "Click!" sounded from behind her. She heard the door unlock. "Good morning, Miss Baker, sorry to keep you waiting," Dr. Dixon greeted in a low baritone, yet friendly voice.

Shannon spun around, slightly dizzy from the shortness of breath, but with a smile, managed, "Good morning, Dr. Dixon, it's so good to finally meet in person."

He shook her hand and led her in past the massive dinosaur skeleton in the entrance, up a flight of stairs and down a corridor to his office. He could see Shannon was eager to get to the reason of her visit, and made an effort to keep the sociably correct niceties to a minimum. Shannon laid out her findings and theories, and they spent the next hours discussing them. He agreed with most of her hypotheses but not all. He felt the ruins were too far from the channel in which invading canoes would approach. Also, on Ua Pou small structures like hers were littered with sacrificial items, some with the remains of human bones but most with animal remains.

Shannon reached into her satchel and pulled out the carved wooden club that was found and inquired if it could be used for sacrificial ceremonies. Now this Dr. Dixon was most interested in. Rising, he said, "Come with me."

He led her back downstairs to the rear of the first floor through a large carved door. Shannon stepped through to a room filled with Polynesian artifacts. A large outrigger canoe stood in the center and on one wall were long wooden paddle oars. Dr. Dixon walked over and reached for one specific oar. He took Shannon's club in his other hand and pivoted the oar horizonal so they could compare the carvings. They appeared to be an exact match. "Incredible!" he said. Shannon was overjoyed with the match but failed to grasp the true significance.

"Shannon, this as you can see, is definitely Marquesan, the oar is specifically from Ua Pou. What I can see from your response is that you don't realize this is the mate to the oar I hold in my hand. Your club was once the top part of an oar. I will bet you my professorship that your club will date back to the same 1500 era as the paddle, made of the same wood. Each warrior would carve a pair of oars he would use as part of a team of rowers. You can see here on the wall we have three of the pairs that belong to the canoe on display. But this oar was missing its partner. Each warrior carved his own distinctive pattern and emblems on his paddles so they could be retrieved once the battle was won." He took Shannon's club and pointed to the narrow end away from the carvings. "For some reason this oar was cut. See the clean end. The oar might have been broken near the paddle head and left as no longer useable. The warrior might have died in the battle, and his one good paddle was brought back to his family."

Shannon stood fascinated by his story and began to conjecture her own theory. "So, it proves the Marquesas warriors came to the island. And it's most likely, the broken paddle was cut down to use as a defensive club. I can further theorize, that the warrior was a watchman at the blind and that's how the club got there."

"That's a reasonable conclusion." He pulled out a magnifying glass from a nearby drawer and slowly looked at the club. The wood carvings were worn but did not indicate deep gashes that would result from beating something with it. It did have the appropriate worn spaces just below the carvings where a rower's hand would have been placed. "It doesn't look like it was used for sacrificial killings, so your theory of a lookout blind maybe correct." He handed the club back to Shannon and then returned the oar to the wall.

"Well, I'm sure the University would be interested in purchasing the club from you, in order to complete our set."

Shannon smiled, "I appreciate the offer, but you understand that in Hawaiian lore, removing certain things from the island is bad luck. Even though it's not volcanic rock, I feel this piece carries the same taboos."

They returned to Dr. Dixon's office and he took careful photos of the club. He agreed to write a letter of confirmation regarding the club and the Oahu ruins as part of the migration of the Marquesas natives. After another hour, Shannon realized it was getting late and Grace would be waiting. Dr. Dixon reiterated his offer to purchase the club, and requested Shannon keep him informed on the progress and unveiling of the Oahu ruin. She tucked the club back into her satchel along with her documents and said she would return for his letter before leaving Boston.

Shannon arrived back at the hotel to find Grace waiting in the lounge. Shannon had missed lunch and was famished, requesting a full high tea of sandwiches, scones, and treats with tea for both of them. Grace could see the excitement on Shannon's face, "It looks like things went well with Dr. Dixon."

"Oh, yes, my club is a match to an oar he had and he concurred with my theories on the ruins." The tea and sandwiches were delivered and Shannon snatched up a cucumber delight and took bites in between trying to tell Grace all that had transpired.

Grace just chuckled. *Not every lady liked talking with your mouth half full. She is definitely thrilled about her success. I wish I could feel the same about finding the desk.*

Once Shannon had mused about all the details of the morning, she finally asked Grace about her meeting with Mr. Stark. It was a pleasant congenial meeting, but not much help. Mr. Stark didn't know anyone by the name of Grandale or the vague description. "He did suggest we check with the local historical societies and museums, that someone might know him regarding his interest in presidential memorabilia," Grace finally added. "I asked the concierge for a list of societies here in Boston. There are six of them, and two are private reenactment clubs of the Civil War. "

They sat and finished their high tea and went through the list of societies. Shannon thought to split up and cover them more quickly, but Grace was rather fearful being in Boston on her own, especially after the greeting they got on the loading dock in New York. Shannon understood. Several were in the Back Bay, which had been known as one of the poorer areas of Boston, but had much improved since the Christian Scientists had built their large church there. Many patrons had moved into the area and it was coming out of its poverty era. Still Shannon was inclined to take her pistol with her, especially if they were to find Mr. Grandale and be confronted by him.

Grace was satisfied with their plan and then wanted to go to the symphony, which was performing that evening. Shannon agreed, thinking their suspect might be in the crowd. They agreed to meet in the lobby and catch a cab. The concert was lovely. Shannon was pretty sure Katherine had played with the Boston Symphony during her career. During intermission, they scanned the crowd for their short little man, and there were several, but they were mostly gray haired or bald. They gave up and enjoyed the rest of the concert.

They slept late the next morning, as there was no need for an early start. The societies didn't open before ten or noon. First on their list was the Boston Historical Society. They hired a cabby with an automobile for the morning, which was driven by a strong middle-aged man. Shannon promised to pay him handsomely for waiting during visits. Inside the Historical Society, they met a spry little woman in her early seventies. She was most eager to show them the museum and Grace indulged her in hopes of gaining her trust and thus the information they needed. As they came to the section on the Revolutionary War, Grace brought up the fact that her great great grandfather served with General Washington, without indicating who he actually was. The host went on about his presidency and a few others. Now Shannon felt it was a good time to ask their narrator if she knew their Mr. Grandale.

"I'm sure you have a lot of Presidential enthusiasts, that belong to your society. We met a gentleman last month that knew all about President Monroe. What was his name, Grace?" Shannon cocked her head gesturing to Grace.

"Oh, I'm not sure. I think his first name was Grandale or Grant, I don't remember his last name as it was foreign."

The woman shook her head. "I know all our members, no one by the name of Grandale. That's an odd name, I would remember it."

They had struck out and so Grace was eager to move on to the next museum. She quickly reminded Shannon of an appointment and they made their way out. It was almost noon and Shannon did not want to miss another lunch, so she asked their driver to suggest a proper place. He drove them to a small restaurant near Symphony Hall and said he'd be back in an hour if he could. Grace looked at their list of societies and picked the South End Historical Society, and then the Old State House. The cab driver showed up just as they finished paying the bill and was delighted to take them down to the south end and wait. The South End Historical Society was housed in an old brownstone, not any larger than Aunt Emma's house. Once again Grace led the conversation with the curator as he strolled them through the Boston treasures from the Tea Party to the War of 1812. Finally, Shannon brought up the name Grandale, this time describing the man.

"I'm sorry miss, but I don't recognize the name."

Grace asked if he would check their membership list, but he said it was confidential. "We're a small society and donations are hard to come by, so we don't share our list. We don't want others pinching our donors." Grace said she understood and once again they made a hasty return to the waiting cab.

Now they headed north to the Old State house. "You ladies really like American history, do you?" The cabby said making idle conversation. Shannon smiled "Well, to be honest, we're trying to locate someone who does. We're just not having a lot of luck."

"Who you looking for? I've been driving cab for years, and lots of people are frequent riders."

Grace was certain he wouldn't know, but told him anyway. "That's slim pickin's to go on," he said.

"You sure it's not Grant Delt I know a young man by that name."

"No, this man is much older," Shannon said with defeat in her voice. They arrived at the State House and once again made their way to talk with who was there. They found another older gray hair gentleman dressed in period costume from 1776. It was late in the day and there were few people wandering around. "Welcome to the Old State House built in 1713 and the site of the bloody massacre leading to the Revolutionary War," he said with great wisdom.

Shannon was not in the mood for another partial tour, therefore quickly moved to the point of their visit. "I'm sorry, it appears you're quite knowledgeable about the State House, but we've actually come to see if you can help us find someone." She put on her most academic voice in hope he would realize she knew a great deal about history and smiled sweetly.

"Oh, in that case, I'm not sure I can help. Most of the people that come are historians in one way or another."

"Then perhaps you will know him. He is a great enthusiast of early presidents. We believe his first name is Grandale or something foreign. We met in New York, and he was very interested in President Monroe."

"Grandale, you say? No one by that name, but we have a Grant and a Gerald on our board. What does he look like?"

Grace described him as best as possible including his Boston accent.

The old gentleman eyes narrowed in deep thought, "Sound like Granville Weltz, he's is a big collector of John and Quincy Adams memorabilia. He's rather stout, likes his beer he does. He must be branching out to other Presidents if he's seeking Monroe items."

Grace's face lit up with amazement that they had actually made a true connection. Grace and Shannon had agreed not to tell anyone why they wanted to find him, only they had something to return to him.

"Would it be possible to get his address so we can contact him and present him with our gift." Shannon asked, *Our gift of police officers. Part of me wishes we had brought the table he sent.*

"Well, we don't give out that information usually."

Quickly trying to think of how to persuade him, she came up with, "I'm sure he will be most grateful to you once he sees that we have changed our mind about giving him an item he was interested in. I'm sure his gratitude will result in a large donation to this historical society." Then adding, "Your board will be impressed with your initiative and your part in obtaining the donation," as she tried to stroke his sense of commitment to the State House.

The gentleman straightened his shoulders just so slightly, "Well, I believe he lives in the Back Bay on Saint Stephen Street near Symphony Hall." He didn't have the exact address, but remembered him saying he often walked up to Symphony Hall.

Grace thanked him profusely, adding she would mention his name, Mr. Chambers, to make sure a donation would be coming. Shannon suddenly felt bad, knowing that there certainly would not be a donation coming from Mr. Weltz and made a mental note that she should send something.

Back in the cab, Grace instructed their friendly driver to go down Saint Stephen Street near Symphony Hall. He smiled, "You found him, did you? I can have you there in fifteen minutes."

Shannon was inclined to explain to their driver what was really going, and shared their predicament. "Now that we have the street he lives on, we need to figure out how to watch the comings and goings on the street to find out which house is his.'"

"This guy is nothing but a high class thief. My cousin will be happy to look him up for you. By the way my name is Felix, and if I can be of assistance other than driving, you just let me know."

"Well, thank you, Felix. I'm Shannon Baker and this is Grace Monroe, but we are not absolutely positive this man actually took the desk. It's just our best lead and guess. We need to see that he has the desk before we call the police."

Felix pulled the cab to the end of Saint Stephen Street so they could observe most of the houses within the two-block-long street. There were only about twenty houses total. They had been parked on the street for several minutes and within that time two men had been seen, one coming out of a house and the other going into a house. Neither man was short, so they ruled out at least two of the houses. "Felix, it's getting late and you have been working all day. Grace and I will make our way back tomorrow and figure out how to watch. You best take us back to the hotel and get yourself home to your family," Grace said, giving a small appreciative sigh.

He drove them back to the Eliot Hotel, pulling up in front and getting out and opening the door for Shannon and Grace. Shannon paid him generously for his time and compassion. "Miss Baker, I'll pick you up tomorrow at nine o'clock and we can stake out the street together, no charge, it's my day off. You will need help, being strangers to town, and my missus would be dismayed if I didn't help."

Shannon started to say no, but realized they did need help. "Felix, you are a good man, thank you. We will see you in the morning," and she shook his hand.

That evening Grace and Shannon discussed what they needed to do once they confirmed they had the right man. "We need to find a way into the house to look for the desk," Shannon fretted.

"I only hope the desk is at the house and he has not hidden it somewhere because he stole it," Grace added.

"From what the gentleman at the State House indicated, Mr. Weltz cherishes his collections and most likely will want to have them on display where he can show them off to friends," Shannon commented to Grace. *Maybe that's how we can get into the house, we need to get him to show us his collection. But we can't ask to see the Monroe desk, he'll be too suspicious since it's stolen and he hasn't had it very long. But if we ask about the Adam's memorabilia that may work. But how do we get an introduction?*

"I'll take the first pass on the street, and then you can take a second," Grace interrupted Shannon's thought.

"We could. But I think we should watch from Felix's cab the first hour. Most men will be leaving for work or errands between nine and ten. After that the houses will be drawing their curtains open so we can stroll by and see if we can get a glimpse of their occupants," Shannon suggested.

Grace agreed it was at least a place to start. It was getting late. She said good night and she would meet Shannon for an early breakfast.

Felix arrived at the Eliot right at nine o'clock and they were parked at the halfway point of Saint Stephen Street a few minutes later. Shannon faced towards Grace and looked out the rear window while Grace looked to the left side and Felix watched ahead. Felix felt it was safe to sit for fifteen minutes in one place and moved to the end of road and park for another fifteen, then finally to the opposite end so as not to draw attention. As expected, several people emerged from the houses: two nannies with prams, a gentleman walking a rather large dog, one man with a briefcase walking up toward Symphony Hall and another walking past the car and turning the corner onto the side street. None of them was Mr. Weltz, but they could eliminate half of the houses now.

As they sat and observed, Felix regaled them with stories about waiting for perspective clients and some of the ridiculous requests, such as taking two or three steamer trunks, even a pet parrot. At about ten o'clock, Grace got out near Symphony Hall and slowly sauntered down the northside of St. Stephen Street. Felix drove around to the other end of the road and parked on the next street over to wait for Grace. As they waited, Shannon reached into the side pocket of her purse for a handkerchief, but at the bottom instead of a handkerchief, she found an old women's suffrage flyer she had folded up. It must have been there for months *Has it been since fall at school when I last used this purse? Surely not!* She placed it back and asked Felix about his family while they waited. He smiled and said, "I have three strapping boys and two beautiful daughters." After about fifteen minutes Grace entered the cab.

"Well, I couldn't see much in the five houses not yet identified. The one at the end of block had very feminine Louis XVI mauve furnishings in the parlor and a vase of flowers on the table. I don't think it's likely he lives there," Grace said. One other had a rather young-looking woman standing at the window, it could be his older daughter but I doubt it. I'd eliminate that one too. The other two I wouldn't rule out," Grace reported.

"Now it's my turn for the other side" Shannon said as she opened her door. "Meet me at Symphony Hall." Shannon turned the corner and looked at the first house. It was hard to tell, no one was in the parlor and was it a maid in the upstairs room? *This is going to be impossible to tell this way. I need to be able to go to the door, but what excuse could I have. For directions; just come out and ask where Mr. Weltz lives, what? Wait, could I possibly? It would be a legitimate excuse, but it will involve taking time. Yet it would further two causes.* She reached back into her purse and pulled out the folded flyer, smoothed it as flat as possible against her skirt and walked up to the first house, then lifted the heavy metal knocker – Thud!

A woman dressed in a floral morning dress answered the door with a puzzled look. "Yes, may I help you, miss?"

"Actually, I'm here to help you," Shannon said, then continuing, "I'm out rallying support for the 19th Amendment. We women are as intelligent and hard working as any man and should have the right to vote. To help shape our town and nation on issues that affect our lives. Do you not agree?" Shannon held the flyer against her waist using her hand to hide the announcement of the lecture date and time. The woman was taken back at first, and then shook her head, "I suppose so, but I leave the politics to my husband."

"Your husband, is he home? Is he a forward thinking man?" Shannon asked.

"He's an honest good man, hard working. I trust he knows best," she replied rather timidly but with adoration.

"Well, Mrs. …" Shannon paused hoping she would fill in the rest.

"Mrs. Parkhurst."

"Mrs. Parkhurst, I'm glad to hear that, but I still employ you to encourage him to vote in favor of the 19th Amendment. I'm sure you have lots to do, so I won't keep you any longer. Thank you for listening." And with that Shannon stepped back from the door and nodded her head. The woman closed the door with a rather confused look as to what had just happened.

Shannon moved on to the next house, four doors down, happy that her idea had worked.

At the next house, an older stern looking woman answered. "What would I need with the vote at my age?"she snapped.

"Don't you want a say on how you will be taken care of after you can no longer work? Voting will give you the right to help make those decisions," Shannon tried to appeal to her. *This one must be a spinster and will have nothing unless her master provides.* Quickly before she shut the door, added "Ah, your employer Mr.… is generous and will provide for you when you retire. How wonderful."

"Ha! Mr. Wiggin provide! Be off with you before he chases you off," she grumbled. Shannon quickly retreated to the sidewalk and made her way to the next block. At the next house a gentleman answered, and was not at all in favor of women voting so she moved on quickly. Once again it was not Mr. Weltz. The last house on her side was an elderly woman, who invited her in to chat. Shannon felt obliged, but quickly realized this lady was just lonely and would have stopped a thief stealing her best silver, to just sit and chat with her for the company. After about ten minutes, Shannon indicated she needed to get to an appointment and stood to leave, but the elderly lady remained seated and continued to ask questions about the need to vote for another ten minutes before finally standing and showing Shannon to the door.

Shannon now worried Grace and Felix were worried and looking for her. She hurried as quickly as possible without running to find them parked at the Hall. As she reached the corner to cross the road, Felix was striding her direction. She waved and smiled indicating all was well. "What took you so long?"

She explained her idea and how she had eliminated the houses on the south side. She wanted to stop at the two houses on the northside that Grace hadn't been able to eliminate before giving up. "Give me another twenty minutes and pick me up at the second house. Then we can go to lunch."

Felix went back to the cab where Grace waited while Shannon walked down to the first house. It was a federal style wood structure with black shutters, with the parlor drapes closed. There was a black metal eagle knocker. It appeared no one was home. Shannon knocked again harder, and was about to leave when she heard the door lock turn. She straightened her dress as a maid opened the door. "Yes, may I help you? Do you have an appointment with Mr. Weltz?" questioned a small demure middle-aged woman.

Shannon's heart leapt, and she frantically thought for the right answer. "Yes, I mean no, I don't have an appointment, but I would like to speak with him."

The woman, looking older than she actually was, said, "I'm sorry, miss, but Mr. Weltz doesn't see strangers without an appointment. If you would like to leave your name and number along with what you like to see him about, I'll give him the message," she said politely.

"Actually, I'm out rallying support for the Nineteenth Amendment. A man's endorsement would be most helpful."

Just then a man's voice rumbled from an open door behind the woman. "Who is it, Minnie?" he asked as he entered the hallway.

Minnie moved aside, so he could see and replied, "A young woman wanting support for the 19th Amendment, sir."

He motioned her to return to her duties, and grabbed the door, "Miss, if the founding fathers wanted women to vote they would have made it part of the Constitution. Women should be seen and not heard," he grumbled as he began to close the door.

Shannon stared into the glaring black eyes of the man they had been looking for, desperate to stall his closing the door and for a peak into the house. She stepped to turn and faked a small stumble and choked, grabbing the door frame to prevent from falling. He just stopped short of closing her hand in the door. "Miss, watch where you step," he scolded.

"I'm sorry sir" she said meekly and pretended to choke and asked, "Again, I'm sorry, I'm leaving, but is it possible I could have a drink of water before..., I've been walking for quite a while." *Hopefully he's an old-fashioned gentleman.*

He stopped and pulled open the door again, "Minnie," he barked. She appeared again. "Get this woman a glass of water and then see her out," and he returned to the room from which he came. Minnie allowed Shannon into the entry to wait while she fetched the water. Shannon took the moment alone to survey the rooms she could see. The hall had a small side table and coat rack, and through the door to her left was the parlor. It was decorated in a rather masculine fashion, with federalist style furnishings. There was a glass case on the far wall. She couldn't tell for sure what was in it, but it looked like books and perhaps a writing quill. The door through which Mr. Weltz disappeared was slightly ajar. Shannon moved closer for a better look, but Minnie appeared with the water, so all she could see was a large desk in front of several built-in bookcases. Shannon took the glass and stepped back towards the front door. She took a sip then thanked the woman and turned to leave. Minnie opened the door and whispered to Shannon as she went out, "I believe women should vote, don't give up," then quickly closed the door behind her.

Shannon's heart was still pounding and a shiver ran through her as she thought about the short angry man. She hurried to the end of the street where Felix and Grace were waiting. *He is going to be a problem. I just know he has the desk, but where?* Shannon climbed into the back seat with Grace, "Felix, we need to move on from here." He started the car and headed back to the hotel.

"You found him! Did you see the desk?" Grace anxiously asked.

"Yes, and No. Number 14 was him alright, a rather curt man, and no, I didn't see the desk. I only got a glimpse into the parlor and barely a peak into, I think, his study. But my senses are screaming he has the desk."

"You ladies need to be careful, especially you, Miss Baker, now that he's seen you. He sounds like he might be dangerous," Felix warned, concerned for his new friends in an older brotherly way.

Back at the hotel, the girls insisted Felix join them for some lunch. The restaurant was serving a hearty pot roast with potatoes, of which

Felix ate heartily. Shannon picked at her food as she contemplated how to get into the house. *We have to make sure he has the desk before we go to the police and accuse him of stealing. What if he didn't take it from the train dock, what if someone else took it from Aunt Emma's back path before Mr. O'Rourke arrived. How do we get into the house?*

Grace had been sitting thinking the same. "What do we do now?" she asked.

"I'm not sure," Shannon admitted.

"Maybe I should go and see if I can get in for some reason," Grace suggested.

"You're going to need a reason and it can't be about woman's rights, he's totally against them, and you will need to make an appointment," Shannon said, rather bewildered.

Felix reviewed what they knew about the man. They knew he collected presidential memorabilia. Shannon was pretty sure he was a bachelor and that he was a stout believer in the founding fathers and the constitution. "That's it, we need to find an early American political item he might want for his collection, or at least want to look at," Felix suggested.

"What might that be and where would we get something like it?" Grace replied. None of them seemed to know. Shannon felt they had taken enough of Felix's time and suggested that each think about it and meet up in the morning.

8

The Retrieval

Shannon had spent a restless night, trying to figure out how to get into Mr. Weltz house, and then if he did have the desk, how to get it out. She wasn't sure they could go to the police. What proof did they have that the desk actually was Grace's grandfather's and now hers?

In the morning, Felix and his cousin Shawn were waiting in the lobby. Felix came from a rather large Irish family with various connections in Boston. Shawn was one of the less reputable family members, engaging in a brawl on a rare occasion, but a good soul deep down. He just liked the ponies and his fingers found their way into a gent's pocket now and then. Nothing serious, just petty larceny. Shawn had a perky grin to his boyish face. He was rather slender, not particularly tall, and slightly younger than Felix but with the same curly light brown hair. Felix introduced him to the girls and suggested they find a quiet place to talk.

Felix had explained the situation to Shawn the night before. Shawn had taken the initiative to obtain a rare personal letter from President Adams written to his son. Shannon gasped when she saw the letter. "You didn't steal it did you?" she blurted out.

Shawn gave her a teasing smile, "I wouldn't say steal, but rather borrowed."

Felix gave him an elbow to his arm. "Stop teasing."

"Alright, no, I didn't steal it, Louise Adams is a friend of mine. She's the great granddaughter of Quincy Adams. It belongs to her.

Mind you, it's only on loan for a day or two at the most. I promised I'd return it to her in the same shape I got it. But I think it should do the trick for an avid admirer of John Adams."

"I would hope so, but how do we introduce Mr. Weltz to it without him getting suspicious," Grace asked.

"Oh, don't you worry about that, people like Mr. Weltz have connections to underground markets and so do I. I'll arrange a meeting with him about the letter," Shawn grinned.

Grace agreed it was good bait. She would take it to him and try to look around to spot the desk. But Shawn said he'd go with her, and while she negotiated with Weltz, he would snoop around the house. Grace would have preferred Shannon be the one to go, but Weltz already knew her. Grace wasn't sure she could do the negotiating and suggested that she and Shawn reverse roles. She would snoop and if caught, she would say she was looking for the water closet.

Felix and Shannon reluctantly agreed, and Shawn said he would set up a meeting for later that afternoon and be in touch. Until then there was nothing for anyone to do. Shannon headed back up to her room and wrote Matty a note telling him that now they were in Boston and what was going on. Shortly after two o'clock Shawn arrived. The meeting was set for three.

Shawn and Grace arrived promptly at three and were shown into the parlor. Minnie, seeing Grace, automatically brought tea and cake. Grace was introduced as Shawn's girlfriend. Grace expressed her delight in his beautifully decorated home and some of the items on display. She had wandered over to the case that Shannon had spotted, and sure enough, there was a certificate signed by John Adams, some sort of Navy commission for a Captain, a pair of spectacles, and quill and ink bottle. She commented on them and Weltz brimmed with pride at their authenticity. But then he wanted to get down to business. Shawn asked if there was a flat desk that he could lay the letter out on that was more private, and away from the staff. Weltz led Shawn into his study to the large desk and Grace followed. Shawn and

Weltz went to the desk and Shawn produced the letter for his inspection. Grace quickly looked around the room for the desk, but it wasn't there. "Shawn, I think I will return to the parlor for more tea, while you men talk," Grace said with a shake to her head, indicating it was not in that room.

Grace wandered from the room and gently pushed the door halfway closed. With the hallway empty she quickly ascended the stairs to check the rooms. Again, the hallway was empty and there were three doors, one half open and she could hear a humming coming from within. *Probably the maid.* She scurried to the first room and stepped in, it appeared to be a guest room, sparely furnished. She returned to the hall and carefully and as quietly as she could tiptoed past the half open door to the other closed door on the other side of the hall and slipped inside the room. This was a large room, obviously his master bedroom. Grace scanned the room: a tall bureau, mahogany armoire, four poster bed and night stand, window... and there in the corner of the room, the desk.

Grace dashed over to it and rubbed her hand across the leather top, her fingers shaking. Suddenly the humming drew near, the knob of the door started to turn. She froze looking for a place to hide. All she could do was dart behind the door itself and hope the maid entering didn't close it behind her. Grace held her breath, her heart pounding so hard she was afraid the maid would hear it. Minnie entered and crossed over to the armoire on the other side of the room and fortunately didn't pull the door closed behind her. Grace could hear her cross the room and peaked out from behind. Minnie had her back to her as she hung something up in the armoire. Grace scooted out and around the door back into the hall almost falling over the basket Minnie had set on the floor. Grace bumped into the wall with a thud. Minnie hurried out to see what it was. Grace had just regained her balance and straightened as Minnie spotted her. "Miss, what are you doing up here. You mustn't be up here."

"I'm sorry, I was just looking for the water closet, too much tea, I'm afraid." Just then Mr. Weltz and Shawn came from the study. Seeing Grace at the top of the stairs and being angry for not acquiring the letter from Shawn for a reasonable price, he shouted, "What's going on? You don't belong up there."

Shawn pretended to back him up, "Abigail, what are you doing? Get down here now, you worthless girl."

Grace hurried down the stair. "I'm sorry, I was just looking for the water closet." Shawn grabbed her arm and pulled her to the front door. "We're leaving. You will just have to wait. Mr. Weltz doesn't value the letter for what it's worth."

Mr. Weltz was right behind them and shouted, "Get out, you riff raff, you arrogant anti-federalist."

Shawn opened the door and hurried Grace out and down the steps to the street as Weltz slammed the door behind them.

Felix spotted them from the corner, where he and Shannon had been anxiously waiting, and drove up to meet them as they walked quickly up the street.

"Well! Was it there? Is he suspicious?" Shannon tried to ask calmly, but it came out excited and hurried.

Grace smiled, "Yes, it's there. He has it in his room upstairs."

"Upstairs, you managed to get upstairs!" Felix commented. "And you didn't get caught? Well done!"

Shawn looked at Grace, "I wouldn't say she didn't get caught. The maid caught her at the top of the stairs and the commotion alerted Mr. Weltz. He and I were basically done quibbling over the price of the letter. He found my price way too exorbitant. Called me greedy, he did."

Shannon looked wide eyed at Grace. "I'm fine, Shannon. They didn't catch me in his room, just at the top of the landing, and I said I was looking for the water closet as planned. That's when Mr. Weltz shouted for us to leave and we did," Grace said triumphantly.

"And the letter?" Felix asked with a bit of urgency.

Shawn patted his pocket, "Safe and sound. I'd best get it back to Louise. Can you drop me there?"

Felix drove to Louise Adam's house and dropped off Shawn, who said he'd meet up later at the hotel. Grace and Shannon were rather weary from all the tension and excitement and needed time to rest. They all agreed to meet at the hotel the next day. Felix said he should to do some driving to earn some money for the family needs. He also thought it best to lie low for a few days to let Mr. Weltz settle back into his routine, whatever it might be. The girls agreed and said they would take the next two days to sightsee. Felix would let Shawn know to meet on Wednesday.

Shannon knew Felix was right about laying low, but her three week's time away from Matty was growing short, with only three days left for obtaining the desk. She and Grace tried to stay distracted by visiting Faneuil Hall and the Old North Church. They avoided going to the Symphony again, in fear of running into Mr. Weltz. Shannon and Grace talked about how to retrieve the desk. Grace wanted to call in the police, saying it was stolen. But Shannon pointed out they only had a bill of lading and so did Mr. Weltz. Both with a brief description of 'small desk'. There was no real way of proving it was Grace's. Grace agreed about the bills of lading, but "I have the letter from my grandfather where he writes about leaving the desk to me and that it has a special present for me." Shannon was puzzled, so Grace continued. "There is a secret compartment in the desk my grandfather told me about where he put something for me. I assume he has put a note there."

This would make a difference. Grace was sure Mr. Weltz nor anyone else knew about the hidden compartment. She would retrieve the note for proof that it was indeed her desk.

Shawn and Felix met the girls around three o'clock on Wednesday. Shawn had done a little snooping on his own and learned that the maid did not live in. Felix also had inquired about Mr. Weltz's interest in the Boston Symphony, that he was a regular patron, and that there was a concert that night. Immediately they agreed. 'Tonight', would be their best chance to get the desk. Grace wanted to go to the police, but Shawn pointed out it would take her weeks to get it that way. Mr. Weltz would most likely protest and take her to court for stolen property. Felix agreed, quoting, "Possession is nine tenths of the law." Grace once again became discouraged.

"Don't fret, Miss Monroe, I plan to retrieve the desk tonight," Shawn said quietly.

Shannon's eyes widened with concern, "How? You can't ask Felix to help. What if you're caught? He has a family to feed."

Felix agreed he couldn't help, but he knew his cousin well enough that he had a plan. "I can manage on my own. You said it was a small desk," Shawn said confidently.

"It's not that small, it will take two people to carry it down the stairs," Grace explained, as she gestured to the width and height of the desk.

Shawn scratched his head trying to convince himself he could still do it alone.

"I'll go with you," Shannon said. "I'm tall enough. Grace is too short to get it quickly down. Plus, if I'm caught, my Aunt Katherine has several influential friends here in Boston. I'm sure one of them can get me released. Plus, I'm just a maid's daughter, it won't sully my name, but it would Monroe. The newspapers would make a big deal out of that name."

Grace and Felix grimaced immediately, disliking the idea, but Shawn admired her moxie. Shannon gave Shawn a confirming glance, hoping the others didn't notice. "Shawn can manage, it's not that big," Felix conceded.

They agreed to meet first thing in the morning at the train station where Shawn would be with the desk. Grace would obtain tickets for the train to Iowa that would then connect to the westbound to San Francisco.

Felix took a sideways glance at Shawn, not sure if he was up to mischief or not. Shawn noted smugly back to Felix as he left, "I'll be fine, don't worry." Grace rushed after Felix to get a ride to the train station to purchase the tickets and arrange for shipping of the desk. This left Shawn and Shannon alone. "Did I understand that look correctly? I'll meet you here at nine o'clock?" Shawn nodded his head and tightened his lips into a slight smile. "Best to wear trousers, if you have them," Shawn whispered as he strode toward the door.

Neither Grace nor Shannon could hardly eat anything at supper and little meaningful conversation was shared. "I'm going up to write Matty a letter to let him know when my train arrives in Sacramento. I'll see you in the morning. Try and get some sleep." Shannon said rising from the table. *I know he won't get it before I arrive, but I need an excuse so I can meet Shawn without Grace knowing.*

"Sleep? I don't think I'll be doing much of that; better I be praying tonight. You?" Grace replied as she tightened her fists to stop them from shaking.

"Oh, I'll definitely be praying tonight, I can assure you," Shannon said smiling and giving Grace a parting kiss to the cheek. "I'll see you at breakfast in the morning." *At least I hope I will.*

~~

Shannon had packed one pair of trousers, thinking she might find time to go riding. She thought to bring the pistol, but she had nowhere to hide it, plus with Shawn she didn't feel the need for it. Just before nine o'clock, she made her way past the front desk and onto the sidewalk. Shawn stepped out of a dark corner and touched her elbow. Shannon jumped and spun around, her senses tingling. "Come with me, I have a truck around the corner." Shannon climbed into a small delivery truck, and didn't ask questions about where he got it. "We'll park out back, and go in through the kitchen. I staked out the place earlier and saw the old coot leave all dressed for the symphony. We should be in and out without a hitch, just stay close to me."

The alley behind the houses was dark. The row of carriage barns was now used for cars and all the doors were closed, indicating the owners were settled for the night. Shawn turned the engine off as to not make noise and let the truck roll to a stop. He managed to park just before Mr. Weltz's back gate. Weltz had left the porch light on for when he returned. Shawn led the way through the old gate and up to the kitchen door. Shannon was right behind him, her pulse racing, watching for any movements in the dark alley. Shawn stooped to work the lock. Clicking noise came from the door as it opened. Within seconds they were inside. Shawn turned on a flashlight he brought and held it low to the floor in hopes it wouldn't shine through any open windows. Shawn led the way upstairs and to the room Grace had told him the desk was in. Shannon was on his heels with her hand on his back to guide her in the dark. She sighed a breath of relief seeing the heavy velvet drapes were drawn. Shawn took a quick look around the room. "Shannon, look here, a letter from George Washington." Shawn was tempted to lift it from it place on the wall, "Don't you dare," Shannon scolded in a low voice. "Let's get the desk and get out of here."

Shawn came and pulled the small desk away from the wall with a grumbling tap tap tap against the wood floor. "You take that side and I'll go backwards through the door," Shawn instructed, now holding the heavy light under his chin. They were just a few steps through the door when, THUD! Thunk. The flashlight was too heavy and crashed to the floor, sending a streak of shivers through Shannon's body at the sound. Shawn picked it up and quickly put in his back pocket. Shannon calming her nerves, once again lifted up her side of the desk and they made their way to the stairs. Shawn stopped and thought for a moment, "What are you waiting for?" Shannon snapped.

"We can't carry it down side by side, we need to turn it on its back. You take the feet and I'll take the top and go first. Just don't push, let me lead the way since I'm going down backwards in the dark."

Shawn leaned the desk onto its rear legs and took the top edge. Shannon grabbed the front legs and lifted them as high as she could. Slowly, feeling for the first step, Shawn made his was about halfway when Shannon slid off a step pushing Shawn forward. He grabbed for the stair rail with one hand while trying to hold the desk with his other, pushing the desk back at Shannon. She went backwards landing on a step with her bottom. "I'm sorry. Are you all right?" she asked, grateful the desk was still there and not tumbling down the stairs.

"BANG!" Shannon froze as she sat on the stair, Shawn did the same but standing. The lights of a car drove slowly past the parlor windows. "It was only a backfire. Come on, keep going," Shawn urged. Shannon stood, now proceeding successfully to the bottom floor. They readjusted the desk to upright and quickly shuffled to the kitchen door. Shawn opened the door and peered out, the alley was still dark and silent. "Go on out, I can take it down the two steps."

Shannon slipped past him and down the steps to the walkway and looked around, then motioned it was clear for Shawn. The desk was awkward to carry, but not particularly heavy. He set it on the ground and started back to the door. "Leave it! He's going to know there was a robbery when he sees the desk gone," Shannon demanded, eager to get the desk loaded and on their way.

Shawn had brought a crate to load the desk into, and with Shannon's help putting the blanket over it, they slid it into the crate. Shawn slammed the truck door a little harder than necessary and the thud rang out into an echo in the ally. They ran for the cab and Shawn started the engine, but just as he put it into gear a car came around into the alley in front of them. They were trapped.

The light glared into the truck, showing clearly who was inside. Shannon turned her head to hide her face, but it was too late. The approaching car stopped in front of them and the driver stepped out, yelling, "What are you doing here? Get out of my way."

Shannon's stomach rolled as she recognized the voice. It was Mr. Weltz. He stormed up to the truck and recognized Shawn as he stepped out. "What are you doing here, I knew you were a thief, what have you taken?" noticing the box in the truck. Shannon now came around full height and determination. "We haven't stolen anything. We're taking what you stole!"

Immediately the stout man knew she was referring to the desk. "I didn't steal the desk. I have a bill of lading in my name," he shouted. A light from the neighboring house came on. Mr. Weltz started to yell, call the police and then hesitated, instead shouting, "Sorry, Charles this idiot has parked in front of my garage." The neighbor sized up the situation and went back inside.

Mr. Weltz in a slightly calmer smug voice, "Do you have proof of ownership to show the police? Well, I do, the crate is in the basement with my name on it and a bill of lading." He turned to the house as if to retrieve it when he noticed the door open. "Ah, proof that you are thieves. My door has been broken open. I shall call the police." He grabbed Shannon's arm and started to drag her into the house. Shawn reacted, pulling the man's hand off hers, causing Shannon to stumble out of the way as the two men began to wrestle. Shawn was no match for Mr. Weltz, being younger and taller.

"Let me go," he grumbled, "or I'll bring assault charges as well." Shawn let go, not wanting to make matters worse.

Shannon stood grasping her arm as car lights flickered into the alley, becoming brighter, stopping just behind Shawn's truck. Shannon's heart sank. She was in over her head and had no idea what to do. Two rather large men stepped from the car, "What's going on here," a voice rang out. Mr. Weltz smugly said, "Now I've got you." Shawn just grinned, "No, I think I have you," as a policeman approached.

"Officer, arrest these two for robbery. They have stolen my desk. It's there in their truck."

"Is that true little brother? Felix, tells me otherwise, that the desk was actually stolen by Mr. Weltz here," Officer Timothy McDowell said calmly.

Mr. Weltz's face paled, feeling suddenly trapped for the first time. Stuttering, "No..no. It-it's mine, I..I. haa..ve a bill of lading."

Felix was the second man. "Tim, Miss Baker here also has a bill of lading addressed to the real owner, her friend Grace Monroe. The problem is they both have no real description of the desk."

"Now, that is a problem, but this desk is in Mr. Weltz possession. Let's see who can describe it best."

Mr. Weltz puffed out his chest confidently, "There's a ledge for pens and ink bottle, the top has an inlay burgundy leather writing pad and lift to a storage compartment. There are two small drawers as well."

"Fine, Mr. Weltz. Seems you know your desk quite well. No special features other than the leather top."

"No, just each drawer has two antique brass knobs."

Tim turned to Shannon and smiled, "and your version, Miss Baker."

"He is correct in the basic description, though one of the brass knobs on the right drawer is damaged. There is also one other compartment."

"You must have damaged the knob loading it. There's no other compartment. Take a look, officer, for yourself," Weltz demanded.

Felix helped Shawn unload the desk into the headlight of the patrol car. It stood just as described by Shannon with the dented knob. Timothy ran his hand over the top leather and opened the lid. "Sorry, Miss Baker. There doesn't seem to be another compartment."

Shannon stepped to the desk and gestured to open the right drawer. "May I?" Timothy nodded. Shannon pulled the drawer all the way out and handed it to Shawn, then reached into the gap feeling along the side until her finger found a button. She smiled with relief and pushed it. Grace had been correct. Click! On the back of the desk a small panel opened. Timothy and Shannon stepped around to see what was inside. There was a very small box and a piece of paper. Timothy pulled them out and took them into the light.

"Seems this desk is Miss Monroe's. The note is addressed to Grace."

Mr. Weltz stood dumbstruck trying desperately to backpedal, "I had no idea it was there. I must have made a mistake, I thought it was my desk. I..I.."

Office McDowell took Weltz and started to handcuff him. "Wait, Tim," Felix said turning to Shannon, "What should we do with him, Shannon?"

Shannon looked at the stout, pale deflated little man. She couldn't help feel sorry for him. "Mr. Weltz, the gentleman at the State House seemed to indicate you were a very honorable man and patriotic admirer of the early Presidents. Why did you take the desk?"

Sheepishly in a small voice, "When I saw it at Mrs. Kelly's, I just imagined President Monroe sitting there, writing the draft for his Monroe doctrine and so many important historical documents. I just wanted to do the same. When I heard she was shipping it her niece at Berkeley, a college student. She couldn't possibly cherish it as much as I would."

"Well, as you can see you were wrong. This desk means a great deal, so much she had me traipse across the country and hunt it down. Never underestimate a daughter of the American Revolution," Shannon said sharply.

Officer McDowell reiterated Felix's question, "What do you want to do? Are you going to press charges?"

Mr. Weltz looked so forlorn, ashamed. "No. We have the desk and are scheduled to go home tomorrow."

Turning to Mr. Weltz, and contemplating for a moment. "Mr. Weltz, I indicated to Mr. Chambers at the State House there would be a generous donation coming, since he had been so helpful. I'm going to trust you with two things: first you will make that sizable donation and two, that you will never STEAL American history again. A handwritten apology to Miss Monroe would also be in order."

"Oh, yes, yes. I assure you this dreadful night has cured me of wrong doing. I like Mr. Chambers and will see him tomorrow at the State House, right after I write Miss Monroe," he said in a very timid and grateful voice. Officer McDowell released him and he hurried into his house. Tim and Felix helped Shawn recrate the desk and load it in the truck.

Shannon rode with Shawn in the truck back to the hotel. Felix and Officer McDowell followed. It was almost midnight by the time Shannon went to wake Grace. Officer McDowell needed to confirm everything and to give her what was in the desk. Grace wasn't really asleep, there was so much to think about. At first, she was angry at Shannon for going without her. Grace dressed quickly, her hair still in its night braid when she sat with everyone. She confirmed everything to Officer McDowell and showed him her bill of lading and the letter she had from her grandfather. Satisfied, he gave her the note and small box they had found in the secret compartment and said good night.

Shawn, Felix and Shannon turned to Grace all curious as to what was in the small box. She read the note and smiled, then opened the small ring box slowly. Inside sat two diamond earrings. Tears welled up in Grace's eyes as she stared at the two single carat pink diamonds that made up the earrings. Shannon gasped, and Shawn gave a whistle.

"They belonged to Elizabeth Monroe, my great great grandmother, President Monroe's wife. Grandfather always said he would give them to me one day."

Shannon thanked Felix for knowing his nephew so well and coming to their rescue. Felix just smiled, "I'm glad you appreciate it. Shawn may not, after his brother gets finished with him. Breaking and entering, you're lucky Mr. Weltz was a weak man after all."

Shawn just grinned, a mischievous twinkle sparked in his eyes. "Oh, he'll suggest I try helping in a more legal manner, and I'll be fine after I buy him a beer or two."

The next morning Felix picked the girls up and took them to the train station. Shawn was there and had made all the arrangements for shipping the desk on the same train. Friendly hugs and good byes were said as the familiar train whistle screamed loudly. Shannon dashed to mail her letter to Matthew that she had written the night before, knowing it probably wouldn't arrive before she did. She looked at Felix and thanked him again, then stepped onto the train and stood waving as the train slowly pulled away.

She found Grace in their compartment sitting quietly. "Well, this has been quiet an adventure, are you ready to join Matt in Sacramento and start working at the museum?"

"It has been a thrilling week and yes, I am excited about being with Matthew."

Grace could see Shannon's familiar uncertain expression on her face, lips pursed and eyes far away. *Is she uncertain about marrying Matt or working for the museum.* Grace didn't ask, knowing Shannon wouldn't have an answer, not until they got closer to home.

9

Life in Sacramento

Shannon stood on the train platform as the locomotive crept into the Sacramento station. She wished it would go faster, the sound of the click, click, click of the wheels taunting her. She would have to be patient another five minutes until she was in Matthew's arms. Before the train stopped, *There, there, he is at the end of the station platform, with flowers for me.* His smiling exuberant eyes met hers as he swept her up and kissed her, as soon as he could reach her. It had only been three weeks and two days since they parted, but it seemed like eternity, so much had taken place. Their embrace, kisses, and hellos now complete, they made their way to the Pilothouse along the river for a late lunch.

Shannon was jubilant in explaining how they tracked down the desk, and the thrilling yet terrifying retrieval. Matt was mortified that she had actually gone with Shawn to break in and steal it back, and more relieved to know Grace and the desk were safely delivered to her parent's home in Pasadena. Shannon realized she had been chattering away since arriving and had hardly eaten anything. Matt on the other hand had finished the last bit of his beef dip, and at last shared what he had been doing.

The exterior of the Hall of Justice Building was almost complete, though the interior finishes still had a long way to go. He had also found Shannon a small cottage close to his place that he wanted to show her.

"You must take me to see your building first and point out all the details that were your ideas," Shannon beamed.

They finished up and climbed into Matt's roadster and made their way downtown. The three-story Beaux-Arts/Neo Classical style building gleamed with its tall floor to ceiling first and second floor windows, topped with the triple window set on the third floor above. These were his contributions. "It's a beautiful structure, worthy of the democracy of our state," Shannon said, as they stood on the street admiring it.

The interior wouldn't be finished for several more months, but they carefully entered so she could see it. Matt held her hand as they climbed to the second floor, as there were no railings in place. But he wanted her to see the view out the upper windows and down into the large foyer. "All the light from the window gives it a spacious, powerful feel. There will be marble floors below that will reflect the grandeur. We wanted the building to reflect the power that justice should exude. Enough of my prowess, do you want to see the cottage I found for you?"

"Of course! But Matty I'm very proud to see you have created such a beautiful and majestic structure." Matt showed her one of the courtrooms, and then they made their way to the cottage.

The small two-bedroom cottage sat on the edge of the park near Matt's house. The white wood cottage, with large porch and roses in bloom, was charming. Inside was a large front parlor with a pink marble hearth and mantle, and pocket doors closed off the small dining room from the parlor. Matt pointed out two doors off the dining area, "That one goes to the small kitchen, this one to a small study. It was the butler's pantry, but the owner converted it into a small office. I thought it would be perfect for your research."

Shannon walked into the small room, the white beadboard and the sheer curtains gave it a warm informal feeling. The window looked out to the small backyard with a small crabapple tree. "It's perfect," she squealed, spinning around in the space, imagining research photos on one wall and shelves of books and artifacts on the other.

Upstairs was a nice size bedroom overlooking the park. A bathroom and second bedroom were just across the hall. Out back was a small carriage house that could house a horse carriage or car as needed.

"Matty, it's charming. You know me well. Of all the places I'm sure this is the one I would pick," Shannon said, putting her arms around him and giving him a kiss. "How far is it from the museum and your place?"

Matt took her to the front porch and pointed north across the park. "My place is there on the other side of the park. The museum is a fifteen-minute walk towards downtown."

Shannon agreed the location was perfect. She loved being across from the park and so close to Matt's place. Matt knew she would love it and had already paid for the first month's rent, so it wouldn't be taken before her arrival. They took the very short drive to Matt's house and he showed her all the changes he had made. Off the back, the small breakfast room with large windows that opened onto the river was now finished. He had increased the size of the kitchen as well.

The afternoon was warm, and they went out onto the back patio overlooking the river. It was cooler under the large oak tree that shaded the house. They sat and discuss what needed to be done to get her settled there in Sacramento.

First, they would go up to Berkeley and pack up her things and bring them back to the cottage. Grace had already moved her things from the apartment right after graduation. They would stop at Oak Ridge at the ranch to spend time with her parents before they returned to Oahu. Shannon wanted to spend a little more time with them, not knowing when she would be back at Mau Loa. *I hardly saw them at graduation. I'd like to go swimming with mother and riding with father before they leave. Who knows it could be another year before I see them again. What with starting a new job and that darn war still raging in Europe, it could spill into the Pacific any time.*

After she visited with her folks and had moved into the cottage, she would seek out Mr. Rawlings, the curator at the Sacramento Natural History Museum, about a position as researcher or archivist. Professor Kroeber, a good friend with Mr. Rawlings, had sent word recommending Shannon. He was positive there would be plenty of work for her.

It was mid-September by the time Shannon visited Mr. Rawlings. He had been expecting her several weeks earlier and was eager to have her start working on researching some Spanish coins and a crucifix from an abandoned mission that the museum had just acquired. There was plenty of proper cataloging of items the museum owned that needed to be done as well. Shannon struck an agreement: she would work from ten o'clock to four o'clock, Monday through Thursday, with Fridays and weekends off to pursue her own research. She still wanted to register the Oahu ruins with the national archaeological registry, yet she was pretty sure it would be some time before she got to Oahu to take up where she had left off in excavation and restoring the site. For now, she would be happy being with Matty and working at the museum.

By first of November, Shannon had settled into her work at the museum. Mr. Rawlings was an encyclopedia of knowledge on California early history but he was a novice archaeologist. They enjoyed discussing various finds listed in the American Journal of Archaeology that came to the museum.

Though she loved her independence, and working for Mr. Rawlings and slowly piecing things together on paper to establish the Oahu ruins, she now longed to be with Matthew more than ever.

Matthew and Shannon were indeed delighted to be back together again. Shannon loved the cottage and was reveling in the love she felt for Matt and he for her. Matthew found it very tempting after a concert, as they settled back at his place for a nightcap, to want her to spend the night. He wanted her to stay and engage in inappropriate romantic activities. It started with a soft stroke to her face, then a kiss on her lips. She in turn gazed into his emerald eyes and drew close to him: this led to passionate kisses and bodies lying together by the fire. Mostly dressed bodies. Yet, instead of taking her up to his bed, he pulled away and strolled out into the cold night air to stop himself. Shannon had expected him to propose after the passionate exchange, but he didn't.

Now I know I truly love him, and I'm ready to be his wife. I would have gone with him to his bed, but once again he pulled away. I do not understand. I know he loves me more than anything, but something is holding him back. Morals, respect, gossip? I know the Justice Building will be done soon and he's been talking about building a bridge near Santa Barbara, but I would go with him in a heartbeat. We could be married and go anywhere his work takes him. My ruins in Oahu will always be there for when it's the right time. Am I brave enough to ask him to marry me, or perhaps he's waiting to ask me on his birthday in a few weeks, or Christmas with his whole family present. Patience, Shannon, patience-- we will have a lifetime together in bed.

They were back in Oak Ridge for Matthew's twenty-fourth birthday. This year it was the Saturday following Thanksgiving. It was a big family affair with one major surprise. Shannon invited Lars to join them, to delight Matt. It was a good weekend and Matt was thrilled to see Lars. She was a little jealous having to share him with Lars as they spent hours reminiscing, and riding around the ranch. Deep down again she hoped he would propose, but he didn't. Shannon decided she would propose to him on the train on their way back to Sacramento, or at least raise the topic.

After Sunday dinner, everyone gathered in the parlor and Katherine played piano. Not before long the conversation had turned to the war in Europe. Eric and Morgan discussing the shortages beginning to occur in the states. The imports of tea, silk, spices and other goods were not getting through to the states, due to the U-boats torpedoing cargo ships and just about anything that crossed the Atlantic out of Europe. Plus, cotton fabrics, sugar and other basics were in short supply as the United States sent needed goods to Britain. All the men were in agreement that before this time next year, the United States would be fighting in the war. "After all President Wilson tried to get Congress to declare war on Germany last April, but the vote in the Senate was insufficient to let it pass. But we can't stay out of it forever, and it doesn't look like the French and British will win without us," Eric surmised. Matt's eyes darted to Shannon, remembering the promise he had made her, not to volunteer. Katherine looked at her two boys realizing they were the right age and asked, "Will you go if you're asked?"

Andrew answered quickly, "I'll serve, I don't need to be asked. If the US is at war with Germany, then that's a good reason and I'll go."

He turned to Matt. All eyes did. "I'll serve my country, certainly. But I'll wait until I'm drafted, for when I'm truly needed. What I'm doing here now I feel is equally important."

Andrew started to argue back, "Buildings are not more important than freedom," Then Lars interjected about soldier's marrying before going off to war, without realizing it was a sensitive topic for Matt.

Once again, all eyes focused on Matt. He stood. Shannon thought he would approach her but instead he strolled over to the mantel and stared into the fire for a moment. There was a hush in the room. Katherine's eyes turned to Shannon, who now was looking at her hands clasped in her lap.

"I don't believe it's fair to a woman for a man to marry her when he knows he's going off to war. Not when there's the possibility he won't be coming back. No man should take the chance of leaving a pregnant woman to fend for herself. If he is going to bring children into this world, he needs to be there for them just as mother and father were here for us."

"That's commendable alright," Lars added. Matt was looking at Shannon for approval. Their eyes met. *Now I understand why he hasn't proposed. He's sure he is going to be drafted. He's waiting for a response, everyone is. Say something, say what he needs to hear.* "And if a woman loves a man enough to marry him, then she will wait and pray for his safety every day until he returns," she softly but reassuringly responded.

Lars, now realizing he had put the two lovers on the spot, "Well, now that's settled, how about a game of cards? Poker, I think is called for, with the gambling of life we're about to embark on."

Morgan and his family retreated to Kalua'ana and Katherine and Abby upstairs for a rest. Leaving Clay, Matt, Andrew and Lars to play. Lars cajoled Shannon into joining them like at college and Matt took her hand leading her to sit on his right. "Oh, no, you don't, if I'm to play, I'll sit on your left. I'd rather bet after you than before," she said taking a seat.

~~

Shannon reassured Matt things were happy between them after their family's conversation by the fireplace. On the train home she confessed she wondered why he had not proposed, and pressed that they should be open with each other to talk about things like that. She may not agree with his thinking, but she would support his decision, and she expected the same in return. Matt was relieved and the tension between them melted away. Shannon tried hard to push her fears about him going to war deep down out of thought, but it was aways nagging from the back of her mind. *You know he will be gone; this war is not ending soon.*

Christmas rolled around quickly and then came the new year, 1917. Matt and Shannon spent New Year's Day at home in Sacramento. There were no fireworks again this year. The headlines in the newspaper noted pleas from England, Sweden, and Spain for peace talks and President Wilson's reply. The number of dead soldiers was staggering and protests to end the war were growing in the States. Other headlines screamed of tax increases and prohibition on alcohol.

Matt's work on the Hall of Justice was in danger of coming to a halt due to federal funding being withheld, as the country was in an economic slowdown once again. Matt's work on the Justice building was basically complete, therefore Leon pulled him from it and had him go to Santa Barbara to survey where a bridge was needed to expand Highway 1 between Los Angeles and Sacramento. Automobile travel had doubled in the last year and bridges over ravines were in high demand. Just north of Santa Barbara, the Arroyo Quemado ranch was willing to help pay for a new modern concrete bridge. Matt and a survey crew were sent to view the terrain and map out the geological aspect of the area.

Shannon, for the first time, was getting a glimpse of an architect's demand to travel to where the work was. *I never realized we would end up in different cities for work. I guess I should have known, now that I think about the Berkeley project he worked on. All of the competing firms were from other cities. The Hall of Justice took almost a year to design, how long will it take to design a bridge? Weeks! Months!*

Now it was her turn to stay and wait for Matt to finish his business and come home. He assured her this first trip would only take ten days and there would be only one-week follow up trips, until the designs were approved by the client. Yet when construction began, he could be gone for a month or more. Santa Barbara was only five hours by train and he promised to be back on the weekends.

Shannon had been in Sacramento for six months now and had established friends at work: the hostess Millie Locklyn, the attendants Bob Rivers and John Spencer, and curator Frances Rawlings. Millie was a little older and lived at a boarding house across town. Millie, a history buff, knew as much about California missions as Mr. Rawlings, if not more. Millie and Shannon took lunch breaks together, often going to Weinstocks on L Street to shop. At the lunch bar, they would hear the men talking about going to war, causing them both to worry their boyfriends would be drafted. They agreed they would have each other for support as they waited for the men to return. Millie and her boyfriend, Jeroen, frequently met up with Shannon and Matt to go to the movies, dancing, and various public talks.

The couples were quite different; Millie and Jeroen were from the growing middle class working families, having lived in Sacramento all their lives, but they were warm and caring and interested in almost everything. They were average height, of English descent with brown hair and hazel eyes, though Millie's hair was lighter brown and wavy, in contrast to Shannon and Matthew with their slightly darker tan coloring and taller stature. They had also seen a lot more of the world. Millie would spend evenings quizzing Shannon about the places she had been and what they were like. Millie and Jeroen had high hopes of traveling the world as a married couple. Shannon was amused by the way they interacted with each other, like polite, playful yet intelligent kittens. *I wonder what they think of Matt and me, are we playful kittens too? No, definitely not, I would say more like high spirited horses with minds of our own but eager to please each other.*

It was the second of April, and winter had given way to spring, the dry grass now green and the river full from the melting snows. Shannon was working on a restoration of an Indian tipi, confirming the tribe's area of habitation along the Sierra Nevada range. It was about three o'clock when Mr. Rawlings came rushing into her lab. "Quick, turn on the radio, the President is about to speak." Shannon turned the small knob until the sound was clear and caught the announcer saying, "President Wilson will speak any moment."

"Dear fellow Americans. Today I have asked Congress to declare war against Germany. The continuous sinking of US passenger and merchant ships by German U-boats just off our coast of North Caroline and the telegram to Mexico imploring them to join them in war, is a threat to our nation. The German submarines' sinking of neutral nations' ships and the loss of innocent lives is a war against mankind. It is a war against all nations. In January we intercepted a telegram from Germany's foreign minister, Zimmerman, imploring Mexico to join them in their fight, promising them our nation as a reward."

Shannon and the others stood listening intently as President Wilson continued saying he expected the Senate to approve his declaration of war in the next day or two and the House to follow. Millie turned pale, "I thought he was in favor of neutrality. Jeroen will fight, I know he will." Shannon put her arm around her trying to keep back the same agony welling up inside her. Bob and John looked at each other. They were in their late twenties, and knew they would be drafted. Mr. Rawlings, realizing the severity of the announcement, told everyone to go home. He would close the museum early.

Shannon made her way home to an empty house. She was desperate to talk with Matty but he was in Santa Barbara for the week. She couldn't sit still, so she walked down to the telegraph office and sent him a message.

Please come home early STOP War scares me

She knew he would understand her need and come. She wasn't the only one sending a message. Several other women were doing the same to sons and husbands.

All the newspaper headlines touched on when the United States would go to war. Everywhere Shannon went in town, the talk was about going to war. She wasn't worried about her family; Evan was too old at 45 and his sons too young, Jeremy only 16 and Henry 14. She stood at the window looking out to the park towards Matthew's house worrying, waiting for him to come home. *Poor Aunt Katherine and Uncle Clay, they have three boys to worry about: Matthew and Andrew but also their grandson, Patrick 19. Will Morgan allow him to fight, if he wants to volunteer? Can Clay manage the ranch without Andrew and Patrick and the other young ranch hands? How am I going to manage without Matty? Why does he have this silly idea about not waiting to get married? I can't believe I'm saying that. You Shannon Baker who wanted time for a career before marrying, happy just to have Matty the way you always have, close but independent. Now faced with losing him. DON'T, don't even go there. We always come back to each other – we always will.*

It had grown dark as she stood there discerning what was to come. It would be another four days before Matthew would arrive home.

The atmosphere at the museum was glum. Hardly anyone had come in all week. Mr. Rawlings was worried. Would he be able to keep the doors open with Bob and John gone, could he hire other women to do their jobs? Millie was in a melancholy mood. Jeroen's grandfather had been an officer in the Spanish American war, and Jeroen had already gone to enlist. Mr. Rawlings started making a list of things needed to be done around the museum, specifically maintenance items, prioritizing them and having Bob and John start on them right away. With the museum quiet and knowing the boys would be gone soon, it was a good way to prepare for the tough times ahead. Painting and display repairs were on the top of the list.

Friday rolled around and Shannon stood waiting at the station for the five o'clock train. Matthew would be on it, and she wasn't sure he would have heard the news that Congress had just passed President Wilson's request to go to war that had been announced only an hour earlier. As of April 6, 1917 at four o'clock the United States was at war with Germany. Life was about to change for the nation. Steam came rushing from the large engine and the screech of the large metal wheels brought it to a stop. Shannon took a deep breath and put on a big smile, trying to hold back the tears as she spotted Matty. He took her in his arms and pulled her close to his side. He could feel the strain of worry within her. "It's going to be alright. I'm still here. I always find you," he said calmly, quietly, as he embraced her. The newsboy came calling "Congress declares war, US to join the fight."

"So, it's official, we're going to war." Matt looked down at Shannon's turned down smile on her face, "Well, we best get home and spend as much time as possible together. Who knows how long we will have?"

They spent all day Saturday together, but on Sunday Matt felt the need to see his folks and how they were planning to manage things. That afternoon they drove to the ranch. Katherine was glad they came and hoped Matt would have some influence over his younger brother's desire to enlist. After dinner, the family settled in the study.

Andrew paced the floor and listened to Matt, Clay and Morgan, debating which ranch hands would be leaving voluntarily. "You're mistaken if you think only Carl and Buck will go. By summer, half of us will be gone," Andrew interjected.

"What do you mean, us!" Clay blared. "I'm going to need you here more than ever if we lose ranch hands."

"I can't stay here; they're going to need men that can fight and shoot. Those city boys have no idea how to rough it or shoot. Matt can stay and help."

There was a lot of discussion for and against Andrew's decision. Amanda, Katherine, Abby and Shannon sat silently listening at first, Abby expressed her disapproval and left in a huff. Amanda insisted her boys were too young and wouldn't give permission, but knew Andrew, like his father, would not be persuaded. Katherine sat next to Shannon on the settee, and quietly took her hand, supporting her fears in silence. Matt stood by the fireplace trying to calm the rather loud dispute going on between Andrew and his father. Once their arguments had been voiced, and hot heads were turning to Matt for agreement, Katherine spoke up to rescue her oldest son.

"Andrew, you are old enough to make your own decisions, we realize this. But right now, we need you here to help with spring round up and branding. If we are going to war our beef is going to be needed to feed the troops. After round up if you want to go, your father and I will not stop you. We will worry every moment you are there, but we are Americans and will defend our country." Clay looked at her and shook his head, but didn't disagree. Then her eyes turned to Matt, "The same is for Matthew."

Matt stepped to the settee next to Shannon, putting his hand on her shoulder, "I made a promise, I would not enlist, but if my country calls me to serve by the draft they are talking about, then I will go. Until that time, I can help here at the ranch, I'm not sure how much architectural work will be needed here during war time. I have the bridge project that should be complete within the next few months."

Shannon breathed a sigh of relief. Katherine, having learned from Clay's mother how to let the men rage and then decree what was best, now invited everyone to come and listen to her play piano and enjoy afternoon tea in the parlor. The discussion then turned to planning spring round up and how they would manage fall round up if the younger men were gone. Clay started to raise concerns again about Andrew, and Katherine gave him a stern glare to remind him the issue had been settled for the moment. She knew it would arise again, but now she wanted harmony within the family. She also wanted her boys to play piano with her, fearing it would be a long time if ever they did so again. They each took a turn playing with her. Matt was much more accomplished than Andrew, and Abby teased him relentlessly for practicing.

Shannon and Matt returned to Sacramento and for the next two months things settled back to a sense of normal. Matt made a trip to Santa Barbara to oversee the first pouring of concrete, while Shannon continued to work on displays at the museum. Bob Rivers enlisted right away; therefore, Shannon stepped in and took his place as attendant. The spring was busy at the museum with school children coming for field trips to learn about native Indians and the missions. Shannon had just finished researching and gathering artifacts from the twenty-one missions in California and set up a display depicting *El Camino Real*, the road the missionaries took.

The end of May arrived quickly, and Shannon and Matt made their way back to the ranch to say good bye to Andrew. Round up and branding were complete and now he was eager to fight. Clay was resolved to his going and Abby was in tears every time she thought about it. Katherine didn't want to make it a farewell party, but kept with the tradition of holding an end of round up dance. Everyone in the valley came, knowing in the back of their minds that Andrew and other young men there, would be leaving and possibly not return. Clay had been lucky so far with only one ranch hand leaving before round up, Pauley was Polish and felt he had to go immediately.

The others, loyal to the Taylors, stayed through round up, but would be leaving as well. Rumors about a draft had been spreading. America didn't have the necessary manpower in its military and the enlistments were not as great as hoped. Every young lady at the dance made sure to dance with as many of the young men as possible, and no one mentioned the pending draft.

Andrew, at one point, took Matt aside away from the gathering, "Matt you know the draft is coming, so why don't you enlist and go with me now, that way we can be together? I'd like to know my big brother is watching my back."

"Andrew, you'll have to watch your own back this time. I made a promise to Shannon that I wouldn't enlist. And we Taylors keep our promises. I'm sure I'll be joining you soon at Camp Kearny because of the draft. But I need you to make me a promise here and now. Mother and I won't ask you to promise to come home, though she would like you to. Promise me you won't be reckless or do anything stupid that might get you killed."

"Me, reckless!"

Matt looked him squarely in the eyes, all seriousness on his brow.

Now all joking aside, Andrew replied, "Yes, I promise, I'll think first before I volunteer. I just hope my officers do the same."

Andrew and several other young men caught the morning train to Camp Kearny, near San Diego, to join the 19th infantry division. They would be one of the first division to be sent to Britain and into the war.

A week later, Shannon and Matt were back in Sacramento sitting on the patio overlooking the river, reading the headline, "Congress Passes Draft". Shannon's worst dread had come to pass, yet part of her was relieved. Ever since Andrew had left, she could see the guilt on Matt's face for not going with him. Now he was free of it and still kept his promise.

She stood still looking at the river, the water slowing flowing towards the sea. She didn't want him to see the tears welling up in her eyes. "So, what now? How long before you will go?"

Matt came up behind her and put his arms around her, "First, all men between 21 and 45 years will have to register. There will be offices opening up all over the country in the next few days. Then they will draw names for the first group to serve, assigning them to camps for fitness exams and where they will serve. It will take months before we go to Europe, and perhaps the war will be over."

Shannon shook her head just so slightly, trying to let out a breath. *Perhaps! No, there will be no perhaps. President Wilson would not have called for a draft if the war was just about over.* "This time just promise you won't do anything too gallant; you don't have to be the one in the front, the hero. Be my hero and come home."

Matt didn't answer but kissed her head and held her as she leaned into him. *I know he can't make that promise. If Andrew or one of his team members need saving, he will go. I just pray God protects him, protects them both.*

The following day, the draft registration office in Sacramento had lines around the block, as did all major cities. Matt was now registered and the waiting began.

Mr. Lionaski took over Matt's Santa Barbara project so he didn't have to travel, and gave him a local minor home renovation project that would only take a few weeks. Shannon, Millie and Mr. Rawlings made plans on how to keep the museum open, but realized the hours would need to be shortened to only six per day, with each of them alternating weekends, their busiest time of the week. They would close on Mondays and Tuesdays. They expected a decrease in visitors, and Mr. Rawlings couldn't afford to replace the men. Shannon and Millie agreed staying busy and working on weekends would be a helpful distraction and ward off missing Matt and Jeroen.

Matt wanted Shannon to move into his place while he was away. "No point paying for your cottage and let my place sit empty."

"Empty... that it will be without you here." *I know Matt's right, but can I stand being in his house with all his things and still maintain my sanity. Or will it be a haunting reminder he is away - in a war! If I stay at the cottage, I can imagine he's just in Santa Barbara on work.*

"What is it? I thought you liked the house and someday you would be here with me."

"I do like the house and I do want to be here with you – someday. I need some time to think about it. To adjust to the idea of being here without you."

Matt didn't press it, and tried to understand, but worried she still didn't want to get married. *First it was Shay Shay that didn't want to get married, then it was me, what with the war and all. Have I blown it? Are we going to have to go through another waiting period after I return? Will she find someone else?*

Shannon took his hand, "Let's cross that road, or should I say park, once the time comes."

He nodded his head, but would make plans to get his business affairs in order and make Shannon the beneficiary of his wealth and house. The next day he caught the early train to Berkeley to visit his Uncle Eric, a lawyer, to arrange for a will and to discuss his holdings. Eric was happy to see him. Since Matt still owed the bank for a third of the house price, he recommended he ask his mother for a private loan. He could pay off the balance to the bank and the house could be left to Shannon without complications. His investment in bonds and stocks he had already designated Shannon as beneficiary. He would arrange to have Shannon added to his bank account so she could pay his electric, water and other maintenance bills while he was gone.

By the end of the following week everything was in order, much to Shannon's surprise and reluctance. Matt explained the house would be hers, that it was all paid for, though he didn't tell her his mother had gifted him the final amount. He still sensed a hesitancy. "You don't have to live in the house. If you choose to move back to Hawaii you can sell it. But if you stay on the mainland, I want to know you have some security, a place of your own."

She nodded her head, realizing this was important to Matt. They tucked the will in a box safe he kept and he gave her the key. "Now can we be done with this and enjoy our day?" she grumbled. It was the end of June and the weather had turned warm with the wildflowers in full bloom. He wanted to take her for a boat ride on the river to their special spot for a picnic.

Matt had arranged for a small row boat and Shannon had packed a picnic lunch. The river near the house was rather fast moving, but further downstream, away from the bluffs, it slowed and meandered. They had a favorite spot where a large willow tree umbrellaed out over the river. They would spread their blanket next to it and eat and read and on occasion sneak under its low-lying branches for a private moment. Today was different, more reflective of all the good times they had growing up together: the secret ruins they ran off to as kids, the college dances, their first career projects, even though Shannon still hadn't officially embarked on her first archaeological expedition. Shannon pulled up her skirt and waded in the water cooling her feet, while Matt skipped stones. They sat and sipped champagne, as he fed her strawberries. All through dessert of petit fours, Matt was quiet, lost in thought, distracted.

"What is it? You're too quiet for a lovely day like this."

"You're right! I should shout from the river's edge, 'I love Shannon Baker and want to marry her'."

"Don't be a tease. You wouldn't."

Matt with a warm smile in his eyes, turned to her and took a box from his pocket. "Yes, I will, if you agree to be my wife."

Shannon was stunned, lost as to what to say. "I. .I.. I thought you didn't want to get married and go off to war."

"I still don't," putting his finger to her lips, "BUT I can't bear the thought of losing you to someone else. I need to know you love me and only me. I need your love to get me through everything I'm going into. I want to say I have a fiancée and we will be married the day I get home. "

"Matthew Taylor, I love you with all my being. I will always love you, no matter where you are. I've waited for the past year to marry you. I will wait until you come home. Yes!"

Matt opened the box with a deep aquamarine stone in a simple silver setting. "This is only the engagement ring. When we set the wedding date, we will pick out a wedding ring to go with it."

"It's beautiful, it's perfect," holding her hand out as he slipped it onto her finger. He turned towards the river and shouted, "She said YES." Kissing her, he pulled her to her feet and led her under the willow tree to be alone with his fiancée.

Upon returning to Matt's house for the evening, they stopped and sent a telegram to her parents.

Engaged Stop Wedding to be when Matt returns from Europe Stop Very Happy

They would call his folks once they were home. Matt carried the picnic things from the car while Shannon stopped and grabbed the mail from the box. As she climbed the front step, an orangish post card dropped from the letters. She froze in her step, fixed on the card lettering: **Draft Induction Notice.** She sank down on the step and picked up the card. She sat with her head bent onto her knees, tears streaming from her eyes without a sound. *No, not today!* And then nothing.

Matt came to the door and immediately knew. He rushed out, taking her in his arms as he sat. Her breath let go along with the sobs and tears. There was nothing he could say that would ease the pain, he just held her tight to his chest, his chin on her head, fighting the tears that wanted to invade his eyes, because of her pain.

They gathered themselves up, and once inside, Matt read the card. 'Matthew Keenen Taylor Order No. 482 Red Ink No. 84. By the direction of the Secretary of War you are hereby ordered to present yourself to the office of the Local Board by 4 P.M. on the twenty-ninth day of June, 1917 for military duty and transport to the Army mobilization camp at Kearny, Calif.'

"Five days, that's hardly enough time to get to the ranch and back."

"True, but at least I will be with Andrew and there's a good chance with Lars. He's from San Diego, close by." *Being with Lars we can watch out for each other. I'm grateful all the house arrangements are made and I proposed just in time.*

They quickly packed bags and caught the six o'clock train to Oak Ridge. Matt didn't want to try to drive and comfort Shannon at the same time. There was no time to alert his parents they were coming. They would instantly know he was there because he had been called up. It would be late by the time they got to the ranch. Matt reluctantly telegrammed Uncle Morgan to meet them, and not to tell anyone. At the last minute he added Engaged! *Hopefully that will prevent any worrisome thoughts.*

10

Saying Good Bye

Morgan and Amanda met them at the train just after nine o'clock, full of smiles and congratulations. Morgan sensed behind their smiles an uneasiness.

As Matt tied the luggage to the car rack, Morgan stepped up to help, "When?" was all he said in a very serious and concerned tone.

Matt instantly knew he wasn't asking when the wedding would be. "In five days."

Morgan put his hand on Matt's shoulder, "We'll look after Shannon until you return."

Clay and Katherine were more than surprised to hear the door open just after half past nine o'clock and Morgan's voice yelled out, "Anyone up? We have a surprise!"

Katherine and Clay came from the upstairs sitting room, as Abby emerged from her room. They were most surprised to see Matt and Shannon, but overjoyed when they announced they were engaged. Kisses and long embraces flew around the group, finally moving to the parlor to sit and hear all about it. Clay turned to fetch champagne but Matt grabbed his arm, "Wait, dad! It's late and once you hear the second part of our news, champagne might not be appropriate."

"Shannon's pregnant!" Abby blurted out.

"Don't be rude, silly," Matt scolded. But from the look on his mother's face, he knew she knew.

Clay moved to stand by Kate and she took his hand. "You've been called up."

"Yes."

Abby squealed, "They can't if you're married."

Shannon stepped over to her and gently said, "Yes, they can and we're not married yet. We will wait until your brothers return home safe and sound." Abby broke into tears and ran up to her room. Katherine started to go but Amanda rose and went after her.

Katherine and Clay had been preparing themselves emotionally for when Matt would be called to war; they just didn't expect it to be at the same time he announced he was engaged. Katherine's emotions ran from overjoyed to helplessly terrified. She suddenly understood the emotional confusion on Shannon's face. Matt and Shannon took the hour on the train to process the emotions and how they hoped to deal with them. Matt was most concerned about Shannon, being all alone and worrying. He knew his mother was strong and had dealt with difficult situations before and she had father and family close by. Clay poured brandy for everyone instead of champagne. Amanda returned downstairs, confirming Abby would be alright. They sat talking for another hour about how the brothers and Lars might be together. Shannon, on the way up in the train, agreed to stay at Matt's house, and perhaps Millie would join her. The hour being late and Katherine wanting a more positive note to retire on, asked how Matt proposed. Shannon delightfully told her, minus the interlude under the tree. Just before midnight Morgan and Amanda left and Matt escorted Shannon upstairs to her usual room, next to his. Katherine and Clay sat a little while longer taking it all in and reassuring each other.

The next morning Katherine wanted to throw a last-minute engagement party, but Shannon wasn't up to all the forlorn looks and questions she would get about how she would deal with Matt away at war. She didn't have answers to this. Matt just wanted to be with family and to make sure Shannon felt loved and part of it. It turned into a day of creating joyous memories. Morgan's boys brought croquet and badminton. Abby with Henry were fierce competitors against Matt and Shannon. At dinner, Clay finally opened the champagne and toasts were made to the couple. For one day they managed to put the notice behind them and dream about a life together. Katherine played piano, and Matt took Shannon in his arms and danced as the family watched.

Before retiring for the night, Katherine requested they all attend church together the next morning, that prayers were needed now. Everyone at church was surprised to see Matt and Shannon and to hear of their engagement. Katherine and Clay ran interference before the subject of war and the draft could be asked. They didn't stay long, using an excuse that dinner at the hotel was waiting, but instead they returned to the ranch for dinner and a few more hours of being a family, all together except one, Andrew.

Shannon and Matt boarded the evening train back to Sacramento. Matt was hesitant to leave Shannon alone at the cottage, but she assured him she would be fine. They would meet up for lunch after they had been to work and notified everyone about what was going on. Shannon knew Millie would be thrilled about the engagement and Mr. Rawlings would let her have a few days off to spend with Matt before he left.

Finally, totally alone in the cottage, the sobs, tears and heartache rang out and enveloped her until she finally fell asleep. In the morning, Matt arrived early with coffee and donuts. "Just wanted to make sure you were alright. It was rough last night. You up to going into work?" *He always knows when I need him. And I so much needed to see his smiling face this morning after the exhausting emotional night I had. I hope it's all out now and I can be strong for him.*

"Yes, I'm sure. No sense in hiding it from you, I cried it all out last night but I'm ready to be strong and take on everyone today."

"Good! You might want to wash your eyes with cold water one more time. They're still a little puffy from crying." She tossed a kitchen towel at him and huffed off to her room to do just that, and to add a bit of powder.

Millie was jubilant when she spotted Shannon's engagement ring, wanting to know how he proposed and wishing Jeroen would do the same. Shannon then explained they would wait until Matt returned and she would take the next two days off. Mr. Rawlings understood right away and told her to shoo and be off, to take as long as she needed, but be sure to return. He would be counting on her, once John who handled the ticket booth was gone.

Shannon wanted to get something for Matt to take with him, but the Army instructions were to bring basically only toiletry and underwear items. *What would he need that could be personalized? Comb, brush, toothbrush, shaving cream, soap... Shaving - a razor and brush would be something he would use regularly.*

She set off to Weinstocks in search of shaving accessories. The clerk was most helpful. "One that is sturdy, not too fancy, but special."

He pulled out three folding blades, one with an ivory handle, a plain steel handle, and a silver handle. *Ivory was too fragile, tin too ordinary, but I could put his initials on it. Silver too flashy.* She picked up the steel blade, "A good practical blade for a practical man," the clerk noted. Then she picked up the silver and opened it to see the blade. "That's a good quality steel blade, it will stay sharper longer than the others. The silver will need polishing but a trick is to use some of the shaving cream now and then to keep it shiny."

Shannon decided on the silver because of the blade and purchased the silver cream brush to go with it. There wasn't time to get them engraved with his initials. *That would make them too fancy, a good blade with a tarnished look will serve him best in the long run.*

It was noon when she met up with Matt at Lionaski's. Mr. Lionaski was very gracious and assured Matt he would have a job for him when he returned. He congratulated them on the engagement and offered Shannon help any time she might need it. He sent them off on their way, shaking Matt's hand in appreciation for the great work he did on the Hall of Justice and the bridge, "Maybe we will call it the Matthew Taylor bridge."

For the rest of the day, they strolled through old Sacramento near the river, looking in the windows of the shops, talking about what shops in Paris were like. Shannon had seen them, but Matt had never been to Europe. They didn't talk about war-torn Paris, only what it was like when Shannon was there, as if the war didn't exist. Matt took her to her favorite restaurant along the river, a string quartet playing softly as they ate. Before dessert he took her hand and asked her to dance with him. There was very little room between the tables, but they didn't care, as others watched on. Everyone in that room had the sense this young man was leaving for war and wanted one last night with his girl. He kissed her and they applauded, causing Shannon to blush and scurry back to their table. Afterward, they went back to his place and watched the stars come out. Shannon gave Matt her gift, "I wanted you to have something from me you could take with you."

"Well, it's pretty fancy for a blade, and I already have something from you I will take with me."

"What? You don't like it?"

"No, I like it, it's very thoughtful and practical."

"No, the 'what' was for the thing I already gave you."

Matt reached into his pocket and pulled out his pocket watch from his mother and chain with the locket she had given him. "I will always carry this with me, the one thing from both my special girls." He opened the locket and looked at her picture, "This will get me through a lot of lonely nights."

Shannon smiled, and Matt began to kiss her passionately, breaking away before he reached for more than he should.

"I could stay the night," Shannon whispered.

"You could, but I.. I'm afraid I wouldn't stop if you did." He took her hand and led her to the door, "I love you too much." The moon was full and the air was cool but not cold as he walked her home. Once they reached the cottage he opened her door, kissed her again, but did not go in. *This is her safe place, if I go in, I may not leave. I will not leave her with memories of regret, not here.* "I'll see you in the morning for an early ride along the river. I'll bring the horses, so dress appropriately."

Matt showed up early with two beautiful horses he had rented from the livery. They spent the morning riding, playing their game of matching gaits, and stopping to watch the river. Matt also wanted to see one more Charlie Chaplin movie before it was too late, and where in the dark, he could kiss her and put his arm around her shoulders, as he had done in college.

After a light supper out, once again they returned to Matt's house. Shannon wandered through it, asking Matt where his favorite spot to sit and think was. What was his favorite thing in the house? He appeased her by pointing to the clock on the mantle he had found in an old house. "Keep it wound for me, will you?" Matt took her upstairs to the room he used for his study. It was now neat, all the papers put in the file cabinet and the books back on the shelves. He went to the large wingback chair by the fireplace that was situated so he could look out the window towards the park. "This is my favorite spot to sit and think of you." He sat her down in the chair and stared at her, taking in how the moonlight lit her face and her smile. "I will picture you here writing letters to me." She had seen him sitting in the chair many times and held that thought.

She got up and walked to his bedroom across the hall. The bed was a large four poster bed made of chestnut wood, with a blue and white star pattern quilt that her mother had made, on top. Matt watched her as she wandered around his room, he so deeply wanted her. She stood by the window overlooking the river. She turned and looked at Matt, calmly and softly, "What can I give to you tonight? Please don't make me go. It's our last night, you'll be gone before dark tomorrow."

Matt stood just observing her figure in the moonlight. He walked over to the night stand and turned on the small light and then walked back to where he stood watching her. She could see the yearning in his eyes, the argument he held within him.

"What?" she repeated softly "What can we give to each other to hold onto."

"I... I want to see all of you, all your warmth and every curve."

Shannon's eyes smiled ever so slightly as she pulled her hair to the front of her neck and reached to undo the top button of her dress. Slowly she turned around and waited for him to undo the rest. He stepped forward and unfastened the buttons down to her waist and kissed her neck, then stepped back again, as the beat of his heart quickened. The dress fell to the floor and Shannon turned around again. She reached out and unbuttoned Matt's shirt, opening it to expose his muscles and hairs on his chest and smiled. Stepping back, she slowly untied her undergarment and slid it from her shoulders. She hadn't worn a corset that day because of riding, and let her undergarment fall to the ground. She pulled her feet free from the bloomers and stepped now fully bare into the soft light of the lamp and stood silently, her one hip slightly forward and her hands at her side. Her dark tan skin glistened in the soft light, and a tingle began to rise through her body.

Matt met her eyes, that rang out with approval and equal desire watching him. Not moving or saying a word, only with his eyes he slowly followed the lines of her body from her soft cheeks, down to her shoulders and the soft voluptuous curves of her breasts, the tan nipples hard and full in the cool air. Shannon watched him as his eyes moved down her body, and could see his own body's manhood come alive. He continued down observing the way the light rested gently on the curve of her rib cage and softness of her stomach. He glanced back at her face for a moment, full with a blossoming blush from the heat rising within her, as she bit her lower lip and smiled, oh so slightly. His eyes returned to her naval and set upon her pelvis, black with hair as it formed a V and joined the fullness of her upper thighs, the light soft against the torso of her hips and pelvis. He took in the shape of her legs, the soft strong line of her upper thigh that tapered to her muscular calves and down to her ankles. He smiled as he spotted her feet, toes he knew quite well from walks along the ocean shores. He stood and took all of her in, closing his eyes, putting all she shared to memory, feeling the urge to have her, knowing he shouldn't let it take control. "You are so very beautiful, all of you."

Shannon smiled and moved toward him. "Are you sure? I will go further than we should, than the caressing of your breasts under a tree." He managed in a low soft voice. *You should say no, but I so want you to say yes.*

"I'm sure," she said as she stepped close and began to remove his shirt. "It would be best to avoid getting pregnant. We can save that until you return. But I want to share as much...." He put his finger to her lips as their eyes met.

He let his shirt drop to the floor next to her dress and moved to the bed pulling the covering from it. He unbuckled his belt and stepped from his trousers, as she came forward observing his firmness and slid her finger into his chest hairs. He took her hand and kissed it and with his other hand slowly moved it down her body gently exploring every curve, her heart now pounding at every touch. He came to her buttocks and stopped. He turned her around and with both arms picked her up and carried to the bed. Laying her down gently and taking another pleasureful desiring look, he turned out the light.

~~

The next afternoon came all too quickly, Shannon now stood on the station platform with several other mothers, wives and fiancées watching the train pull away. It wasn't until Matthew was out of sight, she let go and breathed again, and the tears began to trickle down her cheeks. She walked slowly back to her cottage, not really sure how she got there, the streets and people a blur through the tears. The bright little cottage didn't seem so bright and cheery. It felt empty and all she wanted to do was curl up and cry. *Don't you dare, find something to do.* She had promised Matthew she wouldn't spend her time crying, rather she would be industrious and take this time apart to fulfill her goals, things she was reluctant to give up when she first fell in love with Matthew. She walked into her small study with the picture of the Oahu ruins pinned to the wall and took it down. *This was our secret as children, covered in vines like a cave. Do I really want to share it with the world, our hideaway. Don't be silly, we don't have to hide away anymore. I'm excited to admit I love Matthew... Oh, I so wish you could hold me like you held me last night, right now.* She put the picture back, and looked back through the door to the parlor; the little cottage seemed lonely. She went upstairs to her bedroom and looked around. It was a pleasant room, filled with her mother's quilt and picture of her parents, Evan and family, and Matthew. She glanced out the window towards Matt's, then turned back to her bed, *lonely!* She went to the closet and grabbed a small case then stuffed a few things from her bureau in, and went downstairs, grabbed the key to Matthew's house and walked across the park. She stood at his door, hesitating. *Is being here going to bring back the closeness we had last night or is it going to make me miss him more? Go back to the cottage or stay? Stay. Stay.* She unlocked the door and went upstairs, not to his bedroom, but to his study and sat in his chair. She could smell his scent and feel the contours his body had made in the soft brown leather, and she felt safe and not so alone. As she took in the emotions of the last few days exhaustion finally overtook the overwhelming feelings.

The next morning, she was woken by Mrs. Ling, Matt's cleaning lady. "Are you alright, Miss Baker? Mr. Taylor gone to work already?"

"Oh, Mrs. Ling, I'm fine. I must have fallen asleep here last night. Unfortunately, Mr. Taylor has been called to serve in the war. It happened so quick, we only had five days' notice; he left yesterday for San Diego."

"Oh, I'm so sorry, Miss. What is he going to do with the house? Should I keep coming or prepare it to be closed up until he returns?"

"No, no, Mrs. Ling. Matthew has provided funds and would like you to continue to clean and do laundry. I will be staying here during his absence."

"This is good. I will go make you tea and see if Mr. Taylor has some scones or biscuits and bring them to you.

"That would be lovely, but could you make coffee and I'll come to the kitchen."

Mrs. Ling disappeared, and Shannon took her bag and went to the bath to wash her face and brush her hair. After a few minutes, she made her way to the kitchen. Coffee was simmering on the stove, and biscuits and jam were on the small table in the corner by the window. Mrs. Ling brought a cup of coffee and Shannon had her join her. They discussed what would be needed for the house and laundry. Mrs. Ling would be happy to do Shannon's laundry, as well as the linens. "That won't be necessary. I wasn't raised with a lady's maid. Mother and I always did all the cleaning and washing. Mother was a lady's maid and companion, and taught me to do my own, and not to make my dirt someone else's burden."

"It no burden, Miss Baker. You are a working lady too. You let me help."

Shannon gave in and explained she had not moved in yet but would soon. For today the bed linen and any of Mr. Taylor's dirty items should be cleaned along with the house. Mrs. Ling smiled and hurried off upstairs to work. Shannon sat with her cup of coffee looking out to the trees. *Well, things could be very pleasant here with Mrs. Ling's help. I think Mother would approve, as long as I don't take advantage of her and keep my requests to a minimum. Alright, that's settled, now I'd best get back to my cottage and check in at work.* Shannon finished her coffee and left Mrs. Ling her pay on the counter and headed out, knowing Mrs. Ling would lock up.

Mr. Rawlings and Millie were delighted to see Shannon back with a smile on her face. It had been a busy few days at the museum with summer tourists. John had received his draft notice also and had departed without a word. Mr. Rawlings was down to the two women for help now. They all discussed how to keep things running. Millie and Shannon would trade off manning the admissions desk and being a tour guide, while Rawlings continued with the business end and maintenance. For the first few days Matt was gone, Shannon wavered between the cottage and Matt's house. The second evening alone she sat in his study and wrote him a letter reassuring him she was going to keep herself busy, that she had returned to work and Millie had invited her to a concert on Friday. Matt had promised to write and tell her what unit he had been assigned to and if he had seen Andrew. Until she received word from him, she couldn't address the letter.

She had spent the first two nights at the cottage, and would move her things to Matt's house on the weekend. Friday morning, she received his letter. He was assigned to the 361st Infantry Regiment, of about 100 men, that was part of the 181st Brigade within the 91st division. His commanding officer was Colonel Wise, but that was only for training. She was to send his mail to PR for Private Matthew Taylor, 91st division, 361st Regiment, Camp Kearny California. That first evening, he only had a brief encounter with Andrew, who was being shipped out to England in the morning. He was now a Private Second class and the 19th had been incorporated into the 40th Division. Matt wrote,

He looked good and was in good spirits. This morning as his bus pulled out, he warned me, "Listen carefully to the mustard gas training," and held his nose. I hope him holding his nose, is not the last picture I have of him. I was pleasantly surprised to find Lars here as well. He was assigned to the 362 Regiment, so we will most likely travel and be together, though in different groups. Thank you for our night together. You are beautiful. Gotta Go!

Love you always, Matty

Shannon clung to his letter. At least for now she knew he was safe, even if all the group numbers were a little confusing. Now she had an address to send her letter to, and did so on the way to work.

Shannon, as a tour guide, quickly realized she knew more about the missions than the California Indian tribes. She made a note to talk to Aunt Katherine, who was half Madi, the next time she was at the ranch. She also became more fascinated with the missions, how and where they were built. She wanted to explore more of the archaeological aspect to their sites, having spent a great deal of anthropogonic time on them. Specifically, how the missionaries changed the lives of the native inhabitants and their changes on the land, such as farming rather than hunting. After working at Mesa Verde, Shannon realized adobe could be made several ways with various types of materials and that dwellings were placed in a specific place often because of a geological reason. She approached Mr. Rawlings with the idea of visiting all twenty-one missions and spending a day or two collecting archaeological facts on each mission and then bringing them back to incorporate into the displays. He was all for the project, but not until fall when the museum became less busy and they would start winter hours, open only on Wednesday through Saturday. She could travel on Sunday, collect information on Monday and Tuesday and catch a train home in time for Wednesday. Regrettably the cost of the endeavor would mostly be hers to cover, as they just didn't have the funding. Shannon was a bit disappointed, hoping to get started in August, rather than mid-September. She secretively wanted to start with the San Diego Mission in hopes of seeing Matt before he shipped out. She understood the museum needed her and would plan her own trip to see Matthew in the next few weeks.

They sent letters about every two days. Shannon wrote about the concert, and work, that she now was moved into his place, but had taken up the guest room to sleep. It just didn't seem right in his room, especially without him. He wrote training was fine, a little brutal at times and very dirty. Lars unfortunately or fortunately, depending how you looked at it, turned out to be very allergic to gun oil, breaking out in a mass of red hives. He was now part of the 91st supply unit, since he had a degree in accounting. He wouldn't be on the front lines but would be sent to Europe's headquarters in Paris in a few days.

Within Matt's regiment he had made some worthy friends: Eugene from Stockton, Kevin from Mariposa and Mac a local boy from El Cajon and himself made up the A team of the 2nd platoon. The whole group was comprised of men from California and the 91ˢᵗ was known as the Wild West Division. Andrew, as part of the 40ᵗʰ, was in the Sunshine Division. He couldn't tell her when they would be shipping out and no visitors were allowed during basic training. He would try to send a telegram the day before they left if he could. He missed her as much as she did him, but was too tired at night to lay awake for long thinking about her, before falling asleep.

As July slipped away, Shannon knew Matt would be leaving soon, and she became eager, to the point of urgent, to get to Miramar, California to see Matt before he left. The train stop at Miramar was the arrival point for all the soldiers coming into Camp Kearny. She was just uncertain which station they would go out of to go east. *Will it be San Diego if they sail out of Charleston South Carolina, or Los Angeles if they sail out of New York. Will they board at Miramar and transfer or will they be trucked or even march the twenty miles to the San Diego station. I wish I knew. I'd hate to be at the wrong station and miss him.*

On August 5, Shannon received a very brief telegram.

Los Angeles AM tomorrow STOP Matt

Shannon's heart bounded as she glanced at the clock on the mantle, seven o'clock. Glancing at the train schedule she kept on the table for this purpose, there was a south bound train leaving in thirty minutes. She could just make it if she hustled. She raced up stairs and grabbed a few essentials and threw them into a bag, hurried to the kitchen, grabbed the keys to Matt's roadster which were hanging by the back door, and rushed out. Flinging the garage doors open, she made her way to the driver's side. *Please, please, start. It hasn't been driven for a month ever since Matt left, is there enough gas?* She pulled the choke knob and turned the key, CLICK and then nothing. She pumped the knob again hoping to get gas to the engine and held the gas petal to the floor and turned the key holding it on. CLICK, CLICK, CLICK, BANG, rattle, rattle; the engine came alive. She pulled out of the garage into the street, leaving the door open. It was a twenty-minute walk to the station but only ten by car. She had already spent ten minutes gathering things and getting the car started, now she hoped there was no traffic. At the first two stop signs, she glanced across both directions and seeing them clear didn't stop but sped on through. At the third, a car was there just beginning to cross and she had to slam on her brakes. She was only going thirty miles an hour, but every minute stopped increased the chance of missing the train. She spotted the station. The train was still there, the steam snorting from its wheels. She pulled into the lot barely remembering to put the car in park, and taking the keys she jumped out. Forgetting her bag as she closed the door, she stopped and reached back for it. She could hear the conductor call ALL ABOARD. Running in her long skirt, she reached the platform, and looked at the conductor, "I have to be on this train, but I don't have time to buy a ticket, do I?"

"No miss, this train is leaving now, but I can sell you one on board; come along," and he helped her in to the last car and called FINAL CALL ALL ABOARD as the train began to move. Shannon grabbed the railing as the train jerked forward. She gave a sigh of relief and followed the conductor to a private compartment. "Will this do, miss? Where are you headed?"

"Yes, this will do most nicely, I'm headed for Los Angeles Union Station."

He smiled, I hear the men from Kearney are leaving from there on the six a.m. train to Council Bluffs and then on to New York. Your husband going to be on that train?"

Shannon smiled "Fiancé, and thank you for sharing what I know you probably shouldn't have."

"You're not the first one to try to get a glimpse of a loved one shipping out. Best to stay at the station tonight if you're up to it. It can get pretty crowd and they can arrive anywhere from two hours to forty minutes before boarding. I hope you find him. It will be three dollars and twenty cents for the one-way ticket, or six dollars with the return train tomorrow."

Shannon paid him the six dollars and settled back into the seat for the nine-hour trip to Los Angeles. She would arrive just after four a.m., ahead of Matthew if his information was correct. At about three thirty a.m. the conductor started knocking on compartment doors with warm facecloths for passengers, announcing they would be arriving on time. Shannon quickly washed and fixed her hair. She hadn't changed clothes, and hoped Matty wouldn't notice the wrinkles. As she disembarked, there were a few men in uniforms already milling about. Most of the other passengers departed the station, but she found her way to the main hall. "Excuse me, Colonel, is it?"

"No, ma'am, it's Master Sergeant. You best be on your way; in just a short time this place will be packed with soldiers heading east to fight in the war."

"Yes, I know. Can you tell me when the 361st Regiment will arrive?"

He raised his brow with a grimace, "Ma'am, if you're hoping to find your husband, I wouldn't count on it. We're going to be loading the troops as fast and efficiently as possible. You will just be getting in the way. You best go home and write him a letter."

Shannon could tell she wasn't going to get anywhere with him and turned and headed back to the entrance to the eastbound train platform. *That's what you think, I will see him and he will see me even if it's just a wave.* There were other officers on the train platform, but they ignored her. A train conductor approached as she stood by the archway. "Miss, I'm afraid you'll get trampled if you stand there. Over six hundred soldiers will be coming through here in the next ten minutes."

"Is there a place I can stand and still see the men before they board? Please, I just want a glimpse, I've come all the way from Sacramento."

He was an older gentleman, and had seen his grandson off and knew the feeling and need. "Come over here." He pointed to a large crate just inside the archway. If I was looking for someone, I'd climb up here. Mind you, I didn't tell you to do that. It would be best for you to leave, but who listens to an old man?" He smiled a fatherly smile and left as he heard a large truck pulling up to the station and shouts "Line Up." Shannon scrambled, not very ladylike, onto the crate that put her about two feet over the average soldier's head.

Within minutes, men in two-line formation came marching through the archway. At first, they looked all alike in their tan khaki uniforms with helmet and a small bag slung over their shoulder. A few small whistles rang out as the first group passed by. Shannon was actually glad. *That means they see me and so will Matt.* Each group seem to have forty to fifty men, and she assumed they were the various regiments. As the line of men stopped, waiting to board, she asked "What regiment?"

"363rd" one whispered back.

"What about the 361st?"

"Right behind us in alphabetical squad order."

Another soldier smiled, "He'll see you. He'd be a fool not to notice a pretty girl like you. Thanks for being here, to wave us all a good bye."

Shannon couldn't help but smile, "Be safe", and began to politely wave as the line began to move again. Another two or three hundred men moved past her and she kept smiling and quietly waving. The officers didn't seem to mind since she wasn't making a big fuss.

There was a rather large break suddenly between the men entering. Shannon asked the first Sergeant as he passed by what regiment he was, "The 361st?" and he shook his head and kept walking. Shannon now stopped waving and looked carefully at each face as it passed. A few more whistles sounded, then she heard it, twenty feet away, softly but she heard it, "Shay Shay!"

She looked through the faces and there switching lines to her side was Matt, his green eyes beaming and a grin as wide as his face. He reached her on her perch and grabbed her around the waist and lifted her down, and kissed her. "Keep moving," growled a voice from behind them. Matt grabbed her hand and they walked slowly forward, whispering to each other. At one point the line stopped, in order to start filling the next train car. Matt once again surrounded her and kissed her. Whistles and shouts filled the air from his squad. Shannon held on for as long as she could, until the line began to move again. The sergeant that had told her the regiment number now stood at the train car door, "Step aside, Taylor, and let the men board." Shannon put her arms around Matt's neck again and pressed her head against his chest, taking in the feel of his body and his scent, as Matt did the same to her. Within only a minute or two came the call, "Taylor, get on board, now!"

They gave each other one last deep kiss and then Matt broke away and climbed into the train, turning back for a final look and called out, "I love you."

Shannon stood for a moment and then began to step back out of the way of the men continuing to load, when the sergeant grabbed her elbow," Stay right there, miss." *Oh, I'm in for it now, I hope I didn't get Matt into too much trouble.* The sergeant pulled a small crate forward just behind him, and picked Shannon up by the waist and set her on it. "Miss, if you want to continue to wave to the men, it would raise their spirits, I'm sure."

Shannon was shocked, but smiled and nodded her head. She once again gently waved and smiled at the men, what to her seemed like boys, boarding the train. Matt had been in one of the first groups, so it was another twenty minutes before they were all on board. With the last soldier on board, the sergeant smiled and gave her a two-finger salute, "Thank you, miss."

"Thank you, sergeant. Be safe, and bring them home." Of course, they both knew many would not be returning. She only prayed Matt would not be one of those. "We'll do our best to win," was all the sergeant said and boarded the last car.

Shannon walked up past the cars until she heard it again, "Shay Shay!" Matt dropped the train window all the way down and leaned out as Shannon approached. "You will keep your promise, no un-called-for heroics, and I'll be here waiting for you."

"I promise. We Taylors always keep our promises. I'll be back before you know it." The train's wheels creaked as they began to turn, the engine let out a blast of steam from its stack and began to move. "I love you," Shannon yelled and blew Matt a kiss as she walked trying to keep up with him. He smiled and called back once again "I love you always." Shannon stopped and stood watching the train as Matt moved away, waving gently once again.

With the train gone, Shannon returned to the main hall and found one of the long wood benches and sat to wait until her train back to Sacramento arrived. It suddenly hit her, this was truly good bye, there would be no more chance meetings at the station, no more kisses and hugs. Tears filled her eyes and she held her breath. *Now stop that, Shannon Baker, there are no more kisses and hugs UNTIL he returns. We always return to each other; this will be no different.*

11

Coming Up Short

Shannon returned to Sacramento and to her work at the museum. Walking to work now, she noticed fewer and fewer men along her route. Women were sweeping the sidewalks as they opened the family shops. There were only older men sitting in the barber chairs as she looked in. At work, there was Mr. Rawlings, Millie and herself, the visitors even seemed to be more mothers with children than families with fathers. Every time she noticed the men missing, she wondered where Matt was at that moment. *Is he still in New York awaiting orders, or is he on a boat, heading to where? France or England? Is a U-boat stalking his ship? Heaven forbid, we have lost so many ships. If in France, where is he, is he out of harm's way? Is he safe from the Germans and the Spanish flu?*

Millie would catch Shannon with a long deep furrow on her brow and reminded her worrying doesn't do any good. Shannon would then concentrate on a specific mission or artifact just to keep her mind busy. There were few visitors wanting tours by the time September arrived. Mr. Rawlings was worried about having to close the museum and was seriously considering the need to let Millie or Shannon go.

On September 5, 1917 Shannon received two letters, one from Matt and one from Aunt Katherine.

She worried about the letter from Katherine. If something happened to Matt the army would notify his parents and not her. She set the letter aside and opened Matt's. A letter from Matt meant he was alive.

He was grateful he got to hold her before shipping out. The other guys in his unit ragged on him, but only because they wished their girls said good bye. The letter was vague in regards to details. He was in New York at the moment, but would be shipping out for France. He didn't say on what ship or when. Lars was with him, but would be going to Headquarters to assist with payroll. For the moment, they were healthy, but the returning ships were plagued with men trying to recover from the flu. They were warned to wear a mask while on board and while in port. He missed her "fiercely." Shannon held the letter embracing his words and felt comforted by seeing his handwriting.

Setting Matt's letter down, she took Katherine's letter, terrified for a moment, then, shaking it off, she opened it. Katherine's first sentence was, 'we've heard nothing from Matt so all must be well.' Shannon let out a deep breath and read on. They were in need of help with the fall round up. Over half of the ranch hands had been called to active duty. The army had given them a profitable contract to deliver a thousand head to the San Francisco market. *A thousand head! With only a handful of older cowboys; no wonder they need help.* Katherine was asking if Shannon would come work the round up for a couple of weeks.

Relieved that there was no real bad news, Shannon was quite aware of what was involved with a round up, having helped her father many times. Since she wasn't needed at the museum, she sent word she would be there by the weekend. Mr. Rawlings quickly agreed to let Shannon go for the two weeks, longer if needed. Millie was grateful she could stay and continue to work, since she needed the work to pay her rent. Shannon on the other hand, had let the cottage go and had a free place to live at Matt's house.

Shannon arrived at the Taylor Ranch just after supper, with leather work gloves, cowboy boots and hat. Katherine and Clay were glad to see her, so ready and willing to work. Katherine also would be helping herd cattle, while Abby stayed home and took care of things there. Clay didn't want her and Benton in the house alone, or Katherine sleeping on the cold hard ground, so she would return home before dark each day. Shannon said she would stay with the drive as long as the men were respectful. "Oh, you don't have to worry about that. I'll be there for sure," Clay said in a protective fatherly manner. "No, she won't," injected Katherine. "She will be sleeping here at the house. We'll just have to get up early to be ready to work with the rest of you. Shannon, you'll thank me when you hit that hot bath after the first day." *Aunt Kate's right. It's been a long while since I've spent the day in a saddle, and I'll be hot and dirty by dusk.*

The Taylor ranch was spread out over six thousand acres, almost nine and a half miles of rolling hills, sparse forest and grass lands, with cattle scattered throughout. It wasn't uncommon for it to take two weeks to scour the hills and drive the cattle to the holding pens or into the valley. Shannon would be working with Aunt Kate, Uncle Clay, Uncle Morgan, Patrick and Thomas, Ben, Sam and Miguel their long time ranch hands, and four hands from smaller neighboring ranches that had sold their breeding stock off and could help round up the beef stock. Cattle for meat was always brought to market the last week of September, giving the herds an extra week to fatten up before market.

Monday morning after a hearty breakfast, Shannon walked down to the corral where Katherine had one of her best cutting horses waiting for her. "This is Champ. He responds in an instant and doesn't need a lot of instructions when it comes to herding cattle," Katherine said, handing Shannon the reins. Shannon had a regular saddle she used when at the ranch, and Clay had it outfitted for the hard work with a rope and bed roll. "Bed roll? Uncle Clay, I thought I was staying at the house?"

"First off, best to call me Clay like the rest of the men. You may want it at noon break for a nap," he winked with a grin.

They rode out to the south pasture, and met the men already there. Clay had broken the area up into six sections to be searched by two men each. Shannon was paired off with Ben and sent up to the hill area, as she was accustomed to hunting for cattle in the thick woods of Oahu. Ben had been at the ranch for twenty years and had known Shannon's mother as a young man. Now at age forty-six he just missed the draft. They worked their section weaving in and out of trees, locating several head at a time. Ben stayed with the cattle already collected, driving them down the mountain as Shannon continued combing the woods. Champ was quick to respond to a steer's change of directions, and Shannon began to feel the tiny indicators he gave off before shifting from right to left. Champ's left ear would twitch back when he was about to veer left for one and if going right, he tended to pull his head to the right. Shannon was quick to respond and go with him and not fall off. In return Champ was quick to respond to Shannon's slightest nudge with her right or left knee and turn in the direction. The weather was warm but it was cool up under the trees for her first day of work. Ben was patient as Shannon on occasion lost control of a steer and had to re-chase a stubborn cow. By day's end, they brought twenty head down out of their section and joined up with another fifty head the others had collected. The first day they had covered about sixty out of the five thousand acres and collected about eighty head. They would have to pick up the pace if the thousand head were to be driven to market in ten days.

By late afternoon Ben and Shannon had their twenty head down to the holding area and headed for that night's camp site and food. Shannon was tired, sore, and dirty from riding all day. Katherine was there in camp and had hot water for washing up. Upon putting her hands in the warm water, she suddenly realized how sore her hands were from holding the rope and reins all day. The water felt heavenly on her hands and face. She'd forgotten how hard driving cattle could be. Once cleaned up, she caught the smell of supper and was thrilled to know it was beef stew and not baked beans and bacon. On a drive there was always a pot of coffee ready for pouring. Even late at night, a wrangler always needed to be slightly awake ready for whatever may come in the middle of the night: coyotes, bears, anything that might spook the cattle and cause them to run. Of course, in Oahu it was wild boars that caused the most trouble, since there are no bears or coyotes.

After supper, Kate and Shannon mounted up and headed for the house. Abby met them and offered to help unsaddle and feed the horses for them. "Hot baths are ready and waiting upstairs." Katherine willingly gave her reins to Abby.

"No, no, I'll pull my own weight, at least for the first day. Champ needs to know I care about him," Shannon said as she turned and stumbled over a rock, barely catching her balance, "That is, if I can stay on my feet."

Once they had the horses fed and secure in the barn, Abby took Shannon's arm and walked her to the house and sent her upstairs to the second bath. Benton had just brought up more hot water and added it. Shannon stripped out of her dusty sweaty shirt, her jeans being not quite so dirty because of the leather chaps she wore to protect her legs from branches. As she stepped into the warm water and slid down, every muscle in her body sighed. *I may never get out!*

The next several days went off with very few mishaps, Ben's horse threw a shoe and Thomas's horse stumbled in a deep prairie dog hole, causing Thomas to go flying over his head. Being young, he rolled and managed to end up unscathed, other than a small scratch to his face. By the fourth day, early rising wasn't so difficult for Shannon. Abby would have coffee ready when Shannon came back from feeding and saddling the horses. Katherine held back at the house to give Abby instructions on making more bread as Shannon brought the horses out of the barn to the hitching posts. Star pranced once or twice, but settled at the post, while Champ pawed the ground and snorted, pulling his head away as Shannon led him out. "What is it, boy? Not enough oats this morning?" Shannon went back into the barn to his stall and scooped up a cup of oats. As she turned to exit the stall, the ladder to the upper hay loft came crashing down, missing her by inches and causing her to fall backwards into the stall. The ground under her began to shake and the wood barn creaked and rang out an ominous CRACK. Shannon could feel the ground underneath her roll, as if small waves were passing under her. *Earthquake!* She went to get up, but as she reached up for the stall's wooden wall, again there was a crack, then hard heavy thuds as two bales of hay came crashing down from the loft, hitting the stall wall and smashing down onto her. There was a torrent of cracks, crashes, and thuds as more heavy hay bales came down on top of her. She pressed her arms against the wood wall trying to keep it off her as one bale and then another hit it. The hay bales, as they hit on an angle, broke open and sent straw flying everywhere. This commotion seemed to go on and on, yet it was all over in less than a minute. Shannon lay under the wood and hay stunned, holding her breath, afraid to move and cause more bales to come crashing down. She couldn't see what had given way, but suspected a support beam for the upper loft had cracked and the loft then shifted allowing the stacked bales to slide onto the ground.

Regaining her wits, Shannon managed to free one arm and clear the loose hay from around her face. Her eyes began to focus and in the dim light, she could see five or six bales had landed on top of the wood wall that now pinned her to the ground. She took stock of her senses and didn't feel as if anything was broken, only that she was pinned down and couldn't move. *Okay, I'm a strong young woman, but I don't think even Matt could lift two or three hundred pounds of hay at one time. If I wasn't flat on my back, I could use my feet to push them, but I can't bend my knees from this position. At least one thing is on my side, it wasn't night and I didn't have a lantern in my hand. At least I'm not toast. Or freezing wet like mother was when she got trapped in the stream by the carriage. I wish I could see if the house was alright, I hope Kate and Abby are alright.*

Katherine, Abby and Benson were in the kitchen when the quake began and were able to reach the mudroom doorway. They could hear glass dishes falling from the pantry, but no major crashes, like chandeliers falling. Once the shaking stopped, they made their way outside. Everything up by the house still seemed to be standing. As they made their way around to the back and the barn, they could see the horses standing in the field off in the distance. Not seeing Shannon, Kate panicked and ran towards the barn. "Shay Shay, where are you? Shay Shay!"

Shannon yelled as best she could with three hundred pounds of wood and hay on top of her. "I'm here! In the barn! Kate, I'm here."

Kate reached the barn door and opened it wider to see inside better. The movement caused another bale to come crashing down from the loft just in front of her. "Oh, my God! Shannon where are you?" There were about fifty large bales, some whole, some broken, strewn all over the barn and on several collapsed stall walls.

"Here, the third stall. Careful, hay's still falling from the loft."

Abby and Benson had now reached the barn and started in with Kate. "No, you two, stay outside. I can get Shannon out."

Kate looked up to see where the bales had fallen from. The loft support beam had cracked and the loft floor had dropped about a foot. It looked like most of the bales had slid out from that area, but she knew about fifty more bales were stacked further back. "Are you hurt, Shannon?" Kate asked, as she made her way around several bales.

"No, I don't think so. I'm just pinned down and can't get to my feet."

"Okay, there are eight bales in front of the stall I need to clear carefully, before I can reach you. Just stay calm."

"Mother, let me help. We can move them twice as fast if I help." Abby said, as she started into the barn.

"NO! I don't want you in here. There are still fifty bales of hay up there that could come down. "If you want to help, go back to the corral and check to see what else is down and where the horses are, but stay out of the house in case there is an afterquake."

Shannon looked up to the loft above. *Afterquake? Oh, please don't let there be an afterquake.*

Kate began to pull the bales out of the way, trying hard not to let them thump to the ground or knock against anything. She cleared the last bale and reached the stall. There were five bales on top of the stall wall laying on Shannon's legs.

"Hi, glad you could make it. Sorry I can't get up and greet you properly," Shannon said with a smile.

"Well, I'm glad to see you still have your humor. Now, let's get you out of here."

It was awkward to reach the top bale without stepping on the broken wall and crushing Shannon legs. Kate looked around for the pitchfork, spotting it on the floor across the way. She slowly stepped around more bales and took it. Now, she hoped to use it to pull the bales towards her and away from Shannon's head. She didn't have the leverage to drive it into the bale on the first attempt. Stepping back, they suddenly heard, "Kate, Shannon, where are you?" It was Clay and Ben.

Kate moved back to the barn door as Clay arrived and took her in his arms. "Are you alright?"

"Yes, yes, I'm fine. But Shannon's pinned in the third stall."

Clay and Ben took one look and told Kate to wait outside. He and Ben made their way cautiously to the stall, and Clay with his six foot-two muscular build reached across and pulled the top bale towards him, and Ben grabbing it, set it out of the way. Clay grabbed another and then then another bale, until he could see her face.

"Hello, Uncle Clay, glad you could make it."

Seeing her smile, "You came up a little short, did you? Can we give you an extra hand?"

She grinned as tears tried to well up inside her. She was so relieved to see him. Clay and Ben then lifted the last three bales off Shannon's legs, tossing them a short distance with a thud. Shannon winced and pulled her head back, afraid of more hay bales falling. Clay climbed into the open stall next to her. "Cover your face, I'm going to pull the top boards so I can reach the debris better." He was too big to squeeze in between the standing wall and the fallen boards. Shannon turned her face away and covered her head with her free arm. "Just don't jar the beams too much," Shannon said trying to hide the terror of it bringing the upper loft down on all of them.

Clay yanked the first plank off at one end, as Shannon closed her eyes and winced. With her eyes still closed, she could hear the crack of the second board letting go. "Shay Shay, it's okay, you can open your eyes, the barns not going to collapse." Clay reached in and lifted the fallen wall from his end as Ben lifted the other end. As the boards lifted off her ankle, Shannon gave out a small groan, but with both arms free, pulled herself back out of the way as Ben stepped in, lifting the wall back towards the stall it had come from. Clay stepped over the remaining boards and picked up Shannon and carried her out. Once they were clear, Ben let the remains crash to the floor again. The thud caused another bale to shift above and he darted out of the barn before it fell. This bale teetered on the edge but didn't plummet to the ground. Shannon gave out a shaky sigh and short breaths, no longer able to keep back the tears, so grateful to be out of the barn. Clay held her tight and let her cry into his shirt as he carried her up to the house.

Kate and Ben followed them to the house where they found Abby and Benson on the porch. Benson had not let Abby go inside, but instead went in and inspected things in the house. Clay set Shannon on the porch bench, now calmer, and took a look at her leg, gently running his hand down her right lower calf and ankle. Shannon winced as he pressed her ankle bone, but there was no shooting pain. "Doesn't feel like anything's broken, just badly bruised. Can you stand?"

Shannon put her left foot firmly on the ground and then her right a little more gingerly down. With help from Clay, she stood putting weight on her left leg and then balancing on her right. It smarted a little but held her once she was up. She took a few steps and again there was no shooting pain. "Everything works! I'll be fine in a day; I just don't want to be hitting that ankle again anytime soon."

With everyone accounted for and in decent shape, Clay suggested they stay away from the barn, but going into the house was fine. Kate asked about the herd and if anyone had been hurt. There were about two hundred head that charged off, but Morgan, Sam and Ted Callus were able to turn them and slow them down without incident. Morgan and the boys had gone to Kalua'ana to make sure Amanda and things there were okay. Clay sent Ben back to the herd to salvage things there with the remaining hands, while he and Katherine called on neighbors. Katherine and Clay had seen the aftermath of the 1906 San Francisco quake, and now wanted to make sure the town of Oak Ridge and their neighbors were all right. Clay would need to check on the stockyards and rail lines to make sure they would be running next week. There would be no more round up today.

The girls were to stay at the house with Benson and help put things back in order. Abby was only a little girl when the big quake hit, but she remembered the funeral service for her aunt, and the look on her Uncle Eric's and cousin Nancy's face because of the loss. Shannon also had been exposed to earthquakes on Oahu; there were many small shakes. After all it was a volcanic island. Though Oahu's Waianae and Koolau volcanoes had long stopped erupting, the volcanoes on Maui and the Big Island still roared to life now and then and sent tremors to the other surrounding islands.

By late afternoon, things were calm and orderly again. Oak Ridge had suffered little damage. Only the catholic church bell had toppled from its steeple, tumbling into the grave yard next door. A few fences and one chimney had fallen at a neighboring ranch but everyone was fine. Amanda at Kalua'ana was shaken but okay, relieved to see the boys were safe as well as Morgan. The new horse barns were undamaged but one of the water lines from the windmill had broken and water was pouring into the corrals instead of the troughs. Patrick and Thomas made the way up to the mill pumps and shut them down. By dusk, it too was repaired.

The biggest concern was the dam. Clay, Morgan, Ted Callus and Bill Withers from the town council rode out to the dam to inspect for damage. The dam was only twenty years old and made of reinforced concrete, the first of its kind. A quarter of the Taylor ranch and half of the Callus ranch lay below the dam. If it broke, they would lose use of the land for grazing for years and the destruction down valley would be catastrophic. Upon arrival they could see where the reservoir water had sloshed up to the edge of the dam, but there didn't seem to be any sign of damage from the backside. Using the trail around, they made their way to the bottom of the front side of the dam. It too showed no sign of cracks other than the expected tiny hairlines that had been there. Bill Withers would send word down valley that the dam held and looked to be in good shape. He would request a team of engineers to come monitor it to be sure.

Ted and Morgan returned to their places and would meet up with Clay at the round up camp in the morning. Clay arrived back at the ranch house just before supper. He was eager to get back to the herd and check on things, so he didn't stay the night at the house. Katherine and Shannon confirmed they would be back out in the morning. Katherine and Abby had rounded up Star and Champ and stabled them in the weaning corral, near the house for now. Repairs to the barn would have to wait until after roundup.

The next morning the sun was shining as if nothing had happened. Shannon's ankle was slightly tender, and she wrapped it with a cloth bandage and managed to get her boot on. She and Katherine arrived at the base camp just after seven o'clock. Several of the men were already out once again collecting those steers that had stampeded. Shannon set out with Ben into a new area and resumed herding stray cattle into the main herd. They had lost a full day's work and needed to make up for it. Everyone rode a little faster, checking their areas and driving the steers a little harder to get them to move faster towards the main herd. You could hear whoops and hollers, the slap of ropes against leg chaps and hooves pounding across the valley.

Shannon favored her ankle for a few days and let Champ lead on where to drive a steer. Over the week the herd grew from one hundred to two, then to three as they searched the rougher terrains and higher forest. Regaining momentum, in the lower rolling hills the herd quickly grew to six hundred. Clay and Sam took on the job of cutting out any breeding heifers needed for next year's herd, from those that were rounded up. Patrick and Thomas being least experienced, were the biggest offenders in including the breeding heifers. The boys were just a little too eager to get the count needed and round up over.

By the end of the first week Shannon was beginning to feel weary and bored of chasing rogue steer. Returning to the house at the end of the day to a hot bath was her saving grace. She hoped she would hear from Matt again, but nothing had come. In the evening she struggled to stay awake to write him, telling him about helping with round up and the quake. She reassured him everyone was fine, but didn't mention being trapped in the barn or about her being weary. The address now was APO 91st Division, 361st Infantry PR Matthew Taylor. Where and when he would get it, she didn't know.

At the beginning of the second week of roundup, the herd had grown to six hundred head and working only the lower valleys remained. They would find the most cattle in the valleys where the summer watering holes were located. The heat and dust increased as they moved the large, slow plodding herd down the valleys. Everyone, including Shannon, took their turn at the back of the herd, in the dust rising from the dry fields as the cattle marched across. If a rider was lucky now and then, a steer would break free and head up out of the dust and they could breathe for a moment, until they chased it back to the group. Each evening, Shannon couldn't wait to get back to the house. Her hair was so full of dirt she rinsed it off in the horse trough by the barn, before heading up to her bath and washing it thoroughly. The first time she didn't rinse off the dust, the tub water was so filled with dirt, she didn't feel clean afterwards.

One hot afternoon towards the end of the drive, Patrick stopped at a watering hole and pulled off his shirt to refresh himself in the water. The water dried quickly with the heat, and his strong muscular shoulders glistened in the sun. Before remounting and returning to the herd, he had to relieve himself. Heading to a nearby large sprawling oak, he unbuttoned his jeans and began to pee. "Shit! NO! Get away! Oh, my God, NO! AAAHH." Suddenly, a horrifying putrid stench filled the air. Shannon and Ben, not far from Patrick, heard the screams and started to rush his way and then halted, their horses prancing to an uneasy sudden stop. Miguel came up and met them. "Oh, master Patrick has riled a *zorillo*, I hope he didn't get hit." Patrick jumped back from the very angry skunk he had peed on and ran to the watering hole to try and wash the stinging stench from his bare torso. Morgan rode up, putting his bandana over his nose and mouth, shaking his head but relieved to see Patrick standing in the water. Patrick stood there trying not to rub his eyes that stung from the smell and to see who was on horseback through the blur. Shannon, Ben, and Miguel arrived staying to the upwind side of things. Morgan had dismounted and gone in to rescue his oldest son, who seemed to be unable to see clearly. "You need help, Morgan?" Ben called out.

"Only if you want to help get him back to Kalua'ana, to his mother for a tomato bath."

"I'll pass."

Clay arrived shouting about cattle wandering off from the herd, and ordered Miguel and Ben to "get back to work." He didn't bark at Shannon but gave her a stern glare. Looking at Patrick, now red and squinting, "You alright, boy?" Patrick didn't respond but just stood in wet boots and jeans as Morgan reached him.

Shannon retrieved Patrick's horse, so he could ride back to the ranch. The horse pranced and tossed its head, protesting the smell of his rider. Shannon held the animal's head and spoke softly, until the mare finally allowed Patrick to mount. Clay agreed Morgan should go with Patrick since his vision was so blurry.

"Best get Doc to take a look at his eyes," Clay said as he mounted up. "Come on Shay Shay, there's nothing more we can do here, best get back to the herd."

Morgan returned to camp by supper and reported Patrick would be fine, but Doc wanted to keep his eyes bandaged with warm damp cloths for a day or two. Skunk spray had a lot of acidity, though it didn't appear any had gotten directly into his eyes; the misty fumes had done just enough damage to cause major irritation. He needed to make sure Patrick didn't rub his eyes and cause more damage.

Round up was completed a few days later, but they still had forty miles to go, driving the herd to the stockyards in Stockton. The open range trails for the drive were pretty established with a number of watering reservoirs, but it would take four full days to move the thousand head the full forty miles. The cost and shortage of transport trucks were economically impractical. Clay was concerned about having enough men to drive such a large herd. Patrick's vision still had not cleared completely, and Tim Callus and Bill Withers needed to get back to their ranches, having been away for ten days. Clay had not intended for Shannon or Katherine to help drive the cattle to market. But now with only six men and a mile of cattle to keep in line, the job would be daunting. Shannon couldn't remember being so tired, but she could see Aunt Katherine was struggling to keep going and even more weary. *I can't let Aunt Kate go, and she will if I don't help. And it's not like I'm needed back at the museum. If I get a good night's sleep I can do it, it's only four more days.* "Uncle Clay, let me help with the drive. If we divide the herd into thirds, the seven of us should be able to manage." Clay wanted to say no, but knew even one extra person would make a big difference. Shannon understood there would be four more hot, dusty, hair filled with dirt days and this time no house to go home to in the evenings.

Tim Callus sent his fourteen-year-old son to help. Markus, a tall strapping blond, had ridden in the chuckwagon to Stockton, at the first of September, when the Calluses drove their heifers to market.

Clay would put Markus at the head of the herd to lead the way and Shannon and Thomas up front to wrangle strays that would try to break from the herd. Morgan, Miguel, Sam, Ben, and Clay would take turns bringing up the drag, and wrangling steers from the remaining three-quarter mile of the cattle drove.

Juan, who ran the chuckwagon at base camp, left at dawn to begin the drive. He would travel ten miles and then set up camp and have a hot meal and coffee ready by the time the herd reached him. Clay would start driving the cattle a few hours later and their pace would be slower, giving Juan several hours to set up camp and cook.

The weather had turned a little cooler, this last week in September as fall came on. But the slow pace of the cattle made the first day seem to take forever to go just ten miles. Several times Shannon raced back to see that things at the rear of the drove were okay, just so she could break into a trot bouncing herself awake and create a breeze. Morgan smiled to himself, thinking back to when he and Katherine were teenagers working a cattle drive. Katherine would do the same, anything to break the monotony.

They made the first watering hole after five hours, and rested the herd. The next morning, collecting them back up and onto the trail took several tries as small groups of cattle broke off in wrong directions. Shannon and Clay took off after one group and Clay managed to turn them, but two broke away and got past Shannon. Every time, she tried to turn them, they would split and she would have to chase them back together attempting to turn them again in the right direction. Each time, they were getting further from the herd. Frustrated, she left the more stubborn steer and concentrated on the other, driving it back to the line of cattle. "I've got one other I need to get back," she shouted to Miguel and turned back toward the east.

She let Champ break into a canter until she was back in the general area. It was dry flat land with sage brush clumps here and there. At first, she couldn't spot the steer. Standing tall in her saddle she scoured the landscape. To her left about a quarter of mile away, she spotted him standing by a small seedling. She nudged Champ into a gallop and was about three quarters of the way there when he tripped in a prairie dog hole and she went tumbling over his shoulder. Champ twisted to the left to avoid stepping on her as she rolled to the right away from him, then Champ stopped and pulled up a few feet from her. Shannon was stunned. Her left shoulder throbbed as she rolled over to sit up, spitting dirt from her mouth. She sat with her legs stretched out in front of her, collecting herself for a few minutes. Holding her left arm to her chest, she could move her wrist and elbow just fine. Only her shoulder hurt like the dickens. Bending one knee under her and using her other hand she managed to pushed herself to her feet and took a few steps toward Champ. *Nothing seems to be broken, you were lucky this time. I hope Champ is in as good a shape.*

Still holding her left arm to her chest, as she took hold of the reins dangling from Champs bridle, she stroked his forehead with her good arm. Talking softly, she walked him for a few feet checking to see if he limped. He seemed to favor his right front foot that had dropped into the hole. She stooped and rubbed her hand along his fetlock and knee, but he didn't pull away or shiver. She slowly walked him toward the steer about a hundred feet away. Getting close to the steer she reached and took the rope from her saddle. She usually lassoed cattle from her horse and wasn't sure she had the height to do it from the ground. Getting closer to the steer, she raised the rope over her head. As she began to twirl it around the pain in her left shoulder intensified and the steer began to meander away. *This is not going to work, I'm too short for one thing. Secondly, I can't run and throw the rope and then hold him with one hand. I need to be able to tie the rope off to the pommel.*

She went back to Champ and looped the rope over the pommel. With excruciating pain, she took hold of the saddle pommel fork with her left hand and put her right on the pommel and held on as she lifted her foot to the stirrup. Pulling most of her weight up with her right arm and foot she swung her body up and was mounted. She immediately grabbed her left arm to her chest again, taking a deep breath to relieve the pain. She had laid the reins over Champ's neck and took them in her right hand, as she gave Champ a nudge with her knee. He slowly moved forward; his limp barely noticeable. "Ok, boy we just have to get this one stupid cow back to the herd, then we can rest for the night." She guided Champ up close to the steer, who was chewing on a sprig of grass. Taking the rope once again, she held it up to throw over his head. *Do this right the first time, you won't get a second. Ignore the pain, it's not as bad as it was when you mounted; you can deal with it later. Concentrate!*

She nudged Champ closer and threw the lasso so it opened wider as it left her hand. The steer looked up and the loop caught behind his ears and slipped over his head. Champ instinctively backed up pulling the rope taut as Shannon looped her end around the pommel of the saddle. The steer pulled away but stopped as the rope cinched down around his neck. *Good, he's too tired to fight. Maybe this one isn't so loco after all.* With a little maneuvering and tugging, the steer began to follow Champ as he slowly walked back to the herd.

No one had seen Shannon for some time and Clay began to worry. The head of the drove had reached their stopping point for the night, and the men were busy gathering them into a manageable herd for the night. Miguel told Clay that Shannon had gone after a stray toward the east about a mile back. The sun would be going down soon and Clay and Morgan knew something had to be wrong. They mounted and headed out in the direction Miguel had last seen her.

Shannon had worked her way back to where she had left the herd, but they had moved on. The trail was now soft and every step Champ took raised dust into the air. The pain in Shannon's shoulder began to subside, and she took the reins in her left hand and dropped it to her lap, knowing Champ wouldn't need directing at this point. She loosened the rope to the steer that pressed against her leg, as he had settled into a steady walk. From the east of her, she could hear Morgan shout, "Clay, over here. Clay, towards the trail."

Stopping and gently turning slightly in the saddle to look back towards the east she spotted two riders quickly coming her way. *They finally missed me.* Morgan reached her first, looking to size up the situation before Clay began to shout to her. He asked, "You alright?"

"I will be. We cantered into a prairie dog hole. But I got my steer!"

"Where have you been?" Clay shouted as he pulled up next to her.

"Out rounding up strays."

Clay observing her dirty face and clothes, the way she held the reins in her left hand loosely and the rope to the steer. "What happened? The steer pull you off your horse? Are you alright?" his voice now in a more concerned fatherly tone.

Shannon explained and Morgan took the lead to the steer and headed towards the herd, while Clay continued on to camp with Shannon. Shannon didn't tell him how hurt she was until they reached camp and realized she needed help getting down. "Uncle Clay, I'm too hurt and tired to get off without help. Just watch my left shoulder. I hit the ground pretty hard."

Clay came around to the right side of Champ, not the usual side for dismounting and reached up to her waist pulling her to him as she released her foot from the stirrup and slipped her right shoulder into his chest. Ben arrived and took the horses while Clay helped Shannon to a seat by the chuckwagon. Juan, upon seeing her dirty face, brought warm water and a towel. Clay had seen dislocated shoulders and broken collar bones before, but on big burly men and not on a slender woman. Clay helped Shannon remove her shirt, since she wore an undergarment, and as gently as possible, with his big hand felt across her left shoulder to her blade and up to her collar bone. Shannon winced slightly, but not sure if it was from his cold hand or the ache. Clay couldn't feel anything out of place and Shannon said it only ached a little. Clay soaked the towel in the warm water and held it to her shoulder where it appeared to be swollen. *Aaah, that feels good.* Shannon began to relax.

Shannon's bedroll held a clean shirt, and Juan fetched it and Clay helped her on with it. One by one the men showed up for grub and then went back out to the herd, each taking note that Shannon sat quietly and asking if she was alright. As darkness set in, Clay showed Shannon the surprise he had planned. "Come with me." They walked to the back side of the chuckwagon and there stood a small tent with a cot.

"For me! I think I can really use a private space tonight. Thank you!"

"Your Aunt said it was the least I could do for your help. Now, get a good night sleep. Juan will be moving out just after dawn.

It took Shannon a little bit to find a comfortable position for sleep, but once she did, she was gone. Sleep only seemed to last an instant, however, when Clay gently woke her at sunrise. Shannon sat up and carefully stretched her left arm out and up. The sharp pain was gone, there was only a slight stiffness. She dressed, rolled her blankets, slipped on her boots without much difficulty, and met Morgan pouring coffee. "That for me?"

"Sure. You look like you're better, do you think you can handle things today?" he said handing her the cup. She nodded she was fine and took the plate with an egg between two biscuits that Juan had left for her. Before she had finished the biscuits, Juan had the tent and cot stored in the chuckwagon and was ready to take the coffee pot and cup, so he could get on his way.

Morgan and Shannon mounted and met up with Henry and Clay calling the lead steers to move. They fell in forty feet behind them next to the other cattle and started moving them forward. The others fell in doing the same until all one thousand were once again moving.

Champ seemed be just fine after the fall. Morgan had made sure to check him out that morning. Shannon let Henry chase after multiple strays and only went after the easy single strays the second day. Once the herd was settled down for the night, Shannon would stay awake until late twilight watching the herd, to give the others a few hours to sleep and eat, before taking the night shift. When Sam arrived, she made her way to camp, where her tent and cot were all set up waiting for her. Juan had hot water and an extra towel also waiting. She slipped into her tent, closed the flap and took the hot towel and pressed it to her face, letting the warmth wash away her weariness, then slipped out of her clothes and washed the sweat and grime from her body. She emerged twenty minutes later, dressed in a clean shirt and hair brushed with a little less silt and dirt from the trail. This was her routine for the next two nights. Each night, one man at a time would trade off every four hours, coming to camp to sleep. Juan would wake Shannon before dawn and she would eat and go back to the herd to give Miguel a chance to eat and sleep for a few hours. Being so shorthanded, getting enough sleep had become a problem the final two days of the drive.

The final day, they were still eleven miles out from the stockyards. Everyone was glad it was the last day, but Shannon could hear the men were at their breaking point, the snippy tone in their voices as they shouted at each other. "You're late! You get that one, I got the last TWO," little things. Shannon did her best to stay on top of her part of the herd, but she too was at her weary breaking point, and the extra mile they needed to go today seemed impossible. Clay had to break up Thomas and Markus at one point. The boys stopped for water and were just about at blows when Clay came up pulling his horse between them. "I don't want to hear it. Just get back to work. Thomas, go relieve Ben from the drag." Markus smirked as he grabbed his hat. "Don't smirk, you'll take his place in two hours, don't be late."

It was four in the afternoon as the first of the herd came into the holding pens of the stockyard. Thomas and Shannon were first to arrive, but turned back to help the others, knowing they would be doing the same until all the steers were counted and locked up. Clay was the only one not on horseback, as he was needed to count and confer with the army agent there to meet them. It was after six o'clock when the last pen gate closed and riders took their horses to the livery stable.

Clay had reserved rooms at the hotel in town and Morgan escorted a very tired Shannon to a suite with a private bath that Clay had waiting for her. The hotel maid arrived moments after Shannon arrived, to draw her bath and assist as needed. Shannon was too tired to eat and told Morgan she would meet them in the morning for a hearty breakfast.

Stockton wasn't a tourist town with fancy restaurants. It had more boarding rooms for cattlemen coming and going from the stockyards. Clay planned for everyone to stay in town for two days to rest up before they made their way back to Oak Ridge. It would take three days for Juan and the wagon to get back, but the others would do it in one long day if they chose. Clay, Markus, Ben, Sam and Miguel left early Monday morning to get back that night, while Thomas and Morgan would go with Shannon, stopping halfway in Collierville to spend the night at a boarding house. Shannon came riding into the Taylor ranch about three o'clock on Tuesday and was met by a very happy Aunt Katherine. Morgan and Thomas had gone on home to Kalua'ana, to be with Amanda and Patrick.

Shannon stayed with the Taylors for another week, hoping to hear word from Matthew. "He probably has sent the letter to his house, thinking you were there," Kate said as Shannon searched through the letters that Miguel had brought from town. Shannon handed her a letter from Andrew as she recognized the writing. "You're probably right. At least Andrew has written. Matt should be writing you too, to let you know he is alright." The two of them settled in the parlor and Kate opened Andrew's letter.

He was okay, he'd been in England for a few weeks, but was sent with the British 2nd North Hamptonshire Regiment to Belgium. All he would say about the conditions was, 'no man should have to endure the inhumanity of the trenches. But I'm safe tonight as I write from the supplies center.' Both women were silent, grateful to know he was alive and hoping the same was true for Matthew.

12

A Year of Waiting and Praying

Shannon rushed up the steps to the front door of Matt's house, with key in one hand and her bag in the other. Dropping her bag, she couldn't unlock the door fast enough and reach the mail that lay on the floor below the mail slot. She scooped up three letters with Matt's writing on the front. Each read

Shannon Baker

Future Mrs. Matthew Taylor

15 Riverside Drive

Sacramento California

Relieved, with tears welling up in her eyes, she thought back to the moment she said yes, and how happy it made him. *Future Mrs. Matthew Taylor, how I wish it just read Mrs. Matthew Taylor right now.* Shannon picked up her bag, setting it inside as she closed the door, then climbed the stairs to settle into Matt's chair in his study. She sat with the leather, warmed by the afternoon sun, surrounding her. She imagined Matt's arms around her and looked at the postmark dates opening the oldest first.

My Dearest Shay Shay,

We set sail this morning headed for France. Quarters are tight, bunks stacked three deep filling each compartment with about fifty men. I'm sandwiched in the bunks between Lars and Mac. Boy do a lot of the men snore

loud. Kevin, I think is the worst; poor Eugene is above him. The food was decent at mess tonight. Several men are topside leaning over the rail with seasickness. Thank goodness. I have sailed to Oahu so many times and have an iron stomach.

We have a new commanding officer, Lieutenant Marrelli, that will be in charge of our four platoons from here on out. Sergeant Bill Mason is our platoon leader, Second Platoon. Bill's a fair man, a little older than me, from Redlands CA, been in the army for four years, but hasn't seen combat. He has one heck of an aim with these P17 Enfield rifles.

I dream of you in my arms and it makes me determined to get back to you as soon as possible. Until then I miss you and love you.

Matt

Shannon read the letter over a second time, then opened the next one. It was written two days later, still onboard heading to France. He talked about playing cards, reading a paperback he bought in New York and taking turns on deck. "No U-boats have been spotted so far, but we're still a ways out," he noted. She didn't need to be reminded of the U-boats, but was glad he was keeping busy. Most of all he was safe. The third letter, he wrote upon arriving in port. He didn't say which port, just it was busy like New York, swarming with soldiers. He mentioned one group had been quarantined with influenza, but his sergeant was strict about them wearing masks. He talked about the French people, how they seemed to be going about life as normally as possible; they were very happy to see the Americans. Lars had been sent to headquarters upon landing, but he was currently in a tent located just outside of the port. He wasn't sure when he would get to mail letters again, still he would write even if they didn't get mailed. He added a few intimate messages and closed with *Bonne nuit, mon amour – Matt*

Shannon sat clutching all three letters. *Thank goodness he made it to France safely, with no U-boats attacking or influenza in his platoon. He's healthy.* She could tell from his first letter he was proud to be part of his platoon. In the second letter, boredom was setting in, but in the third, he sounded eager, almost excited to be there. She also wondered if she had been too intimate with him in his last night with her, his words yearning for her and missing her so much already. *No, this is good. It will bring him home to me.*

It had been an exhausting month and Shannon was in need of a good beauty parlor and some pampering. She sent word to Mr. Rawlings she was back but taking a few days to herself before returning to the museum. Shannon was delighted to get her hair cut again, this time a little shorter than usual. A hair style called the "bob" was beginning to emerge, and Warren, creator of Cutex cuticle oil had come out with what he called 'nail polish', a clear lacquer to protect the nails and give them a beautiful sheen. The beauty parlor had just gotten it in and had the clear and a brand new red color. Shannon felt she had been daring enough with the shorter bob, but wasn't sure about having bright red nails and played it safe with the clear.

The following day, the air was crisp, as mid-October began to turn the leaves brown, with a few shades of orange and yellow here and there. Shannon had lost eight pounds working so hard on round up, and most of her dresses now hung like bags. Therefore, she went to Weinstocks to purchase new dresses and corsets. Good fabrics were no longer available, and nothing was coming out of France, so she found a dress rather simply designed, made of a heavy cotton, in a deep maroon color. *It's pretty, but it's so short and no layering of the top coat-style bodice. At least the skirts are full even if they are a foot shorter. What would mother say?* The sales clerk informed her the new shorter simpler styles represented the sacrifices people were making for the war effort. Wools were impossible to get, all of it going to uniforms for the troops, as well as silk for parachutes, making brocades very limited as well. She did like the V neckline with the wide lapel of the maroon dress.

A second dress in a softer deep blue suit style jacket with a straight shirt was more for work at the museum. The clerk convinced her a corset was no longer needed with the new slim cut style waists.

Shannon liked this idea. The dresses were much more comfortable, yet decent without the corset. It was a big extravagance buying two dresses, but she knew Matt would approve. "One for work and one for evenings out." *But who will I go out dancing with?*

Shannon returned to the museum, once again splitting the shift with Millie. With fewer tourists and the school just getting started, Mr. Rawlings had reduced the hours, so the museum was now open Thursday through Saturday, with Sunday open from noon to four. Even with the limited staff and hours, things were pretty quiet and Shannon found time to do research on the missions and various artifacts.

Millie came late to work on the twelfth of November. Jeroen had been called up and shipped out for Camp Kearney that morning. Millie was smiling holding up her hand with a ring on it, when she arrived. Jeroen and Millie had gotten married the day before. Unlike Shannon and Matt, they spent his last night home as husband and wife. Millie's ring was slightly smaller than Shannon's engagement ring, but it was a wedding ring, and Shannon, for a fleeting moment, was envious. The girls made a pact right there and then to be positive and avoid reading the newspapers reporting on the war. As of yet no Americans had actually seen action, though they were in position and now trained. Millie, like Shannon moved into Jeroen's place, being the cheaper of their places.

The day before Thanksgiving, the Sacramento Bee headline read, **"British take Bourion Ridge Americans occupy Cambria"**. It was the first battle that involved American troops and it was impossible for Shannon to ignore the talk around town. *These were British troops. Would Andrew be part of the Americans in Cambria? Was Matt also involved?* The paper reported over 4000 causalities and half of the tank force was immobilized. The campaign overall was a success toward driving back the Germans. *Success! it was a success that neither Matt nor Andrew is a casualty. Matthew, I need a letter, soon.*

By the first week of December, Shannon once again was holding a stack of letters from Matt. With a fire roaring in the study and cozy in his chair, she read them one by one in order of date. He had not been involved with the Cambria campaign. They spent most of the first month improving their combat training, since so many French and British soldiers had been unprepared. Now they were on the march towards the fighting. General Pershing insisted on keeping the American troops as one unit and not disperse them to the various British divisions. He mentioned he was near Joan of Arc's birthplace, and a lot of men went there to say a prayer. He talked about how pretty parts of France were that had not been bombed or ravaged by artillery. But farm lands were becoming graveyards and orchards broken and burnt ghost forests. Shannon's heart ached when Matt described the destruction. But he ended his letters with thoughts of her that kept him going and *Bonne nuit, mon amour – Matt.*

Shannon had not planned to go home to Oahu for the holiday, but Matt's house was so big and empty and Millie was going to her parents. Aunt Katherine expected her to join them as usual, but the closer Christmas and the new year came, she yearned to be with family, to be home at Mau Loa. She regretfully told Mr. Rawlings it was probably better if he found someone to take her place and she understood he wouldn't be able to hire her back when she returned. She confessed she wasn't sure when that would be. It most likely would be several months before she returned to Sacramento. Shannon booked passages on the last ship to Honolulu to arrive before Christmas. She had Mrs. Ling continue to take care of Matt's house and send any mail onto her in Ahuimanu, Oahu.

It had turned cold in San Francisco the morning of her ship's sailing. Nothing had the old familiar holiday spirit. Everyone was quiet, inwardly missing someone. There was no one this time to see her off. Shannon stood on the deck with a few others as the ship pulled away. *I so wish Matt were here!*

~~

Honolulu was bustling as always. Yet in the midst of all the people milling around the dock, she spotted her mother and father with Evan and Lizzy waving joyfully. There was nothing like being in the tight embrace of her mother, after five days of feeling so lonely. Tears came to Shannon's eyes as she hugged her father, *"a'hoe hopohopo."* Shannon began to chuckled; it had been a long time since she heard her father say 'no worries' in Hawaiian. *Now I am truly home.*

It was the twenty-fourth of December, the traditional Christmas Eve party was still planned. Shannon arrived at Mau Loa decorated in lei leaves and red anthurium garlands, a pine tree in the parlor, and the smells of Hawaiian sweetbread and fresh pineapple spiced cider. Shannon's room was the same as it had been before college, soft greens and whites. Her mother had made her a new Hawaiian fruit bread quilt. She unpacked her trunk, putting Matthew's picture on her dressing table and hanging her new maroon dress up, for later that evening. She stood by her window and looked out to the lush green hills and valley. *I wonder what Matt is looking at right now? I hope they hold to a truce for now and he's safe. Probably a lot colder. Remember tonight at midnight to find the moon.*

Guests arrived, bringing food, wines, and desserts. Moria and Sam, with Kai, Keanu and Alana, Sarah's parents the Gilberts, and Kiki and Pauli. The Hawaiian music began to play, and Alana and Kiki danced the Hawaiian hula. With some prodding, Jim got Lalani to dance. Evan made an effort to keep his baby sister from missing Matt and danced with her and coaxed her into playing piano. There was no mention of war and everyone fussed over Shannon's engagement ring and hoped they would be married at Mau Loa. The festivities broke up just after eleven o'clock.

Shannon was just bringing the final cups and glasses to the kitchen, when the clock on the mantel began to strike midnight. "Oh," was all she said and dumped them into the sink with a crash and rushed outside. She ran out onto the grassy lawn, and looked up, turning until she spotted the moon, then stopped. Her father started to follow in concern, but stopped on the lanai and watched his daughter looking up at the moon with her hands to her lips. The silhouette of her dress and face looking up, sent tears to his eyes. There was nothing he could do for her, as she wished Matthew, Merry Christmas. Matt in his last letter said at midnight on Christmas Eve he would find the moon and look at it as if he was seeing her smile. She stood there looking back to him, making sure he would see her smile. But it would really be wet eyes and pursed lips smiling, he would see, as she fought to prevent the tears from falling. For a long moment she stood there looking up, until she gained her composure. Suddenly she spun around on her tip toes. Her dress flew out full and swished then dropped as she stopped and blew out a kiss with both hands towards the moon. Shannon stood looking at the moon with her arms tightly around her for a very long moment, her eyes now closed. *I am with you, Matthew. My love surrounds you and I pray it keeps you warm and safe on this night. Merry Christmas my love. Merry Christmas, Matty.*

Christmas day at Mau Loa was always quiet with just family and a few presents. Shannon had brought a dress for her mother, and a new plaid shirt for her father. She knew both would be difficult to get on Oahu this year. They sat and shared gifts and sipped coffee and cinnamon rolls Lalani had made. At about nine o'clock, Lalani looked at Jim and nodded. "Well, I think it's time you get dressed and take a horse up to the ruins," her father said smiling.

"What? No! I can do that later," Shannon protested.

"Not if you want your special Christmas gift. You need to go now," her mother said, smiling gently. "Go."

What on earth could be at the ruins? It must be important; they both insist I go. While Shannon dressed, Jim went and saddled Gingerbread, Ginger B for short, Shannon's horse. Shannon arrived at the stable with riding gloves in hand. "Take your time, but be back for dinner at one o'clock. You might need this," her father said handing her a large clean handkerchief. *What are they up to?*

"I'll be home in time to help with dinner," she said as she mounted and turned and rode off towards the mountain behind the house. The clean ocean breeze felt wonderful to her. She loved riding to the overlook; but it was a steep climb the final quarter mile and she took it slow. *Falling off a horse once this year is enough.* Ginger B stepped up onto the clearing and moseyed over to the ruin. There was a bouquet of anthuriums laying on the rock wall. Shannon dismounted and let Ginger B wander. She picked up the bouquet and discovered a letter below, instantly recognizing Matt's handwriting. Tears flooded her eyes as she held onto it. She crawled through the opening of the ruins and sat on the floor as she and Matt had done so many times before as children. She pulled the handkerchief from her pocket and dabbed her eyes so she could read his letter.

The writing on the envelope read

Merry Christmas Sweetheart

Shannon tenderly opened it and pulled out the letter. *Surprise my darling. Something in my soul told me you would be at Mau Loa this Christmas and so I sent my latest letter to your folks. I hope you like the flowers. I know our souls are together now and last night as we looked to the moon for each other at midnight.* Tears filled her eyes again, and she had to dry them before reading on. He shared about the cold enshrouding the charming country villages they had trekked past, and that he was holding his own. Tired but healthy. He continued,

Thank you for the beautiful gift you gave me the night before I left. I hold the picture of you in the soft light in my mind and your warmth in my body and they carry me through the cold and lonely nights. I hope I have done the same for you. Loving you now and always. ~ Matty

Shannon clutched the letter to her breast and closed her eyes as before and thought of that last night together over and over again. *Just promise me you will return and we can finish what we started.* Shannon sat in the ruins and thought about all the time she and Matt had come up there as kids, playing pirates and then as teens sharing secrets and dreams. It was here Matt first confessed to her he didn't want to be a rancher, that he wanted to be an architect. He just didn't know how to tell his father. Such wonderful memories she had growing up with Matthew and now she would be sharing the rest of her life with him as his wife.

A gecko ran across the wall and caught her attention, and she saw the sun now overhead. She needed to get back to the house. She stood and looked out over the wall towards the west. France was so very far away, she had never felt so far apart from Matt. She took the flowers in her arm and smelled them again, then crawled out of the ruins and found Ginger B chewing on a patch of grass. Standing for another moment, she mounted and headed back to the house.

She walked into the kitchen to her mother humming a familiar Hawaiian tune. Laying the flowers on the counter, Shannon stopped her mother and embraced her, smiling with such love in her eyes and then kissed her on the cheek. "What's that for? You liked Matty's gift?"

"Oh, yes. The only thing better would be to have him here, but the flowers and letter in our secret place was perfect. But I'm so grateful for you keeping in touch with Aunt Katherine over all these years. It gave Matty and me a lifetime of memories, not just as adults like most married couples, but as children, as far back as I can remember. I love him so much, recalling memories. I think I always have. Now I just want him home."

~~

1918 New Year celebrations came and went, but the news from France was still bleak. By December the Allies had taken Cambria, but at great loss, the influenza epidemic was taking as many lives as the war and the winter in France had thousands cold and starving. The news was slow to reach Hawaii and Shannon was grateful for that. It was quiet, and there was a sense of normalcy at Mau Loa. Evan and their father worked the ranch, with only about five hundred head, which during the winter months needed little managing. Shannon helped check fence lines with her father as she had done growing up, and swam in the bay with her mother. Kaneohe Bay was a pleasant

76 degrees and the beach warmed by the sun. *Funny, when Matty and I swam here as kids, I noticed his muscles as he stood in the water, but I didn't swoon over them like the other girls. Now I can't stop thinking about how beautiful he looked and strong those muscles felt against my bare skin. Shannon, you better not let your mother see what you're thinking. Father or Evan for that matter.*

Shannon couldn't bring herself to return to the mainland without Matty. As January wore on, she spent more time at the ruins and began to excavate around the base where the club had been found. Only a few large scallop shells were discovered, but there seemed to be an additional foundation coming off the downhill side of the ruin. She wanted to clear more of the vegetation to see if there were more pumice blocks that might have made up a structure. But unlike Mesa Verde's low dry brush, the hillside was a tangle of vines, ferns and philodendrons. It wouldn't be easy to clear, nor could she clear it completely without the hillside becoming vulnerable to erosion in the heavy rains.

Shannon was debating with herself about making the ruins open to the public and registering them with the national archaeologic registry. She had started several times, but something kept her from it, interruptions and then hesitations. Her father wasn't thrilled about people hiking through the cattle ranch to get to it and Evan didn't like the idea of cutting a road from the other side. Lalani felt they were sacred and only for the Hawaiian people. Yet they all trusted Shannon to do the right thing. Shannon decided to clear part of the hillside in search of fallen blocks. If she found them, she would make the ruins public, since it was more significant than she originally thought. If nothing else surfaced, then she would keep them private.

Shannon sent word to Mr. Rawlings, Millie and Mrs. Ling she would not be returning until summer at the soonest. She gave herself six months to finish her excavations. Matt had sent three letters to Sacramento and Mrs. Ling had sent them on. Each letter talked about the bitter cold and marching in thick mud and pouring rain to get to their locations, but nothing was said where that was. In his last letter, he mentioned Kevin had come down with pneumonia and had been sent to a field hospital in Chevillon. She wrote him thanking him for the wonderful Christmas present, and she was staying at Mau Loa until summer.

Matt and Shannon settled into writing every week. Shannon received a letter on Thursday, as the mailboat from the mainland arrived on Wednesdays. Occasionally two in one week, but her letter to Matt, usually arrived in bundles of three or four at a time.

Shannon kept her letters as cheery as possible, writing about her work at the ruins as she cleared the hill and general goings on at the ranch and lunches with Kiki. Matt said he wrote when the rain would stop and the air was clear of artillery smoke. That they finally were involved with some light skirmishes, mostly single snipers taking a shot here and there, but no one was seriously injured. He had also gotten very good at poker and had accumulated his share of candy bars. He declined the cigarettes since he didn't smoke. "The candy I gave to the kids in the village of Greux that we pass. Their lifeless eyes flicker with hope for a moment and then they scurry off like mice to their war-torn houses. Promise me, we will never let our children lose sight of hope and living."

By late March, Shannon had cleared twenty feet of vegetation around the base of the ruins. On the hillside only the three original blocks she had discovered were found. She had cleared a fifty-foot path and with a scythe had lowered the vines and ferns on each side for about ten feet. The rocks she encountered were insignificant and natural to the hillside. By mid-April she was convinced there was nothing more to the site than her original discovery and that indeed it was an observation post.

Matt's letters were now coming to Oahu and his last letter was a relief to receive. The newspaper reported the fighting in a place called Somme, that the France and British troops were hit hard but held Amiens. High casualties were being reported. Once again Matt's letter arrived, but it indicated he was not in the northern part of France since he talked about the Mirabella plum and Gingko trees that survived and were beginning to bloom. That France had fewer rainstorms now and the remaining fields were beautiful with wild flowers. Also, Kevin had returned to the platoon, healthy for the most part.

By late June, Shannon felt the excavation of the lookout ruins was complete and had written up her findings and research connecting it to the Marquesas Islands. She sent her report and photos to Dr. Dixon at Harvard as promised. She had contacted the Oahu Historical Society in December 1916 regarding the site and was now ready to file documented information and photos for their records. Ralph Kuykendell from the Society met with Shannon and verified the site, excited to find an observation blind on the west side of Oahu. The large *Pu'u O Mahuka Heiau* ceremonial site on the northside of the island was well known as an observation site for invaders, and *Kupopolo Heiau* on the southside, but this was the first discovery to the east. The direct tie to the Marquesas Islands was also of great interest to him. He inquired if Shannon would be interested in researching the *Pu'u O Mahuka Heiau* site. Since it was abandoned in 1819 by King Kamehameha, the walls and inner building had been crumbling and used for various agricultural purposes.

Before everything was lost, he hoped to preserve the remaining structures and artifacts. Shannon was intrigued and honored to be asked, but she hadn't planned to stay on Oahu, and a project that size, two acres, could take years. She would have to think about it.

Another letter arrived from Matt. This time instead of feeling relieved, she became worried. His handwriting was shaky and smudged. He wrote short disjointed sentences. They had been in their first hard battle. Eugene was killed by an artillery blast that hit where he knelt. Why he and Mac were spared he didn't understand, as they were so close when the artillery shell exploded. The Belleau Woods were splintered into oblivion. And the Germans seemed to be gaining. Shannon wanted to reach out and take him in her arms to reassure him, but he was halfway around the world.

At least he's alive and safe for the moment. When Matt's letters arrived, she always read them as it was that day, not a week or two weeks back. That as she read his letter, he was alive and secure, and not back when he wrote it.

Matt had been gone for a year now. And fighting in Europe didn't seem to be ending. The Germans kept striking out, while the French, British and Americans just kept trying to hold on.

By mid-July, another letter arrived from Matt; this one apologizing for the depressing mood of the last letter. They had successfully fended off advancing German troops from getting into Paris from the east and were now on the march again. He and Andrew had briefly crossed paths in Chateau Thierry. He looked good, but his youthfulness was long gone. *I'm so grateful he saw Andrew. That must have lifted his spirits.*

The Honolulu paper continued to report about the war and the shortages it was causing. Hawaii was lucky there were no sugar shortages there because of the sugar cane fields and mill, but coffee and flour were in very short supply. The Bakers had gone to brewing tea and saving the coffee for a Saturday morning luxury. There being so many Brits on the island, tea in small fields had been grown there for decades. The end of summer had come and Shannon felt it was time to head back to the mainland. The problem was she didn't know what she would do.

Three more letters from Matt arrived by the end of July. Shannon took them down to the beach and sat on a downed palm tree to read. They were postmarked Soissons, France. Her last four letters had finally caught up to him, and he sounded more himself in the first letter she read. They had driven back the Germans a good six miles and secured Soissons. His platoon had taken heavy fire and was pulled out after a week, and sent to Chateau Thierry, to regroup and get much needed rest. They were being reassigned but couldn't say where, only it was a long march and he wished he had his horse. Shannon looked out to the ocean picturing Matt in his uniform and marching. *Marching is good. Soon he will march home to me.*

The second letter mentioned a little town of Braye, where he met a young girl that reminded him of Shannon at thirteen, but she was now head of what was left of her family, taking care of her little brother and sister. 'There's so much hopelessness on their faces, everything they had is destroyed by the war: home, parents, possessions and food. It breaks my heart.' The third letter was sent a week later and again he apologized for being so melancholy. 'I miss you so much but I'm grateful you're safe at Mau Loa. I dream of you at night when I can sleep and pretend to be on a stroll with you as we march. Of course, I'm brought back to reality by the Sergeant's yelling to pick up the pace, but it's my second favorite dream of you. Let's take lots of walks together when I come home.' She sat on the beach staring at his last words "come home." It lifted her spirits. *He will come home and yes, we will take many long walks holding hands... I need to have things ready for when he come home. This war has gone on long enough and we are driving the Germans back. I want him home for Christmas, no, Thanksgiving!*

Shannon now realized she needed to go back to the mainland and make sure Matt's house was ready for him, for them. They would also want to get married as soon as possible. *Do I dare start to make plans for a wedding? I've been afraid to think about it up to this point. But he said when he comes home. Matt will come home.*

Shannon rushed up to the house and found her mother. "Mama, I think it's time I returned to Sacramento and be there for when Matt comes home. I also think I can now think about my wedding, at least the dress."

Lalani smiled. She had dreamed of giving her daughter a beautiful Hawaiian wedding. "Wait here."

Shannon took a seat at the kitchen table and waited, looking out to the gardens her father and mother had created together. *I wonder if*

Matty will like to garden the way father does. I've never seen him plant anything.

Lalani returned with a box, "This is the one thing I have that my mother gave me." She opened the box and pulled out a white chintz wedding gown. On the skirt was printed in black a mountain pattern with flowers and ocean swirls with turtles and stingrays intermixed. Shannon had heard about the dress but had only seen a picture of it. It was beautiful. "My mother made this pattern to represent me, my mountains and flowers and my love for the sea, especially the large turtles that come to shore and the rays that glide below the waves. This dress represents me." At the bottom of the box was another layer of fabric. Lalani pulled it out, "This fabric I made many years ago for you. The mountains with rocks and a horse, for your love of the old ruins and Ginger who took you on your journey through the mountains. The water for your love of swimming and the small canoes represent the boats that will take you to where you belong and bring you back to your island. The flowers for your beauty."

Shannon took the fabric in her arms and touched the ocean and the canoes tenderly. "We certainly have been on a lot of ships to many places."

"Yes, we have, and you and I have loved it. I'm not so sure about your father. That's why I put the horse and the mountain to remind you of all the time the two of you rode together." Lalani gave her daughter a smile and hugged her. "We can take it to Margaret, and she can design your dress. That is if you want this to be your wedding dress."

"Of course, I do, yes, yes. I love the picture of you in your dress with father."

Shannon drove them to town the following day to the dressmaker and to arrange passage back to San Francisco. It would be three weeks before the dress was ready for the final fitting, therefore Shannon booked the SS Maui for August 20th. She also thanked Kevin Kynkendell for the offer to restore the Omake ruins, but declined, since she was not going to be staying on the island. Until her ship sailed, she thought about what she wanted to do back in Sacramento. She knew she didn't want to commit to a long-term project, but something small in the area of research. She wrote to Professor Kroeber to inquire if he had any small projects and to Mr. Rawlings to inquire if the museum would be interested in her original proposal of researching each mission. They could reply to her Sacramento address as she would be there by the twenty-seventh of August. She also wrote Matt and told him she was returning to Sacramento.

By August, Evan and Jim were beginning to prepare for fall round up. They had several men to help round up the small herd and drive them the short distance to the Honolulu meat packing house. Lalani refused to let the herd get bigger than five hundred head, insisting it would anger the land, that overfeeding would not be good. They didn't need to raise more, the herd sold well each year and provided plenty of income. Shannon wouldn't be needed to help with round up. *I wonder how Uncle Clay will do this year. Will he need my help? I need to write and ask.* Lalani and Katherine wrote weekly thus keeping Shannon informed on any word she heard from Matt or Andrew. Katherine hadn't mentioned being short-handed on the ranch. *Was she not wanting to impose this year? Last year was so brutal.* Shannon wrote to Uncle Clay she would come if she was needed, that she was returning on August 27th and planned to go back to Sacramento. A week after writing Uncle Clay, Aunt Katherine wrote back, saying the herd was much smaller only six hundred and they had hired two young men, only seventeen, to help. Shannon wouldn't be needed this year. They missed her and would be happy when she and the boys return.

The day before Shannon was due to sail, Kiki came and helped her pick up her dress and took her to lunch in town. "Well, I guess we're back to writing. Just make it more often." Kiki quipped. They had seen each other a great deal while Shannon was home, and now she would be off again. But this time probably for good, with only an occasional visit for Christmas. That evening Lalani and Shannon carefully packed her wedding dress with her other things. On the way to the dock, they stopped at the post office to check for any mail from Matthew. To her chagrin there was no letter. *He has sent them to Sacramento, that's all. It's only been three weeks since his last letter. I would feel it if something was really wrong. I know I would.* Her father interrupted her as he put his arm around her, "The mail can be slow, and this letter may have been on a ship that was sunk. I'm sure there will be letters waiting for you at home. Now stop worrying. Your mother needs a smile as you depart or she will be in tears all the way home."

"She's always in tears with or without a smile," Shannon half teased and gave him a smile.

13

Troubling Letters

The ship was hit by a late summer storm and was forced to head south to avoid the brunt of it, causing them to be two days late into port. The waves at sea were mountainous and at one point the ship felt as if it would capsize, the deck pitched so far to the vertical. Many of the passengers were seasick, and all were frightened. Shannon herself had never been on such rough seas in all the time she had sailed. She clung to her berth, truly frightened as never before. *Oh, God, please let me be home for Matt when he comes. Please, please, keep us safe.* On the second day of what seemed to be insurmountable waves, the sky cleared and the sea began to calm. Passengers were eager to get word to loved ones, that they were safe but arriving late. They became upset when communications were not being received, due to no other ships in the area, and they couldn't get word to home port. Was the SS Maui the only ship to survive the storm? Why were there no other ships in the vicinity that could relay messages? The communication officer had a sleepless night until he finally reached another ship, and transmitted their location and status: they were safe, but would be two days late to port. Shannon didn't mind the delay, there was no one waiting for her. She was only grateful they had survived the storm. She was also grateful she had never lost her breakfast, causing her state room to smell as others did.

Upon arriving in San Francisco, they learned two other ships had gone down with everyone on board. The bewildered passengers, some still seasick, staggered onto dry land. She contacted Joanna Malcomb and asked if she could stay for a night or two. Taking the four-hour train home to an empty house was a little overwhelming. This voyage had shaken her more then she wanted to admit. Richard and Joanna came and fetched her from the port station. Joanna embraced Shannon upon seeing her unsettled look, and Shannon immediately broke into tears as the pent-up fears came rolling forward. "We almost didn't survive, and two other ships went down. I'm so afraid Matt will not survive," came out, in a breathless whisper.

Shannon stayed with the Malcomb's in Berkeley for several days. Before leaving, she visited Professor Kroeber and again inquired about research going on locally, and if she might be able to help. With the war going on, all local excavation projects had come to a halt. All federal funding was gone, as well as the work force. The best he could offer was a temporary teaching assistant position for next semester. Shannon would think about it.

Shannon returned to Sacramento to Matt's house and set to work airing it out and getting things ready for winter storms. There was only one very old letter waiting that Matt had written back in November. This letter had him at Chateau Thierry still in good spirits, before Eugene's death and Kevin's illness. This was good news. By September 1st, The Sacramento Bee's reporting of the war front was more encouraging. The allies were finally making ground, having taken Arras and Amiens, thus forcing the Germans back to their old line of attack held in 1915. Shannon began to regain her self-confidence and assurance Matt would be coming home. She got active with the Red Cross wrapping bandages, and with the YWCA helping to care for some small children while their mothers worked. With being busy and finding Matt's letter upon return, she did not realize she had not received a letter since before she left Hawaii, almost a month before.

In the evening Shannon often meet up with Millie for supper and caught up on what was going on at the museum. They were putting up a display of pictures showing San Francisco after the 1906 earth-quake, since interest had peaked again after the most current small quake in April. After supper one evening, Millie and Shannon sat talking about the quakes they had experienced. Shannon confessed they didn't seem as scary as the storm her ship encountered. Wanting to talk about something cheery, Shannon shared her wedding dress with Millie. Millie admitted she didn't feel married, since they had only the one day before Jeroen had left. But she was happy to be Mrs. Jeroen Steele. Millie loved the dress and was delighted she would be part of the wedding party. They laughed and made plans for when their men would come home. ... That all changed the next morning.

Shannon received a hysterical call from Millie, so full of tears and sobs she couldn't understand her, yet Shannon knew exactly what had happened and rushed over to Millie's. She found Millie on the entry floor by the phone, with the dreaded orange telegram in her lap, just staring. Shannon reached down and took her in her arms, and Millie began to sob all over again. The telegram said Jeroen had been killed at the battle of Arras on August 18th. Shannon herself was shaken again, the old hidden fears for Matt beginning to resurface. *Stop it, this is no time to be selfish, Aunt Katherine hasn't called. Millie needs you now. You need to be strong for her. Matt will expect me to be strong and confident, for us.* Shannon got Millie to sit down on the settee and brought her a cup of hot tea with a pinch of brandy to calm her. She then called Millie's parents in Morgan Hill. They would be there by noon. Millie finally laid down and fell asleep for a few hours exhausted from the emotions and shock of the morning. Shannon called Mr. Rawlings and informed him. Everyone was very supportive, so many women had received the same telegram over the past six months. Too many!

Jeroen was buried in France near Amiens but Millie would never see his grave. She returned with her parents to Morgan Hill, a widow at twenty-three. Shannon didn't take time to think about Matt in harm's way. She didn't want to at this point. She thought of him only in the barracks playing a piano and playing cards. It was the only thing that could keep her from falling apart herself. She needed to be strong for Millie until she would leave with her parents. After three days, Millie was on the train with her family and what she had packed was in boxes. Shannon would ship them later that week. Shannon walked slowly back to Matt's house and out to the back patio. It had been three days of fighting her fears. She sat down at the table and put her head down and shook from the sobs that came welling up. She hadn't allowed herself to cry in front of Millie, and barely when she was alone. Suddenly she felt as alone as Millie, heartbroken for her sweet friend, and realizing she had not heard from Matt for almost two months. When Shannon woke it was dark, having herself fallen asleep out of exhaustion. She went in and fixed a pot of tea and settled in the study chair and wrote a love letter to Matt.

In the morning, with a melancholy stillness, Shannon called Aunt Katherine to inquire if she had received word from Matthew. She had a letter from him dated August 6, that she had just received a week ago. "He's tired, but fine." Shannon's deepest fears subsided somewhat and raised her hopes again. Katherine wanted Shannon to come to the ranch and not be alone, but Shannon said she needed to stay and help if she could, to keep busy. She would come for a visit soon. Later that day Mr. Rawlings called and asked Shannon if she would come work the museum's admission desk and do tours as needed, now that Millie was gone. Shannon accepted the offer and was there for the weekend tourists. It was a good and sad first day. Shannon was happy to be able to share the exhibits on the missions she had assembled. It sparked her old interest to do more research on them. At the same time, it was lonely. John and Brian were gone and now Millie was gone. It was just Mr. Rawlings that came and sat with her when he had a moment and things were quiet. He did his best to convince her Matt was okay, that a letter would arrive soon. "You know the post; it always takes forever to get a letter from the continent."

Mid-September held onto warm weather and Shannon walked over to the Red Cross headquarters after working at the museum to help roll bandages and fill boxes with supplies for families in need, anything to keep from being alone. She truly missed Millie, and missed Matthew more and more each day she didn't hear from him. After a light supper at a corner café, she reached home and as she opened the door, there it was, a letter from Matt, lying on the floor below the mail slot.

She grabbed it up, dropping her purse and hurried up the stairs to the study. If it was bad news, she wanted to feel his presence around her. Settling quickly in the chair, she took a deep breath and opened the letter. It was dated September 6th, *that's only twelve days ago, oh thank goodness.* Now for certain, she knew he was alive, she sat calmly and read on. They had been pinned down near the Lys River in heavy fighting the first part of September. "I was never so happy to hear a New York accent in my life, when the 369th Regiment arrived to back us up."

He confessed his pocket watch almost fell in the river as he scrambled up the embankment. "The graces were looking over me and it caught on a branch and didn't go into the water. I say goodnight to your picture every night, I'd be lost without it." His sergeant wasn't too happy when he went back to retrieve it, but he would take the chewing out anytime to save it. *Oh, Matty, a chewing out is one thing, but risking your life; is it really worth that? You promised you wouldn't do anything foolish.*

He said they were relieved by the 369th and were being reassigned to a new offensive, so they were back to marching again.

He sent his condolences to Millie; his platoon had come across Jeroen's platoon, and one of his buddies told him he had been killed. Then he promised he was keeping his head down and to keep her letters coming.

Shannon sat as she had with every letter before this, just holding it close to her breast and listening for his voice as she reread his words in her mind. It was late when she stirred again and just had to call Aunt Katherine to let her know she had a letter and he was alright.

Clay answered and would let Kate know, and encouraged her to come to the ranch soon.

The Sacramento Bee continued to report progress, that the German supplies and ammunitions were depleted and rumors about President's 14 point disarmament plan that he had proposed in January were beginning to resurface. Shannon, like so many waiting wives and sweethearts, kept busy with activities at the Red Cross and preparing for when the men would be coming home. Many of them would need housing and time to readjust to civilian life. The YWCA would provide housing for returning nurses and women that had gone over to serve. Shannon helped knit sweaters for the women and sorted through donated clothes for those items that still had a clean fresh look. With the hemlines shorter, she and group of women took on the task of shortening the skirts of older full length style dresses into the new style. Most were from the upper class who could afford to replace clothing rather than alter existing clothes. Shannon had found a few of these dresses at the Salvation Army stores for working on at the museum. It wasn't hard to shorten the hemlines.

By mid-October, Shannon still had not received a letter from Matthew, and she began to worry again. She called Katherine to hear if she had word. Katherine had received a letter dated Oct 3rd from Andrew but also nothing from Matthew. Andrew had been shot in the arm during the Mt. Mihiel advances, and was recovering in Chateau Thierry. It was nothing serious and he would be back at the front within the week. This made Shannon even more concerned, *if Andrew was hit, Matthew could be too.* She began to bury her nose in books written about the California missions for more clues to when and how they were built. Anything to keep her mind busy. She again considered going to each mission for excavation research. Mr. Rawlings needed her there and couldn't afford the trips, therefore every evening after helping at the YWCA, she came home and continued her own book research for clues. After all most archaeology clues come from books, not out in the field. *It's the written word that leads the archaeologist to finding his ruins for excavating.* As the days wore on with no word, her rushing home for the mail, became not so urgent. The odds of a notice from the war department were increasing.

The rumors of a ceasefire were no longer reported as rumors. By November 1st, President Wilson and the allied commander-in-chief Ferdinand Foch were in the midst of negotiating an armistice to end the war, at the request of the German generals and Kaiser William II.

Everyone was hopeful the war would be over by Thanksgiving and men would be returning by Christmas. *Maybe that's why Matt has not written, the army would be sending them home soon, there was no need to continue mail service to families. They will just send us our men. Oh, Shannon you know that's not the reason, but you go ahead and hold on to that thought.* Word spread like fireflies signaling in July, that November 11th at 11:00 a.m. had been set for the ceasefire, pending the final signatures. Specific terms of the armistice were still being negotiated, Britain wanting Germany to be thoroughly stifled, incapable of causing more trouble.

Shannon stood with Mr. Rawlings at the entrance to the museum on the morning of November 11, counting down the seconds as the clock approached eleven o'clock. The clock clicked forward and struck eleven, eleven chimes ringing out; cheers and bells rang throughout the downtown. The sound was wonderful. It was the first time in years people were truly smiling and church bells rang together across the nation.

Shannon reached Aunt Katherine about coming out to the ranch for the Thanksgiving. She was needed at the museum for school tours until Tuesday the 26th, but she would be there by Wednesday evening to help with the final meal preparations. Shannon continued to rush home from work to check the mail, but nothing, not a word from Matt, and fortunately nothing from the war department either. *He's alive, he must be. Otherwise Katherine would have gotten a notice if he was injured or the other.* Shannon refused to let herself think or say out loud the other word. On Wednesday evening, Morgan was waiting at the station for Shannon. "Welcome home, Shay Shay. I'm the lucky one that got to come get you while the others are elbow deep in pies, bread dough, and chores." *Shay Shay, boy I haven't heard it said out loud in such a long time.* By the time they reached the ranch, a simple supper was on the table and all the other preparations for the next day were basically complete. Shannon could only help clear the dishes after the meal. Everyone talked about the men coming home and how much easier life on the ranch would be with the needed help. "I just hope Andrew still likes to eat beef after all that French *paté* and goose livers," Morgan quipped and added, "He will no longer be the boy we sent off, but return a man."

Katherine jumped in, "He will always be my boy, I just hope he adjusts back to civilian life easily."

Clay and Morgan looked at each other. They both had fought in the Spanish American War and knew some men never got used to loud and sudden noises. "He'll be fine, he was raised with the sound of guns," Clay said.

"And your loud boots stomping on the floor and yelling from the bottom of the stairs," Katherine grinned with a teasing demeanor. No one teased about not hearing from Matthew, only offering reasonable explanations: he sent his letters to Oahu, or mail is always getting lost, or he wants to surprise us. Yet deep down Shannon had this troubling sense something was wrong. He wasn't dead, but something was definitely preventing him from writing.

For the next week, Katherine and Shannon took morning rides together. In the flat meadow, both women broke into a gallop, each needing to run away from her worries if only for a moment. The trees were bare, the grass withered to a dusty brown and the winter rains had begun. Shannon wanted to stay at the ranch, but she was still needed at the museum. She would return for Christmas, hopefully with Matthew.

The day before Shannon was to leave, upon returning with Katherine on their morning ride, they came back to the barn which was in total chaos. Katherine could hear Clay yelling and cursing. She jumped from Star and ran in to see Clay lying on the ground in Oscuro's stall, their breeding stallion. Morgan was tying a tourniquet around Clay's right leg where a bleeding gash showed the bone. Katherine raced to help hold the cloth as Ben came with a long board to place under the leg. Shannon took hold of the lead from Sam for Oscuro, still whinnying and upset, and she led him out of the barn. Sam would be needed to get Clay to the house. Juan had already gone for Doc Newell. Clay gritted his teeth and groaned sharply as they lifted the leg to splint it. Katherine told Miguel to get a cot from the storeroom in order to take Clay up to the house. Miguel, Ben, Sam and Morgan lifted him onto the cot, as he gave a grumbling "DAAAMN!"

Katherine held his hand as the men carried him up to the house. They took him to the study and lifted him onto the pool table, a place that the doctor could work. They didn't want to try and carry him upstairs. The bleeding had slowed, but the tourniquet needed to be released in order to let some blood flow to the leg. Katherine and Morgan were just about to release it when Doc Newell arrived.

Doc took over and sent everyone from the room but Katherine and Morgan. Shannon had secured Oscuro back in his stall once everyone was gone and now was up at the house in the parlor waiting with Ben.

Abby had been at a friend's, and as she walked in the front door, Clay let out a cursing yell. "What's going on?" she called and rushed towards the scream. Shannon jumped up and went after her, putting her arm around her as Abby stood in the doorway to the study, stunned to see her father lying on the pool table. Shannon could see they were in the middle of setting Clay's broken bone, and this was not the moment for Abby to see.

Turning Abby away, "He's going to be fine! He fell from the loft and they just straightened his broken bone so it can mend properly. Come with me, they need to finish. But it will be alright." Shannon pulled Abby away, putting her arm around her and led her back to the parlor to wait.

Shannon assured Ben they would be alright if he wanted to get back to his work. "I'll send word once things are settled here. They may need you to get Clay upstairs." Ben nodded and headed back to the barn to clean up things. Benson came with a tray of tea for Abby and Shannon as they waited. Shannon spoke softly trying to calm Abby's fears. After about forty minutes, Morgan came out and, seeing the fear on Abby's face, said, "Your father's going to be fine. Doc has stopped the bleeding and bandaged and splinted the leg. He'll be out of commission for some time. Doc says we can move him to upstairs, so we need Ben, Sam and Miguel again."

"Can I see him?" Abby asked.

"Things are pretty messy in there right now. I think it's best if you wait, until we get him settled upstairs. He'll be up to talking once we get him comfortable in his big bed."

"But I need…"

Shannon cut her off and put her arm around her shoulders, "Abby, we need to go get Ben and the men, that's what we can do to help now. Come on." She led her out to the corral and found Sam and Miguel.

It took another forty minutes to get Clay upstairs and settled in bed. Doc gave him something for the pain and a sleeping power. Clay fought the need to sleep long enough to allay Abby's fears by giving her a smile and a strong, "Nothing to worry about. I'll be up in no time."

Clay slept through the evening, and Morgan and Ben met to figure out how to divide up the work that needed to be done without Clay's help. Katherine sat in the parlor with Abby and Shannon discussing plans for Christmas, trying to distract them from their worries: Abby about her father, and Shannon about Matt. Katherine kept things as quiet as possible in the house to ensure Clay could sleep.

Doc returned the following morning, to check on the wound and to show Katherine ways to help him be more comfortable. Shannon stayed an extra few days to help Kate. By the third day, Clay was more alert and beginning to holler. Shannon worried he would run Aunt Katherine ragged. She took Benson and Abby aside and told them they needed to make sure Kate got a break and enough sleep. Shannon said she would be back in a month for Christmas.

~~

Mr. Rawlings was happy to have Shannon back at the museum. She settled back into Matt's house and thought about how to make it comforting for him. She wrote her mother, telling her the real facts about Uncle Clay's injury, knowing Aunt Kate would play them down. She went as far as to suggest she come and help Kate and it would be wonderful to have them there for Christmas. Shannon received a telegram that father and Evan were needed at the ranch for some major repairs they had put off, but she would come as soon as she could. Shannon was thrilled to know her mother was coming, not only for Katherine's benefit but also for hers.

Everyone was buzzing with plans for when the men returned. The Bee reported the government would be bringing men home in stages and not all at once. The demobilization plan was going to take time to get the ships needed and soldiers to the ports of Brest and Le Havre, from where most would be shipped home. Shannon felt it was important that Andrew return as soon as possible to help. She wrote to her college friend, Maxwell, whose father was at the State Department, explaining the situation at home and the need for both Andrew and Matthew to return as soon as possible to work the ranch. Maxwell wrote back that there was little he could do. The first men to be coming home would be the wounded strong enough to make the journey, then those that had volunteered and served the longest. Shannon had high hopes that Andrew would arrive soon, but concerns for Matt were increasing daily.

The Bee announced some one-and-half million soldiers would be discharged over the next year. Until then, some would be sent into Russia and Germany to oversee the war transition efforts, while the rest were held at temporary camps near the ports. By mid-December, news of the first soldiers to arrive home had reached Sacramento. But along with them several cases of influenza.

Before leaving Sacramento for the holiday, Shannon went and visited Millie to see how she was getting along. Her mother said she had been in better spirits, but now with the men returning she had slumped back into a deep melancholy mood. Shannon stayed and took her shopping and talked about how she was still needed at the museum, that it would be good for her to keep herself busy. It was the only way she was coping with not hearing from Matt for the past three months. Millie admitted she did love her job at the museum and seeing all the school kids come and ask the silliest questions. She would consider it.

Shannon's mother's ship arrived in San Francisco the week of Christmas, and Shannon was at the dock waiting for her. Shannon hadn't realized how much she had missed her. Tears began to stream down her face at her first embrace. "There, there, it's going to be alright. We will get through this together," Lalani said softly. Instinctively, she knew the tears were not out of worry for Uncle Clay and Aunt Katherine, but more for Matt. Shannon's letter had an undertone of fear, and Lalani knew she needed to be at her daughter's side.

They boarded the train for Oak Ridge and settled into their compartment. Lalani sat next to Shannon holding her hand, as she did when Shannon was little and frightened of the thunder. Just having her mother there took away the abandoned feeling Shannon had been fighting for the last month.

Morgan met them at the train station, as usual, and filled them in on things that were going at the house. Clay was up and around. The first day with crutches, Kate couldn't keep him away from the barn and work. Doc Newell had specifically said to stay off his feet, therefore he took the crutches back and provided a wheelchair for around the house. "He's driving us all crazy," Lalani smiled, thinking back to the time he hurt his back, when he and Katherine first met. He drove them all crazy that time too. "He's like a little boy that needs to keep his hands busy. Now that Shannon and I are here, we can help play games, and discuss ranch plans for when the boys come home, and help keep him distracted."

Katherine was overjoyed to see Lalani and Shannon, so grateful Shannon had talked her mother into coming. "Lalani, I didn't realize until just now how much I needed your help, both physical and emotional."

Lalani and Shannon went to the upstairs sitting room where Clay was sitting in the wheelchair reading the newspaper that had arrived that morning. "Clayton Taylor, didn't I tell you over twenty years ago, if you caused my Katherine trouble, I'd come looking for you and give you an earful. Well, here I am. What do you mean, by going and breaking a leg and causing all this extra work and worry?" Lalani said, as she smiled reached down and kissed him.

"Lalani! I know, I know. Maybe you will let me have my crutches so I can get out of this house, and from underfoot. I'm so glad you're here for Kate's benefit. She has missed you."

Shannon and Lalani settled in their rooms, and Morgan and Ben helped Clay downstairs for the evening. Abby had taken command of pushing her father's wheelchair to where he needed to go while downstairs and at supper brought him to the head of the table. Lalani filled them in on what Jim and Evan were doing at the ranch in the way of repairs to the barn and house, and that they thought the herd for spring would be plentiful with spring calves. After supper, Katherine sat and played piano for Lalani. Lalani sent Katherine off to bed early, seeing how tired she looked. They would have some private time tomorrow to share concerns. For tonight she and Shannon and Abby would keep Clay entertained. Lalani and Clay gave the girls a run for their money, or match sticks in this case, as they played poker. "Aunt Lalani, where did you learn to play poker so well?" Abby asked.

"From a very old friend of your mother's. When we lived in England, her friends Thomas and Jessie and I would play. Jessie was a gambler at heart, and taught me how to bluff and bet."

"She sure did!"

"It's late, Shannon, go get Ben and Sam to help Clay upstairs. I will say good night now." Lalani gave her daughter a kiss on the head and whispered "*Moe'uhane hemolele.*"

"Thank you, mama, sweet dreams to you, too."

The next morning, Shannon and Katherine went riding as they had done before. Knowing Lalani was there to watch over Clay gave Kate the freedom to take more time. But it was a very cold morning, and the heavy breathing of the horses could be seen in the gusts of mist they exhaled. They returned to the house and found Abby and Clay dressed and sitting in the upstairs parlor. "How did you get to your chair? Surely Abby didn't help?" Kate asked with a suspicious glance.

"No, no. I got Miguel and Ben to help when he became impossible and started bellowing like a bull sensing a heifer in heat," Abby teased.

"Abby Taylor, what an unladylike thing to say," Lalani scolded as she brought coffee for everyone. They sat around the fireplace quietly talking about past Christmases. Benson knocked on the door and entered, "There's a letter, Mrs. Taylor." Kate didn't recognize the handwriting or the name on the return address. "Kevin O'Brien," she said out loud.

Shannon immediately knew who it was from. "Kevin's one of Matt's platoon buddies." She moved to the settee with Kate as she opened the letter. Their eyes scanned the letter.

Dear Mrs. Taylor,

I'm writing to let you know I have returned home on the same ship as your son Andrew.

"It's about Andrew," Kate said, knowing the others were anxious to hear. Shannon read on looking for word about Matt. Suddenly she was whispering to herself, "No, no, no."

"What is it." Clay demanded and Lalani asked together.

Katherine read on,

Andrew was still recovering from his wounds, in hospital, when he contracted the influenza. The same had happened to me. I had basically recovered from the flu and had written my dad requesting a return-to-work order, which allowed me to come home instead of going back to my platoon. That's how I ended up on the same ship as Andrew.

Apparently, his doctor thought he would be strong enough, since he had survived the worst of it. They were calling off names as they carried the sick off the ship. And I recognized Andrew Taylor. Matt spoke of him often. I only briefly managed to talk to him. He was in pretty bad shape, and I would recommend you come and do what you can for him. They have taken him to General Hospital No. 1 in New York City.

I'm sorry Mrs. Taylor I can't tell you much about Matt. Most of our platoon was sent to Germany for post war duties. I did run across Mac and he lost sight of Matt at the battle of Argonne around the first of November. With the ceasefire many of the platoon and men became scattered and reassigned. He was alive the last time Mac saw him. For now, I thought you should know about Andrew and make your way there as soon as possible.

Respectfully,

Kevin O'Brien

Mariposa, CA

Katherine and Lalani immediately put their arms around Shannon, knowing for themselves, the fear that was tearing through her at that moment.

"We need to go get Andrew and find out if anyone has seen Matt," Clay declared.

"Clay, you're in no shape to be traveling across the country, let alone to Europe," Kate reprimanded.

"You and Shannon go." Lalani said, "I'll stay here with Clay and Abby." She knew her daughter needed to go, to see if she could find Matt, even if she had to go to Germany. Shannon turned back into her mother's arms for comfort.

Abby began to protest, but Clay agreed with Lalani. Abby would only be more of a worry than help. Clay said he would send a telegram to an army general he knew and see if he could find out more about Matt's platoon and whereabouts. Taking action gave Shannon a focus, *Mac said he was alive, he's alive and in Germany. Uncle Clay will confirm it. Matt's alive.*

Katherine and Shannon went and packed, and Clay immediately drafted a telegram to General Robert Alexander. By late afternoon Morgan and Lalani were driving Shannon and Katherine to the train station to catch the four o'clock train to Council Bluffs and then on to New York.

Shannon was finally glad to be doing something about not hearing from Matt. *If he can't come to me, then I will go to him.* Lalani hugged her daughter tightly, so very much wanting to go and be with her. But she would serve the need better at the ranch. "It will be alright. Listen to your heart and your spirit will guide you," she said as she kissed Shannon tenderly, then sent her up the step onto the train. Turning to Kate, "I'll look after yours, you look after mine. And bring them all home safe."

"I will!" Kate replied as the conductor called "All aboard, last call, all aboard."

Morgan put his arm around Lalani as they watched the train pull away. He could feel her desire to go with them. She turned and said, "Let's get back and see what we can do at our end."

It was four long worrisome days on the train for Shannon. Knowing that Matt's platoon had been reassigned helped her somewhat, yet Mac not having seen him since the Argonne battle was not. Katherine was anxious to get to New York to see for herself how Andrew was doing, but relieved he was in the States and getting proper medical care. It was a cold dreary day when the train pulled into Central Station. Shannon had the porter send their bags to the Astor Hotel, while they headed directly to the hospital.

The hospital was huge. Neither Katherine nor Shannon had been in one that large. They made their way to the reception desk, and inquired after Andrew.

"Andrew Taylor, yes, he's on the fifth floor, in the influenza recovery ward. You can't go up there without a mask. Ladies, I would recommend wearing a mask anytime you are around military personal. They have brought the dreaded plague back from Europe, and it's spreading like wildfire. It would be best if you waited until he was out of here and not take the chance of contact."

Both Katherine and Shannon ignored her advice. Nothing was going to keep Katherine from seeing Andrew. The nurse was used to mothers ignoring her warning and handed them masks and pointed to the elevator. "The nurse at the desk on the fifth floor will take you to him. Visiting hours end at 8:00 p.m. "

The fifth-floor nurse led them down a long white hall. One door read "No admittance, active influenza ward." Towards the end of the hall, she led them through a door to a large room with about twenty beds. Some men were sitting up talking to wives or mothers, others were pale and sleeping. Katherine spotted Andrew. He was propped up resting with his eyes closed.

"Andrew Taylor, get your hands out of the mashed potatoes," Katherine said in her most tender but motherly voice.

Andrew smiled and then opened his eyes slowly. "I didn't do it," he said softly. Katherine reached down and put her arms around him, hugging him. He felt so thin and fragile. "Boy, you got here fast. I just had a nurse write a letter to you yesterday. Shannon, what a pretty sight for sore eyes."

"Hi, Andrew, we're so glad to have you home."

"Bet you're even happier to have Matt home, where is that big lug?" he whispered.

Shannon smiled not wanting to worry him in his weakened state, "He's still in Europe, waiting to come home."

Katherine quickly changed the subject back to him. "You always were the one to get sick, and out of having to work. I see you're still pulling the same shenanigans. I think this time you went a little too far."

"Maybe so. It's not been very fun."

They sat and talked for a short time, then Andrew became tired again. They let him sleep, and went to find the doctors about his condition and when he could go home. It took a while until the right doctor was available to talk. Shannon made her way back down to the first floor reception desk to inquire, if by any chance, Matthew was there. "No Matthew Taylor, only an Andrew and Edward. Miss, it's better he's not here, we have had too many pass away, since the men have returned. To be honest, if your family can have private care for your brother, that would be best. We need the beds, and many of the men have begun to recover and then come in contact with the dreaded disease again and die."

Shannon was surprised at the bluntness of the nurse, and glad she had said it to her and not Katherine. "We'll do our best, as I'm sure the doctors and nurses are for everyone." *I guess I'm relieved that Matt's not here and at the same time disappointed. Where are you, Matthew?* Tears began to well up and she fought to hold them from spilling out. The nurse reached and gave her a small wipe she had on hand just for these moments. She had seen it so many times on the faces of wives and mothers looking for their husbands and sons.

Katherine arrived downstairs and found Shannon staring out the front door. She took her by the arm and headed for the hotel. Katherine told Shannon what the doctor said. Andrew was lucky his gunshot wound had healed, and he should recover from the flu with a lot of rest and fresh air. He was in no way ready for a train ride to California, but he did say he could leave the hospital if she could manage his needs, or find someone who could. He warned his nurses were not available for home care. There just weren't enough.

Back at the hotel, Katherine and Shannon made their way to their rooms on the third floor, across the hall from each other. Once Katherine had freshened up, she felt much better and realized they hadn't eaten since breakfast on the train. She went and knocked on Shannon's door, only to hear sobs coming from inside. The door was unlocked and she entered to find Shannon lying on the bed crying. Shannon sat up quickly and wiped her eyes. "I'm sorry, Aunt Katherine, I didn't want you to see how upset I am."

Katherine came to the bed and sat, pulling Shannon into her arms. "Shh, it's alright. You go ahead and cry, you have been far too brave these past months. I too have cried quietly in the night because of Matthew." Shannon tried to stop crying, huffing out short breaths but couldn't as the tears flowed for another few minutes. Finally, she pulled back and smiled, "Sorry, but I needed that. I'm okay now. I'm truly happy we have Andrew home and he will be okay. Now we just need to find Matthew."

The next few days they went to see Andrew twice a day, just sitting quietly with him. Talking too much tired him. Shannon made her way to the army office at the harbor where the men were being processed as they returned home. She was careful to wear a heavy mask and not to touch too many surfaces. She couldn't take the chance of infecting Andrew or herself with the miasma. The sergeant on duty, had three books with the names of men discharged, on the top of his desk. Too many people came in every day to inquire as Shannon was doing, so he kept them handy. Upon seeing her, "Name you're looking for?" he asked.

She smiled and said 'Matthew Keenan Taylor with the 361st infantry. "

He opened the large book with Army stamped across the cover, turned to the 361st and began to scan the names. "Matthew, you said? No wait, that middle name again?"

"Keenan."

"No. No Matthew Keenan, only a Matthew Thomas Taylor. Be grateful Miss, Thomas is listed as a paraplegic, and will never walk again. Your Matthew isn't listed here. He's probably waiting in France to be discharged."

She thanked him for his time, and gained a glimmer of hope that his name wasn't listed as deceased.

Upon returning to the hotel, Shannon found a telegram waiting for her. Uncle Clay had heard back from his general friend.

They have no word on Matt STOP Last seen on October 10 at Apremont France before the Argonne offensive STOP No time to look for wounded or dead STOP Locals best resource STOP Glad Andrew is okay STOP Stay strong Matts alive somewhere STOP Love to you both STOP Clay

Shannon's head was swimming. *No one in the Army knows where he is? Local people will know? Local people.*

Go to France? Can I leave Aunt Katherine with Andrew needing so much help? What should I do? What can I do?

They had been in New York for several days, and Andrew seemed to be improving, after the grueling crossing from France. Katherine was busy making arrangements for Andrew to leave the hospital. She spoke with the hotel about a large suite with two bedrooms, where Andrew could continue to recuperate more comfortably than in the hospital.

A heavy rain was falling outside. Shannon stood at her room window, whispering to herself, "What can I do? How can I find him and not the army? *"Shannon, you're an archaeologist, your job is finding things. So as an archaeologist, where do you start?* "Research!" she said out loud. "We start with books and data, clues that lead to finding where and what it is we're looking for."

Shannon spent the next few days, helping Aunt Katherine with the details to get Andrew moved to the hotel and taking turns visiting with him. In her free moments, she made notes on the information she had about Matt, where he was last seen, and where she knew, from his letters, he had been. Reviewing her notes, she now felt she needed to know the movements of Matt's platoon in order to find him. *Surely the army can tell me that, even so close to the ending of the war. They must know where they sent the 91st Infantry.*

Shannon telegraphed Uncle Clay and asked him to contact his army friend again and see if he could find out where the 361th 2nd platoon's movements from September to the current day had taken them.

Meanwhile she started going over in her mind the last letter Matt had sent. Were there any other clues about what he was doing or going? *There was the river and almost losing his watch, what river?... The Lys, write that down. What else? What was the regiment that relieved them, the one from New York, what was their number? 396? No the 369th Regiment, write that down.* She couldn't remember anything else other than he loved her. The river kept coming back to mind, *what about it?* She remembered him writing he scrambled up the embarkment. *So, he must have crossed the Lys. Where did they cross? Write that down to find out from the general.*

By the end of the week Andrew's doctor was willing to release him to Katherine and Shannon's care. Katherine had moved to a roomy suite with two bedrooms. They borrowed a wheelchair from the hospital and with the help of the cab driver got Andrew in and out of the cab.

Andrew was happy to be out of the hospital and in a comfortable hotel room with a view of Central Park. He was too weak to walk on his own, so both Katherine and Shannon were needed to get him to the water closet and back. The doctor had said to get him up and walking a little each day if they could. Katherine's spirits were much lighter now, with Andrew away from the influenza wards. But she too had growing concerns about Matthew. Why had he not written? When Andrew asked for the third time if they had any news from Matt, they finally told him, "No, not since September." He too became worried. Katherine tried her best to reassure him he was okay.

Christmas was now only ten days away. Andrew was eager to be home for the holiday. But the doctor hadn't been able to visit to say he could go. And until he could stand on his own, Katherine felt it would be too hard of a journey. She was in communications with Clay keeping him informed on his progress and Shannon's attempts to locate Matt. Clay too wanted them home for the holiday. "Katherine, I'm sure he's stronger than he looks. I'll arrange for a special Pullman private car to bring you home. He can sleep all the way here. I'll arrange for your own steward to help."

Shannon received a letter directly from General Billings, saying her best bet for the 361st's movements at the moment was to go to Toul, France, where the communication records with the regiment were currently located. She reviewed the information she had and the only way to get more answers was to go to Toul. Katherine was concerned about her going alone. It just wasn't wise for a young woman traveling by herself. "There are a lot of soldiers over there still, men that may have forgotten how to behave near a young woman," she warned. But Shannon was now determined to go. She just had to find passage on a ship.

She contacted Uncle Morgan and told him she needed help getting Aunt Kate to agree to let her go to France. He didn't completely agree, but said he would help from his end. The next day, Shannon went down to the Cunard office and found there was a steamship leaving in two days for Le Havre, France. It was being used to bring soldiers home. All of the main cabins were booked by returning French families that had fled before the war. There were no cabins available at this late date. The lower cabins had been converted with multiple bunks for the troops and for sick soldiers. Cunard took the return trip to completely scrub and clean them of influenza, hopefully to protect the next group coming home.

Shannon knew that both her mother and Katherine were friends with William and Louise Cunard, the owner of the shipping line. She sent a telegram explaining who she was and what her need was and waited.

Five days before Christmas, the day the Aquitania was due to sail, Shannon received a ticket for a small cabin on deck two, compliments of Arthur Cunard, the Cunard's son.

Meanwhile, Clay had a private train car added to the Pacific Rail to Council Bluffs and would have another waiting to bring them to Oak Ridge. Katherine quickly sent a telegram to Charles Duvaneau, her good friend in France, to have him meet Shannon, and asking him to take care of her, making sure she had what she needed and help in the search. Shannon helped get Andrew to the train and settled on board. "Bring him home, Shay Shay, I know he loves you more than eagles soaring, and is counting on you to find him. He must be lost if he's not here," Andrew whispered.

Shannon kissed him on the cheek, "You take care of yourself and we expect to see you on your feet when we get home."

Katherine walked her to a waiting cab, "You stay out of harm's way. If you need anything, Charles will see to it. Don't take any chances, I don't need two of you lost." Katherine said half teasingly, then embraced her tightly, and oh so quietly added, "Both of you come home safe, …bring him home to me." Katherine eyes were filling with tears for the first time in Shannon's presence, fearful of what she might find.

"Don't worry, I'll find him, I promise. You just get Andrew and yourself home to Uncle Clay. Please try to explain it to mother why I had to go. I'll telegram for Christmas if I can. Tell mother I love her," were Shannon's departing words as she climbed in the cab for the ship.

PART THREE –
Searching for Love

14

Where to Start

On board ship, Shannon learned that one of the head stewards had given up his cabin at Mr. Cunard's request and was bunking in with another steward. She stood in a light mist at the bow as the ship pulled out, this time looking east to France. Once out to sea, she found the steward who had given up his cabin and thanked him profusely. It would take six days to cross the Atlantic. Shannon had purchased a map of France just before leaving and now spent the time marking cities Matt had mentioned in his letter and the dates he was there. She wasn't sure where to start looking: in the hospitals, going to Toul for the regiment movements, or to Lys River from his last letter. Thankfully, her research kept her busy and she was in France before she realized. It was Christmas morning as the Aquatania docked at Le Havre. The port was extremely quiet. Several soldiers hoping to get on the next ship, milled about the docks, but very few French people were to be seen. They were all home this Christmas, thankful the war was over.

She didn't know what Charles looked like, but Shannon looked a lot like her mother and Charles recognized her instantly. As she came across the gangplank, he was there waiting. "Shannon Baker," he said as she reached him. "Yes, you must be Charles Duvaneau?"

"*Oui!* You look so much like your mother; it is a joy to meet you. I just wish it were for a more joyous reason." Charles carried Shannon's case and apologized for not having a car. His had been confiscated by the Germans. They stopped long enough at the telegraph office to send a message to the ranch, letting everyone know she had arrived safe, and writing, *'ma'ma mele Kalikimaka'*, Merry Christmas, mother.

Charles did have what was considered an old fashioned carriage and horse. This was not uncommon transportation at the end of the war. This December, France seemed colder, more desolate than before the war. All the houses seem dingier, the fields appeared disheveled, instead of neat furrowed rows, and many of the linden tree rows were splintered and shattered, not just dormant. The war had taken its toll not only on the people, but also on the land.

Charles and Shannon had time on the ride to the estate to get acquainted and Shannon told him that her mother was currently at the Taylor Ranch to help Katherine with Clay and Andrew as they recovered. They arrived at his estate, just south of Paris, shortly before dark. The main house still stood majestically in the twilight. Henrick met them as they pulled to the front and took the carriage once they were inside. Charles showed Shannon to the parlor, where lights were on and a fire was going. Mme. Fontenelle, the housekeeper and cook, brought hot tea and said supper would be served shortly. The chateau was beautiful to Shannon. The parlor was large, with portraits of Charles' family hanging on the walls. Pine boughs were laid on top of the large marble mantle that included a shield of three grape leaves, the family crest. Once Shannon had her cup of tea to warm herself, Charles was certain she would want to freshen up and rest before supper. He showed her upstairs to the room Mme. Fontenelle had made up with fresh linens and started the fire to take off the chill. It was a charming room with soft blue painted walls. The furniture was French provincial with a four-poster bed. Shannon lay down on the bed, tired and feeling like she was in a dream, a school teacher in a castle looking for her Prince Charming. She thought of everyone at the Taylor Ranch, how it would be a joyous Christmas morning with Andrew home, and then she fell asleep.

The next day, Shannon shared what she knew about Matt's movements, and that more could be obtained at the American Expeditionary Force's headquarters in Toul. But first she wanted to check the hospitals in Paris. Charles offered to take her to the large Army hospital there and a smaller one outside of the city in Creteil, the following morning.

They arrived at the large Army hospital early. Shannon was eager to get there to search the wards for Matthew, half hoping, he was there and half hoping he wasn't. *Finding him there would be wonderful, but it also means he's hurt. I don't care as long as he's alive.* Shannon knew the protocol upon reaching the main desk at the hospital, having gone through it with Andrew. The sergeant on duty checked the roster of patients. Matt was not listed. She asked if there were any from the 361st regiment. He pulled out a different book and looked. "You're lucky Miss, it doesn't look like your soldier has been admitted here. Best to check the demobilization headquarters, they have the list of men waiting to go home." Shannon just had to be sure he wasn't there and asked if she could take a look through the wards.

Since it was visiting hours, he handed her a mask and told her to go ahead to the wards that permitted visitors on the first and second floor. Charles and Shannon wandered through the first ward and then the second on the first floor. Most of the men were in too much pain to notice her. Shannon tried to smile and not stare as she passed bed after bed of bandaged and pale bodies, struggling to be alive. After the first floor she no longer wanted to look, she didn't have it in her. *He's not here, you can feel it in your heart, he's not here. Stop looking here and move on to Creteil.* Shannon told Charles there was no need to look further and they headed back to the main desk.

Charles told her to go out and get some fresh air. He would be right with her. Charles went to the sergeant and asked him to check the other book for the name Matthew Taylor. The Sergeant knew what he was asking and took out a book that was much thicker and turned to the T's and scanned the lists of names. Looking up the sergeant shook his head no, "You're in luck, he's not listed here." Charles said, "Thanks," as the sergeant closed the book listing all the deceased soldiers that had been processed through Paris before being buried somewhere in France.

Before leaving Paris for Creteil, Charles took Shannon to lunch at one of the nicer restaurants along the Seine, that had reopened. They could see the Eiffel tower across the river. Charles talked about taking her mother there and how she climbed to the first viewing level. "When you come back with Matt, we will retrace your mother's visit to Paris and all the sites."

Creteil was halfway between Paris and Lesigny, where Charles' estate lay. This hospital was smaller, with only wounded soldiers and civilians. It did not have an influenza ward. Matt was not registered as a patient, but once again Shannon needed to look for herself. It was much the same; young men, broken and battered by war. This time she tried to smile as she went through. One young man with his chest bandaged stared at her for a moment. "I've seen you," he said, "Or at least I've seen your picture. You're Matt's girl."

Shannon stood motionless for a moment and then rushed to sit by his side. "You know Matthew Taylor, have you seen him?"

"Yah, I know Matt. But I'm sorry I haven't seen him in over a year. We were stationed outside Paris, when we first arrived. He would play piano at the mess hall and every night he pulled out that watch of his and say good night to you. That's how I saw your picture."

Shannon's smile faded away, "Oh, well, I'm glad he got to play piano for everyone."

"Don't worry about Matt, miss. I assume he is just missing, since you're looking for him. He's a darn good soldier and knows how to keep out of danger. He could shoot a can off a fence from fifty feet away. I'm sure he's alright. The paperwork is lost that shows where he's stationed, that all."

Shannon appreciated the effort to assuage her concerns, but they both knew he was lost and not the paperwork. Just then the nurse came to change his bandages. "Sorry, miss, but I need you to leave."

"I was too close to the pesky German artillery and took scrap metal to the chest."

Shannon thanked him and wished him well and a safe journey home.

The sun was beginning to set and the cold dark air began to settle in, as they arrived back at the estate. Shannon was exhausted from the emotional ups and downs of the day, and asked Mme. Fontenelle to bring her some soup to her room, hoping Charles would understand her not wanting to have supper with him.

At breakfast the next morning Charles and Shannon discussed what her next move should be. It wasn't practical for her to go from town to town, hospital to hospital, trying to find him. She needed a starting point. Where was his last known location? Where did people actually see him? She showed Charles her map of locations that his letters mentioned, the Lys River being the last spot. "But the 369th Regiment relieved them from the fighting and they were sent somewhere else. But he didn't say."

Charles knew that a lot of the American forces were positioned at the south end of the front line, while the British were on the north during the final battles of the war. The front line covered over four hundred miles, from Belfort, France to Ghent, Belgium. They needed to find the last place Matt was seen for sure. But how? Charles had worked during the war with the Army supply units. Often mail for the troops came on the same ship as supplies.

"Can we find out where his mail was last sent that would give us a place to start?" Shannon asked.

"I don't think the army keeps track of where mail comes from. It all just go to Paris's central post office for overseas. Incoming goes to HQ, in Toul or Paris."

"What about his pay? Don't they have to pay the soldier?" Shannon perked up at this idea.

"Each Division has a paymaster unit that handles payroll and getting pay to the troops. I could check with a contact I have in the French payroll office and see if he knows who the 91st division paymaster is or at least where it is at this moment," Charles offered.

While they waited to hear from Charles' friend, Shannon took time to write her mother about what was happening. Charles took her riding through the estate each day when the rains had stopped. The rows and rows of grapevines, had been spared from much of the war, the estate being south of Paris. Even in their barren dormant state, you could tell most of the vines hadn't been properly trimmed for this year's harvest. There just weren't enough workers. Charles managed with Henrick and a few women to harvest and trim about fifty acres of the grapes for which the estate was famous. But the other two hundred acres of various grapes had been ransacked by hungry soldiers and starving local people, and Charles allowed it. Charles was delighted Shannon was more like Katherine and loved to ride. It was nice to have company as he made his way to the far side of the vineyards to see what could be saved.

At the end of the week, Charles received a telephone call from his friend. "I think I found who you need to talk to. A Sergeant Larson. He's with the 91st Division paymaster's unit, stationed in Toul."

When Shannon heard the name Larson, her mind immediately raced to Lars, Matt's best friend. Lars being allergic to gun oil was assigned to the clerical pool. His accounting background must have gotten him into the payroll unit. Charles tried to make contact with the Toul Army Headquarters, but it was impossible to get through. Things were extremely busy for the army switchboard operators relaying disarmament and withdrawal orders to all the troops. Civilian calls were not allowed. If Shannon wanted information from Toul, she would just have to go there.

Charles realized it would be difficult for Shannon to find her way around France without help and an interpreter. She needed to be going north where the fighting had been heavy, in small towns, where little English was spoken. He didn't have the time or the energy to go with her, he being almost sixty. He also was needed at the estate and in town as the rebuilding began. Charles insisted Henrick go with her. Henrick had worked for Charles for thirty years, and was in his mid-forties and could help Shannon as needed.

Traveling light was a priority for Shannon, in case she ended up walking. Charles gave her a carpet bag for her things. She packed one extra pair of trousers, one shirt, a few blouses and three days' worth of undergarments and essential toiletries. She purchased a sturdy pair of hiking boots and packed another pair of flat shoes for emergency and extra socks. Charles had a small buckboard wagon and a decent horse they could use. It was old and the seat was hard, but Charles took off a cushion from a settee and fitted it to the bench seat. Henrick packed a box with some food and a few cooking supplies, along with three bedrolls, one for Matt, and rain ponchos, and placed them in the wagon. The buckboard and horse could get over the battered countryside much better than a car, which were scarce and gasoline impossible to find. The horse could feed on grass along the way.

It was New Year's Day, when Shannon and Henrick left for Toul. Charles gave Henrick cash to meet any need that might arise. "Just don't keep it all in one place, divide it up between you and your bags. Shannon, if you need me, just telephone. The French operator will put the French call through first. Don't take any chances and keep me informed of where you are. I really don't want to have to go find you, too."

Shannon laughed, "I think that's what Katherine said to me when we parted."

"Henrick, you take care of her. Your life does depend on keeping her safe, if you want a job when you return. Be wise and be safe. Good luck Shannon," were his parting words.

The morning air was crisp and hints of snow falling lingered. The road from Lesigny to Toul was dusted with snow, but the ground was hard and not muddy. Shannon sat next to Henrick bundled in a blanket and heavy coat, with mittens and a wool scarf pulled up around her head. They hoped to make thirty miles to Cerneux the first night.

Along the road, they passed army trucks full of soldiers heading to Paris and seaports. Each time one passed, Shannon yelled "IS MATT TAYLOR WITH YOU?" A few would yell back. The answer was always no or no Taylor here. They stopped briefly in the few small towns along the way, to get hot coffee. Very few places actually had coffee. Most of the time it was chicory root, roasted and ground to imitate coffee. Shannon quickly came to appreciate the warm drink.

It was almost four hundred kilometers to Toul. By the second day they were halfway. They stopped in Saint-Dizier, where there was a hospital. Shannon just couldn't pass by without checking. The Saint-Dizier hospital was a civilian French hospital and the staff spoke very little English. Henrick asked the nurse at the main desk if a Matthew Taylor an American was there. "*Non*-Taylor. *Nous avion un Paulson, mais il est mort.*" Even Shannon understood the word 'mort' and that Paulson had died. There was no need to walk through the wards. An American would stand out to the nurses. They moved on and reached Maulan by nightfall.

Maulan was a small town and there was no café or hotel. Henrick pulled into a small farm with a barn still standing and asked if they might spend the night there. The old man, seeing Shannon, agreed. The supplies Henrick had brought now came in handy. They ate a simple supper of hard cheese and bread with a bit of wine. Shannon normally didn't drink wine, but tonight it would help keep her warm. The old man brought out some hot water for Shannon to warm her hands and clean her face. Henrick gathered some of the straw scattered about and laid Shannon's bedroll out on it. "It will help a little bit with the cold ground." When Shannon was settled for the night, Henrick placed Matt's bedroll over her. The barn was cold but better than being out in the open. The livestock had been gone for years, so the only smell was from Jacques the horse tied at the far end of the barn, munching away on some of the hay.

In the morning, Henrick gave the old man a few francs for his help. Shannon was eager now to get on to Toul before the paymaster's office would close. It was bitterly cold but at least it wasn't snowing. The military presence on the road became heavier and heavier as they approached Toul. The wagon bumped like a mousse dessert plopped onto the table. Shannon became more uncomfortable and anxious as each truck rolled by. *This road is going to rattle my teeth right out of my head. I just wish I could search each truck for Matt, but that's impossible.* She continued to call out Matt's name or his regiment number. "361st." Again, the answers were no. One soldier called out, "Joan of Arc, save me."

Henrick said the soldier called out Joan's name because they were close to her birthplace, the village of Domremy. Shannon recalled Matthew writing about being there and the house being a chapel of some sort. She suddenly had the need to be there. *If I can at least stand where he stood and share a moment.* It was an hour detour but it was still early. If the road wasn't too muddy, they could make it and then on to Toul before dark. At Void-Vacon, Henrick turned south down a well-traveled road. It was much narrower and some of the forest thickets still lined the road. Henrick explain how people would come to the house and pray to the little statue of Joan for help and then commit themselves to fight for France. It was said in this house she saw an angel that told her to drive out the English and fight for the French king. Since the war began, many soldiers would trek there to say a prayer and ask for strength to fight. Shannon wasn't sure why Matty had been there. He wasn't overly religious, but was intrigued with historical characters. The rain began to fall gently as they neared the house. No soldiers seemed to be there at the moment. She hurried inside to find a small fire in the fireplace that dimly lit the room. The room was empty except for a small table with a small ceramic statue of Joan. Shannon stood quietly trying to sense Matt's past presence in the room. *I know it's silly trying to feel him here. But I can imagine him standing right where I'm standing quietly observing her, wondering about the woman and the courage she had.* "Shannon, come here," Henrick said, pointing to a guest book that sat on a shelf. "When was Matt here, do you remember?"

"It was early, at least a year ago if not longer."

Henrick flip to the front of the large book, October, 1917 was the first date and name. Not every soldier that had visited had signed the book. As they scanned and flipped pages, there on December 10, 1917 was his name. It sang out to Shannon like a whirlwind with his sweeping capital M. She ran her fingers across his writing tenderly as if trying to reach out and touch him. Henrick reminded her they still had several hours before reaching Toul, and that they'd best be off. Shannon turned back to the statue and closed her eyes, *Dear Saint Joan, please lead me to him, lend me your courage.*

The rain had begun to turn the road to mud, and Henrick reined the horse to a fast pace to pull the wagon through it. By the time they reached the road north to Toul, the rain had stopped and the road hardened again. There was only an occasional truck on the road now, as it began to get dark. It would be almost half past five o'clock when they reached Toul and Shannon realized the paymaster's office would be closed for the night. She almost regretted going to Domremy. *No, it gives me hope. The office will be open, first thing in the morning, and there's nothing they can do tonight. Being there, standing where Matt stood, brings us close.*

It was dark as they pulled into Toul. The town was lit with lamps from the houses and men were walking about. Henrick asked one soldier where the nearest pension was located. "Down two blocks and to the right. Not sure there's room, but you might be able to get a bite to eat." There, halfway down the narrow street was a two-story cottage type house, with the sign 'Pension'. Shannon and Henrick were met by a stout-built woman with streaks of gray in her dark brown hair.

"Oh, come in Missy, you look half frozen." She took Shannon's wet coat and gloves and escorted her to a chair next to the fireplace in the parlor.

The boarders had already eaten, but she would bring a plate of meats and cheese and hot tea for them. Shannon explained why they were there and now in need of rooms for the night. "I'm sorry, miss, but I don't have any rooms available tonight, full up with army switchboard operators and clerks. I have been since headquarters moved here. None of the pensions in town have rooms, I'm afraid." Shannon nodded her head in understanding. *At least I'm dry and warm for the moment. A barn will have to do.* Henrick asked about a barn for shelter. "We have one out back, but let me see what I can do first." She disappeared into the hall for some time and they could hear her making telephone calls. She finally returned, "Well, I know the woman that runs the Army YWCA house for the operators and she has one bed Miss Shannon can use for tonight. Henrick, you can bunk here on the floor or in a chair if you like. At least it will be drier than the barn." She gave them the directions to the house and Henrick drove Shannon there, making sure she was settled before returning to the pension, and putting the horse in the barn.

It was late by the time Shannon arrived at the YWCA house. There were twelve signal core girls stationed at the house. Mrs. Hunt showed Shannon to Caitlyn and Margaret's room. Margaret was on leave for a few days, and Cait was on duty and would be back by ten. "If you just sleep on top, I'm sure Margo won't mind," she said pulling two blankets from the big chest for her to use. "I'll let Cait know you're here when she comes in. Bath is second door on the right of the hall." Shannon thanked her as she closed the door and went back downstairs. Shannon was grateful for the comfortable bed and warm blankets, and started to think about Matt and the payroll office, but was asleep before she knew it.

Shannon woke early, noticed Cait still sleeping, and made her way to the bath to change into the one skirt she brought and a clean blouse. Downstairs she found Mrs. Hunt and two other girls in the kitchen. "Good morning, did you sleep well?" Mrs. Hunt asked.

"Yes, very well, thank you."

"Mrs. Hunt tells us you're looking for your fiancé. What makes you think he is missing? I'm Betty, from Chicago," the tall blond said.

"I haven't heard from him, some four months now, and most of his platoon are already home. I just know he's lost. I can't explain it."

"And you're going to find him, when his unit could not?" asked Clair.

"I'm not sure they are even looking. And yes. I'm a trained archaeologist and it's my job to find lost things," Shannon said rather perturbed. *That was rather snooty of you. Shannon, behave like a lady.* "At least I'm going to try. I'm going over to the payroll office to see if I can get a lead on where he was last seen."

"That's a good idea. You tell them Mrs. Hunt said to help, if they want any more of my homemade muffins."

Shannon ate a hearty breakfast of real eggs and bacon, and the muffins were heavenly. Henrick arrived about nine and they departed. Mrs. Hunt offered to let Shannon stay two more days if needed, until Margo returned.

The payroll office was a part of a large building in the center of town. Shannon straightened her skirt and blouse and tried to make herself as presentable as possible. *Now remember to be friendly and smile, take interest in them and just maybe they will be willing to help.*

Henrick and Shannon entered the large building and spotted a sergeant working at a desk. "Can you tell me where the payroll office is located?"

Without looking up, in a matter of fact reply, the sergeant said, "First floor, sixth door on your left." The long hall was lined with doors on both sides, several with what looked like packing boxes sitting next to them. Finally, she came to a dark wood door with the name PAYROLL. *Should I knock, just walk in? this is it, the first real clue, we might find him today.* She rapped her knuckles firmly against the door. "Enter if you must," came a reply.

Surprised to see a civilian, yet a woman, the private squeaked out, "Can I help you, miss?"

"Yes, is this the payroll office that handles the 91st division, 361st regiment?" Shannon asked.

"We did miss, but the 91st as of last week, is paid out of the Soisson office. Why?" He was even more surprised that she was an American.

"I'm looking for a Matthew Keenan Taylor, and thought you could tell me where he was when he was last paid. Do you still have their records or were they transferred to Soisson?"

Sorry, miss, we can't give out information regarding troop movements."

"But the war's over, and no one seems to know where he is. You must have a record of when he was last paid."

"Yes, but troop movements are secure to prevent attacks."

Did he really just say that, doesn't he realize the war's over and no one is being attacked?

Henrick stepped up and in a rather fatherly authority voice, "Look son, we need to talk to your superior. Who's in charge of this office? "

"That would be Sergeant Larson."

"Get him," Henrick ordered. Henrick standing six feet with a large muscular build, rather intimidated the small lanky private. The young man hurried through the door behind him. Shannon could hear voices from the other side. She heard Matt's name a couple of times, then suddenly the door opened wide. Both the sergeant and Shannon stood totally astonished.

"Shay Shay? How in the world did you get here, and what's this about Matt?" Sergeant Larson asked.

"Lars? Is that really you?" Shannon couldn't believe her eyes.

Lars tried to hold his excitement, and gestured Shannon and Henrick through his office door and said, "That will be all, private."

Inside his office, Lars gave Shannon a big hug and kiss to her cheek, both thrilled to see each other. Shannon explained to Henrick, how sergeant Larson, Matthew and she were all at college together. Lars was an accounting major, which explained why army put him in the payroll office.

"What's this about Matt missing?"

Shannon took a seat and explained the situation, that no word had been received since September.

Lars stood and went to the door, opened it and barked out an order. "Private, get me the 91st 361st payroll files." While they waited Shannon filled him in on Andrew and her trip so far. After about thirty minutes, the private appeared with a box and set it on Lars's desk. "That's all for now," he said, and the private returned to his desk. Lars flipped through the fifty or so files until he pulled out a file marked T. He flipped through this until he came to a bundle with Matt's name. These were Matt's records, up through December. Lars flipped one page and then another and then back to the top page. "Well, according to these records, Oct 15, 1918 was the last time he signed for his pay."

"What about November and December?" Henrick asked, knowing payday is once a month.

"Nothing, he never showed to sign for it. We don't give men their full pay in cash. Most wanted it sent home and only take part for personal expenses."

"Does it say where he was when he got his last pay?" Shannon asked with a sense of urgency.

"Sure, the 91st payroll was out of Amiens, and couriers were dispatched to Somme. So according to this he received ten American dollars on October 20th from the Somme office."

"Anything after that?" Henrick asked.

Lars looked at his November and December paysheet. There were no signatures. "Nothing, he never claimed it."

"Can you tell where he was supposed to be?" Shannon asked

"Yeah, November's payroll was after the cease fire and the 91st was sent to Sedan. The 361st was in Montmédy, north of Sedan. Matt should have gotten his pay there. December was from my office here. I was on assignment to Paris, so I missed his regiment while they were here. I thought I just missed him because I was there, not because he was missing," Lars admitted.

"Okay, so we know he was in Somme on October 20th. And in my last letter from him, dated September he mentions crossing the Lys River," Shannon reviewed.

"The Lys is close to Somme, and the fighting there was heavy. One battalion was pinned down there fighting for almost three weeks. I'd say your starting point is Somme. "

"And if we wanted to find Matt's regiment and talk to his commanding officers, do you know where they are now?" Henrick suggested.

"Currently what's left of the 361st is in Avocourt. I just sent the transfer billet for their payroll to go to the Metz office."

Shannon was grateful they had an accurate starting point, but dismayed they still had no idea where Matt was.

"I think we should go to Avocourt and speak with his regiment commander. He can direct us to his platoon leader who probably has the latest info on his whereabouts," Henrick recommended.

"I agree, Avocourt will be on your way to Somme. I'd go with you, but I can't be spared. But if you need anything, call me at the Toul exchange – payroll office."

Lars would have liked to spend more time with Shannon but she was anxious to go to Avocourt, hoping Matt would be there. Lars convinced them to have lunch with him before leaving. He filled them in on his tour of duty as a payroll officer, that he didn't see much cash, and never gold. Most of it was just paperwork, and getting signatures. He had seen Matt in Chateau Thierry, over a year ago, and admitted he would check with a buddy he had at headquarters coroner's office, to make sure Matt and few other friends were not on the list. He showed Henrick the best open route to get to Avocourt, as some roads were so badly bombed, they no longer existed.

Henrick and Shannon were on their way by noon. It would take them a couple of days to get to Avocourt.

15

What Was She Doing?

It was now the first of February and travel to Avocourt was slow as the weather turned warmer and the snow became rain. The roads became deep with mud, making it hard for the horse to pull the wagon. On more than one occasion Henrick needed to find small logs to place under the wheels to get them out of the muddy ruts. Shannon wished they had taken the buggy, that it might have kept them drier. She pulled her poncho down around her legs and tight around her head trying to keep dry.

After they had made some distance that day and arrived in a town with a working pension, Henrick insisted they stop. "It's no good, sleeping outdoors with this rain. We have to have shelter, and who knows if we will find another pension before nightfall."

On the third day, at about four in the afternoon, they arrived at Avocourt and made their way to the Army headquarters. Shannon did not take time to change to a skirt or to dry clothes, but stepped into the office cold and wet. "Brrr!" she said shaking off the water from her poncho. "Hello," she then added.

The sergeant at the desk took one look and, immediately upon realizing she was an American, showed her to a small room with a fire going. Henrick had stayed with the wagon wanting to find food and shelter for them.

"What can I do for you, miss, other than a dry spot?"

"I appreciate this very much, I'm Shannon Baker, and I'm looking for the commander of the 361ˢᵗ Regiment or commander of its 2ⁿᵈ platoon."

"May I ask why?"

"I'm looking for my fiancé. Several of the 361st soldiers have returned home and others are waiting to return, but Matthew Taylor has not been seen. It was recommended he was possibly still with his regiment, since not everyone had been demobilized."

"I see, and you came all the way to France to find him. You couldn't wait for him to return home?"

"I haven't received a letter from him in over five months now. Matthew always writes."

The sergeant, a man in his mid-thirties, looked at the fire for a moment. "Miss, I hate to say it, but have you checked with the war office for men killed in action. We lost far too many good men fighting this war."

"Yes, and his name was not on the list and his folks have received no notice, thank God. I even checked all the hospitals in and around Paris upon arrival. He's simply missing. Something is preventing him from returning. And before you say it, no, he hasn't deserted."

"Well, then, Colonel Johnson is in charge of the 361st Regiment, and he has already departed for Metz, but part of the regiment is still here. I'm not sure it's the 2nd platoon or 3rd, but Lt. Colonel Miles is still here. Their barracks are out on the northside of town."

"That's good news finally; can you tell me how to get there? I have a friend with a wagon with me."

"Why don't you stay here until the rain lets up, and I'll have a private take you to the Lt. Colonel."

He could see she was eager to leave, "Miss, they're not going anywhere for a few days, and it won't do your young man any good if you catch pneumonia. Why don't I call your friend in and I'll get you a cup of hot tea. What's his name?"

"Henrick. He was out front when I left him, but he said something about finding lodging."

The sergeant disappeared for a short time, and Shannon moved closer to the fire in an attempt to dry her clothes. The sergeant returned with hot tea. "Your friend wasn't out front. Just wait here until he comes back," he said, then he returned to his desk. It was about thirty minutes later when Henrick came in and joined her. Henrick had found lodging for Shannon for the night at a small inn. He would sleep in a barn again. The sergeant came back with more tea and biscuits for Shannon and a large cup of coffee for Henrick.

"My assistant is due back shortly, and he will take you up to the barracks, to Miles. You can get a bit of real food at the mess hall while you're there. Miss, I'm afraid I checked the roster for Lt. Colonel Miles's platoon and there's no Matthew Taylor listed. But perhaps he went on with the others to Metz. Miles will know for sure." The sergeant didn't want to get Shannon hopes up but at the same time didn't want to discourage her.

The private arrived a few minutes later and when Shannon had finished her tea, they climbed into the wagon and he showed them the way. Henrick tried to go slow, so the mud wouldn't spray onto the men on the road, yet without getting stuck. The private pointed to a large wood structure that looked like it had been built in a hurry. Next to it was four other small structures, built in the same hurried fashion. The private led them to one of the smaller barracks and knocked before entering slowly. "Lady about to enter, make yourselves decent," he called. A few men scrambled to put on shirts, and the Lt. Colonel stood and met him at the door. "What do you mean, lady?"

Just then Shannon stepped through the door. "I'm sorry Lt. Colonel, but I'm in need of information that you have," she said smiling and reaching to shake his hand.

"You're not a nurse, or with the army. What's an American civilian doing here?" being as polite as he could, and trying to keep his annoyance from showing.

"I'm looking for Matthew Taylor with the 2nd platoon."

"Taylor, the music man? I'm sorry miss, but he's not here. This is the 3rd platoon; Taylor was with the 2nd. Regrettably, not too many of the 2nd survived the fighting in the Argonne Woods. Have you checked the hospitals?" *Why does everyone keep telling me to check the hospitals. He's not there.*

Henrick, spoke up, "We have been stopping as we've been travelling. We will check the one here as well. Is there anyone here that can tell us where they last saw Matt?"

The Lt. Colonel turned to the men sitting on their bunks, "Has anybody seen Matt, the music man, and if so, where was the last time?"

"The last time was when he played that old piano in Toul," one soldier called out.

"If you're quick, a courier for the 2nd was at the mess tent about a half hour ago. You might catch him before he returns. He might know," called out another.

Lt. Colonel Miles could see the spark in Shannon's eyes, "Come with me." He led them quickly over to the larger mess building and upon entering called out. "Anyone still here from the 2nd platoon?"

A man raised his hand, "Who wants to know?"

Lt. Colonel Miles nodded and left Shannon and Henrick where they stood. Shannon walked up to the young soldier and he stood just staring at her for a moment. "Oh, my God, Shannon Baker, Matt's girl. How on earth did you get here?"

Shannon was equally surprised he knew who she was. "Yes, you must know Matt, if you know me. You must know where he is?" she said urgently.

"I'm sorry miss, I wish I did know where he was. Come, sit." He nudged the soldier next to him to fetch some food and coffee. "I'm Mac Garcia. Matt spoke of you all the time, said goodnight to your picture every time we had a chance to sleep."

"Of course, Mac. Matt wrote about you and the others in your team. So, Matt's not here, when was the last time you saw him?" she said, trying to hold back the ache swelling in her chest and tears rising.

"Last I saw Matt, we were charging into the Argonne Woods. We'd been fighting for almost a week, gaining ground slowly. We were coming into a small clearing and the Germans were picking off men as they tried to pass through. Matt and I split up and went around the clearing from opposite sides, intending to meet up once we took out the snipers. That's when all hell broke loose. German artillery had locked onto our location and started lobbing mortars our way. The big kind, splintering trees all around us, sending men flying. Colonel Johnson ordered the entire regiment to move through the clearing and seize the German guns. We took the first guns, but lost a lot of men. As they retreated, we followed. We drove them back about six miles by the end of the second day. But by then I had completely lost track of Matt. Shannon I'm sorry to say but we lost a lot of men in the Argonne Forest and we didn't have time to go back and collect the wounded or dead left behind. The signal corps men are few and far between, for the number injured. Most men were helped by the local villagers. They will bury the dead and if they can, get the injured to the nearest hospital."

"Mac, I just feel in my heart he is not dead. I would know it. What was the last town you were in before heading into the woods and what direction did you go into woods from there?"

"Ah, it was a tiny village, Blain something?" Mac said scratching his head.

"There a Mount Blain not far from here," Henrick said.

"Montblain, that's it. No, Montblainville is it, Mount Blain Village," Mac said relieved. There was a small shop and inn there, not much else. Also, several small farms that were pretty much overrun by the Germans when they were there."

"Okay, that's where we will start. How far from here is it?" Shannon said confidently.

"It's not far, about twenty-five miles. Just north of the next town over. I'd go with you but I'm due back at Colonel Johnson's office tonight. I haven't been discharged yet." The private, who had gone for food, arrived with slices of ham, boiled potatoes, and cooked greens.

"Contact me at Colonel Johnson's office if you need help, currently we're at HQ in Metz. Shannon, I hope you find him. He's a good man," Mac said and rose, asking Henrick to see him to the door. He stopped and put his hand on his shoulder, "Look, Henrick, I didn't want to say anything in front of Shannon. But we lost a thousand men in those woods, and didn't have time to bury them. You need to check the local graveyards. If you're lucky, he will be there. But often locals buried men where they fell and marked the grave with a stone, with a name, if they had one. You may never find where he is buried. Matt was crazy about her, so I hope they are kindred spirits and he is still alive."

Henrick returned to the table and ate his meal in silence. Shannon hadn't realized how hungry she was and ate faster than normal. After a second cup of coffee, she was ready to leave. It was dusk, but the rain had let up. The road back to town was lit by a waxing moon.

Henrick left Shannon at the inn where he had left her things. An older French woman and her granddaughter met her and showed her to a small but clean room. There was no heat, but several down comforters covered the bed. As Shannon climbed into bed after washing up, she wanted to be positive that she would find Matt at the next town in a nearby local hospital. Yet in the pit of her stomach there was an uneasy nagging. *He wasn't with his regiment or platoon as he should have been, if he were alright. Why hasn't anyone seen him in months? Oh, dear God, show me where his is, show me he's alive.* The stress and weariness from concern overcame the coffee and she fell asleep before tears could fall.

She was woken in the morning with a soft knocking at her door. The young girl said her friend was here and breakfast was waiting.

Shannon quickly dressed, putting on clean warm socks for another day of wet muddy cold roads. After a good meal she and Henrick headed west to Varennes which led north to the Argonne woods. It was chilly out, but the road had dried making travel much faster. The linden trees, which once separated the farmer fields, stood like ghostly silhouettes, shattered and tortured with only stumps and broken limbs in the soft morning light. Shannon didn't like looking at them. *So much destruction, so many wounded bodies and for what? Greed?*

It took just an hour to reach the small town of Varennes. Henrick stopped by the church to rest the horse, "Miss Shannon, you stay here. I'll be right back." Shannon nodded and sat trying to warm herself in the little bit of sunlight that now streamed through the clouds. Henrick climbed down and walked around to the back of church to the graveyard. There, at the back, were the rows of what he hoped he wouldn't find. Newly placed white crosses. He slowly walked past each grave, all but two had names, but none were Taylor. The two markers without names, simply read 363rd Regmt. Again, Henrick was relieved; Matt was in the 361st. He returned to the wagon and climbed up to Shannon's breathless eyes. He shook his head and pursed his lips, and she began to breathe again. The town of Varennes was quiet. A few older men sat outside an old barn. Shannon had Henrick stop, "Pardon, are there any American soldiers in town?" They look puzzled. Henrick asked again in French.

"*Pas de blessés ici. Les Americains sont tous partis,*" one man answered.

"*Merci,*" Henrick replied, and headed the wagon north out of town. Even Shannon knew what '*partis*' meant; the Americans had left. Matt wasn't there.

It took them another thirty minutes to come to the little town of Montblainville. Here the forest surrounded the small town, giving it a bleak cold feeling. There were two small buildings and several small cottages. Henrick pulled up to the small shop with a light on. Its front window amazingly was still intact, though dirty. There was a little of everything in the window: a small chair with a few dishes, embroidered dish towel, a large wheel of cheese of some sort and a tin labeled bisques. But there in the corner on a small square of black cloth, it sat. Shannon didn't move as she stared at the shiny object.

"What is it, Shannon?" Henrick asked.

"The watch. I think that's Matt's watch, I don't know how I know, I just feel that it is." She said as she opened the shop door. She immediately went to the window and reached for the pocket watch. Meanwhile a young girl about the age of fourteen came forward. Henrick greeted her, "*Bonjour.*"

Shannon had turned over the watch and found Matt's name and the chain she had given him with the locket still attached. Shannon spun around and looked at the girl. "Where did you get this? Where's the man this belongs too?" she asked in a rather alarming voice. The young girl shrank back afraid.

Shannon realized what she had done and began to try to coax the young girl back to a friendly stance.

Henrick, once again in a soft voice, asked where she got the watch. But the girl was now staring at Shannon.

Henrick asked, "What is it? *qu'est-ce c'est, quel est ton nom?*"

The young girl turned to him and answered in broken English, "I am Maria. She is Shay Shay, no?"

Shannon heart leapt and skipped a beat when she heard her say Shay Shay. Much more gently and quietly Shannon asked again. "Yes, Maria, I am Shay Shay. Where is the man that belongs to this?"

Maria took Shannon's hand and led her to the back of the small store to a couple of chairs and motioned her to sit. Maria sat and in French explained and Henrick translated. "Several months ago, before the big battle a very handsome soldier came to her town and gave her and her little sister chocolate and some dried beef. Her parents had been killed by the Germans and he protected her from some of the more, how do you say, aggressive men. The morning before they left to fight, he came and asked me to hold this for him. He did not want to lose it in the fighting. It was most important to him. He showed me your picture and called you Shay Shay. He said he would be back soon or when the war ended. But he has not come back. I only put it in the window this morning. I am sorry miss, but my sister and I need the money to buy food and it has been three months since the war ended. I am afraid he had died in the battle in the woods."

Shannon clutched the watch in her hand and held it to her breast, as if listening to it tick. Tears began to fill her eyes. *Matty would have never given this up unless he thought he wasn't coming back. It would be like him to give it to help someone else. But he can't be gone, he is coming back. He has to be close by somewhere.* Shannon wiped the tear from her cheek. "*Merci*, Maria, for keeping this safe for him. I would like to buy it from you."

"No, no. It belongs to you. You are his fiancée. "

"Maria, I have to ask, did you look for him in the forest where the fighting took place? Did the men from your village bury the dead?" Henrick quietly asked in French.

"*Non, monsieur.* I am afraid to go into the woods, I don't want to see the dead. The men from our village found many dead soldiers. There is a graveyard out by the north end of town with many markers and names. But I did not know his name, so I don't know if he is there. When the field was full of graves, they just buried the rest where they found them." Maria spoke softly, in respect of the dead but wasn't stunned by the thought of so many dead. Henrick again translated what she said for Shannon, who stood looking at her small thin frame. *For one so young she has seen so much death, has taken on far too many responsibilities.* "His name is Matthew, Matthew Taylor. And I'm glad you are his friend. But now you must let me help you, as you helped him." Shannon reached into her coat pocket and took out her small purse and pulled out several francs and placed them in Maria's hand. "You use these to buy food and warm clothes for you and your sister. You stay safe and grow up as Matt would want you to." Maria smiled and curtsied, as her little sister about six years old came running out from the back room. "*Merci, merci.*"

Shannon and Henrick returned to the wagon and climbed up to the seat. Henrick gave Jacques a tap with the reins, as Shannon stared down the empty road. They were headed for the field of graves.

Just a mile out of town stood a small clearing surrounded by pines and linden trees. These were still standing as if guarding the rows of graves marked by large stones painted white with last names printed on them. Some had dog tags around them, others with only the number of the regiment. Henrick pulled up and stopped, Shannon once again just stared at the field. *Why am I here, what good is it going to do? Why have I come to France if this is going to be how it ends? Alone in a cold empty field without hope. There's no future if Matt's gone. I don't want to look, I can't!*

Henrick jumped down, startling Shannon out of her thoughts. He came around to help her down. She started to reach for his hand and then suddenly drew her hand back. "I can't! Why are we here?"

"It's alright. You don't have to come. Just give me a few minutes and then I will take you back to Paris."

Henrick turned to enter the field of graves. "Wait Henrick. I'm sorry. If Matt is here, I need to know for his mother's sake."

Together they slowly moved among the rows of white stones. Silently reading each name, silently grieving for each mother's loss. Towards the end of the last row Henrick stopped and turned to Shannon. His lips read "Taylor."

Shannon froze looking at the white stone with the name Taylor in bold black letters. There were no dog tags attached to it, but the grave lay silent like the others. The spring grasses had not covered the cold dark earth, the rains had not settled the slight mound of soil. Shannon sank to her knees at the base of the grave. The name Taylor blaring in her mind. *Taylor, Taylor, I so wanted to be Mrs. Matthew Taylor. Matty Matty, I feel so empty. Why don't you comfort me?*

Henrick was speaking to her but she didn't hear him. Henrick repeated his words louder. "Are you sure?' came floating into her consciousness." *Am I sure? No, I'm not sure, I don't want to be sure. How can,*

I be sure? "How can I be sure?" she said out loud, breaking her mesmerism. She looked at the stone again. *It only says Taylor. There are lots of Taylors in this world, in the Army. It was Thomas Taylor in Paris, not Matt. It's not Matt. Please, God, don't let it be Matty.* Shannon stood again wiping the tears from her eyes to look at the grave more clearly. She looked at the grave next to this one, it read Parker, it was longer than Taylor's grave. "Henrick, how tall would you say this soldier is?"

Henrick paced off the length of the grave. One, two, three, four, five, five and half. "Not quite six feet."

"Would you bury a six foot two inch man in only a six foot grave?"

"No. It wouldn't be proper."

"This can't be Matt then. He's six foot one. This has to be another Taylor." Shannon looked around not at the graves but at the woods. Something now told her he was out there. *Somewhere out there.*

16

A Walk in the Woods

Shannon once again began to breathe, regaining her assurance Matt was still alive. But where? Now, where to continue to search? Shannon was emotionally drained from the extreme ups and down she had been put through in the last day. High hopes that this would be the day she would find him, were dashed by his absence. Tracking down his regiment had brought the next lead, and the next. But now all leads led to the woods. The Argonne Forest was about forty miles long. One person could not cover all forty miles.

Henrick and Shannon moved on to the next small town, about four miles north, to Apremont. They found several small buildings still standing for the most part. A woman was sweeping her front stoop and smiled as the wagon approached. Henrick sensed Shannon needed to stop and rest and asked if the woman might spare a cup of tea in exchange for a bit of flour. Flour was in very short demand and she agreed quickly. The cottage was warm and clean. The furnishings were slightly worn but comfortable. Mme. Bodeaux made the tea Henrick gave her and set out crackers and duck *paté* she had made. She did not speak any English, therefore spoke only to Henrick. Shannon sat quietly by the fire and warmed her hands and gathered her bewildered thoughts.

Henrick asked if M. Bodeaux had been there during the fighting or if she had just returned.

"*Non, j'étais là,*" she said.

"You were there!" This sparked his interest, and he asked where the fighting had occurred, specifically where the Americans fought.

"*Au nord d'ici,*" she went on to say. When the Germans realized the Americans were coming, they retreated to beyond the clearing about a mile from there. When the Americans arrived, they swarmed over the little town. But the real fighting began at the north end of town in the forest. It went on for days and wounded men were brought back to her barn. Many died, but some survived, and after the fighting, the local men took them to Avocourt to be treated. Those who did not, they buried in the clearing where they fought.

It began to rain again and Mme. Bodeaux invited them to stay the night. "No need to get soaked. The closest inn is back in Montblainville." Shannon now joined them and listened, not knowing what was said. *Henrick can tell me once we're alone. I wish I could telephone Mac and tell him what's happening. Maybe he could give us another direction to look.* Shannon asked if mail service had resumed, as she wanted to send a letter to Matt's mother. There was no mail in Apremont, but she would take it to Montblainville to mail it. Mme. Bodeaux showed Shannon to a small room off the parlor. It had a small bed and writing desk. The fireplace backed onto this room helping to keep it warm. Henrick took the wagon to the barn and settled Jacques with some hay he found.

It rained heavily through the night. Mme. Bodeaux was content to have company. She even invited Henrick to sleep in the parlor on the settee where it was warm and dry. It was a little short and his feet hung out onto the coffee table. It continued to rain the next day, and so Henrick helped their host with fixing a few things around the house that he could do: a squeaky door hinge, cleaning the ashes from the fireplace and bringing in dry wood for the stove and fireplace from the barn. He took time during moments when the rain stopped to chop more firewood. Shannon collected the eggs from the chicken coop behind the barn and helped with the dishes. In the afternoon, as it continued to rain, they all sat together with a piece of paper, making a map of the Argonne Forest, identifying where the clearing was and the surrounding small towns. Some small farms and houses were scattered throughout the forest. All Shannon could think to do, was to go on foot and begin to search the woods, going from house to house asking if anyone had seen Matt. Since the fighting had occurred a mile north of Apremont and beyond, there were only about fifteen miles of forest to search. Henrick knew in his heart, even this would be impossible. But he was willing to go search the two miles from Apremont to the clearing for now. Mme. Bodeaux told them about her neighbors on the eastside of the wood and another acquaintance on the west.

They spent one more day at the cottage, until the skies finally cleared. They ate a hearty breakfast, and loaded up a backpack that Henrick would carry and a bedroll with their ponchos, for when the rain would come again. They headed down the road, in the direction Mme. Bodeaux pointed toward where the soldiers had gone. Shannon had wound Matt's watch and tucked it in her blouse pocket where she could feel it ticking against her heart. *As long as his watch and my heart are beating together, things will be alright. I'll be led to him.*

Shannon, as they walked along, now began to practice what she had been taught in archaeological excavations, noticing every little twig out of place, every small patch of color, every footprint still visible in the dirt. About a mile out from the cottage she noticed the underbrush of the trees on both sides of the road were broken where men had walked through it. She spotted a worn path from the road into the woods and followed it. It was dark and cold under the boughs of the conifers. Henrick followed, making note of the trees and direction they were going so not to get lost. The path then appeared to split into two other paths that forked off. Shannon stopped not sure how to proceed.

"Henrick, I think we're following a path one group took, but then have spread out to surround the meadow. I think it's best to split up and make our way towards the clearing."

"I don't think splitting up is a good idea. One can get lost in these woods. We need to stay in calling distance," Henrick warned.

I know he's right, but we can't cover as much ground. "Okay, we don't need all three of us lost. I'll go sixty feet ahead of you and then we will together make our way towards the edges of the forest." She pulled out the map they had made and pointed to a neighbor's place to the east. "When we reach here, we can stop and ask."

"Make it fifty feet and I agree. I'm a good whistler. As long as you can hear my whistle, we will be good. Agreed?"

Shannon smiled and nodded her head. Henrick watched her walk through the underbrush until he couldn't see her, then called, "Fifty feet."

"That's good, can you hear me?" Shannon yelled back, "I hear you, start whistling."

Henrick began to whistle a gentle German folk tune as they turned and made their way to the east.

His distant whistling was comforting to her as she now felt alone. Now and then she spotted a piece of fabric from a soldier's coat, a bent small branch on the lower part of the tree where a soldier had leaned. "Stop," she yelled, "Broken trees." An artillery shell had come crashing through hitting a tree and snapping off its top, which now lay in her path. She pulled back some of the branches, checking for any life or signs below them. Nothing. She made her way around and called out "Nothing, let's keep going." After about thirty minutes they reached a small house. They knocked, but no one seemed to be around. Shannon opened the door. The house was empty, no signs of soldiers or people. *Now which way? Do we keep going east or turn back and check more forest to the north?* Shannon stood observing the small clearing by the house, where a field was once planted. Beyond it were more trees, but Shannon didn't see any broken and battered trees from artillery fire. She turned back towards where they came, and in that direction she could see many more splintered and broken tree tops.

They regrouped and paced off another twenty feet from where Shannon had arrived. Then she paced off another fifty feet and she and Henrick began again. Each pass took them about thirty minutes to reach the road, and they found nothing of significance. Henrick realized this was going to take them days, and began to quicken their pace, reaching the end of the grid in about twenty minutes. After two hours, they had only covered about four hundred feet and it was still another two thousand feet to the clearing where the heavy fighting took place. It would take them another seven hours. Henrick suggested they take the road to the clearing and make their way back toward Apremont. Most likely if they were to find anything, it would be closer to the fighting. Shannon hated to skip any of the woods, but knew that Henrick was right.

Via the road, it only took them twenty minutes to walk to the clearing. Once again laying out before them were broken trees burnt and splintered all around the clearing, that was now filled with white stones marking the graves of the fallen.

Shannon sat down on the cold ground, not sure she could go forward and read all the names once again. She listened to Matt's watch ticking against her own heart, that was now racing from fear. Henrick set the pack down next to her and walked over to the far side of the clearing and began to make his way through the first row of names. Shannon sat watching him, unable to move. *So many fallen lives. Matty are you here? I don't want to read all the names, just lead me to you if you're here. Please don't be here.* As Henrick finished the first row, Shannon pulled herself up and stood listening. But all she could hear was the wind in the trees and a magpie calling off in the distance. Matt's voice was not to be heard. She walked down to the third row of names and slowly made her way past each marker: Standish, Wallace, Schwartz, Aruguste… She finished the one row and began the next. Finally, after an hour they finished all ten rows. There were American, English, French and German soldiers buried in the clearing. Shannon didn't hold her breath this time but numbly searched the names. But no Taylor.

It was getting late, and the rains threatened to begin. Mme. Bodeaux had insisted they return and spend the night again. Shannon wanted to make her way back through the woods. It was only just over a mile and at least she would feel better after searching that one brief mile. She spotted a point that seemed to be where the troops entered the field from the woods and took it. They could now see lots of bullet holes in the trees along the front edge of the field. At one point she thought she could see the blood stains from where a soldier had probably died. Henrick took her hand and kept her moving forward, the signs of the battle becoming less apparent. After a few minutes they came across two white stones, marking the dead. One read Quincy Bowler and the other 361st. Shannon's heart sank again and Henrick put his arm around her, moving her forward until they finally reached the edge of Apremont.

That night at Mme. Bodeaux's, Shannon realized combing the woods was a waste of time. The locals had already done it and buried the dead. Yet something kept nagging at her, telling her she was close. *But to what end?* She had a very restless night. Seeing the rows of white stones in her sleep, she woke and lay in the dark, sobbing into her pillow, trying not to awaken the others, her feeling of helplessness overtaking her ability to hold back the tears.

The next morning Shannon felt the need to move on. They had already taken too much of Mme. Bodeaux's food and time. If no one in Apremont had seen Matt, perhaps someone on the other side of the clearing had.

Mme. Bodeaux told them the town of Fleville was the closest and men from there had helped with the search. There was also a small inn there where they could spend the night. Henrick packed up the wagon and made Jacques ready. There was a heavy mist in the air, but the skies showed promise of clearing and no rain. The road had dried somewhat from the heavy rain the few days before, so Jacques was able to move quickly. Shannon wanted them to move slowly so she could scan the woods on the left side of the road, where they had not searched. But the trees were even thicker on that side and she couldn't see very far into the dark thickets. Fleville was normally only an hour from Apremont, but the fighting on the right side of the clearly had been much more intense. The Germans had dug in with large artillery tearing up the road from the movement of the heavy guns and from all the troop's trucks that moved in after that battle. Battered trees had fallen across the road after the heavy rain, one so large Henrick had to unhook Jacques and use him to pull it off to the side.

They reached Fleville about noon. It was about the size of Montblainville. The buildings wore the scars of heavy fighting. Bullet holes riddled every front and most of the windows were boarded up, the glass having been shot out. Yet, there were people moving about. The general store seemed to be functioning and the inn sign read *"Ouvert"*. Henrick pulled up in front of the inn, wanting to get settled first, and figuring the owner would be the best source of information about the war and the people to contact.

M. Le Bon was indeed a source of who and where. He had been part of the men that cared for the wounded and buried the dead. Fleville, like the other towns, had a graveyard for the fallen. Again, Shannon didn't want to search through the white stones, there were already too many haunting her dreams.

"No, no, Miss. There is no need to go to the graves, the major has a list. He sent it with the injured when the army came and took them. Shannon was relieved. *I think I can handle a list, as long as Matt's name isn't on it.* "What name you looking for?" He said in his best English.

"Taylor, Matthew Taylor with the 361st regiment." Henrick quickly answered.

"Taylor, I no remember. You go see Louis, at the store, he has the list. He is our major. But first I show you to your rooms."

Shannon's room was on the back side of the inn and still had two window panes of clear glass letting in the blue sky. Henricks was next to hers. Shannon took a moment to refresh herself and change to her clean skirt and blouse, wanting to make a good impression to gain his help. Henrick had done the same and now they walked down the road to the store.

"*Bonjour*," Henrick said as they walked in.

"*Bonjour*," said a middle-aged man with thinning dark hair. "*Puis-je vous aider?*"

"*Oui*, do you speak English?" Henrick asked for Shannon's benefit.

"Oh, yes! How may I help?"

Shannon stepped forward. "We're looking for an American soldier. We know he fought in the battle in the woods, but he has not been seen since. I'm hoping you have seen him and might know where he went."

The man looked at her with sad turned down lips.

"Madam, we have seen many American soldiers, all those who fought and survived have long gone. Those we found wounded have been transferred to army hospitals. The others, I regret to say, we have buried in the field next to town."

"We understand you have a list of names for the men you have buried. I need to know that Matthew Taylor is not on that list," Shannon said bravely.

"*Oui*, Taylor?" he held his chin thinking for a moment. *Yes, I think there is a Taylor on the list; I just hope it's not her Taylor.* He reached into a drawer behind him and pulled out the list. There were about a hundred names all in alphabetical order. He flipped the paper over to the end of the list. "Strong, Switzer, Talbot, Tyler, Unger. No miss, thankfully for you there is no Taylor, only a Tyler."

Shannon's smile came back to her face. But Henrick had to ask. "What is Tyler's first name, there's no chance they miss spelled Taylor?" Shannon's eyes widened and she held her breath.

"It says Clarence Tyler here. We tried to be careful, knowing loved ones would want to know."

"No, I'm sure you were careful. And yes, they will need to know. The army needs to know," Shannon replied.

"We sent the list to the headquarters in Toul, once it was complete. Though you never know nowadays if the mail is getting through."

Shannon now asked about who helped the wounded and if it would be possible to talk to them.

He told them M. and Mme. Le Bon, the innkeepers, took them in until the army arrived. "They would know, especially Mme. Le Bon. She mothered them like a hen." Henrick thanked him and then purchased a few supplies: crackers, cheese and chicory coffee. Then they returned to the inn to find Mme. Le Bon.

Mme. Le Bon was in the kitchen cooking up a rabbit stew for the midday meal and was about to set the main table. Henrick went to attend to the horse and put him in the barn out back. Meanwhile Shannon, offered to help set the table, figuring they could chat during the meal. There was one other guest, a gentleman with the railroad, who had come to survey the damage to the rails in the area. Mme. Le Bon didn't usually eat with guests, but upon hearing Shannon's request, took a seat next to her after serving her guests. Mme. Le Bon had been a nurse in her younger days, but when she married, they move to Fleville and opened the inn. She said some of the men were in pretty bad shape and she did all she could but still lost too many. "All I could do was hold their hand so they didn't die alone. Then we buried them with their fallen comrades. Others were lucky and we kept them alive until the army could send ambulances and take them back to Vocourt or Paris. She admitted she didn't recall anyone by the name of Matthew. There was a Martin, but no Matthew. She did say, "There was one young soldier so badly hurt from an artillery blast that had sent wood flying, it hit him in the head. He didn't remember his name or what happened."

"What did he look like?" came out urgently from Shannon's lips.

"He was handsome at one time, I think. Dark wavy hair, blue eyes that had such a blank expression."

Shannon pulled out her picture of Matt and showed it to her. "Is this him?"

"No, I'm afraid not, missy. My young soldier had a fuller face, and baby cheeks. I wish I had found your young man. I assume he wasn't on the list. Chin up, miss, you will find him. He's probably in Paris right now waiting to go home. Now finish that stew before Henrick finishes it for you."

"I hope you're right. I wish there was a way to get a telephone call to our friend in Paris. He would have heard if Matt was there."

"I'm afraid the telephone lines have not reached us out here. The closest telephone is in Vocourt, two hours from here."

Shannon finished her stew; it was some of the most flavorful stew she had ever eaten. She returned to her room to rest and try to figure out where to go from there. She picked up Matt's watch and held it. *What have I missed? I have found this. I must be able to find Matt.... Go back. Go back to Paris?*

Light rain began to fall that afternoon and with no place to really look, Shannon and Henrick stayed at the inn. Henrick asked M. Le Bon about the surrounding area and farms. "Is it possible Matt could be at a farm or house near the woods convalescing?"

M. Le Bon didn't think so. Most of the farmers and people that live within a ten-mile radius came to Fleville for supplies. "If he was with one of them, they would have said something to get him help."

Henrick showed him the map Mme. Bodeaux had helped make of the local farms and towns, wanting to make sure she didn't miss any. "No, those are the places I'm aware of on the east side where all the fighting took place. I don't know of any places on the west side close enough to have been involved or where a wounded soldier could have made it, other than the one west of here. I'd know if he was there."

Henrick wiped his hand down his face and nodded his head, now uncertain as what to do. M. Le Bon put his hand on his shoulder, "I think it's time you take her back to your friend in Paris, so she can go home where she will have family when his loss truly hits her."

Henrick nodded his head in agreement and then went and stood by the window watching the rain come down.

17

The Way Back

They had come to a dead end, and now Henrick needed to convince Shannon to return to Paris. That evening he went to her and told her they should return to Paris. There was nothing more here to do. Her head was telling her the same thing, but her heart didn't want to leave. *Matty had been here. He didn't just disappear. Someone along the line has missed something. Maybe Mme. Le Bon was right, maybe he is in Paris, lying in a hospital bed and his name has been misspelled or his file misplaced.* She couldn't think of anything else that could be done there, other than search forty miles of the Argonne Woods. But in her mind, she knew wandering through the woods would not find him. Deep down she knew it would be the same as now. Yet in her heart she felt she had to keep looking, he was with someone somewhere, being helped. She also knew her mother must be worried by now, not having heard from her. The little nagging thought kept coming – go back.

Henrick made ready the wagon with the needed supplies to get them to Paris. It was two hundred and twenty kilometers to the Duvaneau estate and would take them three days, if the rains held off. It was about nine in the morning when the air warmed and they departed Fleville. Shannon was dressed in her skirt and a warm sweater as Henrick helped her up into the wagon. He placed a blanket over her lap to keep her warm against the cool air. She rode in silence as the sound of Jacques's hooves clipped along the road. Her heart was filled with remorse as she held onto Matt's watch. *I promised Aunt Kate I wouldn't come home without him.*

As they passed the clearing filled with graves again, she put the watch in her pocket next to her heart and leaned into Henrick. He instantly put his arm around her, pulling her close to him. He slowed the wagon as they passed but did not stop. There was no need, the answer wasn't there. They continued on about a half mile. Shannon was now staring off to the woods on her left, only trees, thickets, and darkness registering. There was a small narrow road that led off into the woods. It didn't look like it had been traveled in years. But there was something about it. *Did we look down there? Was this on Mme. Bodeaux's map? Is there a farm down that way? Shannon, you're grasping at straws, you know in a mile we will be in Apremont and then there will be nothing preventing us from going on to Paris.* Suddenly she could feel her heart thumping with each tick of the watch and she knew she just had to take one more look. "Henrick, stop, I know it's silly, but we didn't look down that road back there, and I just have to make sure there is nothing there."

Henrick sighed, "We'll have to walk, I can't turn the wagon around here. I can go down to Apremont and turn around."

"No, I'll be right back. I just need to see where it goes."

"It could go for miles, I'll come with you."

Henrick pulled the wagon to the side and tied Jacques to a tree. Then he grabbed the ponchos from the wagon and they went back to the road. There were no rut marks made from wagons and the leaves on the trees weren't broken, indicating no one had been through there in quite a while. They walked on, and the road made a right turn and continued into the dark woods. The sunlight filtered through the trees like stars in a night sky. After another ten minutes, Henrick suggested they turn back. The road didn't seem to go anywhere other than back toward Fleville. "Just a few more minutes, to where the sun is coming through ahead."

They reached the spot where the trees thinned and the sun provided light. Off to the right Shannon thought she could see a building. The road didn't turn towards it, but she could see the grass under the trees had been trampled at one point. She picked up her skirt and made her way over the underbrush and through the trees, until she reached a small clearing where a small house and a barn in need of a lot of repairs stood. The place seemed deserted. Henrick stepped out of the trees, and called, "*Quelqu'un ici?* Anyone here?" There was no answer. Shannon walked slowly around towards the front of the barn. There sat an old man bent over a log trying to saw it. Henrick called out again, "*Bonjour.*"

The man looked up, startled to see strangers. "*Qui êtes vous? Je n'ai rien pour vous.*"

Shannon asked what he said and Henrick told her. He wants to know who we are and said he has nothing for us here.

Hearing Shannon's American voice, the old man looked her up and down through squinted eyes with curiosity. Still, he shooed them away, "*Aller, aller.*"

Shannon turned to leave, but then stopped. "I'm looking for a soldier." Henrick put his hand on her arm, "Shay Shay, he doesn't understand you." Henrick didn't know why he called her Shay Shay. He had never done it before, but for some reason it just came out this time.

Suddenly the old man waved his hand, "*Attendez! ... Tu t'appelles* Shay Shay?"

They both stopped and turned back, Shannon went to him. "*Oui,* Shay Shay." The old man rubbed his chin and mumbled something about *cherie.* He rose slowly and motioned for them to follow him. He shuffled his feet and moved slowly towards the house. Shannon's heart raced, uncertain if it was out of hope or fear. As they came around the corner she saw why. A young man sitting in a chair had his back to her. His head was bandaged and his leg stretched out bound with a wood splint, but she knew at once. Her heart leapt. *Matty... Oh, thank you, God.*

The old man grabbed her arm and stopped Shannon, and said, "*Sa blessure n'est pas seulement à la jambe, mais aussi à la tête. Il ne se souvient pas de grand-chose.*"

Shannon looked at Henrick and he explained, "He has a bad injury to his head and left eye, he can't see well and doesn't recall much." Henrick knew her next question and asked if he recalled Shay Shay.

Non. Je pensais qu'il disait Cherie, quand il marmonna Shay Shay, quand je l'ai trouve pour la premiere fois, mais il n'a rien dit depuis."

Shannon didn't need translating; she understood the first word *non* – no. He didn't remember her. She approached slowly as not to startle him. The bandage came across Matt's left eye. He looked pale and haggard. Shannon tried not to look startled. The old man came close and said "*Matt, ton amie, Shay Shay.*" The name rang in his head and he hunted to recall.

Shannon just stood not sure what to do, giving Matt time to say something. The old man recognized the pursed lip expression, knowing Matt was struggling to remember. He then nudged Shannon to him. "*Dit quelque chose.*" Henrick whispered, "Say something."

Shannon moved in front so Matt could look at her, "Hello, Matt, I've been looking for you. Your mother says it's time to come home."

Matt's good eye squinted trying to make Shannon out clearly. But the voice now sent his mind racing. *Shay Shay, that voice. Shay Shay....Shannon?* "Is that you, Shannon? Shannon Baker?"

Shannon dropped to his side on her knees, grabbing his arm. "Yes, Matt, it's me. I've come to take you home."

Shannon and the memories of them growing up came flooding into his mind. He shook his head slightly, remembering a little girl. Then looking at the dim face beside him, the image of Shannon standing on the steps at Berkeley came clearly. He trembled for an instant, and then reached up to touch her face. *I can't see her that well, but I would know that voice anywhere.* "Shay Shay, thank God, someone has come. I should have known it would be you."

She reached forward and kissed him on the cheek, sending a warmth through him, stirring the emotions that had been hidden along with the memories. Matt pulled her to him and buried his head in her hair and wept softly, adding "Oh, Shay Shay, I'd almost given up hope ever getting home. I don't even know where I am. "

"Shhh. I know where you are now and that's all that matters. We're together." Shannon could feel the exhaustion in his body, or lack of strength as he let go and leaned back in the chair, closing his eyes. Finally, he smiled, "How did you ever find me all by yourself?"

Shannon calmly explained it was his letters that led her, plus help from Lars in Toul. She didn't go into detail about what they found along the way, just that Henrick had been with her. Matt reached a hand out to Henrick, once he was introduced and thanked him for keeping Shannon safe.

The old man had pulled up a chair and sat watching, concerned Matt was overusing the strength he had. While Shannon and Matt spoke softly the old man told Henrick, he needs to rest. He has only been well for this past week. The fever and pain have had him down for months. Shannon looked at Henrick for a translation. "Matt needs to rest. He's only been up for a few days. "

Matt, upon hearing the old man's concern took Shannon's hand, "Shay Shay, this is Albert, I owe him my life. He worries too much." Matt didn't let on that he needed to lie down, but Albert recognized the signs and insisted. Henrick and Shannon helped Matt up and into the house to lay down. "Shay Shay, don't you go away. Just give me a little bit to rest."

"Don't you worry. I'm not leaving. I'll be right here."

Albert and Matthew seemed to have a system to getting Matt in and out of bed, therefore Shannon and Henrick stepped out and let them proceed. Shannon could hear Matt groan and then finally settle. Albert came out and gestured to them to sit. Shannon said "*Merci, merci.* I can't say how grateful I am to you for taking care of him," and Henrick translated. The old man smiled and nodded. Seeing they still had questions on how Matt got there and why he was still there, he began with his full name, Albert Swartlich, he was half German, with a French mother and German father. Because of his last name and the war, he found it difficult for people to accept him, so he kept to himself and preferred living alone in the woods.

He explained he could hear all the artillery explosions and knew the war had come to his woods. But the fighting seemed to be on the other side, near the towns. He was grateful it didn't reach into his land. Once the woods became silent again, he ventured out to see what was left of the towns. Apremont and Fleville seemed unscathed. It had been some time since he had gone for supplies, so he was on his way out the old road toward Fleville, when he came across Matthew sitting up against a tree. At first, he thought he was dead, but when he touched him, he groaned. With difficulty, using his handcart which he often used to transport wood, he managed to get him back to the house. Matt had a deep gash to his head by his left eye and a broken leg. Albert wanted to go for help but he was afraid Matt would die before he got back. It was three weeks before Matt was to the point that he felt he could leave for the four-hour trip to town and back. By that time the army had come and gone, taking the wounded, and the dead had been buried. He sent a letter to the Army headquarters in Toul, but never heard a word from them. "It was in German and I fear they ignored it." He just kept taking care of him thinking the army would show up one day. Or Matt would get well enough to walk out on his own.

He continued saying, Matt's injury to his head had damaged the one eye severely and his memory. He could only recall his first year in the army at Fort Kearney and a guy name Eugene that was killed.

Shannon asked Albert how he knew her name, if Matt couldn't remember. He explained the first night there, his fever was raging and he keep mumbling Shay Shay. He thought he was trying to say *Cherie Cherie*. It wasn't until Henrick said "Shay Shay" that he realized Matt was saying a name."

Henrick asked Albert if he thought Matt would be strong enough to get him to Vocourt where there was a hospital. He nodded his head, but said he didn't have a wagon, adding that the pain in Matt's leg still hurt him and the jarring from the road might make it a very painful ride. But taken slowly a little each day and resting in between to keep his strength up, he could do it.

Shannon and Henrick made a plan, to let Matt rest up for another day and then they would move him to Apremont, to Mme. Bodeaux for a day's rest, then on to Montblainville, then finally onto Vocourt. Albert agreed to let Shannon stay in the house, but the barn would have to do for Henrick.

Shannon was eager to get word to Mac who could get word to Charles and then on to Kate and the others. They decided Henrick would leave shortly and go onto Apremont to make arrangements, then all the way to Vocourt to wire Mac and the others. He would contact the hospital there and see if he could get one of the doctors to come back with him. It would take him the rest of the day to go to Apremont and then onto Avocourt by night fall. He would be back midday on the morrow. He would come back with the wagon, padded with a mattress, if possible, to make the journey more comfortable for Matt. Henrick finished cutting the firewood for Albert and then headed back to the wagon and on to Apremont.

Matt woke after several hours and was glad Shannon wasn't a dream but was really there. She told them of their plan, and he was sure he could make it all the way without stopping. "Well, we will see. The road was pretty bad on our way here and if it rains, we won't be going anywhere," Shannon declared.

She insisted Matt stay in bed until Henrick returned. Shannon took over caring for Matt, giving Albert a needed break. Little by little things were coming back to Matt's memory. He now realized how long he had been gone and how worried his mother and Shannon must have been not knowing where he was. *I should have insisted Albert go for help, no matter what condition I was in.* He wanted to know about

Andrew and if he was alright. He was relieved to hear he was back at the ranch. Shannon didn't tell him about how terribly sick he had been. She told him Kevin was back in the States as well, and Mac had helped them and was in Metz at headquarters. That Lars was safe in Toul awaiting early discharge since he was needed back in the States at the accounting house. She didn't tell him about Clay's broken his leg and that things were hectic back at the ranch. Matt would only feel he needed to get back and help. Albert continued to assist when needed, while Shannon showed her gratitude by doing the cooking and making sure Albert rested as well. Even though there was a language barrier, hand gestures and a few words made things work. That evening Shannon sat and held Matt's hand, until he fell asleep. It seemed comforting to both of them.

Just after noon on the next day, Henrick returned with the wagon. He needed to clear the path through the woods so the wagon could get through. There was just enough room between two trees for a straight path. Albert showed him where his cutting tools were and Henrick went to work clearing the underbrush. It took him until just after three o'clock to clear the fifty-foot path. But now he had the wagon up to the house.

Henrick had made arrangements with Mme. Bodeaux, and she had given him some laudanum to help ease the pain. Matt said he would be fine, but Shannon insisted he take a good dose. With Henrick and Shannon's help they got him to the wagon easily. Getting into the wagon was painful, as Henrick lifted him from the shoulders while Shannon raised the broken leg. Matt gave out a resounding "Aah!", and was relieved to be settled onto the mattress. Shannon wanted Albert to come so people would know how he had helped, but he refused. "I'm alright here. I'm eighty years old and I'll finish my years here, thank you," he said in French.

Shannon gave him as many francs as he would accept and said he would have Mme. Bodeaux look in on him. Matt called him to his side, *"Merci, mon ami! Tu m'as sauvé la vie,"* and shook his hand and patted the old man's face with gentle affection.

Shannon climbed up with Matt and held him in her arms. Henrick tapped the reins and Jacques lurched forward. It was a bumpy ride the fifty feet through the forest. Matt gritted his teeth and realized he probably should have taken a little more of the pain killer. Albert stood and watched, offering a final wave as the wagon made the turn onto the road and then was gone.

It only took forty minutes to reach Mme. Bodeaux's place and she had everything waiting. Matt was tired by the time he was settled into a comfortable bed. Mme. Bodeaux gave him something to help him sleep. Meanwhile Shannon and Henrick ate a light supper and made ready for the next day. Henrick had not spoken with Mac directly but was only able to leave a message, that they had found Matt and would bring him to Vocourt. They planned to leave in the afternoon, giving Matt more time to rest. But Matt woke about eight o'clock and was anxious to reach a telephone where they could let people know he was alright. They told him Mac knew, but he was more concerned about his mother. By ten o'clock they were back on the road headed to Vocourt. This time Matt took an extra dose of painkiller to help get him all the way. They had only been traveling an hour and a half, when the wagon was becoming very uncomfortable for Matt with every jolt. By the time they reached Montblainville, he seemed weak and weary again. *That's it! We're going to stop here. Matt can't take four hours of this.*

On the way to Apremont, Shannon and Henrich had not spent the night in Montblainville. Therefore, she was uncertain about that night's accommodations, but upon arriving in town, was pleased to see a cottage inn with rooms. The innkeeper and Henrick were able to get Matt settled in bed, and Matt didn't disagree when Shannon offered another spoonful of laudanum. It didn't take long before he was sleeping. Shannon was pleased with her room, but didn't use it much, finding it difficult to leave Matt's side.

The innkeeper let Henrick use the telephone to contact the Vo-court hospital to ask if an ambulance could be sent. They called back that morning, to say an Army doctor would be arriving later that day but the ambulance had been sent to Metz. Shannon was thrilled that Henrick's message had gotten through to Mac, figuring he was the one who was dispatching an Army doctor to Vocourt. The laudanum she had was running low and she was very concerned about Matt making the two and half hour trip to Vocourt.

It was raining in the morning, and Shannon was relieved Matt would have extra time to rest before the longest part of the trip. There was no way they could attempt to travel with muddy roads. Shannon sat with Matt and watched the rain. "Shay Shay, we've done plenty of trail rides in the rain. I saw ponchos in the wagon, we should go ahead and leave."

"Matt, the wagon can't make it through the muddy roads. Are you in pain? Is there something worse that you need a doctor now?" she asked, alarmed.

"No, I'm fine. I just need to get word to mother. I know she's worried."

"I'm sure Mac has gotten word to her through Charles. You can't afford to get wet and cold. You're weak enough. I'm sure the rain will stop by tomorrow and we will be on our way."

Matt sighed, he wanted to rub his eyes, but every time he started, he felt the bandages, making him more frustrated. Shannon took his hand and kissed it. She started to let go. "Don't let go, just hold my hands. When I'm frustrated, I just want to rub my eyes hoping to clear my sight and the frustration away. I'm so grateful you're here."

Matt closed his eyes as they sat quietly holding hands. Shannon worried about his eyes and if they were permanently damaged. When Matt wasn't tired, his good eye seemed to focus clearly, only giving him trouble when his strength was drained. She also worried that his leg, not being properly set and now healing, would leave him with a limp. She didn't care, she would love him no matter what.

By noon the rain had stopped and the sun began to shine, warming Matt's room. "Shannon, let's go in about an hour, I'm rested. The roads will dry with this sun." She reluctantly agreed but only if Henrick thought the wagon could make it. Before Henrick had gotten out to the barn to hook up the wagon there was a knock at the inn's door. Shannon was there and opened it. To her surprise it was Mac, standing with two soldiers. "Did you call for help and a taxi?" he said, smiling from ear to ear. Shannon reached out and hugged him. They were there to get Matt back to Vocourt by army truck. Shannon filled him in on his condition on the way to his room.

"Well, look at you, resting on your laurels, are you?"

"Mac, is that you?" Matt said reaching out a hand.

Mac took his hand, "Yeah, it's me. The doc requested a truck for an injured soldier near Vocourt and I knew it had to be you. Headquarters received Shannon's call and I was never so relieved. I thought we lost you. You're a lucky man, Matt. You have a very determined lady that didn't stop until she found you."

"I won't disagree with that."

"Well, you don't belong to her yet. Right now, you belong to the army once again and we've come to give you a ride to where you belong. A proper hospital, so we can get you back on your feet." Shannon left Mac and the orderlies to get Matt ready for travel, and went to find Henrick.

Henrick saw the army truck pull up and knew they had come for Matt. Now he needed to know what Shannon wanted him to do. Make his way to Vocourt and stay with her, or go on home to Lesigny and let Charles know everything. It was about two hundred and ten kilometers to Charles and she knew Charles could use his help. She would stay with Matt until his release, and Mac and the army would help get him home. Still, she wasn't sure the army would take care of her until then. She asked Henrick to come to Vocourt, and help her negotiate finding a room close to the hospital. He agreed and said he would be there by dusk and proceeded to hitch up Jacques and be on his way.

Mac and the army orderlies got Matt settled on a cot in the truck and Shannon climbed up next to him. Mac was driving and tapped on the window giving a thumbs up. The truck rumbled alive as the motor turned over, and they began to make their way toward Vocourt. Shannon wasn't sure the truck was any smoother than the wagon, but it did move faster and didn't seem to get stuck in the mud. It took about two hours to get to the hospital, and the orderly gave Matt another dose of pain killer about halfway there.

Upon arrival, as promised an Army doctor was there to meet them and get Matt admitted. Mac took Shannon to the waiting area and sat with her, while the doctors examined Matt. It seemed like an eternity. Mac went and fetched sandwiches and coffee as they continued to wait. One of the admission nurses came and asked Shannon questions about Matt's family contacts and any allergies they should be aware of. Finally, after another hour the doctor came down and found Shannon and Mac. He reported he had given Matt a thorough examination. His right eye seemed to be unaffected, but his left eye had been creased by a piece of wood according to Matt. "Whoever cleaned that wound saved his eye. He did a damn good job of removing the wood splinters that could have caused major infection and the loss of his eye and life. Right now, it appears the eye is damaged so that he will never clearly see with it, but he can determine light and dark and can see larger objects, though they're blurry. Over time he will adjust to the handicap, but it shouldn't prevent him from doing what he wants to do."

Shannon was glad to hear that Matt would be able to do what he wanted. "What about his leg?"

The doctor confirmed the upper bone had been broken and was mending. But, it was mending slightly out of alignment. Therefore, they had to, in a sense, rebreak it, to straighten the bone and mending tissues. This was not an easy process for Matt, being as weak as he was. But it was necessary, if he wanted to walk properly.

"We have wrapped the leg and it's now in a cast to keep it straight. He's settled in a bed with a leg sling so he can't twist or move it. In time it will heal and be much straighter than it was going to be. Right now, our concern is his very weak condition and his susceptibility to infection and viruses. His body just doesn't have the strength to fight at this point. We will keep him in isolation for now, until he gets stronger. At this point he needs good food and plenty of rest. "

Shannon wanted to sit with him and help in any way she could. She informed the doctor she would not be leaving without him. He was reluctant to have her with him, because of the epidemic spreading though the country. But seeing her determination, agreed, insisting she wash her hands thoroughly before going to him, and recommend wearing a mask in public. "There is nothing you can do for now. We gave him a sedative, so he will sleep until morning. But you can see him for a moment. Then you need to go."

"Show me where to wash."

Mac needed to get the truck and men back to Metz and would notify his regiment of his status. Shannon asked him to contact Lars as well. He gave Shannon a big hug and they promised to meet up in the States once everyone was back. A nurse showed Shannon where to wash and then led her to Matt's room.

The color in Matt's face had faded, and his arms appeared to be thinner now. *Is it just because of the clean white gown and sheets, or was getting him here that hard on him?* She pulled up the chair from the corner and sat opposite his good eye. *Well, my love, we have found our way back to each other once again. I think it's time we make it permanent, no more parting.* Shannon reached up and stroked his hair ever so slightly, hoping not to wake him. His fingers twitched and she took his hand. "I'm here, Matt. It's going to be alright. We're going to go home together, I promise," she whispered ever so softly. She was sitting quietly holding his hand watching his breathing as he slept, when the doctor came in to check on him again. "That's enough for now. You can come back in the morning. I assure you he will sleep through the night." Shannon didn't want to move, but the doctor put his hand on her shoulder. "It won't do him any good, if he sees you worried and worn out. Go get something to eat and some sleep."

Shannon rose, gave Matt a gentle kiss to the forehead and reluctantly closed the door to Matt's room behind her. Shannon wasn't sure where she would go. Henrick had not arrived as of yet, so she made her way back to the front desk. The same nurse who had asked for Matt's information was still there. Shannon asked her if she knew of an inn or room that she could rent that was close to the hospital. She smiled, "There's a hotel two blocks from here and a boarding house on the other side of town, but they do not speak English. Your best bet will be the hotel." Shannon thanked her and went back to the waiting room to think about what needed to be done. She needed to place a call to Charles and send a telegram to her mother and Aunt Kate. Shannon went back to the desk and asked if it would be possible to use the phone for a call to Lesigny near Paris. The nurse shook her head, "Sorry, miss, I can only use it for hospital business. But there is a telephone at the hotel that guests can use."

Shannon grinned, "I understand. I'm Shannon Baker, Matt's fiancée. You will be seeing a lot of me, until he can leave. I guess I'd best go find a room. I'll be back first thing." Shannon suddenly realized she didn't have her purse or anything with her. It was all with Henrick. She was about to return to the waiting room to wait for him to arrive, when he came walking through the door. The moment she saw him, tears began to roll down her face. He reached out and hugged her. "What's wrong? Is Matt, okay?"

"He's okay. They're very concerned, but he's okay for now. I just didn't realize how tiring and stressful today has been." She regained her composure and they walked back to the wagon as Shannon explained things. They made their way to the hotel and obtained two rooms. The hotel clerk spoke English very well, to Shannon's relief. Once their rooms were assigned, she asked about placing a telephone call. The clerk showed her to a booth and helped her place the call, speaking French to the operator.

"It will take a moment, just stay on the line. You will hear a click and she will say '*poursuivre*,' meaning go ahead. Your party should be on the other end."

"*Merci.*" Shannon held the earpiece close and waited. Finally, she heard the click and the operator.

"Charles, Charles, can you hear me? It's Shannon."

Charles was overjoyed to hear her voice. Shannon explained that she had found Matt, and where she and Henrick were. She answered more of his questions and then discussed when they would come to the estate.

"Matt will be better off here than in a Paris hospital. The influenza is out of control there," Charles said.

Shannon said she would send Henrick back in a day or two. It was uncertain when Matt would be able to travel. He understood but insisted she call him regularly regarding his and her situation.

Shannon now needed to send a telegram. The hotel clerk informed her the town operator had been killed and the lines were down. The only way to send a message from Vocourt was from the Army supply station on the south end of town. Shannon was tired and didn't really want to go out again, but it was urgent she did. She went to Henrick's room and asked if he would take her in the wagon. Since he had not unhitched Jacques, he easily agreed.

Shannon walked into the army office and found a sergeant at the desk. "Can I help you miss?"

"Yes, I was told I can send a telegram from here."

"Telegram, well, is it for army business?"

Shannon thought for a moment, *Army business? Of course, it's army business. The army should have been the one to know where Matt was. Now I'm just doing their job of notifying his mother.* "Yes, a matter of fact it is. I need to send a telegram to a soldier's mother, that he is no longer missing." He gave her a questioning look, and once again she explained trying to be as pleasant as she could muster in her exhausted state. He handed her a piece of paper and she wrote out a rather lengthy message. He looked at it. "Miss, this is too long to send." Seeing her bewilderment, he took a pencil and scratched out several words. "Will this do?" and handed it back to her.

"Yes, that will do for now. Thank you for the help".

He had taken out all the details about Matt's condition and left in 'will take time to recover.' Then added 'will be in touch.' He then asked her where she could be reached in case of a return response. Then he took it to the next room, where suddenly, she could hear the tapping of the telegraph. Now she could go back to the hotel to her room and collapse.

~~

Back in Oak Ridge, the telegraph operator wrote out the message and seeing it was about Matt immediately sent a boy to the ranch with it. Lupe, hearing the knock at the door, opened it and took the message from the young man. "What is it, Lupe?" Kate called from the parlor where she and Lalani were having morning tea. Lalani immediately stood, seeing the telegram in her hand. "A telegram for Mrs. Baker," Lupe answered, handing it to Lalani and then disappeared to the kitchen.

Lalani came and sat down by Kate and opened it. "It's from Shannon. Matt's been found." Katherine let out a short breath as Lalani read the message.

Matt injured now in Vocourt hospital STOP Will take time to recover STOP Will be in touch

Katherine grabbed Lalani and broke into sobs. It had been five long months of not knowing if Matt was alive and holding back fears. Now he was safe and all her hidden emotions came flooding out. Lalani just held her and let her get it all out. She too had tears in her eyes, not only for word about Matt but also to know Shannon was safe.

Clay, using a cane, came in from the study having heard the sobs. His face went pale seeing Katherine sobbing. Lalani caught his panicky look, "Matt's been found alive," she said quickly. Clay's face relaxed and he took a deep breath as he made his way to Kate. Kate stood, drying her eyes, "Our boy's going to be okay. Shay Shay has found him." Clay took her in his arms and held her for a long moment, then sat rereading the telegram. Now they had so many unanswered questions. How was Matt injured, where had he been all this time? When would he be coming home? Lalani assured them and herself Shannon would write with all the details, soon, but it would take time for the mail to arrive. They would just have to wait.

"Wait. That's all I've been doing for months." Clay blurted out. "We can send telegrams to this Vocourt hospital and ask what happened. I'll have Miguel bring the car around."

"I'm coming as well." Lalani stood, "I need to know Shannon is okay. She must be as emotionally exhausted as Kate. I need to ask if I should join her."

Clay understood her need to be with Shannon, but he still wasn't fully mobile and Andrew still needed care. Kate went up to Andrew's room and quietly let him know Shannon had found Matt, and he was going to be okay.

Andrew's strength had come back slowly. But the scars of war and what he had seen wore heavily on his mind. He was having a difficult time around crowds and noise and never talked about the war. Now with Matt found, there would be one less nightmare.

Clay, Katherine and Lalani arrived at the telegraph office, and began to dispatch messages.

Where was he STOP How is he hurt

Katherine wanted to know if he could be moved to Charles for care. Lalani sent her own message.

Are you alright STOP Do you want me to come STOP Father on his way to Oak Ridge STOP Do I wait for him or come now

By the time they finished the poor operator had sent three messages to Vocourt France. They all sat down to wait. When the operator finished sending the last message he informed them, he would not get a response until tomorrow at the soonest. The messages had to be sent to the New York international exchange and from there to Paris, France and then to this Vocourt. If Shannon got the messages and responded right away, it would still take another day for the return response. Most likely it would be a few days before he heard back. He assured them as soon as he did, he would send the messages to the ranch. Clay knew he was right and escorted the ladies back to the car. They stopped at Kalua'ana to let Morgan and Amanda know the good news on the way home.

~~

Shannon and Henrick returned to the hotel and stopped in the dining room for a small supper. Shannon was almost too tired to eat, but encouraged Henrick to eat a hearty meal, as he would have a long journey tomorrow. There was no need for him to stay now that she knew where to go and the desk clerk could help as needed.

"Charles needs you at the estate to repair the grapevines. There's nothing you can do here but wait. I'll be fine. I cannot thank you enough for being with me. I couldn't have done it without you."

Henrick smiling, patted her hand and kept on eating.

Shannon finally got to her room and collapsed on the bed. She was exhausted, her emotions wanted to burst and sob, but she didn't have the energy. She pulled off her clothes and crawled in under the covers. She grabbed her knees and sat up just rocking, *I have Matt back. That's all that matters. I don't know what comes next, but it doesn't matter. Everyone knows Matt and I are together again, that's all that matters. So, what's the matter, what are you afraid of Shannon Baker?*

She laid down and reached for Matt's watch and held it. Before she could answer her last question, she was asleep.

She was woken by a knock at her door. "Shannon, it's Henrick." She rose and grabbed a shirt and pants and put them on quickly. "Henrick, is everything alright?"

"Everything is fine. No word from the hospital, I'm sure Matt's fine. But I wanted to make sure you didn't need anything before I left."

Shannon assured him she would be fine and walked him out to the wagon. "*Merci beaucoups,* Henrick." She gave him a kiss to the cheek and hugged him. "We will see you at Charles' before we leave. Safe travels. Wire that you got home safely". She stood and watched him pull away and down the road. Now she was truly on her own. The lonely feeling only lasted a moment when her thought turned to Matt. She ran and cleaned up and made her way to the hospital.

18

Return to Home

Upon arrival at the hospital, Shannon washed her hands and made her way to Matt's room. "Wow, missy, where do you think you're going?" This was a different nurse on duty on Matt's floor.

"I'm Shannon Baker, Matt Taylor's fiancée. I washed my hands and his doctor said I could see him." *Granted that was last night.*

Doris Campbell's eyes widened as she looked Shannon up and down. "I hear you came all the way from California to find him, and you did."

"Yes, and I'm not going back without him. I'm here as long as he is, so I guess we will be seeing a lot of each other. And you are?"

Doris looked at her again, noticing she was clean and her skirt did look like it was of some quality, though rumpled. "I'm Doris Campbell, head nurse of the intensive care wing. Matt is in pretty bad shape, Miss Baker. You can't be chatting away at him wearing him out."

"Definitely not. I just want to sit with him so he knows he's not alone. I can help you in any way you see fit to use my help. Can I go see him now?"

Doris had intentionally been delaying Shannon, in order to give Doctor Franklin, the chance to finish dressing Matt's head wound. "Doctor Franklin is in with him now. You will need to wait downstairs until he's done. I'll ring the station downstairs when he is."

Shannon bit her lower lip, and gave a sigh, knowing she would have to wait. She returned downstairs and took a seat near the admissions desk. It was now about ten o'clock. She sat fidgeting when a private from the army office came in with telegrams. He handed them to the nurse on duty and disappeared. Shannon assumed this was a normal routine.

"Are you Shannon Baker?" the nurse asked.

"Yes. Can I go up and see Matt now?"

"I don't know about visiting yet, but there are three telegrams here, addressed to you. "

Shannon jumped up and took the telegrams and sat back down. The first was from Uncle Clay wanting to know what happened and how he was injured. The second was from Aunt Katherine wanting to know when he could be moved to Charles' estate and then back to the States. The third was from her mother, wanting to know how she was and if she and father should come help. She suddenly did not feel alone at all. She thought about her mother's offer to come help. *It would be nice to have her here. Aunt Kate did need my help when we went to get Andrew. If father is on his way, would he be better help here or to Morgan?*

Shannon was shaken from her thoughts when the nurse repeated, "You may go up now," for the second time. Shannon stuffed the telegrams into her skirt pocket and hurried up the stairs, waving to Doris as she passed by. Doctor Franklin was waiting for her. "He has improved slightly from yesterday's ordeal. He is still in serious danger and his body needs time to recuperate. Don't you go worrying him or making plans. If you want to help, you can help him eat, saving my nurses the time. Best to keep your visit for now to thirty minutes."

"Thirty minutes?" she protested.

"For now, but you can come, this afternoon and again this evening. Let's do three times a day for now. But only thirty minutes, he needs rest." And then he opened the door for her to pass.

Matt was resting with his eyes closed. Shannon didn't know if he was sleeping. She moved the chair close to the bed and took his hand.

Matt slowly opened his good eye and gave a half smile. "You're back!" he whispered.

"Of course," she said and kissed him on the forehead.

"I'd take a good kiss to the lips, but I'm a little too tired at the moment."

"There will be plenty of time for that when we get home. For now, you need to rest and eat."

Shannon pulled out the telegrams and waved them. "They all know you're alright. And sent love."

"And mother's not concerned?"

"She wants to know what happened, but don't you worry. I'll let her know. The doctor feels your leg is going to heal just fine and your eyes are clearing."

"Just fine, but I thought he was trying to kill me all over again yesterday when he yanked it straight. As for my eyes, the one's working better, don't tell her about the other. She'll just worry."

"All right. Now, you just stop talking and rest. I just want to sit here and hold your big beautiful hand."

"You always did have a thing for hands."

"Shhh..." Shannon took the glass of water and Matt nodded his head. She held the straw so he could drink, then he closed his eyes as he relaxed again. It wasn't long before he was asleep.

After about forty minutes Shannon left and walked down to the telegraph office. She sent a reply to Aunt Katherine, writing he had a broken leg and one eye was damaged. They would have to wait to see the results of the treatment. She explained it would take time, possibly a month before he was able to go to Charles' estate. Once Kate's telegram was sent, she sat and thought about what to tell her mother. At last she wrote,

"Come if you can STOP Father stay with Clay STOP I am fine for now"

Shannon reviewed it, then gave it to the private to send.

"If your mother's anything like mine, she will be here before you want her to be," he teased.

Shannon smiled. *I wish she was here now, to keep my mind from worrying. It will take her at least two weeks if she leaves today, what with the train and the ship.* Shannon paid the private and made her way back to the inn. She found M. Maison at the desk and asked where she might buy some clothes. "The general store might have a shirt but that's about it. My wife would be happy to do laundry for you." About an hour later, Mme. Maison knocked on Shannon's door. She didn't speak English very well but enough to get by and understand the guest's needs. Shannon now was in need of more appropriate clothing. One skirt was not going to be enough. Mme. Maison's daughter was about Shannon's height and build and had an extra dress she could use, until she could purchase something or get her things sent from Charles.

The rains had stopped and the sun was finally out, enticing Shannon to do some exploring of the little town. Vocourt was much bigger than the other towns surrounding it. There was a café and a general store, where she managed to purchase toiletries and writing paper, but they didn't have clothing. At about two o'clock she returned to be with Matt, just quietly holding his hand. In the evening she returned to help feed him some vegetable beef soup, mostly potatoes and beef broth.

Doris stopped Shannon on her way out, "I assume you're staying at the inn? May I walk with you? I live just around the corner."

Doris told Shannon when the doctor made rounds in the morning and when the nurses attended to the patient's needs. That half past ten o'clock was the best time for her to visit. Matt would be ready by then. That two o'clock is good and six o'clock if she wanted to help with his meal, then adding if she wanted to stay for an hour in the afternoon and read to him, she would allow it. As long as he continued to improve.

For the next week Shannon visited Matthew three times a day. In the evening he often fell asleep and she just sat watching him until the night nurse chased her home. Matt was slowly improving. Shannon wrote to Aunt Katherine keeping her appraised of Matt's progress, being more specific in her letters than in a telegram. She also wrote to Grace, Millie, and Murry just to fill her hours between visits. After about a week, a trunk arrived at the hotel for her. Charles had sent her things, the clothes and books she had left at his place. She was more than delighted to have them. She often sat and had tea with Mme. Maison, hoping to improve her French and Mme. Maison's English.

After eight days, Matt seemed to be awake more and wanting to talk and be entertained. His right eye was stronger and seeing was easier. Since he was seeing better, Shannon brought him a surprise.

"What is it?" he eagerly asked as she handed him the small box.

"Well, open it and see."

Matt opened the box and there sat his watch on a scrap of velvet. He picked it up, quite surprised. "How on earth, is the girl here? How did Marie find me?"

"Well, I actually found her." Shannon explained how it came to her and how it kept her going through the worst of it. "Now I don't want you lying here, watching the hours pass by. But when it gets a little rough, take a look at it to keep you going. We will be home before you know it."

He pulled her to his side and with his hand on her neck reached up kissed her squarely on the lips. "I've been wanting to do that for a very, very long time."

Just then Doctor Franklin came in, catching the reciprocal kisses. "Ah um! I think it best if you hold off on exchanging germs. Miss Baker, you're still out in public where more and more cases of influenza are showing up. Matt's doing well. We don't want any backsliding."

Shannon blushed a bright red, and let go of Matt. "That's a handsome time piece you have there. Best you keep it for him, Miss Baker. On occasion we do get a few pick-pockets through at night."

Matt handed the watch back to Shannon and nodded.

~~

Several more days went by, and each day Matt seemed to be getting stronger. Shannon was allowed to stay for an hour or more on each visit, and they played cribbage or checkers when Matt was up to it. Shannon, now seeing Matt much stronger, began to make plans to move him to Charles'. Some of the trains were beginning to run between Paris and Toul, with a stop in Vocourt. She questioned the doctor about moving him, but Franklin felt the jarring ride to Lesigny would be unwise. "His leg is still mending, and jarring it won't help."

The wound to Matt's left eye had healed to the point the bandage could be removed. He would have a small scar just below his temple. His vision was still blurry, but without the bandage he had a wider range of vision. Matt hoped glasses would correct the problem, but for now nothing more could be done. As for his leg, the prognosis was good. They began to get him up and standing, without much pain.

"If you keep this up, I might just let you use a wheelchair and go outside. The weather is warming. The blasted winter is just about over," Doris said.

Things were looking up. Then towards the end of the second week, both Matt and Shannon received a big surprise. Shannon sat softly reading aloud *My Ántonia* by Willa Cather Shannon had bought in New York just before she sailed. Suddenly there was a knock on the door. "*Entrer,*'" Shannon said.

"Well, look at you speaking French", then to Matt, "And you sitting up and looking so spry."

"Mother! Oh, my goodness," Shannon jumped up, knocking her chair over as she reached to hug Lalani. "Why didn't you tell me you were coming?"

"Really, Shay Shay. I needed to tell you I was coming?"

"You're right. I knew you would come. You probably were already on your way when I sent the telegram to come. You should have let me know and I would have met you at the station."

"Well, I wasn't sure when that would be. I've travelled so much over my lifetime, it's not like I can't do it on my own. I knew you needed to be here."

Lalani walked over to Matt and gave him a gentle hug. "Your folks send their love and want you home. I've come to help make that happen, sooner than later."

They sat and talked for a while, Lalani sharing her trip and how things were back at the ranch. "Your father should be there by now helping Clay and Morgan. Andrew is only able to help for a short time, before he's tired."

Doris arrived, "Visiting time has come to an end for now. We need to get him up and washed."

Shannon gave him a kiss before grabbing her mother's arm and leaving. "I'll be back in time to say *bonne nuit*."

Shannon was so glad to have her mother with her. They settled in at the pension, sharing breakfast in the morning, and reconnecting for lunch. Lalani sent telegrams keeping Kate informed of Matt's progress. In the evenings Lalani and Shannon would stroll through town and talk about what life might look like once they returned. Lalani shared her first year of marriage and their first trip to Hawaii, how wonderful her father was. She didn't say anything about her miscarriage, only how life has challenges and it's how we deal with them that shapes our lives. Lalani was very proud of Shannon for handling this challenge so wisely.

A few days after Lalani arrived, Matt's commander, Lt. Colonel Johnson, from the 361st came to see him, as he was on his way to Paris. "Well, son, I'm glad to see you made it. I hear you have one heck of a determined fiancée."

Matt smiled, "Now I just need to make her my wife."

"First, you need to get well enough to get out of here and out of the army. These papers will take care of the latter, you'll have to do the work on the former." Johnson handed Matt his discharge papers and said once he was well enough to travel, they would put him on ship for home, no need to be part of the demobilization plan. Matt shook his hand in gratitude and gave him a final salute. Shannon was thrilled to hear he was officially out of the army.

~~

With Matt's good progress, Shannon and her mother made plans to get Matty home. Lalani was in contact with Charles about transporting Matt to his place. They could use the train she'd come on to get him from Vocourt to Paris, but how to get him the twenty miles south to Lesigny?

One morning, midway of the third week Matt had been there, Shannon came as usual for her morning visit. Madge at the admission desk was wearing a mask, and stopped Shannon. "You must wear a mask. We've had an outbreak of influenza in one of the wards."

Shannon grabbed the mask Madge held out, and tied it around her face, as she hurried up the stairs. Doris and another nurse, wearing masks and rubber gloves, were rushing here and there with bottles of antiseptic cleaners. "Shannon, I don't think it's a good idea to be here now. So far Matt hasn't been exposed."

"But he's expecting me. If I don't show up, he will worry."

"Okay, go wash your hands, arms, and face; then grab a pair of gloves from the cart, before going in. Don't touch him! You can only stay for a few minutes. "I'm afraid this wing will be off limits shortly."

"Off limits. It's that bad?"

Doris could hear the fear rising in Shannon's voice. "We'll move him if we can, but it spreads quickly and hits hard, not giving us much chance to do anything."

Shannon went in to see Matt trying to stay calm. "What's going on out there? Why are you wearing a mask? I hear all kinds of running and the smell of ammonia," Matt asked.

"Just a few emergencies, and it must be cleaning day," she replied, ignoring his question about her mask.

Matt knew Shannon was hiding something, he knew her so well. "Shay Shay, what is it? What's going on?"

"Matt, it's nothing to do with you. And before you ask, Mother and I are just fine."

"Then why the mask and gloves?"

"Just a precaution."

Suddenly Matt began to put things together. "It's the flu. It's here in the hospital. Shannon, there's nothing to worry about. Kevin and Andrew got it and the doctors got them through it."

"You're right! But I'd like to get you away from here. Mother and Charles have been making arrangements to get you to his estate. You will have plenty of fresh air and care there. Do you think you're up to the trip?"

Again, Matt could almost hear the pleading in her voice. "Sure, I can make it. If I could get this darn cast off, it would be easy. I'm ready to go home. I just need a ship to get us there. Shay Shay, stop worrying. It's going to be okay. I'm fine." Matt so much wanted to reach out and hug her to reassure her, even if he had doubts himself.

Shannon stayed for a few more minutes, talking about how nice it was at Charles' estate. Then Doris popped her head in saying it was time to go. Shannon blew Matty a kiss and went to find Doctor Franklin. He was in the supply room with another nurse, counting aspirin. Upon seeing her, he stepped out. "Miss Baker, you shouldn't be here. We're trying to ward off an epidemic."

"I understand. But if I can arrange to move Matt from here to an estate south of Paris, with the help he needs, would you release him?"

Franklin thought for a moment. "Depends on the transportation. No more horse and wagon, that would cause a setback to his leg's healing."

"What about the train and then a twenty-mile car ride?"

"That would be acceptable. A van because of his cast would be better. He will need a strong man to help him bathe and other things."

"I can arrange for that. How long do you think it will be before his cast can come off and he can sail home?"

"Shannon, he will be in that cast for at least several weeks. You will need a private state room where he can lie down for the trip. He could probably go home in a month, maybe a week less. The cast could be removed back in the States. Do you have those kinds of connections?"

"I think so, but let me get him to Lesigny first."

"Well, if we can keep him healthy until you can make arrangements, he's a lucky man and I'll release him." He then returned to the supply room.

Shannon made her way back to the pension and asked her mother to contact Charles. By the next morning, Charles had reserved a compartment on the train from Toul to Paris, and was in the process of getting a vehicle for bringing them to the estate. The only problem was the train from Toul to Paris only ran twice a week and it was another two days before it would arrive in Vocourt headed to Paris. Shannon informed Doris that arrangements were made and asked if the hospital ambulance could get him to the station. She didn't think that would be a problem.

Matt had been moved to a new isolation ward, along with two other patients. This was a small room with four beds on the ground floor, furthest from the quarantine ward he had been in. The nurse was doing her best to care for the men. But the moans from the one patient haunted Matt, reminding him of the moans from wounded and dying soldiers. The other man was a civilian, injured when his truck rolled over. They were able to keep him sedated, while Matt lay there in anguish, trying to keep his mind on Shannon and his return home, and not the sights of war or the pandemic infecting Shannon or Lalani.

For the next two days, Matt's ward was off limits to any outside visitors, including Shannon. Sensing Shannon's anxieties, Madge at the desk tried to reassure her it was for the best. If he was to leave on Friday, for now he was fine. Madge agreed to relay messages back and forth for them, that included only a cordial I love you. By Thursday afternoon, they gave Matt something to help him sleep, his angst rising from all the disturbing noises around him.

On Friday morning, to Shannon's surprise, Henrick arrived, having caught the train in Paris. The train went on to Toul and then would return to Avocourt, in several hours, on its way back to Paris. The pension desk clerk also had a brief message for Shannon. It was from Doris at the hospital.

'Don't come to the hospital. We will get Matt to the train. Best of luck. – Doris.'

Lalani took Shannon and Henrick to brunch knowing it was going to be a long day. They ordered a box lunch for Matt for later. At about noon, the sun had come out and the early April air was refreshing. Henrick arranged for Shannon and Lalani's trunks to be sent to the station. The walk to the station was only a half mile, and they arrived just before the train was due. Shannon stood on the platform looking in the direction of the hospital for the ambulance bringing Matt. But the road was quiet, only a woman carrying laundry from the river.

The train came charging into the station with a loud shrill scream of its whistle and slowed to a stop, letting out a blast of steam. Lalani held onto the tickets for the compartment and Henrick made sure the trunks were on board and pulled out the compartment bed for Matt. The train only had a fifteen-minute stop in Avocourt. Shannon became nervous. Matt had not arrived and the train was due to leave in ten minutes. She paced the platform, stopping the conductor twice to let him know a patient from the hospital was coming. He nodded his head the first time and grimaced the second time saying, "I hope it arrives within the next five minutes. We have a schedule to keep."

Shannon pulled out Matt's pocket watch looking at the time. It was three minutes before time to depart. The conductor had called 'All Aboard' once already. Henrick now stood waiting with Shannon.

"Where is he, should I go find him?" she questioned.

Henrick took her arm, "No, getting him up and moved takes time. Once the conductor sees the ambulance they will wait."

She turned back to the train; her mother was standing on the train step with the conductor.

"There," Henrick said. Turning to the conductor, "He's here. Can you help?"

The ambulance pulled up to the platform. An orderly jumped out and came around as Henrick opened the door. Matt sat in a wheelchair with his leg out straight. "Get me out of here, I'm not missing that train." Henrick and the orderly lifted Matt up as he put his arms around their shoulders. The conductor grabbed the chair as they hurried to the steps where Lalani waited. Shannon patiently stood out of the way until Matt was lifted up into the train, then climbed aboard. The conductor suddenly realized the chair would not fit and left it on the platform. The conductor called, "Last Call All Aboard," and grabbed the loading step as he climbed aboard. The train's large wheels squealed and slowly began to turn. The conductor was just about to close up the landing when the orderly came rushing past and jumped to the platform managing to land on his feet.

Henrick and the orderly had just gotten Matt settled when the train lurched forward. Now they were all on board, headed for Paris, and Shannon could be at Matt's side. Matt felt a little weary, but didn't show it. He was more grateful to be on his way home. Lalani had taken a moment upon arriving to wipe the compartment with disinfectant, its scent now lingering.

Matt insisted they open the window slightly, "I'm not riding all the way with that smell. I've had a week of it already. Please, no more."

It was about five hours to Paris with several short stops. Matt sat just watching the scenery go by.

Small towns, battered and quiet. The fields were just beginning to green. The linden trees were still bare, and the thickets of beech and pine where dappled with the sunlight. The train pulled into one small town and a few people disembarked. As they got closer to Paris, the roads along the rail became busier. It was now close to time for those working to return home and the sky was transitioning to dusk.

At about half past six, the train huffed into the Paris Gard du Nord station. Henrick had left the compartment in order to get off just as the train stopped. Shannon stayed with Matt, and Lalani went to find Charles. As she stepped from the train, she spotted Charles and Henrick coming her way. Henrick was pushing a wheelchair, followed by a porter, as Charles waved. Lalani smiled as she embraced Charles. Henrick had snagged one of the sturdier luggage handlers, slipping him a few francs, requesting his assistance in getting Matt off the train. Pleased to have the large tip, he grabbed a wheelchair from the medical assistance office. The two tall men easily lifted Matt and got him to the wheelchair, with Shannon right on their heels. The lad then retrieved the luggage and followed the little entourage out to a waiting vehicle.

At the curb sat an army troop transport truck with Mac sitting behind the wheel. Upon seeing Matt, he climbed from the cab, "Well, there's an ugly face I never thought I'd never see upright again. But, boy, am I glad I was wrong. It sure is good to see you looking better, Matt." Matt reached out his arm and embraced Mac's arm in a hearty welcome.

"It sure is good to finally see you, Mac. Last time, I was pretty out of it and things were pretty blurry. I don't think I gave you the proper thank you."

Shannon was confused, how did Mac manage to be there with an army truck? Mac gave Shannon a hug and, seeing her confused face, "It's surprising how much a case of good French wine can get you. Your friend here knows our commander and sent a case of his finest. And voila! I'm being sent to transport some wounded soldier to an estate in Lesigny. I only wish I could stay and spend some time with you all. But the wine didn't go that far. I'm due back in Metz by tomorrow. How about we get you all loaded and on our way?"

Mac had a cot set up in the back of the truck between the side benches. They quickly got Matt settled, and Shannon climbed up next to him. Mac reached to load the chair, "Oh, that belongs to the station," Shannon said.

"Won't he still need it?"

Charles nodded, as Mac lifted it over his head and into the truck, "Let's hope they have another." Henrick climbed up and secured the back of the truck. Mac thought Lalani would be more comfortable in the cab with him. Charles opted for the cab as well. Finally, they were off. The roads out of Paris were in pretty good shape. It was only the last half hour into Lesigny and to the estate things got a little bumpy.

The night air had turned cold by the time they arrived at the estate. Mme. Fontenelle met them and had a fire going in the main parlor. She had set up one of the small sitting rooms on the main floor for Matt. But Matt wanted to sit with the others in the parlor upon arrival. Lalani, at last, made formal introductions.

"Matt, I've heard a great deal about you from these two women, so let me say I am more than grateful to be able to finally meet you," Charles said.

Mme. Fontenelle brought a light supper and served it in the parlor, inviting Henrick and Mac to join them. They reminisced about Shannon's effort to find Matt and how things were going in Le Havre getting the men home. After an hour, Mac had to leave to get the truck back to the motor pool, before it was really missed. Mac was due to be discharged in another month, and he and Matt agreed to meet up back in California when he was home.

Once Mac was gone, Shannon insisted Matt get settled in his room. He didn't argue. It had been a long strenuous day. Henrick would be his assistant getting in and out as needed, while Mme. Fontenelle would be his caretaker for more personal needs, like bathing. Shannon wanted to protest, but Mme. Fontenelle stoically informed her, it would be very inappropriate for a single woman to see a man, well in his "*état naturel*," and Lalani agreed. "You're not married yet!"

Charles made sure Lalani and Shannon were comfortable in their rooms upstairs and then retired. Later Shannon slipped downstairs and stood at Matt's door just watching him sleep. *I'm so grateful to have him back, safe. I know we will always be together now. I would marry you tomorrow if you asked. I love you Matty Taylor.*

~~

Matt spent the first few days in bed, with only a half-hearted protest, realizing he needed recouping from the trip. He was adjusting to his sight being limited on his left. But his right eye seemed to be compensating for it with a wider range of view. He wrote a long over-due letter to his mother, confessing he wanted to marry Shay Shay as soon as they arrived back at the ranch, that by then he would be able to manage crutches. In the evening they sat and played cards and talked about vineyards and cattle round ups.

Lalani was sure Clay was back on a horse by now, and with Jim and Andrew's help, spring branding would go quickly. Matt wasn't so sure Andrew would be up to the task. The smell of burning flesh Matt couldn't endure, and figured Andrew wouldn't either. Most men had experienced an artillery blast hitting some fellow soldier and the smell of seared flesh, something he would regrettably never forget.

Matt wasn't sure what he would do upon returning. His sight being what it was, he wasn't sure architectural designing would be possible. Shannon reassured him the doctor had said with glasses his sight would improve and then he could draw and design like he did before.

Meanwhile as Matt improved, Lalani and Charles began to make arrangements for a ship home. The Cunards had been so helpful getting both Shannon and Lalani to France, they hated to impose once again. Charles on the other hand, had known them for years. William had long passed, but his son, Arthur, and he had gone to school together. Arthur, now in charge of the shipping company, was more than happy to make arrangements on the next ship to New York, informing Charles he had two very nice first-class cabins available on the SS Mauretania. Civilians were not going to America, but rather coming home from the States after fleeing from the war. He would reserve one for Lalani and Shannon and the other for Matt. He also assured Charles that Matt would have all the help he needed. The one hitch was the SS Mauretania would be departing Southampton on April 22nd, in less than three weeks. Matt was eager to be going home and was all for leaving on the 22nd. Shannon was worried that even though Matt seemed strong, it would prove too much for him. After all they thought Andrew could make the voyage, but when he arrived, he was almost on death's door. *Yet more than anything I want to be home, home with Matt. Besides Andrew was on an army transport ship, full of influenza patients. Matt will have his own first-class cabin, clean and comfortable.*

For the next three weeks, Shannon would ride a horse named Prince Louie out around the estate, often going with Henrick to check on the vineyards. As the last week approached, Matt seemed quite strong, and complained continuously about the plaster cast and his leg itching.

Two days before sailing, Lalani took Shannon into Paris to do some shopping at Le Bon Marché and La Samaritaine, Paris's famous department stores. At Samaritaine's they bought several dresses and a new hat. *It's fun to be shopping with mother, it's been far too long since we have.* Shannon stopped at the jewelry counter in Le Bon's and spotted a man's ring she thought would be perfect for Matt's wedding band, a simple gold band with two leaves barely overlapping, cut into it. Nothing showy, but strong and representative of their unending connection. Before returning to the estate, they had a late afternoon tea along the Seine. Lalani and Charles had a reason for keeping Shannon away from the house that day.

While the ladies were out, Charles had arranged for a doctor to come to the house and check on Matt. Matt was insistent that his leg had mended and wanted out of the cast before sailing. Doctor Purcé, an old friend of Charles, questioned Matt about the break and examined his foot reflexes. Finally, since it had been eight weeks since the bone had been straightened and movement of this foot hadn't resulted in any pain, he agreed to remove the cast. Matt was under strict orders to limit his walking for another few weeks, and crutches were a must. But for the first time in months, Matt was thrilled to sit in a tub of warm water and soak.

When the ladies returned, he met them in the parlor fully dressed standing by the fireplace, crutches supporting him. Shannon was elated and had all kinds of questions. Once they were answered and she and Lalani were satisfied, they made their way to supper in the dining room for the last time.

~~

On April 21st they boarded a shuttle steamer that ran from Le Havre to Southampton as Charles and Henrick waved good bye. Charles was happy to see the young couple would have a future together. The crossing took the entire morning and by noon the morning fog had lifted, as Matt under his own strength on crutches, came across the gangplank onto the Southampton pier.

Now as Lalani stepped onto the dock she stood watching as a whirlwind of an elderly lady came rushing towards her. Matt and Shannon had heard stories about Jessie Roberts all their lives, about her eccentric ways, dressing in men's clothing, gambling, carrying a gun. Shannon had met her in 1911, when she came with her parents to England. And now for the first time, Matt would see for himself that his mother had not exaggerated. Jessie swept around Lalani embracing her like the long-lost friend that she was. It had been almost eight years since they had last seen each other. Katherine and Jessie had grown up together in Pineville. Jessie had come to England with her cousin Thomas, who had become an Earl. Jessie and Thomas then stayed in England while Katherine and Lalani returned to California. Lalani had written saying they would be leaving from Southampton for the States, and regretted there was no time for a visit to London.

On the other hand, Jessie threw regrets to the wind and was there to meet their ship and spend at least one evening together.

Thomas demanded Jessie take Wilkins, her mechanic, to do the driving and to help with Matt. Jessie was rather lead-footed on the gas petal and could cause one's hair to turn gray as she sped through traffic. They made it to the hotel near the harbor and settled in their rooms. At dinner, Jessie regaled them with her wild stories from when she and Katherine were children and her exploits in London. Shannon and Matt never laughed so hard and Lalani was thrilled to hear it. Shannon wanted Matt to rest before the long voyage, therefore they retired early. "Don't go tiring him out with too much hanky-panky," Jessie said as they departed. Shannon smiled, while her mother turned a bright red, adding "Jessie, they have separate rooms."

Jessie wasn't going to let Lalani leave so quickly. They had far too much catching up to do. It was almost one in the morning when Lalani managed to slow Jessie down, reminding her she came to see them off in the morning, and morning was now only hours away.

"You won't be able to sleep until noon like the old days, if you truly want to see us off." Jessie grumbled, but finally walked Lalani up to her room.

The skies were clear the morning of the 22nd, with the promise of smooth sailing. Lalani encouraged Matt and Shannon to join her on deck as the ship pulled out. There was something thrilling about a ship pulling out while loved ones waved on, especially if you were excited about your destination. As promised, Jessie was there waving, her long gray hair a little more disheveled than usual, but her trousers and weskit were neat and strikingly feminine. Shannon had one arm around Matt helping to support him, while waving with the other. Lalani chuckled to herself upon seeing the tears streak down Jessie's face. Some things never change.

~~

The crossing was smooth, and Matt managed on crutches very well. The first night everyone slept soundly. It was the second night that Matt lay awake, now wishing Shannon were by his side there in his bed. His thoughts turned back to that night before they left and his masculine desires began to stir again. He would have risen and gone to her bed, but she was sharing a cabin with her mother. That put an end to his roguish longings and he began to think about what their future would be. *I have the house in Sacramento still, but am I going to be an architect at this point? Can I even read a ruler and measure things correctly with this eye? And what about Shannon? I've been gone since she graduated with her degree in archaeology. What is it she wants to do? Has she completed the work on her Hawaiian ruin? She seems so close to her mother this past month. Does she want to go back and live at Mau Loa? I guess I could become a rancher, that's what I was raised to do. Me, a cattle rancher, surely not. The peace and quiet at Charles's were heavenly. We were in a bubble, in our own world; removed from the horrors of war, the epidemic, and starvation. Mau Loa is like that. What does Shay Shay want? I just want to make her happy. I owe her that!*

Finally, still contemplating all his questions, he fell asleep. In the morning they came haunting back to him, and he knew he and Shannon had some serious talking to do. For the next two days they talked, weighed possibilities, discussed desires, and dreams of children. The only sure thing that came out of the hours of discussion was that they wanted a quiet safe place to raise children and they couldn't wait to get married. They contemplated having the captain marry them, but Lalani convinced them Katherine was already making arrangements for a wedding at the ranch and Shannon's father would be very disappointed if he couldn't walk his daughter down the aisle. So, they agreed to wait.

19

Where Do We Go from Here?

It was a glorious May morning when the train pulled into Oak Ridge. The platform was crowded with Taylors, the whole family there to meet Matt and Shannon. Shannon stepped from the train and smiled, "Uncle Clay, Aunt Katherine, there's someone here that might need a little help getting down," as she motioned them to come. Clay and Katherine walked quickly to the steps as Matt was the first one coming down, using his crutches. Matt then stepped onto the platform and embraced his mother, now crying and holding him in her arms. Clay put his arm around his son's shoulders and kissed his head, something Clay did not do often, but it was for the second time in six months, the first when Andrew came home.

Matt had dropped the crutches and Shannon retrieved them, so he could stand when Katherine finally let go. Abby and Andrew were next to hug and welcome him home. Jim went to Shannon and embraced his daughter, grateful she was home secure and happy, finally reaching for Lalani and including her in his arms. Abby was so overjoyed to see Matt, tears ran down her face, as Matt gave her a hug.

Then it was Andrew's turn, Matt looked at his little brother and didn't recognize the man that stood before him. His little brother's mischief was gone, only an aged hesitant man stood before him. Matt grabbed him and held him tight. Lalani had warned Matt that Andrew was struggling to adjust back to civilian life, and now he realized how badly Flanders Fields had affected him. Andrew smiled, "Glad to have you back." Morgan, Amanda and the boys waited for their turns to shake his hand and hug, along with Eric and Nancy.

The entourage made its way to the cars. Abby jiggled a key in front of Matt, "Oh, no, you don't, baby sister. Not my roadster."

She laughed as she and Andrew headed off together. "We'll race you home!"

~~

There were lots of adjustments to make back at the ranch, now that the house was full again. Jim and Lalani had Miranda's, Clay's mother, old suite, while Nancy shared Abby's room. Eric went and stayed with Morgan. Shannon ended up in the original small guest room at the back of the house, while Andrew and Matt kept their old rooms. It took a few days before everyone began to settle down and stop walking around on tiptoes.

Matt got frustrated with Abby's fussing and concerned about Andrew's withdrawal from people. He and Shannon also found the house too full of people, unable to find a moment alone. They wanted to ride out to their favorite spot, but Matt couldn't ride a horse yet, therefore the back garden became their retreat. It was warm and quiet, Katherine and Lalani making sure to keep the others away. Shannon and Matt were now anxious to get married and on their own.

Katherine had been making a few wedding arrangements, finding out when the church would be available, asking about musicians and having a cake made. She wondered if Matt's blue suit would fit him or if he would be married in his army uniform. Still, it was Shannon's wedding, and Lalani should have been in charge. On a quiet morning Shannon, Matt, Katherine and Lalani sat down to discuss the wedding. Matt agreed Shannon should have a church wedding, but he wanted a small celebration at the house, and he would wear his blue suit. Shannon's wedding dress was there at the ranch already. As much as they wanted to marry right away, Matt wanted to be able to see better and be off crutches and Shannon was willing to wait another few weeks until Matt was ready. *I hope that's all that's keeping him from saying I do.* After a few more decisions, Matt asked about May 12th, if the church would be available. "I'll be off these damn crutches by then and should have my glasses. I want to see my beautiful bride."

Shannon smiled, relieved a date was set. "May 12th it is!" Katherine and Lalani were delighted as well, and could now put the plans made into action.

After a week at the ranch, Shannon and Matt made their way to San Francisco to meet Uncle Richard who had made an appointment with an eye specialist in the city. Doctor Delano had been busy attending many soldiers returning with eye injuries. He took about an hour to examine Matt and finally determined his left eye retina was permanently scarred, causing the blurry vision. He fitted Matt with special glasses, clear lens for his right eye and a heavy lens for his left. The lens allowed Matt to see much more clearly, but not completely. Matt was encouraged with the improved sight the glass would provide. *Perhaps I can still read a ruler.* Delano gave him some eye exercises to help strengthen his eye and hold focus longer. It would take another week for the glasses to be made. They made a final appointment for the following week.

Shannon and Matt had planned to spend the night with Joanna and Richard, but Matt found the noise of the city unsettling. Shannon tried to take the back roads to avoid the traffic and noise. "Shay Shay, let's not go to the Malcomb's. Let's drive up to the Sacramento house. We haven't been alone, close, since before I left. Please I just need to sit by the river and feel at home with you."

"But we don't have any change of clothes."

"Sure, we do. My old civilian clothes are still there, and you must have left something from when you lived there. I'm just not ready to go back to the ranch and face all the questions."

Shannon looked at the gas indicator, it read almost full. She made a U-turn and headed northeast. It would take them three hours to get to the house, but she too wanted very much to be alone with Matt and sit by the river, just the two of them.

It was a little after three o'clock when Shannon pulled into the drive of Matt's house. She hadn't brought the key, but the spare was still under the rock in the garden by the front steps. Matt wanted to carry her over the threshold, but with crutches he couldn't. 'I'll carry you over this threshold soon, once I get rid of these crutches and we're married. Only eight more days!"

Shannon smiled and unlocked the door. The house was clean and tidy. Mrs. Ling had been attending to things as promised. Matt made his way out to the back patio, across the lawn and stood watching the river. The trees were bright with their new spring leaves, and the water was flowing quickly, full from the melting snow. Shannon came up to his right side and he dropped his crutches and just stood on his own two feet. He stared at the chilly rushing waters, and shivered. "Cold?" Shannon asked. Matt didn't answer, his eyes fixed on the flowing water. He was lost at another river, a river with streaks of dark red from the blood of fallen comrades. "What is it? Matt." She took his hand, as it trembled, breaking his trance.

"It just suddenly reminded me of the Lys River. The bitter cold of the war." *She doesn't need to know the horrors that happened there. Let her keep the sweet story of finding the watch.*

Shannon reached up and turned his head to look at her, "You're here with me now, that's all in the past." She kissed him long, until he became engulfed in the kiss and wanted more.

He put his arm around her shoulder, leaving the crutches on the ground, and leaned on her to get them back to the house and up the stairs to his room. He now needed to see her tender silhouette and feel her soft body next to his.

It was dark by the time he woke from their indulgent desires. Matt had been just enough of a gentleman not to take it all the way. He lay wondering if his lustful needs had been too rough. He watched Shannon's bare back as she slept. He leaned forward and kissed her ever so gently on the neck and she began to stir. Turning over and revealing her breasts again, she smiled. *Thank goodness she's smiling and not horrified at what I did earlier.* Shannon pulled the sheet up over her breasts, "Hungry?"

"I'm always hungry for more, but I think I over indulged already. I'm sorry."

"Hungry as in food, silly. Don't worry, we had the right to overindulge, after all we've gone through."

Matt pulled her to him and gently kissed her lips, grateful for her understanding. "Yes, I'm that kind of hungry too." He turned over to get out of bed, then realized his crutches were still in the backyard. He started to stand and realized he had overdone it with climbing the stars, and sat back down.

Shannon slipped out of bed, threw on an old robe from the armoire and made her way to retrieve the crutches. Matt had carefully made his way to the shower by the time she returned. Her first thought was to join him, but then refrained. *We've played enough for now.*

Shannon showered once Matt was done. Then they made their way to the coffee house for a hearty meal. The roads were filled with cars. Matt tried not to cringe at every honk and backfire, but there were now three times as many cars on the road than in 1917. The restaurant was crowded and Matt found it hard to relax, clinching his coffee cup as he sat. Shannon now realized it was too soon for him. He still needed the peace and quiet to wash the horrors of war away. *Hopefully it's not so much as time, but something to do, to keep his mind busy.*

"Since we're here in town, how about visiting Mr. Lionaski, and talking to him about returning to work. It doesn't have to be right away. We have a wedding, remember and a honeymoon. But when we get back."

Matt seemed to respond to this idea and agreed, then turned his energy to where to go for a honeymoon. Shannon could see it needed to be somewhere quiet with few crowds. *Something that won't remind him of France. Definitely not a big city. I feel like I should take him back to Mau Loa, it's tranquil, out of the way, and the vegetation is quite different. Sitting by the ocean, now that would be peaceful and I would like that.*

"Shay Shay, where do you want to go? Do you want to go to Yellowstone National Park?" Matt asked for a second time.

"No, I want to lie on the beach somewhere with you. Somewhere warm and beautiful."

"That sounds like Mau Loa," Matt said with a raised brow.

"No, I don't want to be with family. How would we ever get any privacy? Isn't there somewhere along the California coast we could go, maybe south, where the water is warmer?"

"We could go down to San Diego and see Lars."

"On our honeymoon? I like Lars and I'm sure he's back by now, but I don't need it to be a guy weekend."

"Of course not. There's a little town near the San Luis Obispo mission, Cambria. I went with my folks once. It's a quaint town with a few shops and cafés, and several hotels right on the beach."

"Now, that sounds heavenly."

~~

Shannon drove Matt to see Mr. Lionaski and left them to talk, while she went to see Mr. Rawlings at the museum. He was delighted to see her and hear that Matt was back. She only stayed an hour before returning to pick up Matt.

Everyone at the firm was happy to see him. Matt picked up a design on Mr. Lionaski's desks and tried to make out the figures, but couldn't. Mr. Lionaski could see the distress in his face. "Don't worry, Matt, I've been wearing glasses for years. Once you get yours, it will all come clear. We'd love to have you back, when you're ready. There is going to be lots of building of new homes and stores with the soldiers returning."

Shannon arrived and was glad to hear Matt was still wanted at the firm. Many men that left, lost their jobs to others and had nothing to return to. Returning to his job was good news. They had a house and Matt would have a job. Mr. Rawlings still couldn't afford to hire Shannon as a research archaeologist, only as a part time tour guide. *Sacramento has possibilities, that is if Matt can readjust to the noise and crowds. He's strong, I'm sure he will in time. He doesn't seem to be as haunted as Andrew.*

They returned to the ranch where Matt seemed to feel most comfortable. They became very involved with the wedding, now only a week away. Shannon wished her brother Evan could be there, but he was needed at Mau Loa. Shannon contacted Grace in Pasadena and asked her to be her maid of honor along with Abby. At Shannon's urging Matt called Lars in San Diego, hoping he had returned, to see if he would come and stand with him along with Andrew.

Lars met Grace in Pasadena and they came up together, arriving the day before the wedding. Both were ecstatic to see them. Lars seemed to be his old self, but realized Matt had changed, more reserved like a lot of war vets. Lars went with Matt to pick up the new glasses in the city, diverting to Berkeley for a spin around campus like in the old days. This too had changed, more buildings, more cars. Matt found it difficult to enjoy being there. *So many young faces.* Eugene's face came suddenly into view. "Let's go, Lars. I've seen enough."

Lars looked at Matt and seeing his furrowed brow, agreed it was time to head for home.

The morning of May 12th was warm with clear skies and wildflowers blooming in the fields. Shannon and Matt had at the last minute decided not to get married at the church with a lot of people. Now it was going to be in the ranch garden, off the main house with only close friends and family. Shannon stood dressed in her wedding gown, made with the fabric her mother had designed. Grace and Abby wore soft blue spring dresses. Lalani had collected flowers and made a crown for Shannon's hair and was just finishing pinning it in place. She looked at her daughter and smiled and said, "*Na ke Akua e ho opomaika 'i ia 'oe a alaka 'i ia 'oe i kou ola hou.*"

Shannon turned and kissed her, "Thank you for the blessing."

"What did she say," Abby asked.

"It's a wedding blessing, May God bless you and guide in your new life together," Lalani explained.

There was a knock on the door. It was Jim. Lalani gave Shannon a gentle hug and kiss, then took Grace and Abby and scooted from the room as the wedding was about to begin. Eric escorted Lalani down the short aisle to her seat.

Jim turned to his daughter and handed her a small bouquet, comprised of one pink anthurium he had brought from Oahu, and had been carefully nurturing until this moment. With it were two white calla lilies and a spring of fern, tied with a white satin ribbon. "It's perfect."

"Just like you," Jim said offering her his arm, as they made their way to the garden.

The rose trellis was in bloom and blue iris and columbine filled the garden beds. Matt stood tall, now on his own, the gold chain of his pocket watch glistening from the pocket of his dark blue vest. Lars and Andrew stood next to him, watching Abby and then Grace come towards them. The violinist stopped briefly as Shannon and Jim appeared at the doors to the garden. Matt wearing his wire rim glasses, upon seeing his bride, smiled and he could feel his heart swell as he fell in love with Shannon all over again. She was so beautiful, radiant, as the light caressed her smile. Jim escorted her to Matt and placed her hand in his. "Who gives this woman to marry?" "Her mother and I," Jim announced, then he kissed Shannon and stepped back to joined Lalani. The family minister kept the ceremony simple and uplifting, with exchanging of rings and simple vows, "as one, never to part."

Then Lalani and Jim came forward with traditional ti leaf wedding garlands. Jim took Shannon's wrist and wrapped an end around twice, as Lalani did the same to Matt. Together they repeated, *Na ke Akua e ho opomaika 'i ia 'oe a alaka 'i ia 'oe i kou ola hou.* Then Jim kissed Shannon, and Lalani Matt. They stepped behind them, taking the dangling ends, Jim taking Shannon's across and over to Matt's free hand and Lalani Matt's to Shannon's free hand and giving them a little push. Jim announced, "You are now joined together and you may kiss your wife." Matt and Shannon's kiss lingered softly, until her father's "uh um," and everyone applauded.

The celebration began and all their concerns melted away. Clay stood holding Katherine and whispered, "I remember you standing at that same garden door, the day of Eric's wedding. Like Shannon you were radiant, even if I do say, more beautiful. And I knew right then and there I wanted to marry you. And what a wonderful life you have given me."

Katherine smiled, "It was a beautiful day, just like today. And I know Shannon will give Matt a wonderful life as well."

Jim and Lalani joined them, watching the couple dance and whisper to each other. Lalani took Katherine's hand. "Now we are truly joined forever."

Clay looked at Jim and snickered, "Until grandchildren arrive. Then the negotiating will begin as to who gets them for the holidays."

"Oh, dear God, let it take a while before that happens," Jim replied.

Lalani and Katherine looked at each other. "No worry, we will all go to wherever Matt and Shannon are. Now let's go serve the cake."

The newlyweds would drive down to Cambria the next day, after seeing Grace and Lars off at the train. But for their first night as man and wife they would stay at Kalua'ana, just as each of their parents had done. Both Katherine and Lalani had spent their first night as man and wife in that house and felt it would be a good blessing if the kids did the same. Morgan, Amanda, and the boys stayed up at the main ranch. Amanda and Abby had changed up the master bedroom to reflect a bridal chamber, with champagne and chocolates, including strawberries that were in season. Matt carried Shannon over the threshold and closed the door. This time they would make it all the way as husband and wife, as lovers!

~~

Shannon and Matty spent a week in Cambria, walking on the beach, just sitting, listening to the waves in the evening. They would wander into town for dinner, or go look at the touristy shop items, and buy muffins for breakfast the next day. From their hotel room, they could lie in bed watching the waves lap against the shore, at least when they weren't entangled in loving each other.

Cambria was a good choice for them. They sat and made plans, nothing that they couldn't change their minds about, but for the moment a reasonable direction for work and home, a caring marriage. At the end of the week, they drove the ten hours back to Oak Ridge. To their surprise, Lalani and Jim were still there.

Jim had stayed to help Clay with spring branding. As Matt suspected, Andrew was not able to stand the smell of burning flesh. Clay didn't ask Matt to help finish the drive, now realizing how much the war had affected his sons.

Shannon and Matt laid out their plans to return to Sacramento and resume work at Lionaski's. Shannon would work part time at the museum for now. Doc Newell gave Matt the okay to ride a horse, and they wasted no time riding up to the reservoir and their favorite spot, before they left. Matt had missed his horse Hephaestus, named for the god of architecture, Heph for short, and seemed more himself around him, calm, smiling.

They decided to depart for Sacramento the same day Jim and Lalani would go to San Francisco to catch a ship back to Oahu. The morning before departing, Matt found Jim, just watching Lalani sitting in the garden.

"Uncle Jim, did you ever have any regret about leaving California?"

Jim looked at Matt surprised by the question. "No. Wherever that woman is, makes me happy. When she's here and I'm not, I miss her terribly. Actually Matt, our moving to Oahu was the best decision I ever made, besides marrying Lalani. I'm a simple man. I like it quiet. I like my cattle and my gardens. I like walking on the beach with Lalani, not much for swimming, but I love to watch her swim. No, I have no regrets. Why?"

"Oh, no reason."

"Matthew Taylor, that's bull! You've got something's on your mind. What is it?"

"You're right. Do you think Shay Shay will be happy living in Sacramento, just being a tour guide for a museum? She's worked hard for her degree."

Jim rubbed his chin, and pursed his lips. "If the city is what works best for you, she will be content. I'm sure she will find something more stimulating in time. Shannon's like her mother, she will do what's best. Don't worry, you'll figure out where you belong together."

"Do you think she would be happier on Oahu? Do you think I could find work there?"

"As long as she is with you, she will be happy, never question that. As for work on Oahu, as an architect, the navy base at Pearl Harbor has been growing and bringing in a lot of people. People that need homes. People also need goods and that means more stores will need to be built. So, sure, there could be work. If I recall there is only one architectural firm on the island. Would you move to Oahu? Honolulu will not be any calmer than Sacramento or Oak Ridge. "

"Again, you're right. Honolulu is a bustling city, but if I could have an office outside the city. Shay Shay told me she was offered a job at the *Pu'u O Mahuka Heiau* ruins. We enjoyed being at the ocean so much this past week. It's just an idea rattling around in my mind. For now, we're going back to Sacramento, so I can get reestablished. We're actually excited to be in the house together."

The next morning was hectic with Jim and Lalani leaving early to catch the boat. Tears were flowing once again as hugs and kisses were exchanged. It was only Katherine that was in tears as Shannon and Matt pulled out of the drive later that day, headed for home.

~~

Shannon and Matt settled into the house fairly easily, having breakfast looking out at the big oak. In the evening, they spent time in the study, now with two leather chairs by the fireplace. It was far too warm for a fire, but with the windows open they could hear the birds. They quickly realized they missed riding in the morning and asked Katherine to send Heph and Champ to Sacramento. They found a stable nearby, that would keep them, close to the main riding trail along the river. Matt still didn't enjoy watching the river, preferring to take the road up to the mesa's open field overlooking the valley. On Saturday morning, Shannon and Matt rode down to the river trail to their favorite spot by the large willow. Shannon hoped it was more comforting there for Matt. But there was still something about the way the water flowed she could see that haunted him. *I wish I knew what it was.* She quickly enticed him to disappear under the bow of the big tree to be alone. There the haunting quickly vanished as he passionately kissed her.

Matt and Shannon were delightfully in love with each other and created a secure place together at the house. Riding together seemed to bring a sense of peace and satisfaction to both of them. One evening Shannon confessed the traffic and noise was much greater than it had been. "Wouldn't it be nice if we could live in Cambria, in a house near the ocean? To fall asleep lulled by the waves, and wake each morning with the fresh breezes?" Matt nodded his head in agreement, "It would be nice, but there's no work for me there."

Matt found he preferred to walk to work, leaving late after all the noisy traffic had dissipated, his reasoning being that Shannon would have the roadster to come and go as she needed. Matt's glasses seemed to serve him well at work. Only when the blueprints were old and faded did he have to ask for help.

Lionaski took on a new housing tract that would offer three different size, low-cost houses. Matt was assigned to design the smallest model for the small lots. He missed the challenge of the imposing buildings and freedom to be really creative. He was finding it difficult to enjoy and settle into the work he was given.

It was another month of being woken by cars backfiring and the barking dog on the next street over that seemed to put both Shannon and Matt on edge. Shannon struggled to find interesting topics at work, and not be irritable at Matt's complaining about his boring work and the noise. She begged him to buy a piano, something he used to enjoy playing and now considered it just more noise. They missed being able to go out with Millie and Jeroen. The men in Matt's office were much older and didn't mix with the younger generation socially.

It was a Sunday afternoon when they went riding, Matt wanting to go up towards the mesa to look out over the valley. The horses still weren't used to the cars' noise and became jumpy as they walked up the road to the mesa. Champ tugged at the reins as he reached the field wanting to get off the hard road. Just then, a young man in a car drove past calling out to a friend he spotted walking on the road. He sounded his horn, Uoo Ga, Uoo Gaa. The odd noise sent Champ up onto his rear legs with his front legs pawing the air, then let out a loud whinny, acting as if he was going to gallop off. Shannon leaned into his neck and held his reins tight, as she held to the pommel. Heph pranced around at the noise, but Matt kept control and raced to reach Champ's bridle and pull him down to stop him from charging away.

Champ came down with a thud and sudden stop, sending Shannon off balance. She caught herself by grabbing the pommel and swung her foot loose from the stirrup, enabling her to drop to the ground, just managing to land on her feet. Matt swung down from Heph, taking her in his arms, holding her tight as if afraid of losing her. "I'm okay. Matt, I'm fine. He just surprised us." Shannon held on until she could feel his tension release. Champ stood nearby Heph, eyes wide, watching Shannon. Once Matt let go of her, she reached for Champ's bridle and softly spoke to the concerned animal. Matt was in no mood to ride now, but ran his hand through his hair. He picked up Shannon's hat and handed it to her. "You sure you're alright?" Shannon nodded and gave him a smile. Matt picked up his hat and retrieved Heph's reins. He took Shannon's hand and they walked the horses over to the edge of the bluff and tied them to a tree. Matt stood looking out for a moment, shaking his head oh so slightly and staring off into another place. Shannon stood, giving him a moment seeing he was deep in thought. After a few silent minutes she stepped up and took his hand. "Talk to me, Matt, what's got you so concerned, so deep in thought?"

"Shay Shay, are you happy here? I know you're happy being with me, but are you really happy being here in the city, at your job?"

This caught her off guard. *What has that got to do with Champ. I thought he was going to say having horses in the city isn't a good idea. But am I happy?*

Should I tell him the truth, I'm bored, I miss the ocean. I miss being able to ride in the hills and on the beach. "Well, I like the house we have here in the city. I like visiting with Millie but I have to admit work isn't very motivating. The missions are not my field of interest, but they have an important place in history. Most of all I like doing things with you, seeing you happy. Are you happy here?"

"Happy? I thought I would be. I too like the house, especially how you have made it feel comfortable. But work is not what I expected either. These simple little houses are far from challenging. You... You know I don't like the traffic and the noise. I got so used to the quiet at Albert's and Charles's, even the hospital was quiet. Cambria was so peaceful. I had so many creative ideas flowing in my mind when we were there."

"Are you saying you want to move to Cambria?"

"No. No, I don't think there would be enough work there. I would have to drive into San Luis Obispo every day for work, if I could find work."

Shannon didn't know what to say. Matt sat silent, contemplating what he wanted to say. "Shay Shay, I think I want to move to Oahu."

Shannon sat stunned. Not in her wildest dreams did she ever imagine that. Matt, seeing the sheer shock on her face, went on, "Hear me out. First, you know Mau Loa is like my second home. I've talked to your father about finding work there. He said the navy is building more facilities and housing will be needed along with businesses. I checked with the Department of the Navy and they confirmed they were planning to expand the base at Pearl Harbor by dredging the ponds and clearing some of Sand Island. More and more people are buying homes there. I could do custom designs, not just duplicate shoe boxes. We could find a piece of land on a quiet beach halfway between your folks and Honolulu. We could have our horses and ride every day, walk on the beach in the mornings like we did in Cambria. Also, your father told me the Hawaii Historical Society offered you a job restoring one of the Heiau. You would be close to your family and Kiki."

Shannon's head was now swimming. *Matt's serious about this. He's given a lot of thought to it. But is it what's best for him? He was so much in the middle of things when we were at college. The middle of Oahu, is the middle of nowhere, it would be so different from here. Is that college man really gone or is that man just grown up?... Do I want to return home? I thought I wanted something more exciting, but working on Heiau would be exciting. If this is what Matt needs then, I guess, I'm on board.*

"Shay Shay, say something."

"Matt, I'm overwhelmed. Having our own place along the beach would be wonderful, too good to be true. What about your house here? Your family?"

"We can sell the house and use the funds to build a new one in Oahu. Our families are always together every other year. You know how it goes, the man always becomes part of the bride's family, not the other way around. I think we should give it a try. If we miss the mainland, we can always come visit."

Shannon looked at Matt for a long moment. She hadn't seen him this excited about something, other than marriage, since he had been back. *If he can be his own independent architect and work from a home office, and I could go to the ruins and work it would be ideal. But is he running away? Is this going to help him? We could try it and see if this is what's best.* "Are you sure this is what's best for you, for us? "

"Yes, positive. The potential there is so much greater than here, and raising children there so much safer. But only if you're happy too."

Shannon stood looking out over the valley and at the towns below. Returning and looking at Matt, she could see a quiet yearning, a need, within his green loving eyes. "Well, let's take the first step. Let's get a map of Oahu and pick a place to settle and see if we can do it. My folks will be thrilled. You get the hard job of telling your mother."

~~

Shannon and Matt made a trip to Oahu at the end of June, staying at Mau Loa, enjoying the warm summer waters of Kaneohe Bay. They spoke with several contractors on the island about the need for architects and building the house Matt would design. One of the contractors introduced him to the Naval housing officer, Mitch Frederics, whom he had done a lot of business with. Mitch was very pleased to hear Matt would be moving to the island and had experience with bridges and a large office structure in addition to houses. The Navy indeed was interested in seeing what he might have to offer, as they had plans to reclaim the marsh land for more base facilities as well as housing.

Lalani and Jim scouted out several large beachfront properties that were available, all within an hour of Honolulu for Matt, and an hour from the ancient ruins, for Shannon, and thirty minutes from Mau Loa. Shannon took a liking to one lot near Waikane with a wide sandy beach. Matt on the other hand liked a place on Nu'upia Pond on the north end of Kailua. Then they found a five-acre parcel next to He'eia Park with a stand of koa trees on the west and palm trees and white sandy beach on the east. It had a tranquil beauty to it, and they knew they were home. It was on He'eia Pond, protected from the strong ocean currents and only twenty minutes to Mau Loa by car or fifteen by horse.

Shannon and Matt returned to Sacramento to sell the house and to design their own Mau Loa, forever home, making sure its style reflected the parcel of land they had bought for it. Matt's design included a large space for Shannon's archaeological research, a large architectural office for him, guest rooms, and room for future children. He put all his creative love into the designs. Eventually he would build stables, but for now Jim would keep their horses.

Katherine and Clay were happy for their son. It was as if he had come alive again. They were content knowing they would be at Mau Loa with Jim and Lalani until their place was built. They would come for Christmas, just as they had done twenty years earlier when Mau Loa was first built. Now they would come to Mau Loa Aku, Shay Shay and Matty's 'forever and ever' home.

It was late August, and the sky was dappled with puffy midday clouds. Shannon and Matthew stood on the bow of the SS Maui. Once again, they had said good bye to Katherine and Clay, Abby and Andrew, but there were no tears this time. Everyone knew this voyage was right, everything had come together without doubts or struggles. Shannon had one arm around Matt and tucked securely under his other arm, were their plans for Mau Loa Aku. It lay ahead of them as they cleared San Francisco Bay, now headed for He'eia, Oahu and a bright future full of love, fulfillment, and passion.

About "A Long Journey Home" Series

www.booksbymelody.com

A Long Journey Home Series is about the life journeys, challenges, and sacrifices of several women around the beginning of the twentieth century, and how these influenced them to be strong and independent, to create their own lives. It tells how women make the hard decisions to do what's right for the sake of love.

Book 1 - *A Long Journey Home ~ Katherine*
Katherine's search for independence and purpose
Book 2 – *A Long Journey Home ~ Lalani*
Katherine's life-long friend's search for a place of belonging
Book 3 – *A Long Journey Home ~ Shannon*
Lalani's daughter's relationship with Katherine's son takes a turn, as her life unfolds
Book 4 - *A Long Journey Home ~ Jessie*
Jessie, Katherine's childhood friend - coming 2025

Other Books by Melody Lavrakas

The Need to Say Good Bye – novel
Kristyn had experienced many losses in life and finally faces them
in order to find love.

Wild Things in My Mountain Garden
A memoir about planting a flower garden in the foothills
of Colorado

 Melody Lavrakas was raised in the San Gabriel Valley in California where she grew up visiting the rolling hills of central California and fell in love with the golden grasses and majestic Oak tree that dotted the landscape. In her late teens she owned her own horse, a bay with silver mane, and rode through the foothill of Pomona. Here she would attend California Polytechnic University, Pomona, and graduate with a Bachelor of Science for Business. In her early years her family moved every three years and she yearned to settle in one place and to find lasting friendship. In high school, she found that sister type friendship which led to finding her true love. Melody married John Lavrakas in 1979. They have three children and lived in Maryland, California, Colorado and Oregon. Together they have traveled to Europe, enjoying Vienna, Prague, London, Paris, Holland and Honolulu serval times. In 1988 they moved to Colorado Springs, Colorado, where John worked in GPS while Melody raised the children, gardened, and dabbled in writing.

Melody wrote her first workbook for an after-school program on Oceanography for Kids and taught it to 4th grader. Fifteen years later she wrote Wild Things in My Mountain Garden. With children grown and married, now settled on the Oregon coast, Melody wrote The Need to Say Goodbye and the first in the series of A Long Journey Home (about Katherine). Now she again combined her love for California rolling hills, the discoveries of travel, her sense of heritage and history, with the beauty of Hawaii and a little romantic fantasy and has written A Long Journey Home ~ Lalani, which reflects the love she and her husband have had over their 46 years of marriage. Her latest book "*A Long Journey Home – Shannon*" reflects Melody's thoughtful planning in travel, and her encouragement of her children to commit to a life of caring, adventure, and love.